# Readers love AMANDA MEUWISSEN

## Their Dark Reflections

"I thoroughly devoured this book. Amanda Meuwissen has a gift for creating multi-dimensional characters, full of moral ambiguity, and making you fall in love with them. This book is no exception."

—Paranormal Romance Guild

"The concept of the story was simple, the execution – delightful – one that kept me turning the page."

—Love Bytes

## After Vertigo

"With its endearing main characters and a story that held my attention, *After Vertigo* was a fun read and perfect to unwind with at the end of long day."

—Joyfully Jay

## Coming Up for Air

"*Coming Up For Air* by Amanda Meuwissen is the first book that I've read by this author, but it won't be the last…"

—OptimuMM

By AMANDA MEUWISSEN


Coming Up for Air
Their Dark Reflections

DREAMSPUN DESIRES
A Model Escort
Interpretive Hearts

TALES FROM THE GEMSTONE KINGDOM
The Prince and the Ice King

*Published by DSP Publications*
After Vertigo


Published by DREAMSPINNER PRESS
www.dreamspinnerpress.com

# THE PRINCE
## AND THE
# ICE KING

# AMANDA MEUWISSEN

DREAMSPINNER
PRESS

Published by
DREAMSPINNER PRESS

5032 Capital Circle SW, Suite 2, PMB# 279, Tallahassee, FL 32305-7886  USA
www.dreamspinnerpress.com

Trade Paperback ISBN: 978-1-64405-956-2
Digital ISBN: 978-1-64405-955-5
Trade Paperback published August 2021
v. 1.0

Printed in the United States of America
∞
This paper meets the requirements of
ANSI/NISO Z39.48-1992 (Permanence of Paper).

# CHAPTER 1

REARDON SHIVERED with a bone-deep chill. Despite hugging the thick furs of his winter cloak around him, he thought he might never be warm again.

Ice clung to the castle walls both outside and in, spreading from the corners of the interior chamber like mold. The deeper Reardon went, the less tolerable the cold became, like being dropped to the bottom of a frozen lake with no hope of surfacing.

Here the walls were not merely dusted with ice, they were coated, covered, practically made of it, and so were the ceiling and floor. The décor looked as though it might have been beautiful once, elegant and exquisitely made, but it was all distorted now, the tapestries faded, their original colors impossible to determine.

As Reardon continued, he stopped and shivered for a different reason.

There were frozen remains against the wall.

No, not remains like a pile of bones, but a full, undecayed corpse, with its mouth wide open in a preserved scream.

"That was the last outsider who found his way to my door," a low, resonant voice rumbled through the chamber, making Reardon shiver harder. "He tried to break into my castle, to steal from me, before stumbling across the same threshold where you stand now."

A powerful arm struck out and smashed the body into broken chunks—all clear, like ice, not red and bloody as Reardon had feared. But still, he believed that had been a man once, shattered now.

Dead.

He dared not move to face where the brief glimpse of a bestial hand had come from, but it had to be behind him. He could feel breath like an icy wind on his neck that made his skin prickle.

"And what did you come here for? Hmm? To slay me?"

"If I have to," Reardon answered, because that had indeed been his intention when he made his way to the Frozen Kingdom—to end this once and for all.

"Try it, then," the voice said, "but be warned, if your skin touches me, you will end up just like he did."

Reardon spun, reaching for his sword, but while the monster he expected did indeed tower over him—a great, jagged creature made of ice, with angular features, clawed hands and feet that crunched into the floor, fangs as clear as ice themselves, and its head lengthening upward into what appeared to be an icy crown—the eyes made him pause.

Because those eyes, crystal clear and sparkling blue, held intelligence and curiosity that something otherwise out of a nightmare had no right to—entirely human.

*Blue eyes in a sea of white.*

Just like Barclay's prophecy.


"BLUE EYES in a sea of white? You mean *old*. My true love is aged and wrinkled with white hair?" Reardon exclaimed. He had nothing against those lucky enough to live to see old age, but he couldn't bear the thought of waiting another fifty or more years to finally be happy.

"I didn't say old," Barclay countered. "I didn't *not* say old. You know my visions aren't always clear!"

They sat huddled at the table in the back room of the alchemist's shop where Barclay was apprenticed. They had met right there, years ago, on Reardon's first solo outing from the castle. Or he'd assumed he was solo at the time, though he'd learned later that General Lombard had accompanied him unseen, like a silent bodyguard.

Reardon had always found alchemy fascinating, so the shop had been his first destination that day. Not many practiced the art, but those who did were often great healers, able to create potions that could make someone stronger, faster, more resilient, think clearer, sleep better. The effects only lasted a short time, but it was as close to magic as anyone in the Emerald Kingdom could ever get.

Reardon found magic fascinating too, even more so than alchemy since it was forbidden, but he dared not tell his father or anyone other than Barclay, who was secretly gifted with mystic blood himself and saw visions when he touched people.

Usually it was flashes of the past or present, which could be useful when Reardon forgot where he put his cloak pin or if someone had just nicked something from the shop, but the brief glimpses into the future were what Reardon truly coveted.

"You said 'Love, death, and blue eyes in a sea of white.' How else am I supposed to interpret that? I'm not going to find love until I'm old and dying!"

Barclay snorted. The teakettle whistled on the hearth, prompting him to rise from the table to remove it. "You know I can't always tell what the visions mean. It could be saying that you'll find love during wartime or... um... after stepping on a bug!"

"And what about the sea of white?" Reardon pressed, sitting back in his chair to watch his friend.

Barclay was slight, compact of stature but bursting with energy that made his brown cheeks glow. His long dark hair was tied up messily to keep out of his face while he worked—which he still would be if Master Wells, the High Alchemist who'd chosen Barclay as his apprentice, hadn't stepped out for the afternoon after Reardon came for a visit.

It wasn't because Barclay was a commoner that he was the one making the tea. Reardon never wanted special treatment for being the prince. They alternated. Today was simply Barclay's day.

"Sea of white could be... a shroud. I mean *cloak*!" Barclay corrected.

Reardon groaned. He would be old and creaking before he found true love. He'd lusted before, many times, what little good that did him, but he'd never found anyone who captivated him the way tales of love described it. Not how his father had loved Reardon's mother, Queen Reagan, before she died. Not anyone Reardon could *have*, anyway.

There had been whispers that magic might have saved Reagan where alchemy had failed, while others insisted that hidden magic within the castle was what made her ill. Neither theory changed that she was gone.

"Don't fret so much," Barclay said, pouring the steaming water into their mugs for ginger tea. "It'll be all right."

"How? I'm twenty. Father will have me married by twenty-two to some noblewoman or princess I've never met, and I'll only ever know true love in secret."

"And what do you think will change if you find love before your twenty-second year? That you'll run away with whatever man steals your heart?"

"Maybe...."

Barclay reclaimed his seat, setting the mugs between them, and reached for Reardon's hand. There was only friendship there. Barclay fancied women, and Reardon didn't see his friend that way, but the love they shared was strong because they knew each other's deepest secrets, secrets that would strip Reardon of his crown and risk Barclay being imprisoned or chosen for that year's sacrifice.

Don't steal, don't cheat, don't injure or kill. Most laws were just and sensible. But to love someone of one's own gender was corruption—and so was magic.

Barclay hadn't chosen to see visions. It was something that started happening when he hit adulthood, and if anyone else in his family experienced them, no one talked about it. He had no control over what he saw, just as Reardon had no control over what he desired.

"You'll find love someday." Barclay smiled warmly. His magic required touch, so Reardon felt comforted by the gentle squeeze Barclay offered, since Barclay would be able to see if that wasn't true. "Whatever else my vision means, I'm sure of that."

He squeezed once more and then pulled away to add a dab of honey to his tea.

Reardon added two dabs—more like three—and took a long, calming sip. It may have only been the ginger's natural properties that comforted him, but he imagined there was some soothing potion added. Whether that was true or not, it made him think, however fleetingly, that maybe Barclay was right.

He would find love, even if all he got to know of romance were stolen moments in the night with a man he had yet to meet.

BARCLAY'S VISION couldn't mean *this*, but it was all Reardon could think about as his hand slackened on his sword.

"Is that cowardice? Or fear?" the Ice King boomed, moving fast and powerful like a hulking behemoth that shook the chamber with each stomp forward.

Reardon stumbled, still trapped by the Ice King's eyes—his blue human eyes—and slipped on the icy floor to land hard on his back and the edge of his sheath. He hissed but had precious little time to react before the Ice King was upon him, falling to all fours to claw closer, mere inches from touching Reardon as he'd threatened.

"Perhaps both," the Ice King growled, hovering over Reardon like an avalanche about to crash down upon the side of a mountain. "Not much of a hero if you can't even slay the beast... *little prince.*"

"H-how...?" Reardon quivered, teeth chattering from the proximity of the Ice King's frigid form.

"As if your finery wasn't enough? Only the House of Thom that rules the Emerald Kingdom has eyes as green as yours."

He *knew*. He knew exactly who Reardon was. "My mother...."

"So a queen sits on the throne now?"

"She died. My father is King Regent until I marry."

"Is that what this is about?"

Reardon gaped.

"You're looking for a boon or trophy to gift your betrothed?"

And then he exhaled, feeling very foolish, yet grateful that the cold kept his cheeks from flushing. "I have no betrothed. I came here for my friend."

"YOU CAN'T be serious! It's Barclay!"

"You know what happens if we do not give the Ice King his tithe."

"No, I don't. And neither do you! What does everyone even fear? An army on our doorstep? A plague?"

"Magic's corruption could cause any number of calamities."

"That is ludicrous! Barclay has lived here all his life!"

Reardon stood, fists clenched, in King Henry's personal chambers, just off the side of the throne room. Well, King *Regent*, since it was Reardon who would succeed his mother. He wouldn't normally berate his father so openly in the presence of others, least of all General Lombard or Master Wells, but this matter could not wait for a private audience.

Soldiers had just taken Barclay away in chains.

"You can't do this," Reardon lamented, shifting to appeal rather than anger.

His father was a reasonable man, had been long before he became king and had so many more responsibilities heaped on his shoulders. He couldn't let Reardon's worst fear be realized just because too many people had pointed their fingers and cried witch.

Henry sighed, sympathy creasing the corners of his dark eyes. He was a striking man, taller than Reardon and broad-shouldered, with brown hair and a healthy beard speckled with gray. He rarely wore his crown, only during official summons and proclamations. Like Reardon, he would often go into town with as few adornments as possible, just as he appeared now in a modest doublet. He hadn't been a prince when he married Queen Reagan, only a noble, but while he'd had a high station, he'd never acted like more than a commoner.

Reardon had often been told he was just like his father but that he looked more like his mother, lithe and willowy, with a fair face, auburn hair that could appear almost red in the sun, and the emerald eyes of the House of Thom. Never once had the bloodline's crown king or queen been without them.

"May I speak, Majesty?" Lombard submitted from where he stood vigil at the door.

"Of course, Lombard. What say you?" Henry gestured him forward, and Lombard's armor and the sword at his belt clattered as he approached.

He was near Henry's age, though without any hint of it in his flaxen hair. Unlike most soldiers, he kept his face clean-shaven. He was a handsome but imposing man, who always left Reardon feeling small. Not because he was unkind, but because he'd been the first target of Reardon's lustful fantasies when the stirrings of manhood began.

Even now, a long stare from his piercing blue eyes made Reardon's chest feel hot.

"The Ice King is a magical being, my prince, far more powerful than the elves who abandoned the Mystic Valley and just as un-aging, possibly immortal. He could corrupt this kingdom in so many ways, with plague or war or worse, but he stays on his hill so long as he receives his yearly offering."

"I know the story, Bardy," Reardon addressed him informally, "but every legend about the source, the reason, is different. What if none of them are true? Have you ever even sent an emissary to the Frozen Kingdom?" He returned to his father.

"Your mother's father's father did," Henry reminded him. "You know that tale as well."

"That the emissary's head came back a broken-off chunk of ice, but it too could be a myth. An exaggeration."

"You would risk that when you will be king in less than two years' time? What if you're wrong? You ask me to destroy your mother's legacy, as an outsider of the bloodline."

"Mother hated this tradition too!" Reardon bellowed.

"Yet she upheld it." Henry came closer, and Reardon wanted to back away like a petulant child, but he allowed his father to take his hands. "I have ruled these past ten years in her stead only to hold the line for you. If you wish to bring down all the traditions of your ancestors when you take the crown, so be it, but beware the consequences when you go against the will of the people. We send an offering of corruption at the start of every Winter Solstice, and we are safe from the Frozen Kingdom for another year."

"Barclay isn't corrupt," Reardon choked out, the heat in his chest spreading to his eyes and making him blink away wetness.

"He admitted to the visions," Wells said, a man a good decade older than Henry or Lombard, in robes and a skullcap, with a graying ginger beard much longer than Henry's and what Reardon had once thought were kind amber eyes.

"They're just images in his head, not—"

"It's magic," Henry stated firmly. "Can you really deny it is?"

Reardon wanted to say, "Why does magic have to be bad?" but he knew where that conversation led, especially with Lombard watching, who rooted out those claimed to have magic and imprisoned them just like Barclay. "Choose somebody else," Reardon pleaded.

"Your friend cannot be exempt from the law. I know it hurts you, my son, but there were too many corroborations, including by Master Wells, and he confessed. He is touched by magic. He could bring disaster down on all of us."

"You condemn my friend for superstition!" Reardon wrenched his hands away.

"Magic brings curses in its wake—"

"You only say that because you believe magic killed Mother!"

Henry went cold, but he did not raise his voice, merely looked sorrowful and empty. "What else could it have been? To find her without breath, with no other explanation…."

"Yet alchemy is never a problem." Reardon clung stubbornly to his bitterness, not hiding the sneer he passed toward Wells.

"Alchemy is science," Henry affirmed.

Reardon had never understood why such seemingly simple differences should matter. "Not even you, Master Wells, will vouch for Barclay, after all these years training him to succeed you?"

Wells looked away, but his expression wasn't resentment, or even only fear, but guilt.

"Corroboration including by you, Father said. You turned him in, didn't you? His own family shuns him, yet I thought you, of all people…." Reardon trailed off, too angry to finish the thought. "Of course you turned him in, because you're a coward like everyone else, afraid you'll be counted a witch with him if you don't throw him to the wolves."

"Reardon—" Henry tried, but Reardon whirled on him too.

"You'll never listen. Tradition, old ways, old laws. You'll uphold them even over me." Reardon had never told his father the truth of his heart's desires. How could he?

"When you are king, the decisions will be yours."

"By then it will be too late." Barclay would be gone, and besides, Reardon knew his father was right; that was why he'd never looked forward to his coronation.

He couldn't marry to become king, and then turn around and admit the marriage a sham, changing everything the kingdom believed in. It would cause a revolt. The people already believed that those who yearned for their same gender were corrupt, poisoned by magic somehow too, against science and nature and all that made sense to them. Reardon was helpless and about to lose the one person who understood him.

"When I am king, maybe there will be so little left of me, I won't care if they revolt…," he muttered and turned on his heel to leave before his father could call him back.

Reardon was denied an audience with Barclay until the day came for him to be taken to the Ice King's gate. Reardon had never seen someone bid a heartfelt farewell to those taken away. He tried not to attend the departure of the offerings either, tried not to watch, to will it all away, but with Barclay, he couldn't be so blind and apathetic, not like Master Wells and Barclay's own family.

Reardon went right up to the prison cart that was attended to by Lombard and two of his soldiers. He reached for Barclay's hand through the bars before the cart could be covered and start down the main road, ignoring the confused murmurs from the watching townsfolk.

"I tried, Barclay. I swear I tried."

"I know. It's okay. They were bound to find out eventually."

"Don't be scared. Whatever the stories say, we don't know what happens."

Barclay put on a brave smile. "At least I'll make an attractive ice sculpture. I will, right? And don't only say it because you're my friend."

Reardon laughed despite his tears. "Barclay…."

"I love you, Reardon. Don't do anything stupid, okay? Whatever befalls me, I don't want it to befall you too. Be a good king and wait for your love. You'll find him."

The clop of Lombard's horse coming closer was all the warning Reardon received before the cart lurched forward, tearing their hands apart. Reardon stood in the dirt and watched after his friend until he was nothing but a distant haze on the horizon.

He tried for weeks, *months* to follow Barclay's wishes, wondering if his friend was even still alive. He did not want to believe the stories, but those sent to the Ice King never returned.

Reardon had so few friends who were real, though it wasn't anyone's fault but his own. Both nobles and commoners alike were welcoming wherever Reardon went, appreciative that he was never boastful about his station. Reardon enjoyed their company too, but he felt like a fraud, like a half-formed shadow of himself, except around Barclay, because no one else knew his secret.

It was lonely, and lonelier still with fresh whispers about Reardon's overly kind heart.

"He must have been bewitched," he'd hear someone say, sympathetic, just out of earshot, "to mourn so for one of the corrupt."

"Ever our sweet prince," another would mutter, "too soft, like his mother."

On Barclay's birthday, Reardon got so drunk at the tavern, he couldn't walk straight along the cobbled streets when he tried to go out back for a piss in the troughs. Several of the patrons inside, including the barkeep, had offered to assist him out the door, but he had been too stubborn to accept. He made his aim, thankfully. It was a modest sewer system, but still kept the filth from running into the streets.

Just as Reardon was about to finish doing up his trousers, rough hands seized his shoulders and the world spun.

"If it isn't His Highness," someone said—a tall someone.

And broad. And reeking of ale.

Unless that was Reardon's own stench.

"S'Reardon," he corrected, slurring slightly. "And I don' wanna be prince no more."

"Aw, such a sorry sap," another voice said.

There were two—or was it four?—figures around Reardon. He couldn't be sure if he was simply seeing double. It was dark as pitch, and his eyes refused to focus.

"Lemme go," he said, realizing the larger man still had hold of him. "I'm goin' home."

"Thought you didn't wanna be prince no more," the second man said. He was tall too but stringy, with long, scraggly hair. "Everyone knows what you want, pretty thing, they just love you too much to admit it. When you get pissed, you think your eyes don't wander? Is that why you really miss that last offering, hmm? He bewitch your trousers too?"

Reardon heaved backward, soberer in an instant at what was being implied, but the big man's grip was like a vise. "I'm not bewitched. He was my *friend*."

"Good friend, I bet," the larger man chortled. "You wanna be our friend, pretty prince?" His breath smelled rancid up close, and it mixed unpleasantly with the odor of the piss in the nearby trough, even as they backed him away from it into a tinier alley that had no exit.

"You're talking treason a-and… depravity!" Reardon fought, but he couldn't fight the spinning night.

What did it matter if he was depraved too? He didn't want these men.

"Who you gonna tell, boy?" the stringy one said, a bony hand grasping Reardon's chin while the larger man still had his arm. Meatier fingers started pawing at his trousers. "Gonna cry to the king? You won't even remember what we look like."

Reardon wouldn't. He couldn't tell what they looked like now, in the dark, with their bodies pressing tight and those meaty fingers *reaching*. "Stop—"

The air was cut with a thunderous swish, and the larger man gurgled and fell, his thick fingers leaving with him.

Another *swish*, and the stringy man followed, two thuds on the street.

Reardon squinted through the dark, and when his eyes finally revealed to him the shadow moving closer, it wasn't some bandit, but Lombard.

Ruthlessly, he drove his sword into both bodies, leaving any further gurgling silenced. Then he wiped his blade on the back of the downed men and held his hand out to Reardon.

Reardon took it, pulled powerfully into the embrace of the general, who kept him close to prevent him from wobbling.

"You remember now why I have repeatedly asked you to not go out of the castle alone at night?"

"They were *awful*," Reardon said in reply. "Most people aren't awful."

"You haven't met most people, my prince. Do you think I should have shown mercy?"

"I...."

"Mercy merely means you might end up the dead man instead. Come." He pulled Reardon along, sheathing his sword and choosing side streets and alleys with as few evening strollers as possible.

Reardon was grateful but also surprised. He'd been terrible to Lombard ever since Barclay was taken away.

Sudden fear wrapped around his heart as he realized that Lombard must have been watching him all along. "D-did you... hear...?"

"Their blasphemy? It was obvious in their actions, which was why I cut them down. You need not worry."

That wasn't what Reardon had meant, but if Lombard had heard what they accused him of, he must not deem it worthy of comment.

*Everyone knew*, they'd said.

Did they really? Did others suspect that Reardon was corrupt?

But no. Reardon wasn't the corrupt one. He never would have done what those men tried to do, and Barclay had only ever used his visions to help people and keep himself safe. The real corruption was rarely what people thought.

"Do you really think it was magic that killed my mother?" Reardon asked in the dead of the quiet streets, thinking more clearly by the step, with the castle courtyard coming into view.

"I don't know, my prince," Lombard answered. "No one does. But it could have been."

"If it was... if it *was*," Reardon said, like punching the past with his words, "it wouldn't change my mind. Barclay didn't deserve to be taken."

"Your father can only answer the people's call. There were other criminals who might have been chosen, but your friend was fresher in their minds and something far more frightening, so they cried for him instead."

Reardon knew, of course, and there weren't many criminals in the Emerald Kingdom—not who dared get caught, because if they weren't cut down where they stood, as those deviants in the alley had been, they'd be imprisoned until the next offering. Only if they were passed by as sacrifice could they be considered for release.

But not magic-touched. Not what they'd call "deviants" like Reardon. They stayed in prison indefinitely or were exiled.

"I'll stop it," Reardon swore. "I'll never let them do it again."

"You can try, my prince. And when you are king, maybe you will succeed."

Reardon didn't remember much more about the walk to his room. He awoke in the clothes he'd worn the night before but tucked neatly under his covers. He told no one of what had happened, least of all his father, trusting that Lombard wouldn't either, not when the matter had been resolved. But as he washed and changed and looked himself in the mirror that morning, he became more determined than ever.

The sacrifices had to stop.


"YOUR FRIEND?" the Ice King asked, curious again.

"Barclay, House of Numara. He was last year's offering."

"A rescue mission?"

"And to see for myself if you are like the stories."

Even with a cracked face in shades of white, blue, and gray, the Ice King's expression betrayed his amusement. "And what are your findings so far, little prince?"

Reardon trembled beneath him, but only from the cold.

He wasn't scared. A single touch might turn him to ice like the thief who'd been shattered—and the form of the Ice King, naked but sexless, pure ice from head to toe, was close enough that a touch would be easy—but he felt none of the same helplessness that those men in the alley had instilled in him.

"The truth may be worse," Reardon said. "They call you Ice King, but I didn't think it meant this. If your whole castle is like this chamber, then I fear my friend no longer lives. But then I also have to wonder: Why speak with me at all? Why not kill me outright?"

The Ice King studied him with his penetrating gaze. "Perhaps you'd make a fine ransom, an added bonus to the sacrifices your kingdom sends."

"No, I don't think you're the monster you appear to be. Your eyes give you away, Your Majesty, whatever else you might be."

The pregnant pause that filled the chamber made Reardon fear he'd guessed wrong, especially when the Ice King leaned closer, mist rolling off him, cold enough to frost the ends of Reardon's hair.

"Jack!" a melodic voice cut the quiet, making the Ice King grimace. "The sacrifice didn't come through the gate! The cart left! What—what on earth are you doing?! Who is that?"

As the Ice King lifted off him, all Reardon could focus on was how she'd called him *Jack*, which further proved his point.

The Ice King couldn't always have been like this.

Frost still clung to Reardon, but he was able to take a deep breath and shake some of it from his hair as he sat up and looked past the Ice King, past the window he'd climbed through using a grappling hook and staunch patience, to the formal entrance of the chamber, where the most beautiful woman he'd ever laid eyes upon stood.

She was also monstrous in her own way. Her gown and jewelry were all made of gold, with a delicate crown atop her head, but her hair and eyes and skin were all gold too. The fabric moved like silk as she came closer, and her golden hair, curled in waves down her back near to her waist, shifted around her shoulders like silk, but she was clearly not painted, but made of gold down to every fiber, just like the king was made of ice.

"The Emerald Prince thought to kill me," the Ice King said.

"Only if you'd proven to be a villain!" Reardon protested, confident enough now to stand, though he was careful with his footing on the slick surface of the floor.

"Are you certain I'm not?" The king's fangs glinted in the sun coming in through the windows.

"Prince? Why would they send their prince?" The woman approached more swiftly, practically floating over the floor and bypassing the king without concern. She was even more beautiful up close but still unsettling to look at. "Did you do something vile?"

"*No*. I replaced the real sacrifice and sent him toward the Shadow Lands to make his escape. No one knows I'm here. The soldiers didn't see me make the switch. Are you the Ice King's queen?"

She laughed, and the Ice King snorted.

"His sister, dear. Princess Josephine. Call me Josie."

"Reardon of House Thom, prince and future king of Emerald." He reached instinctively to take her hand, but she drew back.

"Best not do that. My skin is as deadly as my brother's. All I touch turns to gold."

Reardon looked on her in further awe, but still, he wasn't afraid. "You're magical, clearly, but you couldn't have been born like this."

Again, the Ice King snorted, standing to his full height, which made him twice the size of his sister, like some massive ogre. "Our mother would have been quite the sight if we had been."

"Don't be rude, Jack. This castle is cursed, sweet prince," Josie said. "Don't you know that?"

"They know nothing," the king spat, falling back to all fours with a slam and shudder of the room. "Their stories became half-truths and then lies since the curse took us."

"I believe you," Reardon professed. "I suspected as much for years, that whatever you truly are must have been lost to time."

"Careful," the Ice King warned, for Reardon had made to appeal as close to them as possible with a frantic dash forward, yet he understood the need for distance. "I'm still debating whether to add you to my garden of statues."

"You try to frighten me, Majesty, but it's clear you won't risk harming me."

"No? I will not hesitate to kill an enemy."

"And I am not one." Reardon took another step forward, and while there was plenty of space to protect Reardon, they both leaned away, confirming his beliefs. "I only wish to see my friend and know that he is safe.

"Or... has he become cursed too?" Suddenly Reardon wondered if he was also susceptible and already becoming something deadly at his touch.

"The sacrifices do not join in our sorrows," Josie assuaged him. "Only those of us who were here in the beginning are cursed. But there is one boon the offerings receive."

"Josie—"

"No one ages within these walls."

"You mean, the sacrifices from almost two hundred years are all still here and as young as the day they arrived?"

"See what you've done." The Ice King stomped around Reardon. "He'll want to stay now."

"And why shouldn't he? He's this year's offering, isn't he?"

"He isn't—"

"Come, see for yourself." She motioned Reardon toward the doors to venture ahead of her. "They're all eager to meet the new blood."

"*Josie*."

"Hush, Jack. I'll bring him back to you once he sees his friend is safe."

Trusting that the Ice King would not freeze him from behind, Reardon moved as indicated, ginger in his steps, though the closer he got to the doors, the less ice there was to disrupt his footing.

Josie had left the doors open, giant things, three times the height of a man, with the ceiling even higher in this master chamber of the castle. Reardon had chosen wisely, assuming the Ice King would reside where the most ice gathered along the walls outside. Now he found himself assaulted by a surprising but comforting warmth as soon as he crossed the threshold to leave.

He stepped out onto the landing of an immense staircase leading down. As he began to descend, Josie floated out after him to get in front and lead the way—and she did indeed float, for her feet did not touch the ground.

"Which friend is yours?" she asked over her shoulder, keeping pace a few lengths in front of him. "A recent offering?"

"From last year. Barclay, House of Numara."

"Barclay?" She stopped, and Reardon had to catch himself from walking into her. He worried for a moment that something was wrong, that something had happened to Barclay, but she smiled. "Of course. *Reardon*," she said knowingly and continued on without another word.

There were other landings they passed, leading to hallways and more doors, but she brought them down and down, around and around, winding toward the ground floor, where the din of the some two hundred attendants of this castle could be heard wondering where the sacrifice could be.

By the bottom of the staircase, Reardon's hair and clothing were wet from the frost having melted. He felt like a drowned dog, grimy from almost three days travel and restless sleep. It was as warm in this castle as any other, maybe cozier than it should be, considering the chill of the Ice King's chamber.

And it was grand, so grand and beautiful, with tapestries and archways and furniture that belied what Reardon had seen upstairs. Only the Ice King lived in drab darkness. The rest of this castle was a wonder—as were its people.

"There he is!"

"Josie brings him!"

"Oh, he's handsome!"

"And *armed*! Relieve him of all that immediately!"

Reardon was swarmed, feeling the onset of panic, even if he had discovered a different sort of kingdom than expected. Some of the faces were familiar, from the last twenty years or so, a few even looking at Reardon in recognition as well, but there were also elves and half-elves. He'd heard that in ages past elves lived hidden in his kingdom, but he'd never seen anyone of elven blood before, the race most known to be born with magic in their veins.

It was said they'd hidden their ears with magic too, for it clearly gave them away, the full-blooded elves slimmer, with long, tapered ears stretching away from their heads, and the half-elves closer to humans in appearance but still with prominent points to their ears and an extra shimmer in their eyes.

Reardon was so stunned, taking it all in, that he didn't think to fight back as he was divested of his sword belt.

"Are they sending us nobles now?" A woman with dark skin and intricately pinned hair sneered at him as she inspected his sword. "What's your crime, darling? Bugger a few boys?"

"*No*," Reardon exclaimed, stricken by her coming close to guessing the crime that would have condemned him had he been the real sacrifice. "I've never—"

"Reardon!" a familiar voice shouted, and Reardon's head snapped around so fast, he didn't care that some wild-looking half-elf with very strange clothing had just snatched the bejeweled dagger from the sheath on his ankle.

"Barclay!"

The others parted, Josie watching from a safe distance up the staircase, as Barclay appeared, barreling toward Reardon to throw himself on him with enough force that Barclay's feet left the ground. The embrace felt more sound and secure than any Reardon had experienced since Barclay was taken.

"Oh, my friend, I've missed you."

"I told you not to follow me," Barclay chided once he'd finished squeezing Reardon. "But today is the day of the offering. Does that mean you did it? You finally convinced your father to stop?"

Reardon looked down in shame, holding tight to Barclay's forearms to keep him close. "I tried so many times, but he wouldn't listen. I traded places with this year's sacrifice to come free you."

"What is going on?" a new voice boomed over the din of the crowd.

The other voices stopped, and anyone who hadn't slunk away did so now, all save Barclay, who kept an arm around Reardon's waist and turned to face outward as if to ward off some great threat.

Then Reardon saw why, because what came forward through the wide berth the humans and elves of the castle had created had to be another creature of the curse.

Just as the king was made of ice and Josie of gold, this man, big and burly and menacing, was made of flames. He seemed mostly nude like the Ice King, but a long vest hung from his shoulders, made of his element just like Josie's garments.

Reardon leaned into Barclay. He'd rather turn to ice or gold than be burned.

"Why are you clinging?" the flaming man demanded of Barclay. "Who is he?"

"This is Reardon, Branwen. My friend."

"Not the sacrifice?"

"Not technically, but—"

"Then what is he doing here?" Branwen demanded like the roar of a forest fire.

"Calm down," Josie spoke over him. "Prince Reardon replaced the sacrifice. Your temper doesn't have to be as fiery as your face, you know."

Reardon didn't think he could ever get used to reading expressions in elements, but Branwen looked like burning fury. "Jack knows about this?"

"He does. I'll take the prince back to him once he's had a moment to collect himself. Maybe we can clean and clothe him too, make him more presentable. Jack's temper isn't any better than yours these days."

"How many cursed are there?" Reardon asked in wonder after Branwen grudgingly backed off.

"Wouldn't you like to know?" a whispering voice said from nowhere and yet right at Reardon's ear.

He jumped, leaning against his smaller friend again as something began to form at his other side, an outline around a figure that didn't seem to be there but was, like an apparition.

The phantom appeared slight like Barclay and young, though Reardon knew most of the people here were well over a hundred, if not two hundred, years old. This new cursed creature was fully clothed, but his garments were all transparent.

"I'm Spymaster for his royal high-horse up there. Zephyr if I like you." He grinned, his not-there eyes boring right through Reardon.

"What happens if *you* touch someone?" Reardon asked.

"Poof," he said with a pop of the P. "But don't be too worried, pretty prince. There's only one more of us, though he might be the most *shocking*."

Reardon frowned, suspecting hidden meaning in the word—but also not liking being called pretty. While once he'd found the compliment flattering, now it reminded him of those awful men in the alley.

"Go on, Barclay," Josie said, "get him tidied up so we can return him to my brother. Everyone!" she shouted louder, since the crowd had started to titter again. "Make sure the cart is truly gone and that everything is sealed up tight. Nothing changes about the welcome feast unless the king deems it so, and so far, he has not made up his mind. Go!"

Everyone scattered, loyal to their princess, as any good servants would be. She then favored Reardon and Barclay with a warm smile.

Reardon was whisked across the large foyer of the castle with Barclay still holding his waist, leaving Josie behind and the wisp of the Spymaster, and then passing the smoldering Branwen. One more who was cursed, Zephyr had said, which made five in total with the king. What a lonely place this must have been before it was filled with sacrifices. No wonder they welcomed them.

There were so many rooms and corridors and staircases smaller than the one that led to the Ice King's chamber, Reardon would need a guide for weeks to learn this place. At long last, having passed many of the bustling servants preparing for this supposed feast, they arrived at a long row of more closely spaced doors, and Barclay brought him to one that remained open.

"This was to be the new sacrifice's quarters. It's yours, I guess, until the king decides what to do with you."

It was still spacious for a servant's room, even with its own privy, bath, washbasin, and access to running water through a pump. There were clothes of varying sizes for men and women in an open wardrobe, and the bed had a beautiful patchwork quilt in bright colors and patterns.

"I feel like an honored guest in a noble's house, not taking the place of a servant for an enemy king." Reardon spun about to take it all in. "You all have rooms like this?"

"We do. Though they're becoming less abundant. They've remodeled several old guardrooms and larders in recent years. We make do."

*We*, because Barclay was part of this kingdom now, not Reardon's.

As he turned to his friend, he could see how healthy and happy Barclay looked, maybe more so than he'd ever been in Emerald. He no longer had to pretend here, and he was clearly cared for. His clothes looked brand new, and there was an extra ruddiness to his brown cheeks.

"We should get you cleaned up," Barclay said, indicating the bath, which someone had already filled with hot water. It looked very inviting, given the chill that had set in after meeting the Ice King and with Reardon's clothes left damp. "Go on. I'll find something in your size from the wardrobe."

Reardon did as he was told, stripping off what he'd thought was his plainest outfit, though everyone had still recognized his station. He left it all in a basket near the bath. The water was absolute heaven after three days on the road and a brush with being frozen.

"What will they do with my weapons?" Reardon asked after he'd sunk his head below the surface to warm his chilled hair.

"I'm sure you'll get them back. They only take such things until they're sure there's no threat. Branwen will oversee it all. He's master of arms and used to command the king's army—when they had one."

"With Josie as princess and Zephyr the.... Spymaster? Sounds ominous."

"It's a more daunting name than the truth. Zephyr merely watches and listens to be sure there's no unrest. He isn't as sinister as he acts.

Most of the time." Barclay appeared from behind the bath, bringing a dry robe and some soap and oils that he set on a shelf within Reardon's reach.

Reardon utilized the items to clean himself as his friend sat, close but keeping his eyes averted. "You're all servants. Does that mean they force your labor?"

"Nothing like that. We just have our place. A place we got to *choose*. I'm finishing my apprenticeship with Liam, the king's wizard, and Widow Caitlin. She was sacrificed a decade ago."

"Did you say wizard? Magic instead of alchemy?"

"Liam uses everything. I've learned so much this past year, Reardon. Magic is a wondrous thing that can work alongside alchemy to create and heal, not only destroy. You're right to challenge your father."

"I know, I just wish challenging him was enough. Does all this mean you have no desire to escape with me?"

Barclay looked up at him fearfully.

"We can go," Reardon whispered, resting his arms on the edge of the bath. "Right now. Convince my father together. Tell him everything about this place."

"I can't do that."

"You're a prisoner?"

"No. I could go, if I wanted. Everyone is free to leave if they choose."

"Then you don't want to come home?" Reardon's arms dropped back into the water. "Your family stayed silent like all offering families do, but I'm sure they miss you."

"You're sure? Really?"

Reardon hadn't actually seen them—Barclay's parents and older brother. They always ducked away if they saw him coming. "*I* missed you. If I can convince my father of the truth, wouldn't you want to be free of this place? It's remarkable, the people too, but it isn't your home."

Doubt was the only clear emotion on Barclay's face as his gaze drifted, but before he could say anything, the door opened.

The creature that entered was indeed *shocking*, for he was a storm in motion, made entirely of lightning. He entered with a crackle, and all the hairs on Reardon's body outside the water stood tall and tingling.

"Would you hurry up?" His voice snapped like lightning too. "Clean, dry, dress. These aren't complicated tasks." He too had attempted clothing, but only a robe. Anything else wouldn't have held its shape. He also had a face somehow, even eyes, separate from the other sparks of electric light that made up his form, though Reardon wasn't sure how to describe it other than magic.

"Sir Liam?" Reardon asked, hiding his body behind the tall back of the bath.

"Liam is enough."

"As court wizard, serving Josie and Jack? Do Branwen and Zephyr shorten their names and titles as well?"

"Branwen is Bran to some, but if you call Zephyr Zeph, he's likely to take you to bed." Liam laughed—at least Reardon thought the crack was a laugh, though he was busy blushing at the comment. "Formalities don't stick around here long, so don't expect me to call you *Highness*. Now hurry up. Your next audience with the king requires our assistance."

*Our* was revealed as Liam entered fully and a woman came in behind him with long brunette hair and a steely expression, who Reardon took for Widow Caitlin. She carried a potion bottle with a glowing blue substance swirling inside.

He couldn't be sure if her cool expression was simply her demeanor or directed at him as prince of the kingdom that had shunned her. He vaguely recalled when she was chosen, because it had been around the time of his mother's death, and she was one of many called witch that year.

"If you want to avoid frostbite every time you're in the king's presence, you'll drink this," she said simply.

They made no move to turn away, simply stood there waiting for Reardon to get out of the bath.

He ducked down lower.

Barclay scrambled to bring him the robe so he could step out without giving his audience as much of a show.

"Thank you," Reardon whispered.

There was a dressing screen at least, where Barclay had already draped some suitable clothing—basic trousers and a shirt and doublet, with a pair of leather boots. None of it was frilled like a noble would wear, but it was of far better quality and color saturation than Reardon had ever seen on the commoners of his kingdom. Whoever made their clothing was a true artisan. He rather liked the deep red and marigold of his new garments, trimmed in leather to match his boots.

"Do you need someone to help tuck your cock away too?" Liam called when Reardon had yet to emerge from the screen.

"*Liam,*" Caitlin said in a reprimand.

"Please, he's a prince. As if he hasn't dipped his wick in a few brothels."

"He hasn't," Barclay defended, but Reardon did not want that conversation to continue.

Summoning his courage, he stepped out from behind the screen and approached the wizard, careful not to get too close. He imagined that someone who touched him would be struck down like a bolt had come from the heavens.

Caitlin came forward to hand him the potion, and he drank it swiftly. He expected it to be cool, but it burned down his throat.

"This...." He coughed as he handed the empty bottle back to her. "... this will protect me against the Ice King's touch?"

"No, but it'll make it more bearable to be near him. The effects will last a few hours. You'll know when it starts to wear off, though I doubt he'll keep you for that long." Her unfriendliness certainly felt personal with the way she stared him down, but he had little to defend himself with, other than being too weak for too long to stop any of this.

Reardon wondered if there were potions to protect against all the elementals in the castle, but their proximities didn't cause as extreme results. Around Josie there was a slight metallic taste in his mouth, Branwen made him sweat, Zephyr made him light-headed, and Liam made his ears tingle and his hair stand up.

The Ice King was far more potent.

"Come." Josie appeared, floating in the doorway. They all floated in their own way, Reardon had noticed, except the king, who made everything quake with his steps. "Jack grows impatient."

Reardon looked to Barclay, but he'd barely opened his mouth before his friend pounced upon him once more for a tight embrace. Then Barclay gasped, a common enough occurrence when he touched someone, but Reardon hadn't heard that sound in a year.

"A vision?"

"I... I don't know how to explain...." Barclay pulled back, stunned but difficult to read.

"What did you see?"

"I can't say."

"Barclay—"

"I can't say!"

It was then that Reardon realized… he was going to die here. Barclay was never good at hiding his emotions. But if Reardon was headed to his execution, then he vowed to make his time here count.

"It's all right." He coaxed Barclay to return to him, and when he didn't move, Reardon breached the space between them and hugged his friend again. "I love you, and I am so glad I got to see you again. I'll be back soon."

Without waiting to hear Barclay's response, Reardon moved for the door, past the lightning wizard and his sharp-eyed assistant, to follow Josie back through the castle.

Reardon paid less mind to the servants they passed, moving quietly behind the golden princess, lost in thought. He could salvage this, even if he was destined to decorate the Ice King's garden.

"Your hair's still damp, sweet prince," Josie said once they returned to the grand hall that connected to the main doors of the castle and the bottom of the staircase that led to the Ice King's chamber. "That won't do around Jack, even if Liam and good Widow Caitlin gave you some protection. Bran!" she called to the fiery man, who was as large as any normal soldier Reardon had ever met, though not as looming as the Ice King.

Branwen seemed to stomp as he moved toward them, but he too floated, flames pulsing from his body when he came to a halt. "What? Can I turn this brat to ashes yet?"

"No. Just a small little puff, dear, to dry his hair."

Did she mean—?

Branwen snarled like an angry dragon, and Reardon jolted backward as a burst of heat nearly licked his hair with flames, leaving his face hot and his hair completely dry.

"Using me like a bloody barber," Branwen grumbled as he walked away.

"Not quite. We'll need Zephyr for that," Josie said with a scrutinizing frown at Reardon's dried locks falling into his eyes.

"At your service." Zephyr's voice preceded his appearance again, right at Reardon's side, where he puffed a breath, like blowing him a kiss, and the madness of Reardon's hair was suddenly tamed.

"Much better." Josie turned to the wall behind them and touched a dull stone with the tip of her finger, turning it to shimmering gold and reflecting Reardon's image back at him as clear as a calm pool.

The finest barber in all the Emerald Kingdom couldn't have done better.

"No following us the rest of the way now, Zephyr," Josie said, continuing toward the side staircase they had descended before. "You know Jack hates it when you stick your nose where he hasn't ordered it."

Zephyr's translucent face pouted, and then he vanished on the spot.

The ascent to the Ice King's chamber seemed longer than the way down, as Reardon's stomach filled with encroaching dread. "Jack can't be his given name. What is it short for?"

"Crowned King John of the Sapphire Kingdom, but that was a very long time ago."

*Sapphire.* Reardon had never heard this place referred to as anything but Frozen.

Their journey ended abruptly before Reardon could ask any of the questions that had arisen within him. He'd felt the increasing cold as they drew closer to the frosted doors, but it wasn't as unbearable thanks to the wizard's potion, even with only a simple doublet instead of his furs. Once inside, he found his feet didn't slip as easily either.

At the very end of the large room, the Ice King sat with a door on either side behind him. Reardon wondered where they led. The throne the king perched on was magnificent, covered in crystals of ice, yet he lounged in such a carelessly human way.

The throne was so large that he must have barely filled it as a human. Now he took up the entire thing and had to kick his legs over one side of the arm to fully support him—though maybe that was merely how he preferred to sit.

"All pampered and catered to, little prince?" he called down the expanse that separated them.

Josie stepped aside, and Reardon moved forward. As he approached the throne, he soon no longer felt Josie behind him but dared not look back to show weakness.

"This doesn't mean you are safe," the king warned, "or that you are welcome in my home."

"Jack, is it? Far better than 'Ice King,' I suppose."

The king frowned.

"I'll call you Majesty until we trust each other. But on that day, I will call you Jack."

"Is this a game to you?" The Ice King straightened. Reardon stood almost directly before the throne now, chilled and shivering but without any creeping frost on his hair or clothes. "What do you hope to accomplish?"

"My father is wrong for what he does, but seeing this curse on you makes me wonder if he is right about magic's corruption, despite all the wonders it can do."

"Magic alone did not curse us!" the king roared. "One person who wielded it did, and I brought her wrath upon me myself."

That gave Reardon pause. There was so much he didn't know. "You could tell me your story."

"It is a long one, little prince, and I grow weary of your presence already." He stood, crunching down the steps between Reardon and the throne and bringing a gust of icy wind with him.

Reardon sensed how close he was to death but stood his ground. "I only want to bring my people home."

"And where are they supposed to go? *Home*, you say. The thief who almost lost her hands because she was starving, the man who lusted after the wrong noble's son, your friend who has visions—do they have a home to go back to when their own people cast them out as villains?"

"*I* didn't."

"Good for you. You only cared once it finally affected someone you knew."

Reardon's fists clenched to be called a heartless coward, but he'd called himself worse this past year.

He also couldn't overlook the example of a *man* and a noble's son.

"I suppose you've taken in all the corrupted, haven't you?"

"You call them *corrupt*"—the Ice King stomped another clawed foot closer—"yet ask for leniency?"

"I only speak as I was taught. I don't agree with it. I don't believe they're corrupt. Not any of them. I don't want to. If my father understood—"

"He'd still keep up the status quo. Your kingdom shuns what they don't understand because of my curse, yet they don't even remember the time before."

"So tell me! Let me know the truth so we can learn from our past instead of continuing to repeat it." Reardon stepped forward—too close, he knew—but like before, instead of reaching out and ending him, the

Ice King backed away. "You'd really let them all go, wouldn't you? If they wanted it?"

"They don't, but you are welcome to ask them, including your friend."

"Then I am not a prisoner either?"

"That is up for debate."

If Barclay had seen Reardon's death in his vision, it couldn't be now. Not yet. "Give me the chance to prove I will go back and change things for the better. I'll stay for as long as it takes, but once you believe me, once you know me and I know you, let me go."

"And what if I never believe you? You're the prince. You could bring an army to my door after learning my secrets."

"If you never believe me… then you either have another servant or another statue to crush. But that means you take an audience with me every day."

The king scoffed, turning to stomp back up to his throne and throw himself onto it with an elegant ease that should have been impossible. "Sounds frightfully dull."

"Yes, I can see your calendar is quite full."

He rumbled with laughter like a brewing winter storm.

For a long stretch of minutes, he stared at Reardon with his uniquely human eyes—different from his companions. The Ice King was more tied to his humanity, even if he'd lost the feeling of it in his heart, and more cursed and tortured because of it, perhaps.

Yet still he said, "Fine. But make no mistake, little prince, if you prove unworthy or attempt to betray me, I will not hesitate to turn you into frozen rubble like that thief."

All Reardon could do was return his stare and wonder—What was this curse? Why had it been cast? And what had the king been like before it changed him and his kingdom? He had to know, even if a mysterious and frightening future stretched out before him.

*Love, death, and blue eyes in a sea of white.*

Whatever that might mean.

"You have a deal, Your Majesty."


AFTER THE prince left, Jack rose from his frozen throne and lumbered toward the door behind him at his right. The path there led throughout the castle, to intricate passageways only meant for the royal family. These passageways were also frozen due to continued use, but they allowed him to keep watch without forcing his cold on those who served him.

Branwen kept the castle warm and bright. Liam kept everyone healthy. Josie kept them happy. And Zephyr kept Jack informed of all he ever needed to know. Still, sometimes he preferred to see for himself.

He went to the servants' quarters, where he knew they had set aside a room for this year's sacrifice. He did not have doorways into every area, but it was easy enough to remove a small stone brick somewhere unseen to spy on Prince Reardon and young Barclay.

Barclay was... fine. Jack had barely spoken to him in the many months since his arrival. He barely spoke to any of them. That was for his advisors to attend to. But Josie liked Barclay, and he hadn't raised any fuss or trouble with the others. He'd been learning the ways of alchemy and magic from Liam alongside the healer, Widow Caitlin, making a fine addition to their community, a simple man who was unfortunate enough to have been gifted something the Emerald Kingdom feared: visions. His powers required touch, however, and for that, Jack was grateful.

He didn't want to know anything of his own future, spanning endlessly before him.

Watching Reardon and Barclay talk, alone in Reardon's quarters, all he overheard them discuss at first was Reardon's deal with Jack, and then what each of them had been up to during their year apart.

"You see. Just two friends happily reunited."

"Maybe." Jack didn't bother turning to face his sister, who'd come from the other end of the passageway. "Barclay is inconsequential, but that prince...."

"What are you thinking?"

"In the end, he'll try to kill me again. If he does, I'll kill him first."

She laughed, softly so as not to be overheard.

Reardon was beautiful, energetic and bold, and not as afraid as many others, even some who'd been in the castle for decades or more. Jack could admit that he found him captivating, but his heart was as much a block of ice as the rest of him. That wouldn't change. That would never change. And neither would the hard-heartedness of others, the Emerald Kingdom included, even if their prince proved soft.

No, nothing would change, but whatever happened when Jack and Reardon began their "audiences," he hoped the end he foresaw did not come too quickly.

# CHAPTER 2

REARDON WAS a prisoner of the Ice King until he earned his freedom. He might die here, or his fate could be worse, but the people of this place and its curse might finally give him the answers that could change the hearts and minds of the Emerald Kingdom forever.

His father would know he was missing by now but not where he had gone—it could take weeks or even months before they realized the truth. That was all the time Reardon needed. He was on a desperate mission that could doom or save countless lives now and into the future. As prince and future king of Emerald, it was his duty to see this through—even if it was the last duty he ever performed.

Despite all that, his current preoccupation was staring at his reflection in the glass above the water basin in his room, fretting over his appearance for a welcome feast.

His hair was still well-coifed, his new clothes an attractive color combination, though he never thought he'd look so good in red, so used to wearing green. But how was he supposed to face all those people downstairs?

"I don't need a feast. I'm hungry, but… this feels wrong. I'm not really one of them. I'm not the sacrifice."

"But you *are* one of us," Barclay insisted. "You don't have to hide any part of you here. Magic is used freely. People love freely. You could stay forever here and be happy."

"Is that what you saw when you touched me?"

"I…."

Reardon turned to look at his friend, sitting on the edge of his bed. Barclay had brought him several more articles of clothing, traded out for the others now that they knew his size, but he'd decided to stick with the dark red and marigold doublet for now.

"Please don't make me say it," Barclay said, staring down at his knees. "I saw you, I'll admit that much, and you were smiling, but I… I don't know."

"It can't be all bad if I was smiling." Reardon joined him on the bed, creaking the plush mattress as he sat. "You don't have to say more. We'll find out together, like we always do. I know that being here is the right thing, no matter what happens to me. I don't suppose you could simply tell me about this place—the king, his people, the curse?"

"I don't know everything, but I can't say much. We're not supposed to let certain things slip to the sacrifice the first few nights."

"Why not?"

"In case you were a criminal. There have been some sent here, in the past, who deserved to be condemned."

"We're in trouble, then, since I'm such a heinous brigand." Reardon chuckled.

Barclay chuckled too, but his posture was slouched and his shoulders tight with tension.

"Can you really not answer anything? Because I don't understand how Branwen is master of arms but didn't turn my sword belt to flames."

Barclay had returned Reardon's belt and the sword it had sheathed, which were both warm to the touch but not singed or marred.

His dagger was still missing, though....

"They can control their touch if it's on something not living," Barclay explained. "They still give off, well, heat for Bran, that tingly feeling around Liam, and so on, but they can choose to not alter objects. It's things that are alive that are the problem."

"Even plants? Birds?"

"Anything...." Barclay looked away, a shadow crossing his face.

"You've seen them? Kill things?"

"*No*," he said fervently, as if desperate to defend them. "But it can be useful with pests. You'll never find any rodents or insects here, aside from the ones we want, like bees for honey. And, well, there was a thief a few months back...."

"I saw him."

Barclay's eyes widened.

"He made a fitting lesson from the king."

That caused Barclay to shiver as if the Ice King was in their presence now, and Reardon got the impression that the king didn't walk among his people the way the others did. The lack of ice trails everywhere but in his chamber proved that.

"That's it, then? Pests and people who threaten this place?"

"And…." Barclay trailed off once more, twiddling his thumbs in his lap. "*Very* rarely, but… sometimes there are accidents."

Reardon felt a stir of nausea, imagining statues made of ice or gold, piles of ash from fire and lightning, and the nothing left behind from those who went *poof*. "What do they do with—"

"Are you going to keep everyone waiting?" Zephyr appeared like a ghost, just suddenly there inside Reardon's room. He must be able to pass right through the door. "Hurry along now, pretty prince," he said, and vanished again just as quickly.

"Does he often do that?" Reardon rose from the bed with a scowl.

"Basically always." Barclay followed suit. "You get used to it."

"Should I…?" Reardon gestured back at his sword belt hanging from a handle on the wardrobe. "I mean, I usually have it for banquets. It's part of proper dress."

"Reardon, you're not in Emerald anymore," Barclay said with a slight smirk. "This is a nice banquet. I had mine last year, after all. But it isn't *proper*. Come on." He grasped Reardon's hand to drag him to the door. "I'll introduce you to my friends. You don't have a specific place to sit. You can sit by me."

*Thank goodness.* Reardon had worried he might be put on display.

That feeling reignited, however, once they reached the grand ballroom opposite the main entrance that had been turned into a banquet hall with tables to fit everyone in the castle. There didn't seem to be any hierarchy to it, other than the lone table at the very back on a sort of stage with an intricate chair in the center and several smaller but elegant chairs framing it.

The king and his elementals were not yet there, but everyone else was, and all two hundred some pairs of eyes turned to look at Reardon as he and Barclay entered. Barclay hadn't let go of his hand the entire way, and for that, Reardon was grateful, clinging tight as his friend led him to one of the center tables and they took two empty seats.

On Reardon's other side was the dark-skinned woman who'd asked if he'd "buggered any boys," and across from them was the half-elf with curiously bright and mismatched clothing.

"Aren't we lucky you know our little fortune-teller," the woman said, as everyone else murmured and continued to gawk at Reardon. "Shayla. Thieving. Forty-five years." She held out a hand, sporting fingerless gloves and black-painted nails.

Reardon tried to accept the hand as he would a noble lady, to which she laughed and put her hand in his with a shake. "S-sorry," he stammered. "But... thieving? Forty-five years?"

"It's customary to introduce yourself with the crime that sent you here and how long you've been in the castle," Barclay said.

"Oh."

*Forty-five?* Shayla didn't look any older than Reardon or Barclay, yet she'd been here for decades.

Widow Caitlin was there as well, beside the half-elf, giving Reardon a calculating stare.

"Nigel." The half-elf waved. "Charlatanry. One hundred and seventy... oh who knows anymore. Two maybe? You're a fun addition." He laughed when Reardon held out a hand to him as well, and he stood to accept it—which showed the jeweled dagger on his belt.

"That's mine." Reardon reached for it, but Nigel pulled away to reclaim his seat.

"Ridiculous. I've had this dagger for ages."

"You most certainly have not—"

A bell chimed, and the din of the room instantly quieted. An unseen door opened behind the head table, permitting the elementals in order— Liam, Zephyr, Branwen, Josie, and finally, the Ice King himself, who brought with him a wave of cool air that made everyone shudder.

*Jack.*

The names, so human, did not fit such mystical creatures.

The Ice King took his seat, frosting it ever so slightly, as if the control the others had with nonliving things was less possible with him. His sister and Branwen each sat next to him, with Liam and Zephyr in the chairs farther down. They were a sight all together, like something out of a storybook or fantastic dream.

That's when Reardon realized that all the tables were laden with food—game, vegetables, cheeses, and bread. He was ravenous, but he'd been so distracted by the eyes on him, he hadn't let his attention wander or his mouth salivate.

But unlike the feast before him, the head table had nothing.

"They can't eat," Barclay whispered. "Not like that."

"Then how do they...?" Reardon started to ask but thought better of it. Everyone was waiting for the king to speak.

Once the room was still, the Ice King stood, large and looming above everyone. "Another year, another sacrifice," he bellowed. "But as you know, we were robbed of that sacrifice today, for the prince of the Emerald Kingdom deemed us *unworthy* and released the offering to escape into the wilds."

Reardon hadn't deemed—

"Make no mistake," the king continued before Reardon could protest, "he is not a replacement. He is not a guest. He is here by my grace alone, and it will not be lasting. He wishes to change your fates, and so I ask you now, so he can have part of his answer early.

"Would you return to the Emerald Kingdom if given the chance?"

"Never!"

"No, my king!"

"We serve you, always!"

A resounding chorus rose up, and Reardon shrank in on himself as the voices grew and more and more of them cried out to say the same.

The Ice King looked so smug, his eyes piercing as he hushed the crowd. "There you have it, little prince. But I suppose you think yourself a hero anyway, hoping to prevent persecution of the *corrupt*. He claims he wants to know me," he returned to his people, "know us and our ways, our curse, to bring an end to the Emerald Kingdom's follies. Maybe he is honest. Maybe he hopes to overthrow me."

"Wait—" Reardon tried.

"He is the future king of our neighbor, after all!" the king cried louder. "I wonder what to do with him...."

"Kill him!" someone shouted.

"Stop the Emerald Prince!"

"Freeze him now, Majesty!"

"No!" Barclay burst up from his seat, drawing the angry eyes of his fellows. His friends had not erupted with such words, but many others had. "Please. He means well. Truly. I know he means to help. He's not like the others. Reardon has been my friend for years with no hope of gain for himself."

"No?" Widow Caitlin said, cool and expressionless. "He did not know of your visions or benefit from them?"

"He... did, but... but I offered my visions, he never asked—"

"Sounds like a charlatan to me!" Nigel cackled.

Shayla laughed, and many nearby laughed with them, leaving Reardon certain that his death was imminent, but the Ice King quieted the crowd once more, as Barclay sat with a distressed frown.

"Let the prince speak," the king said. "Go on, tell us. What makes you not like the others of your land?"

With all eyes on him, as pointed as the tips of pitchforks, Reardon hesitantly stood. The seats Barclay had chosen for them were almost perfectly in the center of the room, making him feel surrounded and very aware of the peril he was in if they called for his death.

"I don't believe in corruption," Reardon said, causing an uproar of fresh murmurs. "I don't! Not like they say. Not for loving someone or having magic inside you. I only wish to understand to be able to better convince my father."

"He's not one of us!"

"Kill him anyway!"

"How can we trust him?"

The voices of dissent returned, and Barclay looked to Reardon pleadingly to say more, to say the truth—that he *was* like those who the Emerald Kingdom would call corrupt if they knew his secret. But Reardon had held that in for so long, he didn't think he could admit it here, like this, in the middle of a crowded room.

The voices rose higher, and Barclay's stare grew more insistent. Reardon had to speak to save himself, and as much as it shook him, he readied himself to do just that, when the Ice King hushed the crowd like before.

"I hear you, good people, but I also hear disagreement, and not everyone has spoken. Let us take it upon ourselves to make the Emerald Prince prove himself. We will have our feast, but as the days and weeks pass, I will look to all of you to help me decide what to do with him.

"Make sure the prince pulls his weight and that he is worthy of whatever fate he earns."

There were stomps of feet and a clatter of dishes as people pounded the tables with their fists like some tribal ritual, a promise between them that cast even more menacing stares Reardon's way. The king had painted a target on him, ensuring Reardon's time here would not be easy.

"To the feast!" The Ice King clapped, and the resonance of his large clawlike hands cast an extra chill through the room that spurred his people to attack the hot food before them.

Everyone started filling their plates, but as famished as Reardon was, his stomach churned at what had transpired. He was in enemy hands and had no idea how to gain their trust.

"Relax. No one will dare touch you now." Shayla smacked his back so hard, his chin nearly collided with his empty plate. "They'll leave that to the king." She snickered, smacking him again before reaching for a large leg of juicy game meat.

"At least it'll be quick." Nigel snickered in kind.

"*Stop*," Barclay pleaded. "They're only joking." He filled his own plate and then started to fill Reardon's, nudging him to eat.

Maybe Shayla and Nigel were only joking, but Reardon could feel eyes on him from all sides, and Widow Caitlin kept passing him her frosty stare. She might as well have had the same powers as the Ice King for how chilly she appeared.

"Eat." Shayla nudged him as Barclay had. "You're no good to anyone sulking. Make friends! Get the people on your side and the king will have no choice but to spare you."

"How do I do that?" Reardon muttered. "Everyone hates me."

"Prove you're useful." Nigel shrugged, tearing into his own leg of meat. "That's what we did."

"More wine!" someone shouted. "And how about a tale from the good bard?"

An echo of like requests resounded, and when Reardon looked around to see who they meant, he realized everyone's attention was on Nigel.

He winked at Reardon and hopped up onto the tabletop, sliding platters and pitchers out of his way with his feet. "Are the masses demanding a tale?"

"A legend!" another voice called.

"Tell us about our fletcher, Nigel!"

"The first sacrifice!"

Since there was no hierarchy to who sat where, there was no way for Reardon to tell at first who the fletcher might be, but he saw a few heads turn toward a table behind him at a man with a blond beard and hard eyes, holding a very pretty young woman at his side who wore tiny round spectacles.

Though Reardon supposed neither of them was truly *young*. The man was over two hundred if he'd been the first sacrifice.

"There's nothing I like better than a proper redemption story!" Nigel cried. "And I can say that; I met him when he was still insufferable!"

The crowd laughed.

"Someone pass me that wine!"

A full goblet was handed up to Nigel, and he took a healthy swig before beginning, "*There came the night!*"

Everyone cheered, and then quieted after what must have been a familiar opening.

"*There came the night!*" He stomped his feet, keeping time with spoken verses.

> "*When a rich man's son who dallied*
> *owed more than he could rally*
> *to the tavern in the square.*
>
> "*And hence it was he was indebted*
> *for all the women bedded,*
> *and his father kicked him out to earn his fare.*
>
> "*But oh alas! He had no skills but the thrills that he had*
>       *wasted*
> *and liquor he had tasted—*"

"Still true!" someone shouted, and another round of laughter filled the air.

"*—and liquor he had tasted to get by,*" Nigel ended, balancing ginger steps on down the table with nimble leaps and flourishes to the crowd's delight.

> "*The rich man's son did wade and wallow*
> *and become so very sallow*
> *like a man cast adrift on a lonely, empty isle,*
>
> "*But soon he turned his eyes to thieving,*
> *blind from all his stealing,*
> *and picked the temping pocket of the wrong kind of*
>       *smile.*

"*There came the night!*" he called once more, starting a clap with his stomps that got the crowd clapping with him.

*"When he stole from worse than merchant,*
*who wondered how far he bent,*
*and lured him in with cloak and soak to keep the chill*
       *away.*

*"Alas again! He tried to run,*
*but the seedy slaver won,*
*by giving chase into the night for fight was yet a plight*
       *to be made right!*
*And was he caught?"*

"No!" the crowd cheered.

*"He ran and ran,*
*with cloak in hand*
*and emerald crest on emerald seaming,*
*lovely bright and gleaming*
*to the north!*

*"But lo, the land was quiet,*
*yet he would surely riot*
*before he stopped,*
*lest he drop,*
*as he reached the gates at hand.*
*And was he caught?"*

"No!"

*"Bright magic lit the dawn*
*as he dashed across the lawn*
*like a shot*
*fired taut*
*as an arrow to our king.*

*"Those others green,*
*left unseen,*
*learned to fear,*

*while he did cheer,*
*and swore to Emerald no longer*
*—a frozen arrow's stronger—*
*the fletcher ever after and bow master!"*

He stretched his arms wide with a final stomp, but then pulled one hand close to his mouth and whispered, *"Just a pity it took a hundred years instead of any faster."*

The crowd cheered again with a smattering of laughter and applause.

"We all know whose bed that cloak's on the end of now!" someone called, and the fletcher pulled his woman closer against his side.

Only when the laughter died, with Nigel bowing low to accept his accolades, did the fletcher speak.

"*Five* years. It took five years before I surpassed the king's master of arms with a bow."

"It's true!" Branwen called from the head table.

"And only twenty more to lose his good humor!" Nigel shouted back.

"Whose fault was that?" the fletcher responded.

"But!" Nigel cried to keep everyone's attention on him as they laughed louder. "But. I say to you all now… *here comes the night*!" he cried, and then bent to speak directly to Reardon. "And on this night, sweet prince, how would you tell that tale?"

Reardon's cheeks burned hot and his heart jumped into his throat. "I, um…."

"Go on. I'm curious what the Emerald stories say."

"I-I thought… bards were supposed to sing."

"It's better this one doesn't," Shayla murmured.

"Free verse is allowed." Nigel scowled as more snickers arose. "You want a song, give us one. How would you sing the tale of the *Emerald Arrow* first fired into the heart of this place?"

Reardon felt more on display than ever, with every table watching him, including that of the Ice King and his court. "I know a different version."

"I'll bet you do." Nigel hopped down to the floor but remained standing. "Maybe a dozen or so? And what's your favorite?"

"The story is similar but paints the slaver as a noble."

"He was one," the fletcher chimed in, eyes hard again and smile thin. "He was both, but history is sung by the victors."

There was a tense silence where Reardon wasn't sure how to proceed, but then a clear, melodic voice rose up beside him.

> *"Beware the lure of passion's ploy to take what's not*
> *your own."*

Reardon turned to Barclay. They were both sitting, facing each other, and Reardon smiled as he jumped in to join him on the verse.

> *"By king and country, you'll be caught and exiled from*
> *your home.*
> *As once a thief in dark of night did rob a noble's*
> *horse*
> *And run when he was chased off road beyond a noble*
> *course.*

"*And the thief ran on,*" Reardon sang powerfully on the chorus, with Barclay falling to harmony as they had done many times before.

> *"Swallowed up by greed,*
> *Toward a hungry maw*
> *On the hill.*

"*Those in pursuit were sieged by death and magic in the air,*" Reardon led, and Barclay came in later to add harmony they had not used the first time.

> *"Held back by frozen gates ahead and all they'd known*
> *to fear.*
> *The thief escaped beyond the wall, assured that he was*
> *free*
> *But down the Ice King came to feed and warned the rest*
> *to flee.*

> *"And the thief cried on,*
> *Swallowed up by greed,*

*But the hungry maw*
*Had enough.*

"*So, beware the vice that will feed the story's end*," they sang in unison, "*for the next year comes again too soon.*"

Barclay nodded for Reardon to give the final line, and he did, softer now but loud enough to fill the room, "*And the Ice King sings the final tune.*"

The ceiling was high, so that Reardon's voice echoed long after he'd finished, and while he continued to smile at his friend, the silence that reigned in the absence of their song drew his eyes to the head table, where all other eyes had turned too, because the Ice King was staring stoically back at him.

Those eyes nearly glowed, cutting across the expanse between them, but Reardon knew it was not magic. His eyes were simply that blue.

"Well now," Nigel cut the silence as sharply as the king's gaze, "the story might have been shit, but your singing's not half bad. Our young fortune-teller too. We'll have to teach them something more fitting for next time, eh?" he called, and another rumble of laughter filtered through the hall.

Reardon blushed at the shouted compliments and applause, thinking that a few of the eyes on him were a little less unfriendly now, even if the king said nothing.

Nigel sat, and with his departure from the stage, the din of separate conversations took over the hall once more, allowing some of the blood to leave Reardon's cheeks. He watched Nigel add food to his plate, reaching over the woman next to him to grab an especially large piece of cheese. She shoved him back into his seat with impressive strength, and as he laughed, unruffled, the jeweled dagger smacked the tabletop and unhooked from his belt with a clatter.

Reardon nabbed it, but then grandly handed it back to Nigel. "Let's say I get that back on my own someday. *Without* you noticing. Then can it be mine again?"

"Good luck with that," Shayla snorted, as Nigel held the dagger delicately between his fingers.

"I'm the talented one around here at making things… *disappear.*" Nigel waved his hands around the dagger, covering it from Reardon's sight, and when his hands parted, the dagger was gone.

"Magic…." Reardon gasped.

The woman next to Nigel sneered, "Nobles. Can't tell the difference between magic and basic sleight of hand." She was beautiful but had a lethality to her that told Reardon she had likely been a soldier or an assassin, especially given the defined muscles bulging through her shirtsleeves.

"It's an illusion," Nigel said, lifting the dagger from his lap. "Not real magic. But this beauty is still mine." He grinned as he hooked it back onto his belt, eyeing Reardon in challenge.

"Until I earn it back," Reardon promised, to which those around them snickered. It wasn't some grand family heirloom, but it was precious to Reardon—a gift from General Lombard on his eighteenth birthday. He'd learn everything he could from these people and gain both the dagger back and their trust.

Reardon began to eat more normally then, chatting with Barclay, Nigel, and Shayla, with occasional additions by Caitlin, though she never addressed Reardon directly. As the feast waned, he realized that the room had grown darker and more torches were lit to fill the hall with light. But while the evening shadows had indeed crept upon them, the room also felt warmer, and he soon saw why.

The head table where the elementals had been watching and talking amongst themselves was now empty, the Ice King's chair looking wet as the frost melted without his presence.

"They don't stay out at night," Barclay said.

"Part of the curse?"

"Yes...."

"What?" Reardon pressed when he sensed that Barclay was keeping something from him.

"I'm sorry. I can't say," Barclay whispered. "I'm welcome here in ways only you ever welcomed me back in Emerald, and for that, no one will ever replace you in my heart as friend and brother, but...."

Reardon shook his indignancy away as he saw his friend's pinched frown. "I understand. I'm meant to earn learning the rest, and I will. I will change things like I promised, even if you never want to come home with me."

Barclay took Reardon's hands beneath the table, like a silent apology for wanting to stay. "Eventually we'll be able to talk about everything, and then I can explain why I'm so happy this is my home now."

Reardon supposed he'd never envisioned what a place where he could be himself would feel like. He wasn't sure he knew *how* to be himself. Barclay knew his secret, but Reardon had never been able to tell anyone else or openly express romantic affections for another man. He saw men and women express it to each other all the time, but….

But here there was so much more to be amazed by.

A pitcher held aloft at the end of the table caught his attention, and when he looked, he saw that no one was holding it. It *floated*, moving down the table to the waiting hand of an elf.

The elf was broad-shouldered and handsome, with black hair and an unruly curl hanging across his forehead. He poured water for himself, and then some for the human woman next to him, who sat close, clinging to his arm.

They were clearly a couple, something that would have condemned the woman too, just for that—lying knowingly with someone of mystic blood. Perhaps that was what had happened, him sent here, discovered as an elf, and her following, called corrupt, right behind him.

Fewer eyes were on Reardon now, and it afforded him the sight of *casual* magic being performed all around, as well as other mixed couples showing affection. More items floated rather than having to be handed down. There were simple transformations, like bread becoming cakes and the white meat of the game birds becoming dark for those who preferred it. Even mending could be done at the wave of a hand, fixing a stain from an overzealous wine drinker or a button that had fallen off someone's tunic.

Reardon stared at it all in awe, but maybe more so at the couples, so comfortable and unafraid together, whether elves and humans or half-elves and—

His heart jumped, all other focus draining away, as he looked back to the muscled woman beside Nigel, who had a beautiful dark-haired half-elf beside her. She was cupping her cheek, whispering sweet words that had them both smiling. Then she *kissed* her, simple but bold, right there at the table for everyone to see.

No one else seemed to care or even looked their way. And they weren't the only ones. At other tables there were other such couples, just as brazenly holding each other or enjoying brushes of their lips—women together, *men* together. Suddenly, Reardon noticed all of them and couldn't look away.

"You're safe here," Barclay whispered, noticing his diverted attention with a soft smile.

Reardon smiled too, because these daring couples gave him hope, even if he wasn't ready to sing his own secret to the rafters like he had the thief's tale.

He shook his head when Nigel tried to fill his empty water goblet with wine, but Nigel insisted. "It's your party, even if much of the room is being poopers about it. Have one glass or you will deeply offend me."

Reardon had two, enough wine that, combined with his exhaustion, his eyes soon started to droop, and his head nearly slumped into a pudding.

Barclay coaxed him out of his seat to lead him from the hall, assuring him that he could go to bed whenever he wanted now that the king was gone, even if there were a few jeers thrown their way as they left. Barclay's friends had all departed too, though he wouldn't have pegged them for early retirees.

"Where's your room?" Reardon asked, waking up more as they walked, alone now in the corridor to Reardon's chambers.

"Right next door," Barclay said. "People change rooms sometimes, but generally, each new sacrifice is next to the previous year's. Easier to expand that way.

"Nigel and Shayla aren't so bad, right? And Caitlin will warm to you. She just doesn't talk much until she gets to know someone."

"And here I was taking it personally," Reardon joked. "They're lovely, really, but an odd match for friends, especially since you've all been here a different amount of time."

Barclay wrinkled his nose.

"It just surprised me!" Reardon amended.

"They all have other friends too, and so do I. Everyone is friendly here. They will be to you too, I swear. But the four of us have... a lot in common."

"Caitlin also works with the wizard?"

"And Shayla. She collects most of the supplies we use. I'm sure you'll see for yourself. They'll all think of ways to put you to work."

"Is that what they did to you?"

"To start. To gauge what sort of person I was but also my interests. It'll be fine," he reassured him, taking both hands again. "How can it not be when you were nothing but honest in there?"

The knot in Reardon's stomach twisted to remind him that he wasn't as certain as he pretended. "Do you think we offended the king with that story?"

"He isn't easily offended or I wouldn't have started it."

"His gaze was just so...."

"Intense. I know."

They both shivered, and after another tight squeeze of Reardon's hands, Barclay let him go.

"Sometimes, in my dreams," Barclay said, "I see a world where magic is used openly everywhere, where people love openly whoever they want. I like to think that's the future, and not too far off."

"Maybe it is," Reardon agreed. "Good night, my friend."

"Good night, Reardon. I'm so glad you're here."

Reardon didn't bother lighting any candles or lanterns when he entered his room, finding his way easily enough in the dark. The idea of sleeping in a real bed reminded him of his exhaustion, and he barely took the time to strip before he climbed under the covers.

The quilt smelled like lavender. They really had done everything they could to make the sacrifice feel welcome, even if they were cautious of anyone new.

As Reardon closed his eyes and started to drift off, he wondered where the elementals had gone when the sun set and what they did during the night. One of the many mysteries he had to solve, he supposed, and come morning, he'd be ready to get to work.


JACK STOOD in the same passageway he'd watched the prince from earlier, seeing the bed clearly through the hole he'd made by removing a carefully chosen stone. His goal wasn't to peep, and it was far too dark to see much of him undressing anyway, but the faintest flash of bare skin made his chest feel warm—and nothing felt warm to him anymore.

The young prince was just so beautiful. And he had a voice to match—one that had enchanted Jack, so much so that he hadn't dared speak after the tale Reardon sang for fear of his own voice breaking, even if the words had painted him as the villain.

Jack *was* a villain, worse than any bard's tale could say. His people were too forgiving, but then, none of them had been there in the beginning, only those who carried the curse with him.

He'd been keeping his eyes on the banquet hall and knew the moment when Reardon and Barclay left, but now the prince merely slid into bed, planning nothing untoward but slumber.

Jack had to admit that Reardon seemed earnest with no ulterior motives, but there was no ending to this experiment where over two hundred years of dissenting beliefs was resolved by a single hopeful boy made king.

Turning from the even breaths of the prince, who had already fallen asleep, Jack replaced the stone and moved quietly back down the passageway to his chamber. He knew where his court members were, but for him, there was nowhere else to go but back to his icy halls.

He shivered as he crossed into the main room, a sensation that made him smirk, and then continued behind the throne to the other door, the one on the *left*, where no one else was ever allowed to go.

The next morning, Jack was shocked—and possibly a little irritated— to leave his private room, just after the crack of dawn and planning to sprawl himself across his throne dramatically before calling for the young prince, only to discover Reardon already waiting for him.

"I expected a chronically late and ambivalent young royal, and yet... here you are," Jack sneered, crunching one clawed hand onto the armrest of his throne.

Today Reardon was dressed in complementing green and blue, accentuating the hue of his eyes, with the contrast and bright light of the sun making his auburn hair far redder than before.

The boy was a royal, gorgeous, and seemingly smart and talented— surely he had to have glaring faults hidden away, or was otherwise secretly daft or entirely full of himself. Yet, despite the haughty smirk he wore as he bowed low in Jack's presence, his eagerness seemed genuine.

"Majesty," Reardon greeted as he finished his bow. "Widow Caitlin left several draughts in front of my door to keep back your chill, so after scavenging for some quick breakfast, I came straight here for our inaugural audience. Princess Josie assured me you would be ready."

"I'm sure she did," Jack grumbled. Gripping the side of his throne more tightly, he made a show of easy strength by swinging himself up onto it with a loud crash and burst of icy wind that made Reardon shudder.

The prince remained undaunted, however, and steadied himself with a shake of his hair. "I understand certain things have been kept from me. Barclay is loyal to you, aside from sharing what he deemed safe, but I intend to learn the rest, as I told you."

"You will know me, and I you," Jack recounted. "So far, I have learned that you are equal parts bold and meek, completely ignorant of my kingdom, an admittedly impressive bard... and quick to blush."

Reardon's cheeks went instantly scarlet.

*Ignorant again?* Jack wondered. *Or merely bashful?*

"One would think you'd be used to having attention on you, little prince."

"N-not volatile attention."

"You sure? Not everyone is tolerant of princes, not even your own people."

A scowl crossed Reardon's face, like he knew of some not so well-meaning subjects, but he kept that story to himself. "I apologize if my naivete is a concern to you, but that is why I wish to learn. The banquet... I know it was not really meant for me, but it was still wonderful."

"Yes, parlor tricks, wine, and amorous strangers." Jack trailed the tips of his claws down the front of his throne, watching Reardon's body language and the way he bit his lip. "I bet you thought you were right at home, like in the cellar of some sleazy tavern."

"I have never frequented brothels, if that's what you're implying!" Even Reardon's ears went red at that. "Your wizard said the same, but I am not like that."

"It's easy to pretend you like magic and mixed company when it's a novelty instead of a way of life."

"Knowing each other means putting aside assumptions, and you are making a lot about me."

If that scarlet color was as real as it seemed, Jack wondered how naive Reardon truly was. "So, convince me you're interesting enough not to simply banish you from my sight."

Something seemed to spring to Reardon's mind immediately, but he dismissed whatever it was and emboldened himself with something else. "I told you my mother died. I was ten years old."

"And how old are you now?"

"Twenty-one."

Maybe a rebel then. If his father was Prince Consort and only King as placeholder, then Reardon was meant to marry within a year and take the throne.

"Her death raised many suspicions," Reardon continued. "No one could explain it, and so magic was blamed. But I never believed that. There was no evidence; people simply chose something they didn't understand to be the scapegoat because they saw no other answer."

"Your point?"

"I never jump to conclusions. Not about anyone or anything. I'm a scientist. I would have apprenticed as an alchemist right along with Barclay if I'd had the option. But I also believe that magic can't be any eviler by default than alchemy. Nothing is evil by default, only by choice."

A philosopher too, but that wouldn't change anything.

Lurching up from his lounged position, Jack took great enjoyment in the way Reardon scrambled back as he began to lumber toward him. "You might be everything you claim to be, little prince. But your task here is also to convince me that releasing you won't bring doom upon my kingdom."

"When I am king—"

"You will still be at the mercy of your people."

"I can sway them—"

"With what? What will your arguments be?"

Reardon floundered, starting and stopping again many times, before giving up with a defeated sigh. "I don't know, but that was why I asked to see you each day. I can only discover the answers by learning. I appreciate all the time you are willing to give me."

Jack could move upright like a man, but it was easiest on all fours with how large and changed his form had become. Regardless, he remained tall, looming over Reardon. "You get until I notice your potion has begun to wear off. No longer."

"Why don't we start with a walk?"

"W-walk?"

"So you can see my *garden* for yourself."

Turning around, Jack headed for the door to the right of his throne. When he reached it, he looked back to see that Reardon had not yet moved.

"Well?"

Clambering forward, Reardon showed commendable speed to catch up, long limbs flailing, yet he was still somehow graceful. He shivered as they moved into the passageway, but there were no signs of ice crystals forming on his skin or clothes.

Jack had to hunch to traverse the corridors upright, knowing each path by heart as he led Reardon through halls and down several staircases, all paved in ice, toward the ground floor and a door to outside.

It was early morning and late in the year. The sacrifice arrived the first day of winter, and so today was the second, meaning that outside was just as cold as in Jack's chamber as they stepped out into the sun.

Reardon was as impervious to this cold as to Jack's with the potion in his veins, and he smiled as he tilted his head toward the light. "It was freezing following the caravan all those nights. How wonderful to be outdoors in winter in nothing but a doublet and be this warm."

Naive, ignorant—but filled with wonder that made his lovely face light up like the dawn.

Jack turned away before Reardon could notice him staring. "I don't feel the sun at all anymore."

As Jack moved down the familiar path, Reardon detoured off the walkway into the dead grass, allowing him to get closer to Jack's side without slipping. "That sounds awful. You never feel warmth? Ever?"

"Tell me, little prince," Jack asked without stopping his progression down the path, "how could I, while I am made of ice?"

Reardon gave no answer but followed quietly, beginning to look around and take in the grounds.

They had exited from the side of the castle. In spring, only Jack's path would be dead and frozen, the rest surprisingly lush with greenery that various people of the kingdom kept tidy. Over the years, more and more planting had begun. Now, even in winter, there were a few smatterings of color.

Reardon gazed fondly at the bright yellow winter jasmine that dangled like ivy along the wall. Jack was leading them along a purposeful path to look out beyond the castle, opposite the Emerald Kingdom, a view Reardon had likely never seen. There was a second gate there, not easily reached.

Jack's castle stood atop a hill like the song said, and out that gate was the path toward what once was the rest of his kingdom. He paused as they reached it and let Reardon wander to the chilled bars that separated them from what lay outside.

"I always wondered...," Reardon said, taking it all in—the sprawling city below that was desolate now, with collapsed houses and not even the scurry of animals, like a wasteland. "Only your castle was ever spoken of, but as grand as it is, it's still only a court. What became of your people? Your original people?"

Jack stayed on the path, for if he drew closer to Reardon, he'd inevitably lean out toward his empty legacy, and he did not wish to endanger the young prince.

Yet.

"Some left before I was cursed. The rest after. Beyond the city, farther down the hill, you can see the start of the Mystic Valley. Some went there. Some to Emerald. Some beyond to lands unknown. No one stayed behind but my inner circle. We had many years alone before the story of the first sacrifice you heard last night."

"He wasn't really a sacrifice."

"No, but he was the beginning."

"And what of before then?" Reardon insisted.

Jack held his head high, the shape of it formed together with his crown feeling forever heavy, but he did not answer.

"You're not going to tell me what the curse is, are you? Not without effort."

"You can see what it *is*, little prince." Jack gestured at himself with one of his massive hands and at the trail of ice behind them. "But come now, we barely know each other to be spilling such intimate secrets." With a grin, he moved on, expecting Reardon to follow, which he did, and brought them around the side of the castle toward the front courtyard.

"You said some of your people escaped to the Mystic Valley," Reardon said, falling in beside Jack again, "but the elves have been gone from there for centuries. It's as abandoned as your city and farms."

"Is it?" Jack tilted his head, and when Reardon's brow furrowed, he laughed coldly but didn't elaborate.

Pushing forward, they reached the true garden of the center courtyard that had been well-kept by the people of the castle, though the fountain held no water this time of year. Reardon looked at it with as much awe as he had the flowers, but Jack steered away from it to bring them closer to the gate, where the *other* garden existed as upright sentinels to ward off any who entered uninvited.

Reardon's posture changed immediately, seeing the multitude of frozen figures like the thief Jack had shattered in front of him.

"More unlucky cutthroats who didn't realize where they were. And some who did, sent here like the others, but they chose to not belong."

"Barclay said the same, that some of the criminals sent here deserved it." While Reardon held himself more stiffly among so much glaring death, he walked unafraid through the statues, almost touching one before he pulled back.

"Does that assuage your guilt?" Jack asked.

"No."

Jack waited for Reardon to return to his side before continuing. He had to make him understand. "You've heard the story of our first offering, now hear the truth of our first death."

Watching the way Reardon's face paled further, Jack moved on down the path to the other side of the castle. His garden was not merely the guards past his gate but also figures lining the walkway along the right side, since it better faced the Emerald Kingdom.

"She was a sacrifice, you see, after nearly a decade of people wronged, only hoping to find sanctuary. She tried to swindle me. *Me*. Swore allegiance, acted the part, and then, once she had gained our trust, she attempted to make off with trinkets she thought would fetch a nice price in other lands and fled.

"On her way out of the castle, she stabbed a young elf gifted with beautiful magic who tried to stop her. He didn't survive. The thief didn't get far, however.

"How did you put it? *But down the Ice King came to feed*," he sang softly, haunting and low. "I swooped upon her like a storm. I knew what my touch would do, though I hadn't seen the effects on a human yet. In that moment, I wanted to freeze every highwayman that had ever lived, every liar, everyone who thought they could claim their place and then simply be gone when it no longer suited them.

"If she wanted out, then she was out. I caught her before she reached the gates and laid my hands on her without mercy. She froze on the spot... right here where I left her."

Jack saw Reardon stumble, the young man not expecting to be brought before the subject of the story, yet there she was, untouched by time. Jack rarely shattered statues, preferring to keep them as reminders.

Her expression was preserved in mute shock, the trinkets she carried frozen with her in a bag at her side.

"Was I wrong?" Jack asked as he stopped in front of her.

"I... don't know," Reardon said. "I can't say I ever agree with someone being killed. But you certainly seem to be the hero of your story."

"I'm no hero," Jack snapped, lunging toward Reardon more closely than intended and causing him to stagger back. "That is not the lesson here. I earned my curse, but the people your kingdom sends to me did not. Even ones like her...." He glanced at her frozen body, remembering the sweet smile she'd afforded everyone in the castle, like she was a doppelganger of her own self once the truth was revealed. "I can't say if she deserved her fate, but as I said—"

"You won't hesitate to kill an enemy," Reardon finished. "But like I told you, Majesty, I am not one. I believe all of this. You don't need to frighten me. We can end this. Together. The sacrifices. Maybe even the curse. Just tell me. Tell me what caused it."

What caused it... was that Jack had proven to be the real monster of his kingdom, far worse than the jagged edges his body now displayed. He hadn't killed or robbed or bedded anyone unwilling. He'd done worse.

Apathy was so much worse....

"Please." Reardon inched closer. "Do you think I can't sympathize?"

Jack fell to crunch down into the frost at his feet on all fours and leaned close to Reardon's face. "I think you will realize that this curse cannot be broken and all you hope to accomplish will fail. When you can no longer deny that is true, you will see no other answer but my death. And I will not allow that to happen."

"Majesty...." Reardon shuddered.

A small part of Jack would have preferred to end this now, before he had to again be disappointed, but the sweet face before him... he didn't want to see it frozen. "We're done for today," Jack said and turned to move back toward the castle.


REARDON HAD the entire day ahead of him—but for at least a quarter hour he didn't move from the garden.

He walked back through the statues of ice, staring at each expression, at each look of terror or surprise, and understood why the Ice King didn't believe him or his ambitions, but he couldn't give up after only one day.

He hadn't seen Barclay yet that morning. Maybe he could find him—

"Thinking of fleeing already, dear prince?"

The familiar voice spun Reardon around.

*Shayla.*

Even in the bright light of morning, she wore dark colors, making her stand out starkly against the frost on the ground, with her equally dark skin and black hair. Adornments hung from her ears, and her lips were painted burgundy. She looked like the type of thief the Ice King had talked about, especially with a large knapsack thrown over her shoulder, yet she had proven herself welcoming and clearly had her place here.

"*Dear* prince, *sweet* prince, *little* prince. Can someone just call me Reardon?"

Shayla laughed, reaching him and giving his shoulder a firm smack like last night. "Reardon it is. Still have some time left on your cold potion, *Reardon*?"

"I think so." Reardon didn't feel much chill, and Caitlin had said the potion should last for hours.

"Then come on." Shayla motioned him toward the gate, which Reardon had assumed didn't open much outside the acceptance of annual offerings, but apparently he was wrong. "You said you wanted to earn your place. It's my day to go foraging, and around here, no one leaves the castle alone. You're coming with me."

# CHAPTER 3

THE EMERALD Kingdom was to the south, the Mystic Valley farther north down the opposite side of the Ice King's hill, but Reardon followed Shayla to the east toward a clearing and the edge of a thick wood that he knew would eventually join with the Dark Forest to the Shadow Lands.

He hoped the true sacrifice had made it there safely and that he hadn't doomed them instead. The Shadow Lands were just as much a mystery as the Ice King's castle.

Reardon wasn't sure what he and Shayla could find for alchemy components while the ground was frozen with patches of snow. That's what she was mostly foraging for, she'd said—*components*. Reardon's knowledge of alchemy was focused more on the mixing and application after ingredients were gathered. Barclay would know better what could be found in wintertime.

"You realize this is an enchanted castle, right? That includes the surrounding grounds," Shayla said, smirking as she looked at Reardon's furrowed brow.

"Are you saying the plants here can withstand winter?"

"Some, and several things grow here that normally wouldn't be found together. But a few useful items—rosemary, thyme, mint—they always thrive in winter." She knelt a few yards from the line of trees, and indeed, several varieties of plants were clustered around their feet, green and lush and overlapping out of the snow. She began picking them with adept precision, taking string from her bag and bundling like plants together before filling the bag with her spoils.

After watching her a few moments, Reardon mimicked her efforts, and she smirked once more, inspecting his work with an approving nod.

"A prince who doesn't mind getting his hands dirty. Who knew?"

She worked twice as fast as Reardon, however, and occasionally she'd toss a plant aside that didn't look quite right to her eyes or tell Reardon to lighten or fatten a bundle before completing it. She'd obviously done this many times before.

"Violets." Reardon pointed behind her, closer to the trees. "They're good for sore throats, aren't they? Would Liam want those too?"

"Knowledgeable, are you? They're on the list. Though not for sore throats. They can be manipulated for other purposes. You won't see anyone from the castle getting ill, but we can be injured or killed."

*Enchanted indeed*, Reardon thought, though he mostly cared that he was continuing to learn about the castle, its curse, and its people.

They were essentially immortal as long as they didn't get hurt, and Reardon would be too while he stayed here.

"Barclay said you knew alchemy, but I didn't realize how much," Shayla said. "That's rare around here. Most of the occupants are magic users. I have basic knowledge. Otherwise, it's mostly Caitlin as our healer, and Liam with his enhancements and experiments. He's a good wizard, but he's blown up his lab a time or two as if a storm blew through it—pun intended." She smiled fondly, like she knew him well.

"A true education involves rough hands and calculated risk," Reardon said with a smile of his own, looking at his dirt-smeared hands, wet from the snow. "My mother used to tell me that." The memory of it brought a soft warmth to his chest. He'd grown beyond feeling a constant ache at the loss of her, but he still missed her every day.

"I remember when the Emerald King announced her birth," Shayla said absently, causing him to snap his attention to her, because he kept forgetting how much older everyone in the castle was compared to him. "So that's where all that *red* came from." She reached out to muss his auburn hair, her hands wet and dirty too, yet the touch felt more playful than razzing.

"She must have grown up well, considering you're not so bad a bastard," she continued, returning to her work. "It was her father, you know, who decided three strikes as a thief was enough to call for one's hands. Only a plea to be sacrifice could stay the butcher's blade. I took my chances."

*The thief who almost lost her hands because she was starving*, Reardon recalled the Ice King saying. He hadn't known his grandfather. That king died before he was born.

"I'm sorry," Reardon said solemnly. "That's awful. They don't do that anymore. But then, thieves might still be chosen as sacrifice if they get enough voices raised against them. My mother did away with many barbaric practices, but she never dared change the larger laws.

"*I* will when I am king. I have to. Especially after meeting all of you."

"That's rather noble." Shayla slowed the pace of her foraging. "I'd think you were all fluff, but you don't seem the type to be made for lying. Maybe you really aren't so bad."

"I'm still sorry."

"I'm not. Ending up here was the best thing that ever happened to me."

Barclay had said the same, and while immortality, food, shelter, and a caring monarch were reason enough to warrant such a response, Reardon had the feeling that there was something more.

Soon they had gathered everything they could from around their feet, and Reardon went to the edge of the wood to pick the violets, while Shayla headed farther down the clearing to shave off bark from a specific patch of trees with one of her blades.

He hadn't noticed initially, but she was armed with twin daggers almost as long as short swords, as well as a hunting knife at her ankle. Reardon felt the loss of his own dagger then, and the sword he might have brought along if this outing had been planned, but he'd left his weapons belt in his room, knowing he'd be seeing the king.

It was in that moment, wondering about his promise to Nigel to steal his dagger back and glancing at Shayla using her hunting knife to chip away bark, that he heard the first growl.

Reardon tensed, because that was no mere wild dog, judging by the resonance, although that would have been bad enough. Turning his head to look deeper into the wood, lush and dark despite the early morning sun, he saw a pair of eyes glowing and the measured steps forward of something larger with a snarling maw.

"Shadow beast...."

"*Wolf*," Shayla corrected, her voice coming steadily from his right. "If shadow beasts exist, they stick to the Dark Kingdom. Now, back away slowly and don't lose eye contact. Whatever you do, don't turn your back on him."

Reardon knew that, but his instincts still told him to do the opposite and *run*.

Steeling himself with even breaths, he stood upright and began a slow shift backward into the clearing, keeping his eyes on the wolf—a *dire* wolf, or at least it had been once, he realized as it materialized more clearly. Its size was impressive, but it looked emaciated.

It was alone. There were no signs of any other wolves, no pack it had come from, which explained its weakened state—weak enough to be ravenous and exceptionally feral.

A whistle rang out from Shayla to draw the wolf's attention, but its eyes remained on Reardon. He didn't dare look at her himself, but he could see her out of the corner of his eye, her hunting knife and one of her daggers in either hand.

"I'm going to throw you a weapon, but he'll probably leap the moment your eyes are off him."

"*What?*"

"Be ready. Try to defend more than harm. He's only hungry."

"Wait—"

"Now!" she cried, and Reardon jerked his head toward her, arm already reaching to catch the dagger his eyes found and locked on, and a moment later he had it with a twist of his wrist and swipe forward just as the wolf lunged.

Its teeth caught the blade instead of Reardon's neck. If this had been a healthy dire wolf, he would have been helplessly bowled over, but he stood firm, pushing back on the blade until a great shove forced the wolf away from him. Reardon swung the dagger around to slice at each of its legs, just enough to wound it, and then scrambled back to keep out of reach.

The cries the wolf made were pitiful, but the narrowing of its eyes was murderous as it readied to lunge again.

Shayla darted forward as fast as if she'd appeared from nothing, slicing first with the hunting knife and then with the twin of the dagger she'd thrown to Reardon. She raised the blunt end of the dagger and rammed the hilt down into the wolf's temple, at which it dropped like a drunk in a tavern at the end of a long bar fight.

Reardon gasped, adrenaline pumping and weapon tight in hand. He'd fought in the past, trained in multiple forms of combat, but he'd never had to fear for his life.

"You know how to handle yourself," Shayla said through panted breath.

"And if I didn't?"

"Then I couldn't have helped you." She grinned, nimble fingers effortlessly twirling her dagger and knife before sheathing them. "But I still tried."

Reardon watched her kneel beside the fallen beast, recognizing how close he'd come to being rent in two without accomplishing anything of real note, other than coming to the Frozen Kingdom to rescue his friend. Knowing Barclay was safe did not change that Reardon was glad he'd fought to get here, but there was so much he hadn't confessed to. So much he hadn't done.

Shayla pulled a vial from her belt and tipped the liquid down the wolf's throat.

"What is that?"

"A sort of healing draught. When he wakes, it'll be as if he's slept and eaten well for a week, his stamina entirely returned to him. What he does after that is up to him. After all, we don't know his story or why he's a lone wolf so far from friends."

"Such mercy," Reardon noted, wondering if the numbness settling into his fingers was from his own draught wearing off or the grip he had on the dagger.

"It's easy after being shown mercy yourself." Shayla stood and came over to take her dagger back from him. "Funny how people work that way."

*Mercy merely means you might end up the dead man instead.*

Reardon liked Shayla's lesson better, but he still had to say, "Most of the people in the castle didn't act that way toward me."

"Many of them are still angry, but while they may gnash their teeth, none would actually harm you. They just wanted to push you, see how you'd react. They trust their king. If he was willing to give you a chance, they will too."

Reardon wasn't sure yet if he had been given a chance or merely a temporary stay of execution.

"We get protective is all," Shayla said, gesturing him up the hill, away from the wolf and the line of trees. She must have deemed their spoils enough—or it too risky to wait for the wolf to wake. "We're family."

*Family.* Josie and the Ice King certainly, but the others too in more than blood.

Just without children.

So many of the people in the castle were paired off, and while not everyone, it made the lack of children suddenly apparent, though Reardon hadn't realized until now.

"If no one here ages... then children can't be born either, can they?" he asked as they headed home.

"One of the downsides. For some. I find it freeing. *Lots* of worry-free sex."

Reardon tripped, face red and hot in an instant.

Shayla laughed but didn't take back her statement.

"Y-you have someone?" Reardon stuttered. "I didn't see you and Nigel with anyone. Unless...."

"It's not Nigel," she said as though the idea was preposterous—and it certainly seemed to be from their lack of romantic chemistry. "Keep on as you are, Reardon. You'll discover all the castle's secrets eventually." Without elaborating, she kept on up the hill, her bag full and her steps sure.

Reardon's potion *was* wearing off, he decided, as he shuddered beneath his doublet, wishing for a warm fire when they returned.

Shayla noticed. "There should be a cloak with your new clothes."

"It's too short. Which is a shame, because it's lovely. I can use the one I came in. Though that was taken away to be cleaned...." He stopped short, thinking of his dagger again. "I'm not getting it back, am I?"

Another warm laugh bubbled out of her. "I can take you to your cloak later. Clean it yourself and you might get to keep it. Does that mean you're enjoying your new clothes?"

"Very much. The colors, the simple but flawless craftsmanship." Reardon returned to her side, picking at the brilliant blue and green of today's garments. "I honestly think this is better than any of the frilly noble wear I've had to endure. And the quilt! Does everyone have a quilt like that? It's like a rainbow of patterns, and so warm."

"Flatterer," she said, opening the gate for them with an extra-wide smile. "I was rather proud of yours, but not everyone has a quilt yet. I started with the newbies and have been trying to backdate. Nigel was jealous you got one before he did."

Reardon stood for several moments inside the archway before he realized what she meant. "*You're* the tailor?"

"Not the only tailor, but I did make your doublet, the one you wore last night, and your quilt. Why? Do I not look like a tailor?" She planted her hands on her hips, which only accentuated the presence of her daggers.

"More like a...."

"A...?"

"A cutthroat," Reardon said honestly, not surprised when this seemed to please her.

"Then I haven't lost my touch," she said, spinning about to continue toward the castle—past the guardian ice statues that didn't falter her steps in the slightest. "Come on. I'm not abandoning you yet. Time to deliver these components to our wizard."

The castle would still take Reardon weeks to learn in full, but he memorized as best he could the path Shayla took him on to travel from the main doors to Liam's laboratory. She explained that he had his own wing of the castle, partially for storage and experiments, but also to accommodate living quarters separate from others, like all the cursed had, as well as space for his apprentices to work.

Caitlin was beyond a mere apprentice now, really Liam's second, standing in where he was limited by touch. Barclay was the one learning, a rare breed, apparently, since Caitlin had been the first in a generation to hold up to Liam's standards for alchemy.

Much of the castle had high ceilings and open space, but Liam's lab felt immediately stifling, like an overstuffed library, closed in by shelves filled with a combination of books, equipment, and messily labeled bottles.

The smell was also… interesting, like bread and sour fruit. Once Reardon saw the setup for fermentation, he realized why.

"You make ale and wine in here?"

"Reardon!" Barclay exclaimed upon seeing him enter behind Shayla. He and Caitlin were huddled together over a cluttered worktable making a large batch of some potion or another in a cauldron, just like Reardon had seen Barclay and Master Wells do many times back home.

Liam was there too, though standing farther away, choosing ingredients that he set on the table. "Where else did you think it came from?" he grumbled, sparking jolts of lightning from his body.

Reardon hoped an errant spark wouldn't have the same effect as his touch.

"Behave," Shayla chided him. "I did your grunt work, and I expect compensation." She set her bag on another table along the wall.

"You let the prince help you?" Liam sneered, eyes glowing brightly like two pinpricks of stars in a night sky. "Am I going to be picking weeds out of those bundles?"

"Only what you'll be picking out of your ass." She extracted a bundle to show him, which easily could have been hers or Reardon's, since their finished work had ended the same. "Relax. He's a good kid. Fended off a hungry dire wolf without getting so much as a scratch."

"What?" Barclay abandoned his work to rush to Reardon's side, causing Caitlin to scramble to pick up the slow stirring he'd been doing with a ladle, her lips pursed but silent.

"I'm fine," Reardon said. "Just a reminder to watch my back. Outside if not in," he added with a smile at Shayla—though Caitlin and Liam both shot him steely glares to remind him that he hadn't won over everyone just yet.

"Did things go well with the king this morning?" Barclay asked, hurrying back to Caitlin to reclaim his ladle, which allowed her to add another ingredient to the bubbling pot.

"It didn't go… terribly."

Shayla snorted, and Reardon wondered if she'd been watching long before she called for Reardon to help her forage.

Looking over the ingredients more closely, Reardon recognized everything that had been added to the pot, and when the wizard started straining juniper berries, he was certain of what they were making—a regeneration potion, similar to what Shayla must have given the wolf, but for slower-acting effects that replenished a person's energy throughout an entire day.

It was strange seeing a being made of lightning handle, well, anything. Liam could clearly still hold things, and yet it almost looked as though the carafe the berries were in, their yellowed juice ripe for use, merely floated amidst a tiny storm.

Reardon frowned at the strained juice when Liam set it on the table. "If I may say, sir, muddling juniper berries instead of infusing water with their juices allows for better sustained regeneration, even for soldiers doing long patrols."

Liam crackled, his fierce eyes shooting to Reardon like he might fire a bolt at him.

"I mean no disrespect! But the difference in stamina is staggering. Barclay and I helped our High Alchemist test it when we were teenagers."

"I've tried telling him," Barclay muttered.

"And I've said no," Liam snarled. "This is how we have always done this recipe."

"Even with a second voice added, speaking the same logic?" Reardon tried.

"If it will shut you both up, fine," he snapped, turning to retrieve a bundle of fresh juniper that he threw on the table beside the juice, along with a mortar and pestle. "I don't need two of you nagging me. But if you know a thing or two, Emerald Prince, then you do the work."

Reardon did know a thing or two and held his ground, sliding the mortar closer and placing the berries inside. He mashed them swiftly with the pestle, breaking the skins and keeping them as part of the mixture to be added to the potion. The final product went down more thickly, but it did work better.

"Barclay is a good teacher," Reardon said as he ground the berries. "Alchemy isn't part of just anyone's education in Emerald, only if one chooses it, and I wanted to learn."

"Reardon is a quick learner." Barclay continued stirring the potion, a necessary step until everything was added. "He takes to alchemy more naturally than almost anyone else I've ever seen. Better than me, really. You'll want him as my replacement before you know it."

Reardon blushed at the compliment.

Liam regarded him more carefully then, following his movements as he finished mashing the berries and added them to the cauldron in slow chunks while Barclay stirred.

"Any magical affinity?" Liam asked.

"I don't know."

Another crackle of lightning rose from him, and he pointed a sparking finger at Reardon, drawing a design in the air that formed a visible rune, like an M or a gateway door, simply hovering there. Reardon didn't know what the rune meant, but he watched in awe at the way it glowed a brilliant red, and then pulsed away from Liam right toward him.

Reardon flinched, but the rune didn't pass through him; it paused just in front of his chest and shone its soft red light all across his body. The light felt warm, like standing in a pool of sunshine, but when it faded, the rune turned gray and fizzled like falling ashes.

"Not an ounce," Liam said in distaste—causing Reardon's chest to feel like that fallen rune, scattered into dust, though he'd never realized how much he might want to be magical. "Which makes you useless."

"Like me?" Shayla said, arms tightly crossed as she stared him down from her perch beside the other table.

If a demon made from the eye of a storm could look like a child caught doing something naughty, then Liam managed it with a ripple of light across his features. "You're not completely devoid of magic. Most people have at least some affinity. Besides, you're skilled in other ways."

"Not ways you'll be experiencing any time soon."

Liam crackled, and Reardon's face burned hot. They must be close if she could tease him like *that*.

The silence was as charged with static as Liam himself. Reardon looked to Barclay, but he and Caitlin were distracted by the final steps of the potion, adding the last few ingredients, and then—*poof*, a cloud of purplish smoke billowed up as if a person were inside puffing on a pipe. Barclay ceased stirring, and Caitlin moved off to get several vials for them to fill.

Reardon tried to take the second ladle she returned with, but she ignored him and kept it for herself. She still hadn't spoken to him directly since showing up with Liam in his room yesterday. Leaving more cold-resistance potions outside his door had helped her avoid him yet again.

"Did you have magic?" Reardon asked Liam for something to fill the air other than smoke and irritation. "Before the curse, I mean?"

"All elves have some magical ability," came his reply, eyes remaining on Shayla. "I was the king's wizard long before I became this."

An *elf*. Reardon hadn't realized, but as he looked at Liam now, he saw the lightning forming long points at the end of his ears in perfect outlines of the real thing.

"Magic simply means learning to harness the power within you so that alchemy isn't necessary to cause the same results. I can cast a spell that has the same effect as one of these potions, but it takes a toll, has a price, energy that needs to be replenished. Understand? That is magic, though there are a few exceptions, people who have special abilities unique to them that may or may not have a similar cost. Like Barclay."

Reardon edged around the table, moving cautiously closer to Liam. The Emerald Kingdom only taught its people to fear magic, not how it worked. "Do you have one? A unique ability?"

The bite to Liam's gaze softened as he looked at Reardon. "In the spring, when it's been too long without rain, let's just say… sometimes there is a sudden *storm*."

The thought of all that power made Reardon light up with excitement. Control over weather. That explained why he'd become lightning. "How wonderful."

"See," Shayla said. "I told you he was a good kid."

Liam shifted, like he'd once again been caught doing something he didn't want others to see, but his crackles dimmed, and the comradery between him and Shayla bloomed once more as easily as the awkwardness had withered it before.

These people weren't monsters—not the king's court or those who had been sent here. The elementals were frightening, the Ice King most of all, but whatever their curse, even the king was more than what he seemed.

Like with Liam, there was also something about *Jack*, something soft and entrancing within his jagged, frozen lines, that Reardon swore he would suss out.

The king's eyes proved it.

*Blue eyes in a sea of....*

A jolt of anxiety shot up Reardon's spine, as if he'd been struck by Liam's lightning. He'd had the thought once before, but the old vision couldn't mean the king... could it? It involved Reardon being here, clearly, but either he would only know true love through his friendship with Barclay or, if romance was in his future, then maybe with someone else within these walls.

It couldn't be the Ice King. That was preposterous!

But it made Reardon really want to talk with Barclay.

"Barclay, do you have time to—"

"He's working," Liam said shortly, though perhaps a touch less menacing than before. "You did your duty, now go bother someone else. Collecting these potions is delicate work, as I'm sure you know, if you're so knowledgeable."

"I can meet up with you later," Barclay said without taking his eyes off the careful ladling of potion into one of the vials. "We can have lunch. I'll meet you in the hall at noon."

"All right...."

"Let's leave these wily wizards be." Shayla moved from her vigilant post, leaving her bag on the table. "We have laundry to attend to. Or did you plan to skip that part of today's labor?"

Reardon felt marginally better about his standing here, having gotten a little on Liam's good side and being productive, even if Caitlin still wouldn't meet his gaze, and he did appreciate Shayla being his unofficial guide. "I'll help."

"And don't worry," she said, patting his back, firm but affable. "Liam's only 95 percent asshole."

"Shayla...," Liam called as she tugged Reardon toward the exit.

"Till next time!" she called back and kept on walking.

Reardon could ask about the vision later—the old vision, not the more recent one that Barclay was unwilling to talk about. Reardon knew there were more important things than his love life, but oh, wouldn't it be something to finally know another man's touch? If ever he was going to find romance, it had to be here, where love wasn't limited by law.

*"You're safe here,"* Barclay had said. There were others like him in this castle, many others, who loved without fear.

Reardon tried to pay attention to the route Shayla took him on to better map the castle, but his thoughts strayed—especially when he caught the attention of a passing elf. Most people he came upon cast him wary glances or avoided him, but this tall, lanky figure smiled like he hardly knew how not to, handsome in a pointy-featured sort of way, with dark hair and red-and-purple accents in his clothing.

As Reardon and Shayla moved past him up another set of stairs, Reardon couldn't help staring at the elf, who scanned down Reardon's body with a stretch to his smile and a funny little wiggle to his nose—and then winked.

Reardon slammed into the banister, whirling his head around to grab on to it and keep from flipping over the railing and dropping the very long distance down to the main floor. Shayla didn't notice, but when Reardon glanced back, the elf was still smiling.

*Wouldn't it be something?* he thought again—as long as it didn't cause him to plummet to his death.

Looking away with his face flushing, Reardon hurried after Shayla. Although the elf's grin had been attractive, all Reardon could think was....

He didn't have blue eyes.


"EVEN I feel your chill today," Branwen's voice echoed off the ceiling of Jack's chamber, drawing his attention from the spot on the wall he'd been staring at while lounging on his throne.

Branwen moved from the entrance like flames eating up dry wood in an impossible-to-stop wave, yet since his feet didn't touch the ground, he didn't so much as singe the floor or melt any ice. They didn't know if they could be affected by each other's touch, but they'd never dared test it to find out.

"What are you sulking for?" Branwen barked. "Thought the pretty princeling would be yacking your ear off."

"I sent him away." Jack kicked his legs over the arm of his throne.

"Already? He's that bad of company? At least he's a better view than this shithole."

Ages ago—literally—when Jack first chose his court, Branwen was the only non-noble, a soldier who'd proven himself and become Jack's friend. Jack didn't care how the choice had been sneered at by the high-born, because he knew Branwen was the best man to lead his army and protect his castle, crass or not. Tactlessness meant he never hesitated to speak his mind, something Jack valued.

Usually.

"The view will be short-lived. He's young and idealistic and thinks he can change the world with nerve and good intention."

"Classic fool, then. Still pretty." Branwen was only harping on that to annoy Jack. Branwen liked pretty things too, but not men.

"Worry about the fire in your own loins and stay out of the business of mine."

"What business?" Branwen pulsed red-hot flames as he stood at the foot of the throne's steps. "I don't see any *business* at the moment."

Jack clenched his fists with an icy creak, kicking his feet down again with a crunch into the frozen pedestal. They were all sexless in these forms but hardly devoid of wanting. But Jack's anger couldn't last, and he let his tension go. "He's pretty. He's not worth futile dreaming."

"Let's get rid of him quicker, then. He's all set to play champion. How about I put a little scare into him? See if the princeling can fight. Get Oliver to help for some early morning yard training tomorrow." A menacing smile flickered across Branwen's face. "The good fletcher will jump at the chance after that song last night."

The suggestion had Jack mirroring Branwen's grin, fire and ice in warring parallel, though he still wondered at his friend's motives. Regardless, if there was a way to break Prince Reardon of his foolish notions, this might be a start. "Do it. If he wants a crusade, let's see how he battles."

Branwen gave a mocking and mischievous bow before turning to leave, though not without adding, "And do something today, will you? You're not a damn cat."

Jack kicked his feet over the arm of the throne again just to spite him. Thinking *was* doing something. He was strategizing. Admittedly, normally this time of year, he'd be watching the new sacrifice with an eagle's eye until there was no doubt whether they belonged.

The prince should not be an exception.

"Zephyr!" Jack called, swinging his legs around once more to get to his feet.

"Yes, Majesty?" Zephyr popped into existence at Jack's side. He might honestly always be watching, lurking wherever he pleased, but whether he was hiding in a nearby corner or on the other side of the castle, he always heard Jack—he heard everything—and could appear in moments.

Every court needed a steward, but Jack understood that anyone who ran a castle was obviously more than a mere butler. *Spymaster* was more accurate even before Zephyr's hearing and mobility became supernatural. He'd been a noble but was tossed aside when his family discovered he had no interest in carrying on the family line.

Jack had snatched him up immediately. The fact that the disrespectful brat hated the idea of bowing to anyone only made Jack like him more, especially once he discovered what an ear Zephyr had for gossip.

"Where's the prince?" Jack asked.

"Getting his hands dirty—or should I say *clean*—helping with the washing."

"He's doing the washing?" Jack couldn't decide if Reardon continuing to surprise him was irritating or intriguing.

"Took off his doublet even," Zephyr said with a whistle. "Very fetching, that prince."

"Not you too." Jack scowled.

The translucent nature of Zephyr's form was eerie to some, but it only reminded Jack that he had nothing solid to swat at, just the faint outline of a young man looking well-dressed and smug. "I'm just enjoying the view," Zephyr said, floating leisurely in front of Jack. "Don't pretend like you haven't been stealing peeks."

Before Jack could snark back at him, Zephyr poofed away. He could very well still be right there, but that didn't stop Jack from turning toward his secret tunnels, even if he did hear giggles following him.

He'd ended his time with Reardon early; the least he could do was see what he was up to.

The washing room was in the cellar, with a large basin fit for half a dozen people to encircle it around a water pump. Jack knew exactly how every contraption in his castle worked, but much of the ingenious additions had come after the curse, created by the people sent here, whether through magic, engineering, or both.

The pulley system and rows upon rows of line above those doing the washing allowed each person to hang their finished garments without moving and then send them aloft. Prince Reardon was among them, a seventh to the usual six, given room by Shayla, who stood just off his shoulder. Reardon knew how to scrub and rinse and wring, but the pulley system was clearly a fascination for him, a smile adorning his face whenever he used it.

Everyone in the castle rotated as a washer throughout the week. It was the sacrifice's job to be added to a shift their first day, but Jack had never seen anyone excited by it.

The other five in attendance were a mixed bag of older and newer offerings, including an elf, nearing almost one hundred years here now, who'd created that pulley system and improved it over time. He got enthusiastic every year on the night of the offering, eager to meet someone new, but he'd remained quiet last night upon discovering that Reardon was the Emerald Prince.

Now he looked as eager and enamored as usual.

"It's really very simple," he said with a shrug, seated beside Reardon.

"But at such scale!" Reardon exclaimed. "Look at how many clothes it can handle, and barely a drop on any of our heads while they dry. It's marvelous! I'm sorry… what was your name again?"

"Wynn," the elf replied, holding out a hand slightly wrinkled from the washing—even though it had been another Emerald Prince who discovered the glamour hiding his ears so many years ago and banished him to the Frozen Kingdom. "Discovered as an elf, ninety-two years ago. It's nice to meet you, Reardon."

"You too."

Even the veterans were falling for Reardon's charms, unable to resist the way he looked at the whole world seeing rainbows behind his eyes. But that was easy for a well-fed royal who'd never had anything to fear. Even in this castle, surrounded by people who should be his enemies, Reardon believed he was in no peril.

*Naive. Ignorant.* Jack kept thinking those same slights, yet he was drawn to Reardon as well and watched raptly from his hidden corridor as the prince worked just as hard as anyone else and made quick friends of everyone around him.

"Looks like that cloak of yours has a ripped seam." Shayla nodded upward at the cloak hanging with the other drying clothes—deep purple, edged in gold embroidery and lined with thick tan fur. It was beautiful, but there was an obvious tear near the clasp at the collar. "I can fix it for you once it's dry."

"I can sew," Reardon said proudly. "I don't mind mending it myself. But maybe you can show me how you would do it. I'm sure your techniques are better, given these garments." He indicated the shirt he wore, his doublet folded up nearby, as Zephyr had said.

With his sleeves rolled up, the emerald green shirt brought out his eyes even more, and his forearms strained with taut young muscle as he worked.

He was indeed fetching, especially with his front laces untied to reveal the line of his collarbone.

Jack saw the people around the basin sitting closest to his spying wall shiver, and he pulled back, realizing he'd gotten too close and had pressed a hand to the stones, causing them to frost over. If any of those who'd felt the cold realized what the chill meant, none paid any mind.

"My mother taught me how to sew," Reardon continued, "and I always mend my own clothes if it's simple enough. I'd hoped to learn weaving eventually too, and embroidery because... well, it's fun, isn't it? Having something new and interesting to wear, especially if you made it yourself? Barclay likes tailoring too."

"I didn't know that," Shayla said in surprise. "Once Liam found out he'd been an alchemist's apprentice, he stole him away from anyone else. I'll have to conscript him sometime. You as well."

Reardon flashed his lovely smile at her over his shoulder—and then hissed as he scraped a shirt down the washing board. Jack thought it was because a knuckle had missed the barrier of the fabric, but when

Reardon pulled his hand from the water, there was a cut that had to have been made from something else.

"I guess the wolf got me after all."

*Wolf?*

"We have supplies down here," Wynn offered, rising from his work to head toward a row of shelving along the wall. "Let me wrap that for you."

"I won't be able to help then. It's not so bad."

"Listen to you," Shayla huffed. "Fended off a dire wolf your first day and taking it in stride."

*Dire wolf?*

The closer row of washers shivered again. Jack needed to stop leaning in.

Thank goodness Shayla had been with Reardon. Jack still wanted to see the prince's fighting skills, but it appeared he had a way of averting the danger snapping at his heels.

"Yet you only got that small scratch after leaving it alive." Wynn shook his head, gathering some ointment and bandages, obviously having heard the tale before Jack arrived. "Don't fret. If you'd still like to help, you can switch to gathering up the dry garments. Everything gets folded and placed on top of these shelves, and anyone waiting on clothes pick them up themselves. Easier than remembering who wears what."

Wynn sat with Reardon, attending to his wound as if they'd known each other for years, which was saying something for an elf who was so much older than he looked. Almost everyone here was older than they looked and set in their ways. Too often Jack felt his two hundred plus years compared to the young king he'd been when his life changed.

"Did you build anything else in the castle?" Reardon asked Wynn with an earnest scoot closer.

Excitement and new things to learn and be enchanted by were what made age irrelevant. Jack saw it in Wynn's face as he explained the plumbing and various machines throughout the castle that he'd created. Shayla looked the same. The others did too, just from watching Reardon listen and engage with fervor.

It had been a very long time since Jack felt the age he'd lost.

Before long, more time had passed than he intended, and Reardon headed to the hall for lunch. Jack wasn't surprised to see him meet up with Barclay, though Shayla and Wynn joined as well, along with a few others from the washing room.

Jack couldn't tear himself away, following Reardon from one part of the castle to another. Though others went their separate ways, Reardon stayed with Shayla, taking his cloak to the tailoring room. His excitement never seemed to fade, and he entered the spacious chamber covered in fabric and various things being made or mended, and he made friends there too. He was far from being deterred by the few cold shoulders or distrustful glances he received.

"What are you doing?"

Jack flinched, a burst of icy wind pulsing from his body.

Josie stood in the corridor behind him with her delicate arms crossed and a golden eyebrow raised.

"What I always do when someone new enters the castle."

"Lies," she dismissed. "You watch some, yes, but not like this. You trust your people. You trust me and your court to let you know if anything is amiss. You're supposed to be taking audiences with the prince, not prowling."

At least she was keeping her voice low, but Jack still slid the stone from his spying spot back into place as he turned to her. "Our audiences will resume tomorrow. I wasn't in the mood this morning."

"He's getting to you already? I'll have to get to know him better, then. Maybe tonight."

"No." Jack stomped toward her. "You know the rules. And make sure everyone else holds to them as well. Not at night. Not yet."

"Please, Jack. None of your people would dare betray our secrets before the designated time. Two weeks for anyone new." She rolled her eyes, finishing with a mockery of Jack's voice, "Only then can they prove trustworthy."

Two weeks was bare *minimum*. Josie had pushed for only one once, but that first frozen statue on the lawn… she'd been in the castle six days before her betrayal.

A week wasn't enough.

"I'm allowed vigilance," Jack said.

"You like him."

"I'm keeping my eyes on him."

"Because you like him."

"Because I'm concerned and waiting for the ax to strike!"

If possible, Josie's golden eyes rolling at him showed even more exasperation than her original blue. "Prowl away, then. I think I'm going to go help the tailors." She turned to head down the corridor that would exit her right outside the tailoring room's door.

Jack bristled, but then promptly removed the stone again to watch her knock and go inside, keeping her distance as needed, but engaging Reardon far too pleasantly. She even dared to glance wickedly over at Jack with a wink.

Josie often spent time in the tailoring room, inspecting the newest creations, but she was an awful traitor. She looked as sincerely enamored with Reardon as everyone else, however, when he asked if she'd ever tried making gold thread.

Jack could only watch for so long with his sister there, goading him, but after leaving Reardon alone, he eventually wondered where he was again, and found him at dinnertime back in the hall. Nigel and Caitlin had joined the group, Caitlin the only one who remained frosty toward the prince. Those who had yet to cross his path kept their distance, but more and more people were treating him like one of their own.

Jack and the other court members didn't go to the banquet hall outside the welcoming ceremony—not until the grace period lifted. If the offering proved to truly belong after two weeks, then they were brought into the fold, not before.

Reardon was swindling everyone after only one day!

It had to be a swindle. Only charlatans won people over this quickly.

Barclay knew him, though—a commoner, best friends with a prince. It made Jack wonder. After dinner, the pair went to Reardon's room, merely sitting on his bed, talking about their day as any true friends would.

The sun had set, but Jack barely noticed, until he shivered as he stood watching from the same spot he had last night.

"Did you want to talk about something earlier?" Barclay asked. "Something specific?"

Reardon glanced away, a rare glimpse of him being caught off guard. "It's nothing. I mean... it's everything, but I think I'll go mad if I try to figure out your visions."

Barclay nodded, understanding whatever was left unsaid with a thin smile.

What visions did the fortune-teller have of Reardon, Jack wondered. It couldn't all be a swindle if the boy who could see the future loved him.

"What I can tell you—" Barclay took Reardon's hands, a gesture, such easy touch, that they enacted often. "—is that I think you're right. This is where you're meant to be."

Reardon nodded in kind, making Jack even more curious about what they were talking about.

After another quick squeeze of Reardon's hands, Barclay rose. "I'm off to bed."

"Already?"

"I… had a long day."

Jack huffed. He knew that wasn't the real answer, but Reardon didn't notice the deflection.

"What about breakfast?" Barclay offered.

"I think I'll grab something early again. I'm not letting the king banish me so quickly tomorrow."

*Optimist.*

"Good luck," Barclay said.

While Reardon's brightness never fully dimmed, he was noticeably sadder, sitting there alone, but that only rooted Jack more firmly to his spot. He tried to pinpoint what it was about Reardon that kept captivating him.

Reardon was all the things Jack had told Branwen earlier—young, idealistic, foolhardy in his confidence that he could set things right, whatever the cost. He was also beautiful and warm and had charmed a few dozen members of Jack's kingdom today.

At first, Jack thought it was because Reardon so obviously didn't belong, the curiosity of the unknown in an outsider, but he'd certainly put in effort to belong here, and every so often, Jack would see a shadow in Reardon's eyes that said he might belong more than first guessed.

What was that shadow that had darkened the young prince's life like the others sent here? Merely guilt? His mother's death? Or something more?

As Jack continued to watch, Reardon inspected the work done on his cloak, half sewn by Shayla and half by him, and hung it in his wardrobe. It was early, but although Reardon looked toward his door a time a two, as if debating going out to explore or find some of his new friends, he eventually chose to go to bed.

Tonight there were lanterns and candles still lit that he didn't snuff out before undressing. As soon as his trousers came down, Jack lowered his eyes, but it was difficult not to look through his periphery at the much clearer view of the young man's lean, muscled form.

It was when Reardon settled but still left the bedside candle lit that Jack looked up again.

The covers weren't pulled all the way to his chin, only enough to cover his nakedness, as he tilted his head back on his pillow and let a hand drift down his chest beneath the quilt.

Jack looked away again. He certainly couldn't watch *that*.

But just as he turned to leave, he heard Reardon whimper.

"Please. Oh please... let me find him here."

*Him.* What nameless, faceless figure did Reardon conjure in the private dark of night?

Jack hurried away before he could be pulled into further deviance, but distance from the prince and what he was undoubtedly doing now in the solitude of his room did nothing to dull Jack's errant thoughts. It had been so long since Jack had touched someone, since someone had touched him, and Reardon was something special but dangerous that shook Jack to his core and made him wonder what it might be like to melt.

# CHAPTER 4

THAT NIGHT, Reardon slept with straying dreams of blue eyes, handsome smirks, and broad muscled shoulders of no man in particular—but oh, his phantom figure could touch and kiss and hold him too tightly like he'd always wanted. He found himself half-awake as the sun rose, hard and leaking fresh sin onto his sheets. He would have let a straying hand drift between his legs again like last night, but not when he had somewhere to be.

He mixed a black shirt and black trousers with his scarlet doublet, and today he affixed his sword belt before taking his daily draught to face the king.

His treks with Shayla through the castle had taught him a few new routes, so he took a shortcut to make his way to the kitchen, swiped meat and a chunk of bread that one of the workers he'd befriended in the tailoring room allowed with more of a smile than yesterday, and then took another new route toward the king's staircase.

On this path, he passed a row of paintings, some of landscapes and animals, but others of well-dressed nobles. Former royalty, he supposed. He came to a glaringly empty spot on the wall before reaching the last— an elegant brunette woman with sharp blue eyes. It took him a moment of staring at her remarkable beauty to realize that, while the hues had changed, the face remained.

It was Princess Josephine.

"I hated sitting for that portrait."

Reardon spun around, surprised yet again by a court member, always so good at sneaking, given that their feet didn't touch the ground. "Princess." He bowed his head. "You are as lovely now as you were then."

"*Josie*," she reminded him, floating closer, but not too close. She was truly ravishing in monochrome gold, but the painting added depth that she clearly missed as she gazed upon her portrait. "And you're sweet. It's a wonder this ever got painted. I get restless sitting still. Jack too. Even when he lounges like a contented cat, he's always shifting or fidgeting his hands."

That drew Reardon's eyes to the empty space where another painting might have hung. "Are there no portraits of the king?"

"None that survived." She turned to him, offering a melancholy smile. "He won't look at himself anymore, who he used to be. To him, he's only the monster." She gestured down the corridor for them to walk. "You're getting to him, though. I can tell."

"It didn't seem that way yesterday." Reardon barely had the king's ear for half an hour.

"Give him time."

There were other members of the castle up and about, but not many, giving them solitude to speak, yet there was only one thing on Reardon's mind as the puzzle remained unfinished. "Josie… would you tell me about the curse?"

"You'll have to get the story from Jack if you want to win him over. Some things will reveal themselves in time. What I'm sure I don't need to tell you is that he blames himself, but we all deserved what became of us."

Ice and gold, the royals of this cursed kingdom were both made of seemingly unfeeling things, yet they lived as vibrantly as anyone, and neither was truly cold, not even King Jack for all his attempts to act that way.

They were sad more than anything, and for that, Reardon wished he could reach out and place a comforting hand on Josie's arm.

"He told me he earned the curse," Reardon said as they began winding up the staircase he'd climbed many times now. "Says he's a villain."

"The king before, our father, was the real villain. He was a true tyrant, and his reach was vast. Our kingdom is only this castle now but growing again, almost more than we can contain within these walls, and we're happy here with what we have.

"We're not heroes, Reardon, but I like to think we're not villains either."

"And before?"

A sigh passed her golden lips, accompanied by a faintly derisive chuckle. "We might as well have been a gallery of rogues."

While each member of the court was unconventional in their role compared to what Reardon was used to for a kingdom, he didn't think any of them roguish.

But then, just as they reached the door to the Ice King's chamber, Zephyr appeared to block their path, causing Reardon to lurch backward and wonder if at least *one* member was a rogue.

"Sorry to interrupt." Zephyr grinned, though he kept a safe distance. "The king would like to take today's audience in the back courtyard."

"You mean the training yard," Josie said with a frown.

"Same thing."

"What is Jack plotting?"

"I couldn't begin to imagine. But he did say he'd prefer that I show the young prince the way."

The Ice King was getting rid of his sister, the only member of the court who'd been truly kind to Reardon. Liam had seemed tolerant yesterday but not exactly friendly, and the rest... well.

Reardon didn't trust the look on the Spymaster's face.

"If he gets hurt, whoever does the maiming will answer to me," Josie said, her golden sheen practically glowing as she projected the same aura of authority that her brother commanded so well—not that it softened use of the word "maim."

"Don't worry, Reardon." She shifted seamlessly back to a benevolent princess. "He simply hopes to test you and push you into a corner. You push him right back."

That was Reardon's whole intention of taking audiences with the king—to push him and learn everything he could so that they'd come to an understanding and end this division between kingdoms. If he could take knowledge back home that could help sway the hearts of his brethren to be more accepting of the things they feared, all the better.

Still, he was glad he'd worn his sword belt this morning.

"Perhaps I'll see you in the tailoring room." Reardon smiled at Josie with another bow. "I'd love to discuss uses of gold thread."

"An eye for fashion and pleasant to look at." She smiled back at him. "Don't you let any of the castle's brutes best you. Be a rose, like me—soft and lovely, with sharp edges to sting anyone who wrongs you."

Reardon could sting better than most, but her words helped lift his head higher as he followed Zephyr along a different path, back on ground level to a door leading behind the castle.

More people bustled about, but with Reardon trailing behind Zephyr, they all seemed to be laughing at him.

"Should I be worried?" he asked.

"Always." Zephyr peered over his shoulder with another ominous grin. "It's just a shame that if they scratch that pretty face, I can't patch you up personally."

Reardon stuttered to a halt, though he could see the door they were headed toward. The Ice King was the only member of the court with human eyes to know their true color. The rest all matched their element, so Zephyr's were a milky gray.

A cold sweat overtook Reardon as he wondered if they'd once been blue.

"Not used to being an object of desire, pretty prince?" Zephyr floated back to him, so close that Reardon would have known his true eye color if they were more than mist. He was drawn to broader men, and Zephyr was slight like Barclay, but he was handsome in his own way, slender and impish.

"Wh-whose desire?' Reardon stuttered.

"Daft, are you? Or only interested in ripping bodices?"

"*No*," Reardon blurted, but then years of training to not admit such things made him fumble to correct himself. "I-I mean, I... *have* desires, but I'd rather not rip anything."

"That's no fun." Zephyr winked.

If Reardon had a banister before him, he would have plowed into it again. He felt faint, like the floor had dropped beneath him. How did someone become so free that they could express their desires that openly?

"I-I-I...." He had no idea how to follow suit.

"You are a mess. We'll have to work on opening you up." Zephyr grinned again, and Reardon felt his cheeks catch on fire, completely mute when the imp blessedly turned forward.

Willing his cheeks and heart rate to calm, Reardon had the distinct impression that he was walking into a trap. He itched to grip the handle of his sword but didn't want to appear combative.

His tune changed quickly once he got outside.

Combat was clearly what they had in mind, because all the large, imposing members of the castle were in attendance, the soldiers and mercenaries for hire who'd been sent there—including the fletcher, the first sacrifice.

He might have been noble once, but he was a solid pillar of muscle now.

Zephyr couldn't be Reardon's love, but the fletcher's figure stirred his passions easily.

*And* he had blue eyes.

He also had a woman, Reardon reminded himself, spotting her pretty bespectacled face behind the figure of the blond and bearded fletcher. Reardon needed to focus on more pressing concerns—like the sword in the fletcher's hand.

"I hear you can sew and wash and mix potions," the crackle of a gruff voice spoke, drawing Reardon's eyes to the sidelines where Branwen stood beside the king with a flaming sword. "I also hear you fended off a dire wolf. A future king must be skilled in many things, including how to fight."

"I can fight." Reardon stood proudly, allowing his hand to touch his hilt now. He had barely moved away from the door, but space had been cleared for him and the fletcher. Dummies and weapon stands spread about the perimeter of the yard with the watchers forming a circle, the cursed in their own fantastical line that Zephyr joined.

"Then show us," the Ice King said.

Reardon had a short sword, the fletcher a long sword—no, *great sword*—that he clearly could have wielded in one hand but slowly gripped in two. Reardon didn't feel the chill from the frost-covered ground or crisp winter air, but despite the fletcher being without his shirt, showing a swath of impressive scars, he gave no sign that he felt the cold either, and Reardon had a feeling it was without any potion.

Cautiously, he moved forward and drew his short sword to a smattering of laughter when they saw its size.

"You're welcome to select a more suitable weapon," the fletcher said with his thin, appraising smile, squaring his stance.

"I haven't mastered wielding anything heavier." Whenever Reardon tried, it unbalanced him, his strength refusing to grow beyond its peak.

"I can teach you how to handle a *larger* sword!" Zephyr called, and laughter roared once more.

Fighting a return of flushed cheeks with so many eyes on him, the king's most heavily, Reardon scanned for friendly faces in the crowd. He saw no one he'd gotten to know yesterday, not even Shayla, but then his eyes found Nigel.

"Knock his block off, fletcher!" Nigel cried.

So much for finding a *friend*.

There was a chaotic energy about Nigel, certainly, though his uncharacteristic snarl seemed to be directed at Zephyr for some reason, with furtive glances passed between them.

"May I at least know your given name, good fletcher?" Reardon asked the man before him, circling closer and imagining how painful the first clang of blades would feel. "Or is it merely *Emerald Arrow?*"

The fletcher's smile barely twitched. "It is until you prove yourself."

He rushed Reardon without warning, and instead of bracing his sword upward to deflect the coming blow, Reardon spun out of the way and waited for his opponent to stumble.

He didn't.

Far swifter than anyone with a great sword had any right to be, the fletcher pivoted and rammed his hilt into Reardon's side. Reardon gasped, breath lost, and nearly lost the grip on his short sword.

"Don't assume your opponent's abilities without proper assessment," the fletcher said like a scolding tutor. He reminded Reardon of Lombard—blond, beautiful, and severe. Lombard had taught Reardon to fight, but he'd clearly gone easy on him. Reardon couldn't approach this battle thinking the rules would be the same.

The fletcher let him catch his breath, and then squared his stance again.


REARDON HAD indeed never been to any brothels or known the comfort of another. If he had, he would have risked being discovered as a deviant and been banished from his own kingdom. There was no denying it now, though initially that had not been the purpose of this sparring match.

The way his eyes raked bashfully over Oliver's rippling bare chest proved to Jack the truth, as much as the young prince's blushing cheeks and utterances the night before of finding an unknown "him." He wasn't the first to prefer like company who had darkened Jack's door. It shouldn't have mattered, and yet the knowledge made Jack's eyes narrow that much more closely on Reardon's movements.

He was… capable with a sword. Few were as skilled as Oliver or Branwen with any weapon, but then, they each had a couple centuries of experience to call upon, and Reardon was a mere boy of twenty-one.

Still, each time Oliver sidestepped Reardon and threw him to the ground, or simply overpowered him with a clash of metal, his great sword dwarfing Reardon's smaller blade, the prince got back up, took a breath, and tried again. To his credit, it took Oliver longer to best him each time, with Reardon's eyes trained on his movements and learning, waiting, calculating openings and how he could use his speed to his advantage against a stronger, more skilled opponent.

When it seemed to all those jeering for Oliver to finish him that Reardon was sure to call for a reprieve, that was when the prince struck.

Oliver weaved and swung, and Reardon ducked out of the way, but when before Oliver would surprise him with a sharp jab of his hilt, fist, or sweep of his leg, this time, Reardon saw every countermove coming and responded in kind. He weaved, twisted on the hard, frozen ground, swung up with his blade like he might slice Oliver cleanly, and then, at the last moment, rammed his hilt into Oliver's shoulder and kicked the side of his knee to send him sprawling.

A surprised silence fell over the crowd, for few had ever brought Oliver to his knees save those he'd trained himself. But after Oliver let his great sword hit the ground, he left it there, lifted his head to look at Reardon, and accepted the hand offered down to him.

"Oliver," he said as he was hoisted to his feet. "Not bad. For a noble born."

"You too," Reardon said, squeezing his hand fiercely in reply.

"And how are you with a bow?" Oliver nodded at the targets and archery sets nearby.

"Awful, to be honest."

"That won't do here." Oliver sized Reardon up like he did all those he intended to teach. "You need to master the skills you have, and what you have is speed. You've seen Shayla fight with her daggers? You could dual-wield just as well with two short swords and be a menace against any opponent, but you let your eagerness get the best of you."

"You aren't the first to tell me that." Reardon smiled with a distant fondness in his gaze like he was thinking of someone specific.

Jack squelched the wave of jealousy that struck him.

"Who says besting the fletcher proves his mettle?" Branwen boomed beside Jack, bringing him back to himself and reminding him that they were not alone in the training yard.

Branwen stomped forward, causing anyone too close in the crowd to back away as all members of the kingdom had been taught, and for

Reardon's eyes to widen into emerald saucers when he was left standing alone as Oliver backed away too.

Grinning in a way that seemed too wide while he was made of fire, Branwen squared his stance as Oliver had, his much larger great sword, crackling and aflame, looking insurmountable and reflecting in Reardon's eyes to turn them amber.

"Come at me now and see how you fare," Branwen goaded.

"I… but…." Reardon stammered.

"Blade to blade won't set you on fire, boy. Now, how do you face a real challenge?" Branwen puffed out his chest, sending a burst of flames to explode outward like a stove stuffed with too much kindling, losing his definition before he became once more a brimstone fortress of a man.

Jack's instincts were to cry "No, enough!" but he'd been the one to ask for this to see what Reardon was made of. He just didn't want the depths of the prince to be revealed only to be turned to ash.

"If I was elsewhere and presented with an opponent like you," Reardon said, raising his short sword with shaky arms, "I would desperately seek a parley."

"Not all opponents are swayed by words," Branwen spat.

"Maybe not beasts or monsters, but men can always be reasoned with."

Branwen howled, and Jack felt the heartache in his cry like few could, for only the cursed knew how they had bartered and bargained and been denied.

Reardon spun away as he had with Oliver, barely missing having a chunk of his shoulder sawed at by a flaming edge. Branwen wasn't thinking, seeing an enemy where Jack had merely wanted him to see a pretender—when he still thought Reardon was pretending.

Branwen spun in kind, swiping out in a wide flaming circle that might have taken Reardon's head off if he hadn't ducked. All those watching backed up in equal measure like one great mass. But Reardon didn't understand. He'd avoided clashing with Oliver too much blade to blade, knowing he'd be overpowered, so he tried the same with Branwen, but there was nothing of Branwen he could cut or touch!

Darting forward, he sliced at Branwen's leg, only to have the blade pass through him as if he'd swung at a bonfire. He teetered from the force of the momentum and started to fall—*into* Branwen, something Branwen couldn't see because he was midturn, swinging toward Reardon, where they would clearly collide with more than blades.

"Stop!" Jack bellowed, and with his cry, he struck out, like throwing an ax across a battlefield.

A cascade of ice shot over the ground from him to the dualists, not capable of freezing Reardon but still deadly if it sliced through him. Instead, it sliced between, snuffing out Branwen's closest flames and toppling Reardon into a wall of ice that made him hiss at the freezing temperature, shaking frostbitten palms when he reared back.

The crowd went silent again, Oliver standing tall and vigilant, ready to race to Reardon's aid if Jack decreed it, as Branwen realized what had happened. They all got caught up in their vices sometimes, but it had been years since any of them had... an accident.

Jack waved his hand, and the wall of ice crumbled, melting into the frozen ground. He would have told Oliver to go forth and help Reardon, crouched and holding his stinging hands, but Nigel ran to him first.

Zephyr lurched forward then too, but held back, remembering his own deadly touch and that he could do little more than watch. He and Jack watched together as Nigel took Reardon's hands and placed his palms over them.

"Now you see it," Nigel said playfully, a glow forming where their skin touched, "now you don't."

The strain in Reardon's brow lessened, and when Nigel pulled his hands away, Reardon looked entirely at ease, staring at unmarred skin. "You're a healer?"

"Just an elvish parlor trick. It only works on minor wounds."

"Thank you," Reardon said, and then turned his eyes to Jack, as if to pass those same words to him.

Branwen said nothing, brooding and bitter that he'd nearly lost control when this had been his idea. Jack nodded at him to let it go, before returning his eyes to Reardon.

"Be more vigilant, little prince. A future king can't be a klutz. Now come. We'll finish today's audience in private. Oliver can teach you the bow another day." Jack turned to head for the staircase behind the castle entrance, winding upward to the ramparts. He heard the crowd murmur and disperse, followed by Reardon's dutiful feet.

The prince said nothing as they ascended to the top of the wall. From there, all the lands could be seen, including a better view of the Mystic Valley.

"Majesty," Reardon said when Jack merely gazed outward, "I must say that I am truly grateful—"

"I do not need any undue deaths on my conscience. If you die here, you'll earn it."

Reardon quieted, only to sigh and stand taller. "I'd rather earn your trust. You care deeply, allowing everyone here the greatest of freedoms. You even protected me when you still see me as an enemy. That is the mark of a good king."

Such naivete again, but Jack was beyond believing there was any act to it. He gazed down at Reardon, the wind from being up so high further tousling his hair, sweat on his brow from his fights and resolution in his expression.

Jack was resolute too.

"Making up for past mistakes does not absolve them."

"Perhaps not, but if you were a bad king, you wouldn't care to make up for anything." Reardon shifted closer, too close, only a foot from certain death, despite how close he'd come to it down below. "Please, Majesty, tell me of the curse. Have I not proven myself enough?"

*Not enough for everything,* but there were layers to this tale.

"Do you know whom you will marry?" Jack asked, watching the expected reaction of Reardon's cheeks flushing and his eyes going wide.

"I... no. My father has not yet chosen anyone or introduced me to candidates. I expect it will be soon, though."

"When my father introduced me to mine, I told him to marry them himself, for I'd sooner see his decaying corpse on the throne than ever rule."

"You did not wish to be king?"

"I did not wish to be beholden to anyone but myself. As prince, I had everything I wanted. Money, power, prestige. I could do whatever I chose, and no one questioned me. But if I was king, I would have responsibilities.

"My father was a traditionalist, like the worst of those from your kingdom. He didn't scoff at magic, as long as he controlled those who wielded it, but he believed elves should only lie with elves, men only with women, and the lands must always be ruled by a firstborn son of our line—married and with at least one heir on the way before they took the throne.

"I wanted none of it. Least of all a queen."

"What did you do?" Reardon asked with rapt attention.

Jack leaned his massive head down to him. "I fucked all the stable boys."

"R-really?" Reardon sputtered, face flushing as scarlet as his doublet.

"Not only the stable boys," Jack amended. "More so as many men as I could. Out of desire, certainly, but also to spite my father."

"And—" Reardon reached for the stone wall as if to steady his footing. "—did they want to be taken by their prince?"

"Are you asking if I forced myself on them?"

"I-I wouldn't presume—"

"Rest assured, little prince, it was always mutual want."

The tension in Reardon eased, but his mind was clearly working through the implications. "Is that what cursed you?"

"You think lying with men could curse a whole kingdom?"

"No! I don't agree with the teachings of my kingdom that it's wrong. I *can't*, not when I—" Reardon snapped his mouth shut before the truth could escape him.

"Not when you lust for no queen either," Jack finished.

The tension returned tenfold, Reardon's blush draining away to leave him pallid. "Am I so obvious?"

"No, but I've seen enough. You're used to hiding yourself." Jack steeled his gaze on Reardon sharply. "You will not hide from me. If you wish to know me and for me to know you, then you will be as transparent as Zephyr. Do you understand?"

"Y-yes, Majesty." Reardon regained his composure with a stalwart breath. "I did not mean to hide my... wants. I've just rarely spoken of them. Barclay is the only one who knows. But you are right. I have no desire for a queen."

"Then what do you desire?"

Epic tales could have been written with the many thoughts that played behind Reardon's eyes, his gaze clouded as he considered his answer. "A choice."

Jack turned back to look upon the landscape beyond them. "So did I."

"What happened?"

"My father died, and I became king anyway."

"You changed things then, before the curse?"

The bitterness that had not dwindled in over two hundred years made Jack's lips curl. "I certainly did."

"Is that why you allow such freedoms here? Because you were the same?"

There was no such scorn in Reardon, only the innocence of a youth who'd been hiding all his life. "I allow it because who one loves or lies with shouldn't matter."

Reardon smiled, and if Jack had still had doubts about him, all would have been banished in that expression, catching the warmth of the sun in his ruddy cheeks. "I wonder if my father could ever understand that."

Not if he was anything like Jack's, but Jack couldn't imagine this young prince turning out as he had with a cold, brutish figurehead raising him.

"Majesty," Reardon asked with sudden hesitancy, his eyes falling to the drop-off of the wall, "when you approached other men to… be with, what did you say? How did you win their favor?"

"Besides asking if they wanted a romp in the stables?"

"Surely it wasn't that easy?" Reardon's cheeks burned brightly again.

"Sometimes it was. Do you know nothing of wooing, little prince?" Jack asked, knowing the answer, but it still surprised him how virginal those green eyes looked when they blinked at him.

"Isn't that for women?"

*Oh, dear boy.*

Reardon was a man, and yet also only on the cusp of manhood, shielded from knowing all he might have asked of the world.

Leaning low once more to bring their faces as close as he dared without risk of unintended touch, Jack dropped his voice low too. "You tell me. Wouldn't you like to be wooed?"

Reardon dropped his eyes to the stones at their feet. "I… suppose I would."

"And how would one woo the Emerald Prince?" Jack asked—foolishly, because Reardon's thoughts could never stray to *him* when they went distant with reverie.

"I… would want us to understand one another," he said sweetly, sighing with the first breath of anyone young and yearning to find love, "to have similar wants and goals, similar likes. I would want to be drawn to them as I am a good friend, but with that stir of passion that is impossible to explain."

"You speak from experience?"

Reardon glanced up fearfully, but then relaxed, as if he had to remind himself that here he could speak openly. "The first man I ever loved... was the worst candidate. Our master of arms. He's older. Strong, dependable, handsome. But he is the very man who would have seen me to the gates upon my banishment if I were discovered. I could never be free to love him, blue eyes or not."

"Blue eyes?" Jack repeated.

"Oh, um... it's nothing." Reardon's gaze darted fearfully away again. "He was always there when I needed him, but he also helped me to be self-reliant. He taught me to fight and to stand proud during court like a proper prince. He could weave tales almost as good as a bard, to the point that I often didn't know if what he told me actually happened or was a legend spun for my amusement."

"You enjoy stories? I suppose your singing suggests as much."

"I do, but really, I enjoy the ways people can connect, maybe because I had so few I connected with back home. The people were always wonderful to me, and I tried to be wonderful to them, but what I have with Barclay is unique. It's difficult to befriend a prince who can't be honest about who he truly is." He fidgeted with his hands, mesmerized by the smooth skin that had so recently been burned by ice.

Something startled Reardon then, and he pulled back, looking at Jack in full and at their surroundings.

"I've... never told anyone all that. Not even Barclay knows about Lombard."

*Lombard.* Jack disliked this "master of arms" immediately, silly as it was to care about Reardon's infatuations. "Why tell me?"

"You *asked.* And I promised we would know one another. Isn't that easier with a connecting thread? We are not so different."

They were different in all the ways that mattered, because Jack could have been like Reardon, good and wanting to do right by others despite being barred from his heart's desires, but he chose a selfish path. Reardon reminded him of all he might have become if he'd been better, and although that truth and their similarities might have made Jack hate him, he felt warm in the prince's presence.

Their eyes locked, sapphire on emerald, and with the wind and the sun and Reardon's rosy cheeks, he looked far too beautiful and breakable to be standing before a monster that yearned to touch.

Reardon shivered, sharp breath escaping his lips, and Jack reared back, too much mist and power emanating from him.

"Your potion wears thin," Jack said, drawing up to his full height to turn and head across the ramparts away from Reardon. "We'll continue tomorrow."

"But… you didn't tell me about the curse!"

"Tomorrow," Jack said again.

Perhaps, once he had, Reardon would see the monster more clearly.

REARDON WASN'T sure if the potion really was wearing off. It shouldn't be. He hadn't shivered from the cold, after all, just….

The king's eyes could be so piercing.

So *blue*.

And he too had been a prince who loved in a way that others saw as wrong.

Well, maybe *loved* was the wrong word—*fucking stable boys*. Reardon blushed at the thought. Oh, to have been that bold! He wondered more than ever what the Ice King had looked like when he was human. Josie was breathtaking; surely he was too.

The king headed off along the ramparts to reenter the castle another way, making it clear that he did not wish for Reardon to follow him, so Reardon descended the stairs. When he reached the training yard, most of the crowd had gone, but Nigel and Zephyr remained, talking heatedly about something that they hushed when they saw him.

"Just remember, Spymaster," Nigel said, loud and snappish, "I can find almost anything funny—but not *that*."

Zephyr huffed, crossing milky arms as he floated before Nigel. "Like you've never done the same," he said and poofed away.

Nigel bristled, visibly upset, only to pivot and smile maniacally. He was once again dressed in bright colors with conflicting patterns. "Ignore him. Preferably always. Let's get out of the cold, shall we?" He swooped forward to take Reardon's arm and swung him around toward the door. "I didn't really mean for Oliver to knock your block off, you know. Which he didn't, thankfully, though Branwen could have done worse."

"Thank you again for my hands," Reardon said.

"Of course! And you can make it up to me. I hear you were unjustly torn from the princess's side this morning. Did you know she's rather talented with a lute? Let's see if we can make a real bard out of you." He tilted his head up toward Reardon's cheek and whispered, "But upstage me too much or too often and I will have to destroy you."

Reardon laughed, feeling rather confident despite his near-miss with Branwen. He'd beaten the fletcher—*Oliver*—and earned his respect, the Ice King himself had rescued him and conversed with him more than a mere exchange of barbs, and he hadn't lost any new friends.

He did wonder what had Nigel so upset with Zephyr, though.

Inside the castle, Reardon continued to map the paths he was taken on. Today he traversed even more areas he hadn't yet been and continued to be impressed by the palace's size. Nigel took him to a music room packed with instruments and hand-written sheet music. Josie was there, along with several others, including Wynn at a harpsichord with a quill in hand, as if writing music that very moment.

"I see you survived," Josie greeted with a smile, near the wall with her lute, away from the others, while some had flutes or other stringed instruments, and one had a simple drum.

"Best not tell her what happened," Nigel mock-whispered.

"Why?" Josie asked slowly.

"So as not to spoil your lovely mood, of course. What are we playing?" Nigel pulled Reardon into the room, releasing him to take up a tambourine.

"Are you a music master too, sir inventor?" Reardon approached Wynn at the harpsichord.

"Our princess is more the master, just you wait, but building...." Wynn patted the side of the harpsichord and then tapped his parchment. "That I can do."

"You built that? And wrote all this music?" There were shelves of bound pages all around Reardon.

"Not all of it," Wynn said. "There are stories too from Nigel for when he wants accompaniment. What songs would you hear, Emerald Prince? We learn new ones from every offering. We might know something you're familiar with."

"Can all of you sing?" Reardon asked the small gathering of musicians.

"Best if I don't," Nigel said.

"Or me," Josie added, "but a plucked melody I can handle just fine." She strummed a perfectly tuned chord that lifted Reardon's spirits further. He missed the times when he and Barclay would simply sing together or when Barclay would play on the old harpsichord in the palace that Reardon's mother once used.

"Do you know 'The Ride-Along Bard' about the traveling minstrel who keeps finding faulty heroes? That one always makes me laugh." It had been Reardon's mother's favorite when he was little and she'd sing by his bedside.

"A classic!" Wynn said, setting his quill aside to straighten on the bench and starting right in on the introduction without needing to change sheet music.

Josie strummed, and the flutes started up, the lone drummer pounding out a beat as Nigel held his tambourine under his arm and clapped along.

Wynn began with a beautiful tenor.

> *"There once was a humble bard*
> *Setting off to tell the greatest of tales,*
> *Seeking heroes and knights in every tavern she fared.*
> *She was never short of volunteers."*

He nodded at Reardon to continue, who knew the song well.

> *"The first she rode along beside*
> *Was a fabled hero of legend,*
> *A lady knight besting dragons and beasts,*
> *Then besieged by cutthroats and brigands."*

Wynn joined on the chorus.

> *"For no bard is humble,*
> *And no hero's flawless.*
> *All that matters is the stories we tell."*

This time, Wynn nodded for Reardon to start.

> *"The next the bard chose as her muse*
> *Was a bright young hero who'd vanquished a lord,*

*Freeing peoples and lands from the overlord's hold,*
*Then he conquered and ruled just the same."*

Wynn nodded again, adding harmony as Reardon led.

*"She tried a noble king all adored,*
*Hearing praise of peace and riches.*
*Indeed, the king was everything claimed,*
*But he ate his enemies whole.*

*"For no bard is humble*
*And no hero's flawless.*
*All that matters is the stories we tell."*

Reardon motioned for Wynn to take the final verse, and he did, high and true.

*"For years she tried to find a true song*
*That wouldn't end in heartache and gloom,*
*But all the heroes were lies or had died on their feet,*
*So she drank and lied her way too."*

They finished strong together.

*"For no bard is humble,*
*And no hero's flawless.*
*All that matters is the stories we tell.*

*"When the dark falls,*
*And swords clash in the night,*
*Strong ale is better than a fight."*

Wynn trilled through several loud ending chords, and Nigel gave an impromptu shake of his tambourine, making everyone laugh. Reardon's mother had often said it wasn't a funny tale if one listened closely, but it always got a crowd roaring and made Reardon smile.

He took a seat beside Wynn at the harpsichord. "Can you teach me what you were working on when I came in?"

They played and sang for nearly an hour more before the door to the music room burst open—to reveal Barclay, looking put out that he hadn't been invited.

"Now, now, poor slave to our weather wizard," Nigel exclaimed, "how did you know to escape and join us?"

"Zephyr told me." Barclay rushed over, squeezing onto the bench with Reardon and Wynn like it was commonplace for the three of them to play together. "I begged Liam to let me leave early for lunch once I finished a few things. What are we singing?"

Reardon noticed a funny look on Nigel's face that was quickly replaced by a smile.

"Glad you could join us," Josie said, moving to take a spot in front of the harpsichord, where she smiled at Barclay with all her golden beauty. "Music isn't the same without you."

"And there would be no music worth singing without you," he answered—only to catch himself like he'd said something he shouldn't, darting his eyes at Reardon. "I-I mean...."

"Shall we try another?" Wynn spoke over him. "How about 'Moonlit Lovers'?"

If the princess could blush through her golden sheen, she certainly did, and it struck Reardon as suddenly... sad. Barclay had always been a disaster with women, which Reardon said was his fault for being the worst sort of second, but it didn't surprise him that his friend had found a better voice here.

How unfair, though, for it to be with a woman he couldn't touch.

"Shouldn't the bard get a turn?" Nigel blocked their view to Josie by draping his arms over the harpsichord, tossing Wynn some new sheet music to be played with spoken verse, and the merriment played on.

They stayed in the music room for what must have been hours, leading up to lunchtime. When they did finally agree that hunger meant it was time to disperse, Wynn patted Barclay's shoulder for his lovely additions to their harmonies, and Barclay's eyes went blank.

A vision.

"Wynn—" Barclay turned to the elf as they stood from the harpsichord. "—there's an issue with the sewage pump, a faulty valve you need to tend to that might break in a few days."

"Good to know! What would we do without you?" Wynn patted his back again.

Reardon wasn't used to Barclay being able to express his visions without having to think up some elaborate lie for why he knew what he did. Here it was just a part of life.

Josie smiled at Barclay as she floated out of the room after most of the others had gone, his eyes following her the entire way, until they reached Reardon watching him.

"What?" Barclay startled.

Reardon could have brought up the princess but decided to be kind. "It's just wonderful seeing you so carefree about your visions. These people are remarkable." He looked to Wynn, last to leave, waiting for them at the door.

"They are," Barclay agreed, "but it's not only that. My visions here are usually... smaller. In Emerald, I could encounter people from all over the kingdom, and it always felt so big. We're like a small village in the castle. The future is filled with simpler things, like faulty sewage valves." He chuckled. "It's only the past sometimes that reminds me what everyone here has been through."

"Like you," Reardon said, gripping his friend's arm.

"And you," Barclay returned. They had all been shunned for things they couldn't change. Then Barclay looked at where they were connected. "Did you want to know more—"

"*No.*" Reardon let go. He never wanted Barclay to think the only reason he touched him was for a peek at the future. "I mean... did you see more?"

"Nothing new."

"Then no. I'm finding my way here." Reardon gestured toward Wynn so they wouldn't keep him waiting. "I'm going to stay on this path without doubting where it leads. Starting with telling the truth."


JACK HAD watched it all like the day before, following Reardon as soon as he returned indoors, from the music room to lunch afterward, where Oliver and his wife joined the friends Reardon had made.

The prince's secret was out, not only because he'd had to be truthful with Jack, but because he chose to confess to his new companions too. As he explained what he had in common with many of the denizens of the castle, others turned to listen, and the darkness in Reardon's eyes gradually lifted, finally free of their burden. He was acclimating quickly and being welcomed faster than few ever had.

But he was not meant to stay. If all Reardon wanted from his time here came to fruition, he would return to his own kingdom someday, not become part of Jack's. That truth drained the warmth Jack had felt outside, reminding him of his own eternal chill.

He lost track of time watching Reardon until darkness fell, when he retreated to his rooms. He'd managed to avoid Josie, ducking away whenever he heard her coming—especially after she learned the full scope of events in the training yard.

"Jack!" She pounded on his door. He couldn't hide any longer after the sun set. "What were you thinking? He might have been killed!"

Jack stood in his private chambers, a place no one else had been since the curse was cast, not even his sister. "All ended well. Leave me be."

"They ended well, but they might not have," she called more softly. "Do not tempt fate. You know how accidents haunt us."

"Everyone I've frozen has earned it."

"But the same cannot be said for all of us."

Jack closed his eyes. He hadn't meant to put Branwen in that position, or to remind Josie of events that haunted her. He didn't know any longer what he wished to accomplish with Reardon. He'd been consistently surprised by him. Maybe Reardon could convince his kingdom to change, go home and make a new world of the Emerald Kingdom. Jack's own kingdom would stop growing then, and perhaps some of his people would leave, at least to visit, if not return to their old homes for good.

That would be the only happy end any of them could hope for, yet it filled Jack with an ache to imagine all he knew coming to an end. To lose any part of this home he'd built, to lose any of its people, even Reardon, who'd only been here for a few days....

"Jack," Josie called again, very soft now, defeated on the other side of his door.

"I won't endanger him again. He'll only do that himself. No more tests. But the two weeks stand. I've been wrong before."

"What is it about him that has you so vexed?"

If only Jack knew....

He did know, he supposed. It was everything about Reardon, including what they had in common.

"Please, Jack, talk to me. Let me see you." A faint thud sounded at the door, as if she'd pressed her palm there.

"Tomorrow," Jack said, not turning or making any move toward his door.

She did not plead again, knowing he wouldn't budge. Eventually, her silence gave way to the soft padding of retreating feet.

Jack's mind swirled with all he'd discovered of Reardon and all he'd seen. His love of stories. His voice. Jack used to spin tales too, for the sheer joy of weaving prose.

Now he drifted toward his writing desk, covered in neatly stacked parchment that he hadn't touched in ages. Carefully, he sat and picked up his quill, allowing the words to flow.

> *The noble prince went on his quest*
> *To become a greater king*
> *Than those before who'd shamed their lands*
> *And bards denied to sing.*
>
> *He traveled far to learn abroad*
> *How other kings reigned just*
> *But for all he found who'd earned their crowns*
> *Men made beasts ruled thus.*
>
> *He pitied one such beast*
> *To turn him from his ways*
> *In hopes that tenderness might win*
> *And pierce the heart that strayed.*
>
> *Hearts made of ice aren't made for melting*
> *But the prince did burn so bright*
> *That he reached the wayward beastly king*
> *And found him in the night.*
>
> *Lips and hands and hearts did touch*
> *Knowing pleasures lost before*

*And the prince did reach the king at last*
*As the beast became no more.*

Jack crumpled the parchment and chucked it across the room, angry at himself for writing something so... juvenile. He was no bard, and he shouldn't be a dreamer.

There was no end to his curse, least of all through a hapless fairy tale.

# CHAPTER 5

REARDON WAS sore at the end of another long day, especially after his adventures in the training yard. Now he sluggishly wandered up to bed, Barclay having already retired, as well as Shayla and Nigel, though Reardon had stayed in the banquet hall nursing a cup of mead with Wynn while getting to know Oliver and his wife, Amelia, who he liked too much to be jealous of for having snagged the heart of the handsome fletcher.

Wynn was the castle's main engineer, but she was a close second, and Reardon was enthralled to hear about everything the pair had invented to make life better here.

The hour was drawing late, however, and he needed rest to be up early for his next audience with the king. Reardon's wing of the castle was quieter than others, less full, he supposed, with many of the rooms still empty.

As he neared his corridor, he saw Widow Caitlin leaving it, briskly moving in the opposite direction. He still hadn't spoken to her and wondered where she was off to so late and at such a persistent pace.

He knew little about her and hadn't thought it right to ask Barclay, like some meddling gossip. He hadn't even known that her room was down their same hall, though it made sense, with quarters handed out as new offerings came to the castle, and she only having been there ten years.

Surely, more drastic measures were allowed with someone determined to avoid him. He was meant to discover the castle's secrets, after all, and wanted to befriend and understand everyone he could.

Slowing his steps and glancing behind to be sure no one else was nearby, Reardon flattened himself to the wall before continuing. When he peered to see how far she had gone, he saw her disappearing down another hallway. Hurrying after her, quiet but swift, he peered around the next corner—but saw no sign of her.

"Spying, Prince Reardon?"

Reardon jumped a clean foot off the ground and spun to find her behind him.

*How?*

"Well?" Caitlin crossed her arms, clothed simply like everyone in the castle but with deep hues to her dark blue kirtle over a silvery-gray smock. She wore her long brunette hair down, with only the front few strands pinned back. She was a lovely woman but painted over with a sheen of severity.

"No." Reardon straightened. "I was just hoping to talk to you, since you seem so set on not talking to me."

"Do we have something to talk about?" Her words dripped scorn that would have deflated Reardon if he hadn't accomplished so much today.

"You must hate me greatly, but I was only a boy when you were sent here. Let me understand—"

"Your father was not a boy. He was king, and he made a choice to follow the will of the people, despite my pleading." The ice in her expression was indeed as piercing as the king's, even with brown eyes, but she seemed to calm herself as she finished, "He was grieving, I understand, but so was I."

"You were grieving?" Reardon looked through her veiled expression, realizing that the bitter cold was to shield a broken heart. "Of course. That you're a widow precedes you."

Her arms dropped, and she huffed a dejected sigh. "You lost your mother, and that same night, I lost my husband."

"The same night?"

"That fact only condemned me further. General Lombard stormed my home, found my potions and teachings unsanctioned by alchemy, and called me a witch. They assumed I killed my husband and your mother, but they had no evidence other than magic in me."

Reardon hadn't understood how the offerings worked back then, but he remembered whispers of a witch—of many witches, then and in all the years since. "They've condemned others for my mother's death, never sure, just speculation. I'm sorry that while you suffered your own loss, you had to suffer being blamed for it too." It did not even occur to Reardon that either accusation could be true. "May I ask… who was your husband?"

She hesitated, keeping her distance from him. "Stephen, a guard in the castle. I called him Stevie."

"Stevie?" Reardon exclaimed. "I remember him! I knew he was married but not to who. I didn't learn he died for months. They sent so many soldiers away after my mother's death. He was a serious soldier, but when no one was looking, he would smile or wink at me or even crouch to play."

The barest twitch of a smile touched Caitlin's lips. "He always had kind words for your parents and fondness for you too. When I confessed my fears about starting a family, knowing our child could inherit my magic, he used you as a reason that it would be all right, saying the kingdom was in good hands.

"Maybe I was wrong to cling stubbornly to thinking otherwise...," she said quietly, only for her expression to harden again. "But you haven't changed Emerald yet, and actions speak louder than empty promises."

"My promises are not empty," Reardon swore.

She stared at him for some time, and then nodded.

He would have accepted that as a truce and let her pass, but the knowledge of Stevie's death plagued him. Caitlin was young—or had been when she was sent here. Stevie had been the same, midtwenties, he remembered, not much older than Reardon now.

"Stevie dying the same night as my mother can't be a coincidence. Do you know how he died?"

"He died as your mother did, the very same way."

"What?" Reardon's stomach roiled. "You know how my mother died? Was it magic as everyone feared? Please, I—"

"No." Her hard eyes turned sympathetic, but she held out a hand to halt him. "There were components missing from my home. The High Alchemist reported some missing from his shop too. Science killed your mother, with elements taken from various sources to cover the killer's tracks.

"Stevie must have seen them or caught them in the act, and they forced him to drink or be doused in whatever substance they used. I tried telling all this to Lombard, to your father when he questioned me, to anyone who would listen, but I was just a witch in their eyes, easy to condemn and dismiss."

"But what *exactly* was it?" Reardon pressed. "What potion did the killer make? What did they steal to do it?"

"Wormwood and rose petals were missing from the High Alchemist. Wormwood can be a poison, but Lombard would have detected it on its own. He said the bodies had no trace of anything, that only magic could be blamed, but I know it is more complicated than that."

"What did they take from you?"

"Dried spider's eye and wraith's teeth."

"Wraith's teeth?"

"A fancy name for ice, key in many potions, and by raiding my home, they discovered my secret." She turned her hand palm up, and tiny shards of ice began to form before Reardon's eyes. "I make the ice myself."

Elemental manifestations were some of the most common forms of magic found in the people sent as offerings. Those who could conjure water—and therefore ice—were considered the most dangerous, because everyone associated that magic with the Ice King.

"I don't know exactly what killed Stevie and your mother, but it was science, not magic, and whoever used it was no one in this castle." The ice retreated into her palm as if it had melted away. "They never told you any of this? Your father? General Lombard?"

"No." Lombard never shared anything with Reardon about that night, and whenever he pressed his father, Henry looked so sad, voice catching as he tried to speak, that Reardon would backtrack and tell him it didn't matter.

He'd always hoped it hadn't been magic, but to learn so much more of the truth didn't assuage him.

"Thank you for telling me now," Reardon said. "Perhaps, one day, I can change the hearts of our people and get justice for all our loved ones."

Like before, Caitlin stared at him for a long time, her subtle smile peeking through more broadly. "That really is all you want, isn't it?"

"What else would I want?" He tilted his head at her, only in the crease of her brow recognizing that she had expected different of him, some other version of a prince, and looked—at least he hoped— pleasantly surprised.

"Keep on as you are, Emerald Prince. You're faring well so far." She nodded once more and moved to slip past him, heading back down the hall she'd initially begun to trek.

It had been a productive day, no matter how wary it made Reardon to finally know that whoever caused his mother's death had gotten away with it, and he still had no idea how or why.

He also realized that he hadn't discovered where Caitlin was headed, but he knew better than to try following again.


JACK DIDN'T need sleep. The curse saw to that, though occasionally he and the others still chose to, if only for a quieting of the mind.

Last night he hadn't rested at all. He'd been too agitated, leaving his crumpled bit of poetry in the corner of his room for hours before he finally retrieved it, smoothed its edges, and left it back on his desk. He should tear it into pieces or freeze it to dust, but he couldn't bear to part with it just yet.

Today he graced his throne minutes before Reardon's arrival. He would not be beaten again.

"Follow me, little prince." Jack got down as soon as the young man drew near, turning toward his secret tunnels. Where he wanted to have their audience today was somewhere he could only reach through the hidden passageways or risk icing far too many halls.

He saw the awe on Reardon's face as they entered the initial corridor. Jack kept looking back as he led Reardon, since the space was tight. His own hunch and slow gait ensured Reardon also had to walk slowly or risk running into him.

Eventually they came to the room Jack intended, and he moved the hidden door aside.

"Do these tunnels lead everywhere in the castle?" Reardon asked.

"For the most part." Jack backed away, leaving Reardon plenty of room to exit. "Go on. I have a feeling you haven't seen this room yet." He couldn't come right out and say that he knew Reardon hadn't because he'd been spying on him since he arrived.

Cautiously, Reardon ventured forth. Though the tunnels were slick and icy, his potion guaranteed steady footing, and he gave no sign of shivering, though a gasp did leave him once he'd cleared the exit and saw what lay on the other side.

The library was a masterwork, boasting the highest ceilings in the castle and bursting with tomes. The last two hundred years had only seen its shelves added to by works of the people here, which wasn't many, but the original collection itself was vast. There were no windows, sparing the books from the power of the sun dimming their covers, but the great hall with its many rows was lit up brilliantly, one of the brightest rooms in the castle, because Branwen always spared a part of his power to keep it lit, just as he kept the castle warm.

Branwen came off as harsh, but Jack knew him to be an avid reader, as well as a contributor to their bard tales, though for prose only, not singing, and not publicly.

"You may leave the path," Jack said. "It was made for me, since this is one of few rooms I was not willing to give up, even if I do leave an unfortunate wake."

Only then did Reardon look down to see that he stood in a hollowed-out groove in the floor like a forest path, leading many different directions throughout the library. It kept Jack's ice and subsequent melting from getting near the books.

Reardon turned to look at him with a boyish smile. "How clever. But how do you read if you can't touch the books?"

Jack gestured ahead, and Reardon stepped gingerly out of the path to walk along the main floor. A few rows down was a pedestal with an open book, surrounded by one of Wynn's clever contraptions. It connected to a pair of pedals on the floor, and with a simple step on one of them, the connecting mechanism gripped a page and turned it.

He showed Reardon by turning to the next page, and then stepped on the opposing pedal to turn it back. "I need assistance when the time comes for a new book, but this serves its purpose."

"What is this one?" Reardon stepped up to the pedestal to investigate. "*The River Princess*? That's a romance!"

"A king can't enjoy some sordid fun? I thought we discussed that already. Admittedly, I prefer to reimagine most damsels as—"

"Stable boys?" Reardon teased. "Though I suppose in this case it would be a prince." What he'd said seemed to catch up to him, and his sweet smile dropped. "I-I mean… uhhh…."

"I never had a prince," Jack said. The words slipped free as easily as any confession to Reardon so far, because the bashful way he lowered his head and fluttered his emerald eyes, only to flick them back up and center on Jack, seemed to say his wants focused there too.

Not on Jack. It couldn't possibly be that. But on a prince of his own.

Jack sat in an extra groove built like a bench, and Reardon pulled a chair over to sit close at the edge of the path. There was barely the length of a man separating them, and yet, in his trough to protect the world from his frozen form, Jack felt leagues away from Reardon beside that pedestal.

"How might a prince have changed things?" Reardon asked.

"Maybe not at all," Jack said. He needed Reardon to understand that there was no changing anything—not here. "I wasn't prepared for my father's death. I thought I could put off the inevitable forever. I was young, like you, and felt invincible, constantly thwarting my father's plans for me.

"When he died, I had a wicked and terrible idea. Thrust into my role as monarch and expected to marry, I vowed instead to change everything, to make a mockery of what my father thought a kingdom should be and create a land free for everyone to live as they pleased."

"Wasn't that a good thing?"

"Have you ever heard what the road to damnation is built with, little prince?"

Reardon's twitch of a smile said he had.

"My intentions weren't good. I was really only thinking of myself and the freedoms I wanted. I dismissed my father's advisors, even the most well-respected ones, and chose my friends as my court. We did whatever we wanted, telling our subjects to do the same.

"Not to say my court isn't each capable in their position, but back then, we had no plan or sense of gravity to all that fell under our rule. And let me assure you, there is nothing quite as dangerous as giving people exactly what they think they want.

"What happened wasn't on them, however. They soon saw the folly of it all, that yes, everyone should be able to love and exist and pursue their heart's desires—or at least most did—but there must be order and responsibility too. A kingdom should not rule every part of a subject's lives, but freedom shouldn't be a guise for apathy. There must be a balance between control and personal liberty or everything crumbles."

"I understand," Reardon said. "I wish to change the laws of the Emerald Kingdom, to not condemn anyone without a true crime against them, but not to abolish all law and tradition entirely."

"Then you are far better than I was. A tyrant in power isn't the answer, but giving everyone everything eventually collapses. Bandits arose, unrest, famine, and the people looked to me to fix it. But all I cared about was… my stable boys," Jack finished wryly. "A system is only as good as its worst person in power, no matter how well-intentioned.

"More and more people left for other kingdoms, where crops were plentiful and soldiers dependable. Freedom didn't matter when it came from a king who didn't care—or certainly didn't seem to. Eventually, my Sapphire Kingdom caught the eye of the Mystic Valley. The Fairy Queen had grown concerned about so many flocking to her lands, so she came to investigate."

"The Fairy Queen?" Reardon's eyes shot wide.

She wasn't really a fairy. Fairies were myths or whispers of the Shadow Lands, but the Fairy Queen was such a powerful ruler of the elves that she had myths of her own. Elves of the Mystic Valley were said to be un-aging because of her magic.

Jack could see in Reardon's eyes when he realized he should have guessed where the curse came from, since the castle's inhabitants were un-aging too.

"She came with a small contingent of her people, and we threw a banquet in her honor."

"That is the proper response for a visiting ruler."

"Naturally, but at the time, my lands were half-abandoned, and the castle was a mess. We may as well have been drunken revelers, feasting from our stores, while the few remaining outside were starving.

"The Fairy Queen sat in silence through it all, as we made fools of ourselves. I even attempted to bed a human in her company who turned out to be her Prince Consort."

"You didn't." Reardon paled.

"I did. It was clear that my kingdom would implode in months if not weeks, so, before the night was through, she stood from where we dined, and with a flourish of her hands, all the candles lighting the room snuffed out, and only she glowed, radiant in the center."

Jack could still remember it so clearly, though he'd been well on his way to inebriated by that point. As he recited to Reardon what she said, he heard it in his mind in her powerful voice.

*"You are not a king or a kingdom. You are a menace, even to your own people. Now I see why they come to me or run off to distant lands. I could let you continue wasting your resources and losing your subjects over time, but that would be cruel to everyone.*

*"Instead, I will give your people a choice—to stay or be welcomed into my lands instead, while you and those who rule beside you are taught a lesson."*

Her voice had resonated with even more power as she cast her spell.

*"Your kingdom's folly ends tonight
and you will live until it's right
for you are cold and full of wanting
like molten gold
that burns without warmth
and stinging power made for haunting
the invisible that you forgot.*

*"Be what you are and have neglected
until you find your way.
See what you should be in your mourning
before you rule again someday."*

"I felt it then," Jack said, "though I couldn't describe it as anything more than a chill and tingle down my spine. She turned to my friends, as she sent her own people away, and said, 'If you protect him and believe in him, you will see this curse through. When his heart melts and he is a true king, then the spell will be broken.'

"She warned me that a return to my father's ways was not the answer. All power or no power is never the answer."

"Balance." Reardon nodded thoughtfully.

"There are things to be learned from all ways and all people. There is no single answer to how to rule well. I don't claim that how this castle runs now is best, but it is ours.

"When the Fairy Queen left that night, Josie, the others, and I soon found ourselves alone, but we didn't believe anything would come of her words—until dawn, when we began to change."

"And all the people she asked to seek refuge?"

"Every last one of them accepted her offer and left."

"Then came the story of the fletcher?"

"Yes, though we had some years alone first. I suppose you could say that Oliver gave us a project, and we decided to stop wallowing in our solitude."

With the story at its end, a reaction Jack had not anticipated burst onto Reardon's face.

He smiled.

"This is such wonderful news."

"What?"

"The curse," Reardon said, serious but full of energy. "It's only meant to be temporary. It has stipulations. It can be broken!"

"Don't you understand? I allowed my subjects to starve and die while I rejoiced in my wealth and position."

"I do understand. You and Oliver were very much the same. Do you hold it against him, the rich man's son he once was?"

Jack wasn't sure how to respond to that.

"The only thing I don't understand is why the curse still stands. Clearly, you have lived up to your end of what the Fairy Queen requested."

"You aren't listening," Jack bit out sharply.

"I am. I have. She cursed you to find your way to becoming a better king, and that is exactly what you did."

"If that were true, if that were all it took, then I would no longer be this." Jack lifted one of his clawed hands, large enough that he could have gripped Reardon's head with ease and crushed it. "Yet here I am. There is no cure. There is no end."

Reardon's need to rail back—to *defend*—rose within him, but then he exhaled with a slump in his chair. "Perhaps we simply need to find the right answer."

He was foolhardy indeed, but not because he was wily and selfish. He was kind and wanted everyone to have what he sought.

"Maybe that's for another day," he said before Jack could answer, not pushing, merely leaning forward on his knees, as close to Jack as he could without being in the trench with him. "Tell me more."

"More?"

"About your favorite tales, maybe? What tomes have been your favorite?" Reardon looked curiously around them, leaving talk of the curse behind as if it changed nothing of his opinion of Jack or his court. "What types of stories warm the mighty Ice King? Always romance?"

Jack couldn't express, didn't dare, that the only thing that had warmed him in over two centuries was sitting right in front of him. "Have you never ventured into those depths, little prince?"

"I have. In books anyway." Reardon blushed.

Jack didn't want to inspire pity, but the truth was it was always romantic tales he pursued, because after years of dallying with no substance, now he could have neither, and substance was what he craved.

Though dallying still held its appeal.

He couldn't remember the last time he'd spoken this freely. Not to Branwen. Not even to Josie. But with Reardon, it came so easy. "My favorite was a rare tale, because it wasn't traditional romance, but the love story was clear between two knights who appeared to be best friends. The author must have been trying to tell the real story in secret. The truth was in the underbelly, waiting for anyone clever enough to see it.

"The knights, both men, never once kissed or intimately embraced, yet their passion and loyalty to one another was stronger than most obvious romances I've ever read." Jack smiled to remember it, how the knights were the perfect examples of stalwartness, especially when protecting each other, and he'd often close the book while reading it to imagine unwritten scenes where they ravaged one another.

"What was it called?" Reardon asked, looking around again with an eager eye.

"I can't remember. You'll have to see if you can find it."

"Seriously?" Reardon balked. "That could take years without knowing the title!"

The amusement Jack had been feeling, and the soft, wonderful warmth Reardon instilled in him went suddenly cold as he recalled that *years* wasn't part of the bargain. "When do you plan to leave?"

Reardon startled, as the truth must have only then washed over him too. "You'll... let me leave?"

Somehow, Jack had forgotten that he'd initially promised not to. "I require that you stay two weeks to prove you aren't an enemy in disguise. After that, the choice is yours."

Because after two weeks, Reardon would know the final secrets of the castle.

They spent hours trading stories, Reardon perusing the shelves and occasionally finding a tome that he loved and placing it on Jack's pedestal for them to read his favorite passages. Jack could almost have forgotten that he was a monster in a ditch, unable to touch the young prince who stood just out of reach.

They might have stayed hours more if Reardon's stomach hadn't grumbled.

"Is it lunchtime already? Let me put your book back for you." Reardon traded out the book he'd been reading from, careful to return to the exact page the original book had been on. "If it's any good, Majesty, perhaps you'll loan it to me. I can imagine a princess is someone else too." He flushed, ever so quick, to slips of phrase that he didn't seem to intend.

Jack stood to head back into the tunnels, while Reardon started for the door, but then the prince stopped with a glance over his shoulder.

"Oh, um… you could come with me, Majesty. I know you don't eat but—"

"I have very specific places I tread, little prince, or it leads to messy cleanup. And we don't have quite that much potion to spare for everyone."

Reardon hadn't shivered once during today's audience, and he didn't now, though his potion had to have worn off. "What company do you keep," he asked, smiling as he finished, "when bothersome princes aren't around? Oliver, I suppose? The other soldiers with Branwen?"

Reardon guessed that because they were the only people he'd seen Jack with, but the truth was… Jack was usually alone. "Not often."

"Then…?"

Jack couldn't answer, but Reardon didn't leave him at a quiet stalemate for long.

"Then I look forward to tomorrow." He bowed, and only after Jack nodded did he turn to take his leave.

Jack had almost made it to the entrance into the secret passages when he looked back and, realizing he was indeed—*again*—alone, decided he would stay and read, and maybe the title of that long-forgotten book would come to him.


REARDON WAS hungry but also distracted as he left the library and contemplated all he'd learned. One phrase from the story of the Fairy Queen stuck with him, though he hadn't dared mention it aloud.

*When his heart melts….*

The curse could be broken. The Ice King didn't believe it, but Reardon knew it could be. He just had to figure out how to melt the beast the king believed he'd become.

He may have gotten a little too distracted and excited, because he didn't know this part of the castle, and he was definitely lost now, with no one else anywhere around. Looking behind him, he wasn't sure he knew how to get back to the library either.

"Left unattended, pretty prince?"

Reardon jumped at the appearance of Zephyr, fading into existence at the end of the hall. "I don't like that name," he said, harsher than intended as adrenaline tore through him.

"Oh? Which part?" Zephyr's grin gave its usual teasing twitch.

*Either*, Reardon thought, but then he'd started to think that he did want to be prince if he could make his time as one count and become a good king.

"Strange you wouldn't want to be called pretty," Zephyr went on when Reardon didn't answer. "Do I sense a story there?"

Reardon's cheeks flushed with shame, and his instincts were to deny it and keep that memory to himself, but Zephyr's transparency reminded him of what he'd promised.

Relaxing, he walked toward the invisible steward. "After Barclay was sent here, when his next birthday passed, I drowned my sorrows at the tavern. A couple of men tried to take advantage when I was alone on the street."

Zephyr's expression slackened.

"Our master of arms came to my rescue before anything happened, but *they* called me 'pretty prince.' Now it just makes my skin crawl." He shuddered to think of it and wrapped his arms around his middle as he came to a stop before Zephyr.

"For me it was 'darling,'" he said, causing Reardon's eyes to bulge, "though we were still indoors. I was drowning my sorrows over my parents kicking me out of our home. The brutes who had me wouldn't let me out of the corner. Had me boxed in at the least visible part of the tavern, blocking any view to freedom or a savior.

"Then *our* master of arms saved me, long before he was made of flames. Funny, isn't it?"

"Funny?"

"How different people in different lands at different times can still have the same story." Zephyr smiled. He always smiled, but there was sadness to the expression now and the slightest sweetness that Reardon realized was the real Spymaster beneath his sharp-tongued guise. "So…. Reardon it is, then, even if you are still pretty. Come, I'll show you to the dining hall."

As Reardon followed, he realized he hadn't seen Zephyr since yesterday—since the argument he'd witnessed between Zephyr and Nigel. "Did I… say or do something yesterday morning that I shouldn't have?"

"Meaning?"

"You and Nigel seemed upset. Was it something I did? Or maybe something I can help with?"

Zephyr paused. "You didn't *do* anything, and you can't do anything to fix what's wrong. I'm… maybe not the most tactful person in the room most days."

"You hurt Nigel's feelings?"

"When you've pushed people away all your life—" Zephyr glanced over his shoulder. "—it isn't easy keeping them close, even after years of practice. Who we were in the beginning…." He trailed off, lifting the palm of his hand to stare at it. "Haunts us."

"And who were you?"

Zephyr smiled, and while he was still an imp, the comradery that had been missing before shone brightly in his clear eyes. "An *ass*, couldn't you tell? Hurry up now. I can hear that lovely lean stomach of yours growling. Nigel's headed to the dining hall too, wondering if one of us *ate* you."

Reardon chuckled as he continued to follow. He forgot sometimes that the Spymaster could hear all that went on in the castle. Smoothing a thumb over one of his own palms, he thought back to yesterday again, which brought his eyes down to his sword belt.

The smaller sheath for his dagger glared emptily back at him.

"I was so grateful to Nigel for healing my hands, I forgot all about reclaiming my dagger. I promised to steal it back. I don't know how stealthy I can be, though. I tried to be with Widow Caitlin, and she caught me straight off."

"I know." Zephyr glanced back again. "I saw."

"In my defense, I was stealthy enough to swap places with the sacrifice!"

"Were you? Or was it because the guards were terrible? Caitlin is good. Nigel is better. If you want to steal that dagger back, you'll need to catch him unawares."

"Best I learn the castle without getting lost, then."

"There are other ways. Do you know how I sneak around so easily?"

"You're an invisible wind?"

An airy chuckle responded. "Also…." Zephyr stopped before they crested another corner to tap a place on the wall that opened into the secret passageways.

"Of course." Reardon peered inside. "The king showed me. Is it okay to use these?"

"As long as you're invited. Left to start. I'll direct you so you can learn."

Reardon nodded gratefully and ducked inside. As they went, he noticed elemental markings on the floor and walls that he hadn't noticed with the king. There were ice trails, but also scorch marks and occasional swaths of gold.

"Right next," Zephyr said. "These are important skills to learn, you know. Stealth. Subterfuge. Misdirection."

"Are you teaching me to be a thief?"

"Isn't that what you asked? And if you want to avoid being targeted by a real one again, you should know how they operate. You can't tiptoe after someone and think you're invisible. Left."

The direction came so seamlessly, Reardon almost missed it, but turned left at the next fork.

"Balance is important to better distribute your weight. Even your breathing too. Most people breathe louder when they're trying to be quiet. Find your shadows, the person's blind spot, and consider ways to distract them toward the opposite direction of your approach."

Reardon attempted to do all those things as Zephyr mentioned them, even as he was still safely in the passageways.

"And finally—stop. Listen for the right cues, almost like meditation, to drown out everything but what you want to hear—*without* closing your eyes."

Reardon had been about to close them but resisted, keeping as still as he could with even breaths. He could hear Nigel! And Barclay! They were just ahead, almost directly beyond another secret door.

Whenever they opened, they did so silently, so Reardon took the risk and pressed his palm against it. Not a sound came as the door slid open, and Nigel and Barclay's voices grew louder. They were discussing *Reardon* and where he might be, since no one had seen him since morning.

Pausing before stepping out, Reardon considered the way their voices carried. Barclay clearly faced toward him, but Nigel must be faced *away*, which was when Reardon noticed the alcove across from him. For once, Barclay not being able to school his expressions might help.

Reardon stepped into the corridor, waving to get Barclay's attention. He looked immediately startled, prompting Reardon to dart quickly to the opposite side of the hall.

"What?" Nigel asked, turning as Reardon had expected.

"I, uh...."

"Is someone in the passage?" Nigel approached it, left open with no sign of Zephyr, bringing him perfectly into view of Reardon with all his attention elsewhere.

Reardon swept forward, reaching for his dagger—

—only for Nigel to spin, grab his wrists, and twist. The next thing Reardon knew, he was on his back, staring up at his friend's face.

"Sneak!" Nigel cried joyously. "You almost had me! Who showed you the tunnels?" He helped Reardon up with a firm hoist of his forearms, and the way he and Barclay laughed made it impossible for Reardon to feel like a failure.

"The king did first." Zephyr appeared, just suddenly there like always.

Nigel's smile dropped.

"He needs to learn, doesn't he?" Zephyr continued. "As it turns out... *Reardon* isn't completely useless."

"He isn't?" Nigel prompted.

"Not entirely. But don't you have lunch to get to?" Zephyr blinked away again, as quickly as he'd come.

Reardon wasn't sure he understood what had just transpired, but at least the expression on Nigel's face now was a pleased one. "Just you wait," Reardon promised. "I'll get that dagger back yet."


JACK WAS so engrossed in his book, calmer than he remembered feeling in a long time, that it was almost sundown before he realized the day was over. He retired, finding himself thinking of the young prince again. He didn't need to spy, but he still felt the urge to, if only to see Reardon for as long as he could.

Which he didn't think would include sharing their audiences with others.

"There are certain places in the castle I don't go," Jack said when Reardon requested he accompany him to the tailoring room the next morning.

"I know, but I also know that you have ways to get anywhere in the castle, so that is not an excuse. As long as we take the tunnels, the cleanup won't be too bad. Don't you miss spending time with your subjects?"

Jack sensed a trick, but he couldn't figure out what it was. "We don't have enough potion—"

"What do you think this is for?" Reardon hefted the rucksack he'd brought to Jack's chamber, which clattered with an obvious collection of potion bottles. "Caitlin helped. We'll choose one room a day. She said she can keep up with that demand. Today we're going to the tailoring room. Go on." He motioned Jack toward the entrance into the tunnels. "I'm sure you know the way."

Jack stomped his foot in irritation, being told where to go in his own castle, but no gust of bitter wind or show of strength affected the prince—not anymore. Jack had no other recourse but to obey.

No opening of the tunnels went directly into the tailoring room, but it took only a few steps from an exit to reach the tailoring room door. Reardon went ahead of Jack then and knocked before entering, warning all inside that they had a guest, before Jack slowly ducked in after him.

The small group of people inside bowed as Reardon went around, handing out potions. None of those gathered seemed surprised to see Jack. Reardon must have told them ahead of time, and Josie, in the corner, looked so smug, turning spools of thread into glittering gold.

"You realize I can't touch anything," Jack grumbled at Reardon.

"I know. But I believe you have a keen eye." He returned to set his now empty rucksack aside. "Shayla and Josie are helping me with two doublet designs, and I'd love your thoughts, Majesty."

Shayla was indeed there, one of Jack's most capable hunters, foragers, and artisans, and one of the first who'd become taken by Reardon. She brought over two swaths of fabric, one a beautiful emerald and one a deep sapphire blue. She also held a square of practice cloth with various embroidery samples.

"I taught our Emerald Prince this one." She showed Jack a square embroidery stitch like the links of a chain. "And he taught me the other." Then she showed one in a diamond pattern.

"Josie can do two types of gold thread," Reardon said, snatching up a couple finished spools. "Aren't they beautiful?"

One was her usual yellow gold, but the other was silvery white. The way they glittered was quite enchanting, and Josie glowed with pride in a way Jack hadn't seen in years.

"Very beautiful," he admitted.

"I was thinking yellow gold for the green, and silver for the blue," Reardon said, "but which style for which? I'd like to practice both."

"I don't have the skills—"

"It's not skill I'm after. It's your opinion, which I value very much."

That rare warmth filled Jack's chest. He considered the fabrics, the thread, the embroidery styles. "Squares in gold. Diamonds in silver."

"I thought so too." Reardon beamed. "Do you want to see how each is done?"

Jack sat in the corner of the room, slowly frosting the stones beneath him, but those with him didn't seem to mind. While Reardon sat close to show Jack his embroidery, Shayla chatted with him as well, as did others, bringing their creations over for Jack's commentary.

A bitter part of him wanted to say that his opinion didn't matter since no one had seen him in clothes in two hundred years, but he held his tongue because they all looked genuinely pleased to have him there and appreciative of his responses.

After Josie turned a small pile of thread into dazzling additions to their trimmings, she whispered, "Still waiting two weeks?"

"Yes," Jack said without falter.

He'd wait longer if he could. Once Reardon knew everything, he'd be ready to leave.


AFTER THAT day in the tailoring room, they no longer took their audiences purely alone. Day after day, Reardon dragged Jack all over the castle using the hidden passageways—to the alchemist tower, for example, to assist Liam, Barclay, and Caitlin. The widow was no longer cold to the Emerald Prince, but gentle and patient, as she taught him basic transmutation, which he took to as adeptly as he could sew.

Reardon wasn't quick with everything, however. He really was awful with a bow when Oliver tried to teach him, but they considered it a win when he finally hit the target—albeit not the actual target but the stand holding it up.

He was better with a short sword and quickly mastered how to handle two, trained as equally by Shayla at that point as Oliver. His old short sword was left in his room, replaced with twin blades made of hard steel and gold-colored hilts, forged by Branwen's fire.

Each day was mixed with an audience between him and Jack and adventures throughout the castle, Reardon learning much, becoming one of them, even though his time there was only temporary. Not a soul was left in the castle after the first week who thought Reardon didn't belong. He became even more popular as he learned favored bard tales, singing them at dinner—sometimes alone, sometimes with Barclay or Wynn or both—or giving a pretty refrain to accompany Nigel's spoken verse.

Reardon confessed to Jack, traveling through the tunnels after spending time in the music room, that what made him love bard tales so much was that his mother had loved them too.

"I never thought to ask, Majesty. What of your mother? I've only heard you speak of your father, the king."

If anyone else had broached the subject—if *Reardon* had on his first days—Jack would have grown angry, but there was very little ire left in him where this young prince was concerned. "A quiet, lovely woman, given to my father, not in love, who couldn't keep her light alive after Josie was born. She'd borne too much by then, and I don't only mean me.

"My father, the life she'd been given, it whittled her away. She died before Josie was a year. No one is meant for a life they didn't choose for themselves."

The gentle affection and understanding Reardon offered still caught Jack off guard, but despite Jack's beastly form, Reardon never shied from looking him in the eyes. "I am sorry, Majesty. We have much in common, even the sadder things, the harder times, the losses, but I am glad I have come to know all we have in common that is good."

He turned to continue moving through the tunnels, and it was just as well, because the warmth Jack felt then was so intense, he'd swear he felt a drip of water streak down his face.

There was less need to spy on Reardon after so many days, but still Jack did, if only to keep that warmth tended to like a smoldering fire. It had not yet been two weeks, but a long ten days, when Jack watched Reardon head down to the cellars at the behest of the kitchen staff to fetch a few bottles of wine to bring up for dinner.

Branwen was there, sitting at the tasting table, with several bottles already and a goblet before him.

"What are you doing?" Reardon asked. He hadn't crossed Branwen's path since the training yard, for the twin swords had been presented by Shayla.

"Waiting for nightfall," Branwen grumbled, and then turned and saw who had joined him. "You."

"Yes." Reardon sat beside Branwen, closer than most would dare, especially after almost being burned.

Branwen sat up taller, his flames dimming to a soft orange. "You got a death wish, princeling?"

"No. But I haven't seen you lately. I never got to thank you for my swords. They say you forged them especially for me." Reardon wore them now and touched their hilts with reverence.

"Didn't want you falling like an idiot again," Branwen said, shifting uncomfortably, but it would be difficult for him to get up and leave without shifting too close to Reardon. "Those swords are perfectly balanced."

"They're magnificent. I didn't realize you could forge. Did you make all the weapons in the castle?"

"Do you ever shut up?"

As usual, Reardon wasn't deterred, but gave a gentle laugh. "I doubt the king thinks so."

Branwen wasn't much of a talker, and Reardon did indeed talk incessantly, but for once, he sat still and quiet, waiting for Branwen to speak again.

"If you're going to stay, then drink with me," Branwen barked, moving the empty goblet toward Reardon.

"But you can't... a-all right," Reardon stuttered, taking the open bottle and pouring some to fill it halfway, only for Branwen to huff disapproval, so he filled it to the top.

Jack had seen Reardon drink before. He could manage a glass or two, but anything more than that left him utterly sloshed.

Reardon started with a small sip.

"Pfft." Branwen's next huff produced a burst of flame like a dragon snorting. "If you can spew so much out of your mouth, then you can take more too."

The flush that filled Reardon's cheeks was not from wine, though Branwen didn't mean it the way Zephyr might have. Regardless, Reardon tipped the goblet back to bring the wine nearly below half again.

Branwen snatched the bottle to fill the glass back to the brim. They sat close, enough to make Jack nervous, especially with Branwen plying Reardon with more wine, but Reardon wasn't shying away, and it dawned on Jack how much Branwen needed this.

Jack hadn't seen Branwen much either in the past week. He should have been the one to check on his friend, instead of neglecting him. He'd spoken to Branwen, but he never knew what was right to say when accidents—actual or merely close calls—always felt like they were his fault, since none of this would have happened without him.

Yet there Reardon went, being everything Branwen needed just by being himself, undaunted and friendly, like a pillar of virtue.

That was it! That was the title of Jack's book, the one he hadn't been able to remember, resounding suddenly in his head—*Pillars of Virtue*. The knights in that story had displayed all the chivalrous pillars—courage, mercy, hope—and the sexual tension between them had fueled many of Jack's adolescent fantasies.

He watched Reardon now, much like those knights, not pushing Branwen to talk about what had happened, but simply being with him to show that he wasn't afraid or resentful.

"I'm not much of a drinker," Reardon said, even as he tipped back his next few gulps.

"That's coz you're a twig. Keep training with the fletcher and Shayla. You'll toughen up."

"And with you?"

"Suppose so. If you take good care of those swords. And learn to hold your liquor." Branwen pounded the table, flames bouncing across the wood but never causing it to catch fire.

Reardon took another gulp. "My only wish is that you could be drinking with me. Perhaps someday."

"Oh?" Branwen straightened again.

"No curse lasts forever," Reardon said.

*Naive and ignorant.* But oh, how his hopefulness was infectious, because it made Branwen laugh. "Says the twenty-year-old."

"Twenty-*one*," Reardon corrected.

"Nothing left to learn, then?"

"I have everything to learn. And I'd like to. Everything I can. Including about you, Sir Branwen, if you'll tell me."

"I'm no bard," Branwen said with a wrinkle of his nose.

*Lies.* Though maybe not spoken.

"If every story was the same or told the same way, they'd be very boring indeed," Reardon said.

He drank, not saying more, until eventually Branwen began to talk. He didn't look at Reardon, and he didn't tell stories of the castle, as Jack would have expected. He spoke of a quiet boy with a hard father and a too-soft mother—very relatable for Jack—but who'd always been seen as too brutish to think for himself.

None of it was likened to a life Reardon could relate to, but that didn't seem to matter to the young prince. He listened and he drank until Branwen ran out of things to say.

Reardon was on what must have been his fourth glass of wine, slurring as he said, "M'sorry, Bran… if my stumbling scared you."

The silence stretched, but finally, Branwen said, "Me too."

When next the quiet broke, it was with a hum, followed by the tentative flow of song.

> *"A raging fire must first be lit*
> *By sparks we plan or cannot see.*
> *Tended slow to not burn out*
> *But watched to calm when it burns free.*
>
> *"Hark! The fire in all,*
> *The fire in you,*
> *The fire in me.*
>
> *"Oh gentle hearth that crackles warm,*
> *Others' care is who you'll be.*

*Consuming pyre or saving grace,*
*The choices made save you and me.*

*"Hark! The fire in all,*
*The fire in you,*
*The fire in me,*

*"The fire in all who long to be."*

Reardon chuckled and took another gulp from his goblet.

"You just made that up?" Branwen gawked. "Right now?"

"I did. Drinking must agree with me," Reardon said with the start of a hiccup.

"Reardon!" Barclay exclaimed, rushing down the stairs with Josie close behind. "Where have you been? They suddenly remembered in the kitchen that they sent you down for wine, and you never came up."

"Bran!" Josie scolded, seeing the state of Reardon when he turned to his friends with a wide, rosy grin. "What did you do to him?"

"He's the one who wanted to drink with me," Branwen protested.

"I made a new song!" Reardon said too loud at Barclay's ear, when he hurried over to heave him up from the table. "It's about, um… fire! I think…. Yes, definitely fire!" He burst into giggles, and Branwen chuckled with him.

"You're not so bad, Emerald Prince."

"You too, Sir Bran! A true de-*light*." He giggled again, all semblance of sobriety gone.

Barclay looked exasperated but mostly amused, and Josie smiled too, sharing the warm expression with Branwen.

"Come on." Barclay hefted Reardon toward the stairs. "It's almost nightfall. Josie, can you get someone to grab a couple bottles for the kitchen?"

"I'll do it!" Reardon broke away, bolting for the back-cellar door.

"No!" Josie cried.

Reardon almost had it open before Barclay, the only one who could stop him without turning him into *another* accident, slammed the door shut again. Only the barest hint of gold had been seen, but Reardon didn't seem to have noticed.

"*Not* where we keep the wine," Barclay said. "Someone else can do it."

Josie and Branwen shared soberer looks, but a true spiral from the current merriment had been averted, and while Barclay brought Reardon upstairs to feed him water and bread and whatever else he could get into him, Jack decided not to follow.

Instead, he headed for the library. There was a mere twenty minutes before sunset, but although he still didn't know where to find his favorite book, now he knew its name.

And he was determined to find it.

"Zephyr!"

SOBERED AND not at all sick or miserable-feeling thanks to water, nourishment, and some combined healing from Nigel and Caitlin, Reardon slogged upstairs to bed. Everyone had adamantly made sure he was okay before taking their leave of him, but he'd assured them he was fine.

Branwen was one of the few remaining in the castle who he hadn't spoken to at length before that evening, and while Reardon didn't fully remember everything about their hours together, he was confident he'd made headway.

He was tired when he got to his room, so tired that he almost didn't notice the book lying on his bed until after he'd removed his sword belt and doublet. It was beautifully bound, with red-and-gold lettering to state the title and two jousting knights carved into the leather.

*Pillars of Virtue.*

It had to be the king's book, his favorite, he'd said, about two knights who might have been written as in love if the author had been bolder or lived in a different time. Reardon had never read it, but to find it like a gift waiting for him felt like the most intimate thing anyone had ever given him. Surely it was only to borrow, but still. The king must have had Zephyr set it there, for there was not a single mar of ice upon it.

If it wasn't nighttime, Reardon would have gone to the king right then to express his thanks and ask if they could read the first chapter together. But he couldn't. He wasn't allowed anywhere near the court's private chambers after dark.

He needed to tell someone, though. Reardon had accomplished so much in his week and a half being here. If he was right that "melting" the king could break the curse, surely a gift like this meant he was close.

Close to melting him back to Jack—because they were *friends*.

Reardon clutched the book to his chest. He didn't even know what Jack's real face or body looked like, only his eyes, and yet he couldn't help wondering....

Couldn't help wanting....

He had to see Barclay.

Still clutching the book, barefoot in his trousers and untucked shirt, Reardon rushed next door and knocked.

No answer.

"Barclay! I'm sorry if I'm waking you, but I need to talk." Reardon knocked again.

Still nothing.

He knew Barclay was a light sleeper, and Barclay had definitely said earlier that he was going to bed.

"Barclay?" Reardon tried one more time, but when once again, no answer came, he opened the door.

Barclay wasn't there, but several candles were lit—and one of the secret passageways was open, leading right into his bedroom!

Reardon clutched the book tighter. Barclay wasn't the type to go snooping around, but then, where had he gone?

Edging closer to the tunnel, Reardon peered inside. There were torches lit along a path leading to the right, like a beacon telling Reardon where Barclay must have trod. He followed, and the farther he went, the more he noticed swaths of gold on the walls like he'd seen elsewhere, but here there was only gold, no sign of ice or scorch marks.

The path eventually stopped at another open tunnel entrance. Reardon was cautious, but his curiosity had been piqued too much to not go in. The room on the other side was opulent, with plush pillows, a beautiful vanity, elegant dresses in wardrobes, and a wall covered in jewelry hanging for selection.

There was also a dress, a pair of trousers, a shirt, and various other clothing in a pile on the floor.

And a bed with bodies moving on it and the distinct utterance of a familiar voice that *moaned*.

"Barclay?"

Covers tumbled from the shoulders of the most visible occupant on the bed, revealing Barclay's brown skin and the pale limbs of someone tangled with him. He yelped when his eyes met Reardon's and scrambled to cover himself.

"Reardon! How did you... *when* did you... why are you here?"

Reardon was too mortified to look away, staring openmouthed at having caught his friend in the throes of passion with what he soon saw was a very beautiful brunette. "Sorry! I-I saw the tunnel, a-and I didn't realize, I...." Still staring at the woman's face—grateful as he was that he could only see her *face*—it suddenly struck him that he had seen that face before.

In a portrait.

"Josie?"

# CHAPTER 6

JOSIE LOOKED human.

Normal.

Just like her portrait.

The curse was broken!

"It's only at night!" Josie cried, sitting up fully while holding the sheets to her chest. She was radiant—blue eyes like her brother, wavy locks of soft brown hair, and youthful glowing skin. "The curse still stands, but what we hadn't yet told you, Reardon, is that we get reprieve when the sun sets.

"I'm sorry. We're vulnerable after dark, so we always wait a full two weeks to reveal that secret to newcomers, ever since... we were betrayed."

Josie's sorrow made Reardon sag and hug *Pillars of Virtue* more closely against him. "The thief," he whispered. She clearly meant the statue in the garden of the thief who'd tried to run after killing one of their own. They couldn't risk someone untrustworthy discovering that the court could be killed too if the time was right.

No wonder they were still sane and able to rule well if, after dark, they existed as they once were and could touch those they held dear. Barclay hadn't fallen in love with someone out of his reach. He already had her.

Which meant all the other members of the court were human now too!

"Reardon!" Barclay called, as Reardon turned and fled back into the tunnels.

He ran anyway, returning to the entrance into Barclay's room but moving past it, certain in his use of the tunnels lately that he knew how to reach each of the court members' chambers. Or at least how to get close enough to find their wake trails, like Josie's tunnel was covered in gold.

He had to know. He had to see for himself if the same was true for all of them.

First was Liam in the alchemist tower. He and Branwen both left scorch marks, but Liam's were finely focused like jagged lines of lightning. The closer Reardon got to the tower, the more concentrated the scorches became until they suddenly stopped.

Pushing on the wall where they disappeared, Reardon revealed another doorway, leading into another bedroom, this one filled with alchemist tools overflowed from the laboratory.

And another pair of moving bodies on a bed, hidden by covers.

Reardon hadn't hoped to find the same type of interlude, but given the circumstances, he couldn't say he was surprised.

"It is true!" he cried, hearing a feminine yelp and rustle of sheets before Shayla appeared with her usually pinned hair wild and curly about her head.

"Reardon! How—?"

"What are you doing here?" Liam shouted.

Shayla sat atop his hips, keeping the sheets around them, but Reardon could see Liam's face. He never would have known it was Liam if not for his voice, but that was indeed the wizard. He could have been a brother to the fletcher, really, if not for his elven ears. He and Oliver shared the same blond hair and blue eyes.

These eyes didn't give Reardon pause, however, or wonder at Barclay's vision, since he knew this man was another one spoken for.

"You were all so obvious, yet I didn't see it," Reardon said, unable to keep the smile from his face, even if he was being terribly intruding, because the court was not made of the lonely creatures he'd thought. "Nigel…," he said in realization and turned once more to dash back into the tunnels.

"Where are you going?" Shayla yelled after him.

"Wait!" Barclay cried, not far behind, as he and Josie gave chase.

Still, Reardon ran, elation fluttering in his chest, finally understanding what Barclay's friends had in common.

He didn't know where Zephyr's chambers were, but he knew Nigel's. It only dawned on him now that he had seen evidence of a wind elemental in those tunnels and in Nigel's room more than anywhere else—grooves in the stone like decades of erosion.

There wasn't a tunnel exit directly into Nigel's room, but there was one outside it. As Reardon burst into the room through the main door, Nigel spun around wide-eyed, in the process of changing for bed.

"What is that rack—ah!" Zephyr appeared—*naked*—from the wash area and clutched a robe he'd been carrying between his legs. "Don't you knock?"

He had blue eyes too, though Reardon had dismissed Zephyr long ago, fair though his face may be, and clearly, he was also taken.

With color filling his usually translucent form, his cheeks held a warm glow, dark hair messy and damp from bathing, with the otherwise same slender form Reardon had seen floating.

"You *were* fighting about me," Reardon said, "because Zephyr kept saying lewd things to me!"

"Nigel forgave me for that!" Zephyr defended.

"Reardon…." Nigel dragged a hand down his face. "We—"

Reardon spun on his heels to continue his journey, pushing past Josie in a silken robe and Barclay in a barely held up pair of trousers.

Only he couldn't reach the tunnels this time, because Shayla and Liam were coming out of them, equally half-dressed, and Liam looked far less understanding than everyone else. His physique matched the fletcher's too, but Reardon didn't have time to admire it.

Sprinting the other way, he mapped out in his mind which tunnels would best lead him to the basement. He vaguely remembered from his drinking with Branwen that the master of arms said his chambers were down there, close to the wine and ale. Now Reardon knew why: he *had* been waiting for nightfall so he could drink when the sun dipped below the horizon.

"*Stop!*" Barclay tried again, but Reardon knew his stamina would win.

He had three couples chasing him as he worked his way to the lower levels of the castle, finding larger scorch marks with smears of blackened soot along the walls. When at last the scorches stopped, he found the expected door.

"Reardon!" Caitlin yelped—from a *desk*, thankfully, with a large, imposing man standing over her shoulder, both fully clothed.

This room was more utilitarian but covered in parchment and scattered tomes, which surprised Reardon, as it seemed Branwen was dictating to Caitlin.

"She's my scribe," he growled, like some hasty defense.

Branwen was as broad and burly as Reardon would have imagined, with mild scruff, a mostly shaven head, and pale eyes that also looked blue. Every single member of the court had blue eyes, but none of them were the eyes that mattered to Reardon.

"If you're with Bran, then…. He doesn't have anyone, does he?" Reardon asked Caitlin, turning equally imploring eyes to Branwen. Hearing the others pour into the room behind him, he turned to them as well. "He doesn't, does he? I know he doesn't. He can't."

"Reardon," Barclay said with a sigh, reaching out to touch him—only to gasp.

*A vision*, Reardon thought as he surged forward, realizing then that he still clung to the king's book, and Barclay's slack expression made him clutch it tighter, like salvation. "It's him, isn't it? It has to be him."

"I… I don't know." The strange expression on Barclay's face didn't change, but he blinked the vision away and gave Reardon's arm a firm squeeze. "I didn't see the same thing just now. I'm not sure what I saw…. There was a woman with dark skin in brilliant finery, and… and someone in armor of the Emerald Kingdom, bookending you like a prize between them. You guarded someone from them that I couldn't see."

"The *king*," Reardon said without falter. "It's him, Barclay. It has to be, and I stand before my love, between my kingdom and the past."

"Your love?" Josie repeated, stepping from the others—Liam and Zephyr, who looked annoyed, and Shayla and Nigel, smiling in delight. Josie's robe was neatly tied now, black silk trimmed in gold.

"Just as all of you found someone," Reardon said, "I am meant for him. That's why I'm here. My purpose here. I'm sure of it."

"Hang on," Branwen said, no change to his gruff voice even when lacking flames. He held a goblet, finally enjoying his wine. "Don't get any ideas that *we're* together like that." The faintest color filled his cheeks as he said it, and he wouldn't meet Reardon's eyes, something mirrored in Caitlin which told Reardon that, despite their protests, they clearly wanted what they hadn't yet had. "She helps get my ideas down, that's all. Nothing like these rutting maniacs."

"Rutting?" Liam threw back. "Shayla ignored me for a week because of this princely brat. Who *is* useful," he amended when Shayla glared at him, "and not all bad most days, but I'm allowed my ire!"

"Maybe sometimes you take for granted what you have," Shayla shot back. "You don't need Reardon's presence to require occasional reminders."

"Sounds familiar," Nigel muttered.

"You forgave me!" Zephyr cried again, looking rumpled in just the robe he'd been clutching earlier.

Nigel pulled Zephyr against him, quieting him in such a sweet, reflexive manner that Reardon had kept his smile. He was right. He had to be right. They'd all had lessons to learn, but they'd needed someone to melt their hearts as well, someone who had nothing to do with this place in the beginning—a sacrifice freely given.

Wasn't true love always the epic end to a curse?

"I only found Barclay a year ago," Josie said, taking his hand to pull him close too. "They've all had each other for decades. I'll rut as I like."

Barclay blushed far darker than Branwen or Caitlin, a beautiful hue, because Reardon had never seen his friend so happy.

"Four days left, and we have to do this in *my* room?" Branwen grumbled, taking a gulp of wine.

Reardon turned to him, to all of them, understanding that he had broken the rules, however unintentional at first. "I'm sorry I made you all run, but I had to be sure. I understand now why you said fourteen days. Any shorter could allow a swindler to betray you as that thief once did."

A solemn expression touched each of the court members as it had Josie, but she was the one who spoke. "We told her the truth after six days, so certain she posed no threat, just another one of us welcomed into our company. But then she knew, you see, that we were vulnerable at night."

"But... the king did freeze her," Reardon said, confused, as the implication was that she had betrayed them while they were flesh and blood.

"She planned her theft for early morning, just before the sun rose, but she should have given herself more time. Before she reached the gate, the sun was up, and Jack caught her. Before then, she still got to one of us." Slowly, Josie pulled aside the edge of her robe to reveal a scar beneath her collarbone.

"The king said she killed an elf." Reardon scrunched his brow in further strain. "Someone with beautiful magic."

"It was beautiful," Josie said softly. "The most powerful healing magic of anyone here. The thief got to me first, knowing my chambers held the most gold. I gave chase, even with my injury, and he saw us in the halls. He tried to stop her, but she was too swift.

"I was already weak, but I struggled to help him, and sweet thing that he was, he still tried to heal me, even as I was trying to stop *his* bleeding, flowing so much more freely than my own. I... I was still touching him when the sun came up...." Her delicate hands clenched into fists, and Reardon didn't have to ask what her touch had done.

Barclay slipped an arm around her waist, and she leaned gratefully against him.

"I understand why Jack wanted to wait with you, Reardon," Josie said, "as we have with everyone else since then, but I also don't want to let the past haunt me. None of us do."

As Barclay held her, the others all vigilantly silent, Reardon recognized why the princess had only found love so recently, despite two hundred years having passed. It was too difficult for her after causing someone such awful harm. Though Reardon also believed she had needed to wait for the right person.

He had not seen any statues made of gold in the king's ice garden, but now he wondered what had become of the... accidents.

"I swear to you that I am not your enemy," Reardon said. "I never will be. I don't only want to understand your curse and change my kingdom. I want to break the curse and save everyone."

"And you think loving Jack will do that?" Branwen asked skeptically.

"Could have skipped the interrupting-us part," Liam muttered, and Shayla smacked his chest.

"I don't even know his real face, yet I feel...." Reardon stroked the cover of the book, holding it out in front of him to look at the carved leather. "I know the days have been few, but as each one passes, I find myself more amazed by him. With our audiences, I always want them to last longer."

"You love the king while he looks like *that*?" Zephyr sneered.

Reardon couldn't truly say he loved the king, but the draw he'd felt for only a scant few, it was the same for Jack as for anyone he'd ever lusted after. "If not yet, then I think I could. I need to see this through, to know his feelings in return. To truly know mine. Only then can I be certain if it's enough to break the curse."

"What do you intend to do now?" Josie asked.

"I intend to see him. Would any of you stop me?" Reardon hugged the book once more.

There was a shift of glances between them all.

"That's the book the king had me scouring for in the library," Zephyr said.

"Yes, and place on my bed."

"I didn't place it on your bed."

Reardon's eyes snapped up from looking at the cover again.

"The sun was already setting," Zephyr explained. "He ordered me out of the library after I found it. If it ended up on your bed, Emerald Prince, then he's the one who put it there."

The resolve in Reardon strengthened, knowing the king had been in his room, risking getting caught after nightfall.

"You are a wily one," Liam said, trying to pull Shayla against him like the others, which she allowed after a weak show at struggling. "You might even be right."

"He means *mad*," Zephyr said, and then when Nigel elbowed him, added, "but we're certainly not going to stop you."

Branwen and Caitlin were different—quiet, stubborn creatures, maybe only commiserating, though Reardon did wonder what the master of arms had Caitlin writing for him. Still, they were hopeful sentries, with Caitlin rising from the desk to stand beside Branwen, both offering encouraging nods.

Lastly, Reardon looked to Josie and Barclay, his first friend among the court and his oldest friend of all. Whatever Barclay saw when he touched Josie, it filled his face with peace and fondness that Reardon hoped to one day know for himself.

"Wish me luck," Reardon said and turned, one last time, for the tunnels.

JACK'S REAL chambers, his private rooms that he never entered during the day, saving them from his horrible ice trail and frigid touch, sprawled beyond his frozen throne and the main entrance into the hidden passageways. No one else was allowed there, ever, but especially at night, when his earned isolation was absolute.

He couldn't bear to see his own face, his own form, so no one else could either. While the rest of the court looked as they once had when night fell, Jack, just as his curse was different during the day, doomed to leave an icy residue and stomp upon the ground like a plague, wasn't the same when he was human either.

He was *human*, but the damage….

Sitting beside his bath as it filled with heated water, he hated what little of his skin he could see, sleeves rolled up to his elbows.

His rooms were warm, as warm as he could make them, but he still started most nights with a soak. He never seemed to get warm enough, no matter how hot the water or how many layers he wore or blankets he piled on his bed. He rarely slept anyway, since the need was gone with the clutch of the curse. He dreamt, though—daydreams of what might have been if he hadn't been such a fool all those years ago.

The washroom had steps up to the large bath and many wardrobes around it, and continued farther on to his bedroom, where Jack's large bed sported four ceiling-high posts and heavy bedcurtains. Closer to the door was his antechamber and study. Josie loved her gold, but Jack had always preferred silver, even if it was less kingly. His rooms were the same, covered in those colors, in stone and cool woodgrains and varying shades of blue.

The rug that adorned his study led beneath several bookcases and his desk. Behind the desk wasn't a normal chair but his original throne, which had once been in the other room where the frozen throne now stood. Jack had moved it here as a reminder, closeting away what he hadn't been able to live up to.

The throne wasn't wood but polished white stone painted in gold and silver. It was too grand to sit behind a desk and as tall as Jack's ceiling, blocking much of the view toward the bedroom and bath. Jack preferred it that way, to be blocked off from everything.

He ran his fingers through the warm water, deeming it high enough to turn off the pump, and tried not to cringe at the sight of his ruined skin.

Closing his eyes, he attempted to think of anything else, something good, something sweet—and wondered if Reardon had discovered the book yet.

"Majesty?"

Jack's eyes flew open.


THE DOOR wasn't locked. *Why bother*, Reardon supposed, since no one would dare do what he was doing now—ignoring the very serious mandate to never disturb the court at night.

Well, once someone was trusted, the court wasn't off-limits, Reardon knew now. But the king never allowed anyone in, and he was encroaching on the king's privacy anyway, untidy without his doublet and clutching an old leather book.

"Majesty, I know you're here," Reardon called again, softly shutting the door behind him.

This was a king's chambers indeed, the grandest Reardon had seen tonight. The rooms seemed to go on forever beyond the antechamber, with an overlarge throne behind an ornate desk. And it was so warm, the coziest room in the castle, contrasting starkly against the chill on the other side of the door. Only the door itself and a bit of the floor right in front of it remained wet and cold, where the king must stand as his form changed.

"Please, Majesty, I didn't mean to discover your secret. I only went to speak with Barclay and found...." Reardon trailed off, nervous amidst the silence that greeted him. Still, he crept forward toward the desk with its elegant throne. "I saw Josie. I've seen everyone. All that remains is you."

Even as Reardon came around the desk, he heard no sound. Maybe the king hadn't returned yet. He'd been in Reardon's room. He might have gone somewhere else. But then the barest peek toward the washroom showed that the bath was filled with steaming water, ready for someone to sink into it.

"Don't be angry. You can't leave me this gift and not expect that I'd want to say thank you. There is so much I want to say to you." Without any rustle of noise or answering voice, Reardon sighed and turned to the desk, his back to the washroom as he moved beside the throne and set the book down, peering over the desk's contents.

In the center was a crumpled piece of paper smoothed out, like the king had thrown it away and then changed his mind. Reardon picked it up.

*The noble prince went on his quest—*

The air was knocked from him as a body slammed up against him from behind, arms wrapping around his own to pin them to his body and cause the rumpled paper to drop.

"You come into my room and rifle through my things?"

The king, his voice unmistakable—with *his arms* wrapped around Reardon.

Reardon didn't dare move but couldn't help leaning subtly against the warm body pressed to him, not some large, hulking figure, but a man, about his own height, with tan arms, much of the skin visible, as the sleeves of a simple shirt were rolled up.

"Forgive me," Reardon said, holding still and forgetting the parchment as he made to turn his head.

"*Don't.* You will not look. You will not see me. If you do, I swear I will throw you from the window you first climbed through."

The words were cold, but the body was warm as he held Reardon. He *held* Reardon, touching him, which had to be the first time he had touched anyone since—

The king squeezed so tight, Reardon gasped for reprieve.

"P-please! I won't look!" Reardon promised, keeping his head forward but glancing down at the arms around him, at the glimpse of skin and humanity and....

*Scars*, countless scars, covering so much of the king's arms that Reardon hadn't noticed for how many overlapped and ran together.

"Is this what you wanted?" the king roared, shaking him. "To see the true, *ugly* me? Ugly and earned, have no doubt about that."

"No, I... I could never think you ugly, Majesty, no matter what the rest of you looks like. Please, I have seen too much beauty in you to see ugliness."

The hold on Reardon slackened but did not release. "Then you are a fool. You learned our secrets early, which means I can choose to cast you out or imprison you, maybe freeze you come morning."

"You won't."

"So bold and foolhardy, little prince?" The king's voice was ice where his touch was not, sharp and biting, but Reardon saw through him.

"No, but if you had such hatred for me, you wouldn't have left me that book. *You* left it, Zephyr said, not him."

A puff of air disturbed the hairs on Reardon's neck, as warm as the room and enough to make him shudder. "Damn gossip."

Reardon smiled, because the king hadn't denied it, and his hold was loose now, just their bodies flush and those arms around him. No one had ever really held Reardon before, besides a brief embrace, and certainly not like this, intimate and caging. Reardon should have been unnerved by it, but the king never instilled that feeling in him.

"I won't look if you do not wish it, Majesty."

"I do not. But I also do not believe I can trust you anymore."

"Then let me prove myself again. Let me know you. Isn't that what we promised?"

"You *broke* our promises."

"I didn't mean to! It was an accident. You can ask the others."

"Was coming here an accident too?"

"No. But I hoped you might make an exception for that."

Another silence, as if the king wasn't sure what to do or whether he dared release Reardon—and honestly, Reardon did not want to be released. He felt improper stirrings low in his belly at being so securely detained by the mighty Ice King.

"May I ask...?" he ventured quietly, still looking at the scars and seeing a hint of the king's bare feet too. He was otherwise dressed like Reardon by the feel of him, in only a shirt and trousers.

"Part of my punishment," the king said, hot and close at Reardon's ear. "I don't feel pain. Or if I do, I have grown too used to it to notice. The others become their element at sunrise, but I am trapped inside. Every day, these two hundred years, the ice cuts deeper. I don't have wounds come nightfall, only the scars.

"If you came here looking for a handsome face that only looks unfortunate in sunlight, you will be disappointed."

The harshly spoken words did not change the stirrings Reardon felt. "That does not matter to me. It wasn't your face that first showed me who you are. A face is not what warms someone the way knowing them can. The way... a touch can." He lifted his hands just enough to alight a soft caress on the king's forearms.

A howl was the only precursor to Reardon being slammed onto the desk, the king releasing him but for a hand pressing to his shoulder and another at his lower back, keeping him down. The king's hips were close at the curve of Reardon, bent to his will.

"I will not touch you," Reardon swore, biting back an unbidden moan, "but if you asked... oh, Majesty, if you asked... I would, and I would welcome you touching me."

The grip on Reardon faltered. The king wasn't hard behind him but very present along Reardon's backside. "You know not what you say."

"I do. Believe me, I do." Reardon arched backward, as bold as the king had accused him of being. His captor might not be hard, but Reardon was, twitching in reaction to being pinned when he knew there was no danger. "Please," he said, shifting his legs to spread wider and splaying his arms across the desk.

"I saw you," the king said in answer, and for the first time, Reardon felt the king tremble. "I… watched you in the night."

Reardon tilted his head, though not so much as to risk peeking over his shoulder.

"It was your second night in the castle. I watched you, I am always watching, but I saw something that night that I shouldn't have and almost didn't turn away. You undressed and retired without snuffing out the candles and reached down your body beneath the sheets."

Recognition made Reardon throb at the thought.

"I didn't stay beyond that moment, but that's how I knew your desires, because I heard you speak them as I left, longing for a 'him' instead of a queen. You think you know me, but I have not changed since the days I bedded my stable boys."

"But you have," Reardon said, not sobered or ashamed as the king surely wanted him to feel with that admission. All he could imagine was those brilliant blue eyes on him. "I'm glad you told me, and I forgive you, because you did turn away like the good man I know you to be. All I ask is that you offer the same mercy to me. Forgive my coming here… and give me what I beseeched of the fates that night. If you want me, take me." He flattened more wantonly on the desk. "Take me and let me know your touch."

The hand on Reardon's shoulder loosened like it might lurch away, but the one on his back shifted, sliding down his hip slowly, and then hungrily over his ass with a firm grip, as the king twitched tellingly where he teased between Reardon's thighs.

"*Yes*," Reardon gasped. "Please… let me be yours."

"I forbid you to look at me."

"Not once will I attempt to see you, Majesty, unless you ask it of me."

"I will not. And I will not give in again. This is only for tonight."

Reardon gave no answer to that, because he refused to believe it would be true.

He closed his eyes.

The king squeezed his backside again, and then brought both hands around the line of his untucked shirt. His palms raked up Reardon's skin beneath the fabric, and though even his hands felt scarred, that did nothing to diminish Reardon's wanting.

With an insistent tug, the king tore the shirt from Reardon's head, returning his hands to travel down the same route they had gone up. Even without seeing him, the contact offered a promising thrill. Reardon didn't care how many scars marred the king. In his mind's eye, he conjured a powerful, faceless man with those intense blue eyes, wearing a blue doublet with white-gold embroidery. Before knowing the king became human at night, Reardon had already been making it for him.

Textured palms slid around Reardon's waist, up his chest and down like had been done to his back, feeling him everywhere with slow precision. Long fingers spread over every part of him, applying the perfect pressure to make him shiver. With the king's hips pressing in flush against Reardon's, a lone hand strayed beneath the band of Reardon's trousers, through the coarse hair there, and right to his burning flesh.

No frantic touch of his own could compare to someone else wrapping their fingers around him or passing a warm thumb across his slit. Reardon whined, hips rocking in reflex, which both pumped his cock into the king's hand and pressed the curve of his ass against the hardening length behind him, but Reardon's trousers were too tight for the king's hand to move much while merely down the front of them.

"Take them off," the king ordered.

Reardon fumbled to obey him, hands trembling uselessly, but once he got the ties undone, his trousers fell loose to his ankles, leaving him naked and still bent over the desk. Sordid tales of romance told Reardon what came next. Basic anatomy, secret whispers, the instinctive straying of his own hands—he knew what came next, and he longed for it in ways no solo pleasuring or pining after a man could satisfy.

The king was still dressed, though, still holding Reardon down and stroking him, making Reardon's belly hot and his loins ache.

"Please, Majesty. *Take me.*"

"So impatient, you don't even know how much more pleasure there is in waiting." His grip tightened, but the movement of his hand slowed, an agonizing slide, as the king's hips began to rock forward, subtle teasing of his clothed cock between Reardon's cheeks.

"I *have* waited…. My whole life I've waited, please."

"I will, but you need to slow down." The king's free hand pressed so hard on the middle of Reardon's back to keep him in place, he had trouble taking a deep breath. "Do you want me to hurt you? Because it will not feel nice if I fuck you raw like you think you want. There is an art to this, little prince, like clothing crafted or a bard tale composed. Do you understand? Or do you want the culmination to be a disappointment?"

The warning came with immediate reprieve, the pressure on Reardon's back lessening while the hand between his legs gathered every bit of slickness leaking free and pumped harder. "S-slow," Reardon conceded. "Whatever pace you set."

The whole of the king's body molded over Reardon, the feel of soft fabric tickling his bare skin, and then breath tickled his ear as the king whispered, "Good little prince."

REARDON WAS a virgin, of that Jack had already been sure. Long as it had been since he'd known the feel of another's body beneath his hands, he couldn't simply *take* Reardon, thrusting like some drunk in the back of a tavern. But if the young prince was so needy, so full of lust and certain that he wanted Jack to be the first to ravage him, then this act was going to be savored.

Reardon hadn't shied from his touch yet, not the feel of scars or the brief glimpse of them on his arms. Jack couldn't bear for those emerald eyes to land on his full form, but he could accept Reardon's body as tribute, eyes closed and unseeing as Jack devoured him, to make up for the slight of crossing his threshold.

After all, Jack was the monster of this story. He would take his tithe like a troll beneath a bridge, and it would only prove his point.

That was why he chose to give in, because he was owed, and Reardon had asked, and there had to be a balance, an exchange of power that kept Jack in control. If he gave too much to Reardon, he didn't know what might happen.

Rolling up from lying over Reardon's body, Jack brought the hand not touching the prince to the ties of his own trousers, letting them drop and his length free. He teased the budding wetness at its tip along Reardon's crease, and the whine Reardon released was more enticing than any stable boy Jack had ever had.

"Reach back," Jack commanded, much as he enjoyed Reardon's arms akimbo on the desktop. "Touch me as I'm touching you."

Pausing for breath, Reardon brought his arms in first to lift himself and not crush his cheek to the wood when he reached back, left hand grasping for Jack until he had him.

"Feel how hard I am?"

Reardon gave an initial shaky stroke. "Yes."

"I'm not yet where I will be." Jutting his hips forward, Jack dragged his tip along Reardon's crease again so he would understand his size and that he was not yet full. "Keep on. Get me there." Jack rocked into Reardon's hand and against those parted cheeks, his arm coiled around him to continue offering similar strokes—an infinite loop of pleasure building.

Each pump from Reardon's hand pressed his own knuckles against his backside, and the tip of Jack kept teasing there too. In turn, Reardon's motion rocked him into Jack's hand, with mewling whimpers and gasps spilling from his lips. Despite the pooling wetness between them, however, it wasn't nearly enough.

And Jack couldn't prepare Reardon the way they were now.

He stilled his hand and grabbed Reardon's wrist with the other. "Do you want me to stop?"

"No!" Reardon cried. "Please, Majesty—"

"Then don't open your eyes. I will stop and banish you from my sight if you do."

"I swear."

Jack released him and stepped back.

"Majesty—!"

"I am only disrobing. Stay as you are."

The sight of Reardon's body displayed with open thighs and cock dripping between them made it difficult not to stroke himself to completion just from the view. Jack kicked away his trousers and threw off his shirt.

"Get the rest of your clothes from around your ankles."

Reardon did so without using his hands or shifting much from how he remained bent over the desk. He seemed to like that position, and Jack might have kept him there, but he had better supplies in the other rooms.

Reardon's skin was a perfect pale swath of peach, lean muscles down his legs, taut shoulders, narrow hips, and a budded entrance waiting for a slick touch....

"Majesty?"

"Still impatient, little prince?"

"No. Well, yes, but... I will keep my eyes closed, but please, I want to pleasure you as well, whatever ways you want from me."

Jack stepped toward him. "Being inside you will accomplish that."

"Y-yes."

"But...." Cupping both spread cheeks before him, Jack squeezed the flesh being offered, his cock bobbing forward with its ready tip. "Your mouth would be a good start if you wish it. Eyes closed." He hooked an arm around Reardon's knees and scooped him into his arms, eliciting a quiet gasp. Lumbering like an ogre had made Jack stronger, or perhaps Reardon, for all his height and long limbs, was simply that light.

The prince flailed to cling to Jack's neck but kept his eyes closed as promised. Sure steps brought Jack into the bedroom, hard and weeping though he may be, and he laid Reardon upon the bed with his feet facing the top. Reardon seemed reluctant to be released and dropped his arms slowly from around Jack, fingers brushing lightly across Jack's cheek. There were scars there too, but Reardon remained content without flinching as he stretched upon the bed.

Turning from him, Jack went to the bath to gather oils. Reardon didn't disobey by trying to steal a glimpse, merely craned his ears and waited.

"Have you decided, then?" Jack asked when he returned.

"Majesty?"

Jack gave his length a few firm tugs before setting the items he'd gathered on the bed. The back view of Reardon's prone form had been tempting, but like this, Jack could see the lines of his hips pointing to tantalizing hardness, wet and scarlet red. His lips were equally colored, pouty and parted, as if already answering Jack's question, "If I may have use of your mouth?"

"O-oh...." Reardon blushed far too prettily, too virginally for Jack to not want to have those lips on him every way he could, but he needed Reardon to say it. "Yes, Majesty. Gladly yes."

Climbing onto the bed, kneeling at the foot, with Reardon's head between his knees, Jack began to lower himself. Reardon tilted his head back and opened his salivating mouth to take Jack in.

And oh, the *heat*—Jack had forgotten how good it felt to be enveloped by such warmth. He trembled as Reardon trembled, the prince's hands clutching the sheets with nothing else to hang on to and sucking him in a good two, three, four swallows without stopping. Jack's moisture was lapped up, but Reardon's mouth's own watering overflowed past the corners of his mouth, just as his eyes began to water too. Yet he swallowed Jack in again—and *again*.

"Slower." Jack barely bit the word out, afraid the young man, supposedly inexperienced, would cause himself to choke. He had unknown talents, because he didn't gag as he swallowed Jack deeper and then pulled off. "What was that… about never frequenting brothels? Perhaps not as a client."

"I-I'd never—"

"I know, but then you are a natural." Jack dipped to Reardon's lips again, and Reardon sucked him in past the tip without prompting, farther, *farther*, and then off again.

"D-does that mean I please you, Majesty?" His mouth looked sinfully red and shiny with drool still leaking from the corners.

"You could please me more." Jack dropped his hips more insistently, forcing Reardon to take half of him at once, but from there he let Reardon control how much he was willing to swallow. Inexperience gave way to instinct as Reardon found a rhythm, taking Jack in and out, *in* and out, a little deeper each time.

No bath, no clothing, no covers had made Jack feel this warm in centuries, rocking down between the pliant lips of the Emerald Prince.

"Keep on… but touch yourself while you do."

A grateful hum responded, Reardon's left hand twisting into the sheets while the right found his length with practiced ease and started pumping madly.

"*Slower*. But suck harder."

Reardon whined, so close to finishing, Jack knew, because he could see his hips stuttering and stomach clenching with the need that wasn't being met. Jack needed it too. He was having trouble keeping his thrusts into Reardon's mouth civil. How easy it would have been to fuck that mouth raw, willing and open beneath him—but Jack wanted this to last, wanted Reardon's thighs quaking from a much better connection.

"Up. Forward on your knees. Now." Jack lifted away to keep from listing to one side as he calmed the mad thrum in his ears and reached for the oils.

"But Majesty—"

"*Now*."

The strain in Reardon's face as he stopped stroking was pitiable, but he simply didn't yet know how much better this could be. He listened, lifting with effort to get onto his knees, head pointing the correct direction now, as he leaned onto his forearms, keeping his ass up and his knees parted.

Jack squeezed himself to still the growing ache, made no easier by that stimulating sight. He'd leave Reardon a blissed-out, gibbering mess if he did this right—and he intended to.

The oil he chose was thick and moisturizing for after a bath and smelled faintly of cedar and roses. The large bed barely shifted with his slow crawl toward Reardon, but he knew when Reardon was aware of just how close he got, because he thrust his hips backward.

"So warm…," Jack said, cupping Reardon's ass while his oil-slicked fingers trailed down between his cheeks, teasing lightly at the puckered skin.

Reardon mewled and thrust back harder into his touch.

"So sensitive and desperate, but you have to be patient… so you don't spill all over my sheets when I first *press*—" Jack reached the waiting entrance that flexed at his approach, giving way the moment he pushed in the tip of a finger. "—inside."

"*Jack.*"

The utterance made Jack falter. He'd heard Reardon say it before, but not directly calling him that. In such a plaintive voice, it made him want to wring more sounds out of the prince.

"Is this what you envisioned?" Jack twisted his finger in deeper.

Unintelligible murmurs replied.

Jack took that as permission to begin a gentle thrust. Reardon was tight but open enough that a single finger found its way inside without trouble, discovering the slick curves that would soon encompass Jack. Reardon stopped trying to hold himself up and became a limp and submissive puddle, weak sounds of discovered ecstasy catching in his throat as he rocked back and back and *back* to pull Jack in deeper.

Jack twirled a second finger over Reardon's hole, picturing the way the prince's lips had enveloped his head. He pressed a second digit inside.

"Ah!" Reardon's head snapped up with a pained gasp.

*Virgin*, Jack reminded himself, returning to only one. "You're tight."

"Th-that's… good?"

"It can be. But too tight hurts. I won't be fucking you tonight, little prince."

"But Majesty—!"

"I will not hurt you. But I can still give you a taste and take my pleasure too."

Removing his fingers entirely, Jack dripped more oil to coat them, finding that the slide of two fingers, even eventually deeply thrust, made their way in more easily after a time. With each renewed twist, Reardon's tension receded, any signs that it was too tight or painful banished, as his breathing picked up in their stead. Still, Jack could tell that anything more would be too much.

He started his thrusts slow but gradually began to increase the rhythm. Fresh whines floundered off Reardon's tongue, fingers clawing into the sheets like before, with his forehead pressed to the mattress.

"Oh… oh… *Jack*," Reardon moaned again, as Jack fucked him with a kind hand, his own length leaking rivulets onto the sheets behind the entrance he so wished to ravish. "Are you certain you can't—"

"I am. But I promise the taste I do give you will be sweet."

Thrusting deeper and harder and as fast as he could, Jack soon had Reardon crying out in unrestraint, made even more vocal by Jack reaching around him with his other hand to grip Reardon's soaked member and pump in time to the twist of his fingers.

The dual touch upon Reardon brought Jack's hips closer, his hardness finding refuge against Reardon's thigh. The searing hot skin made Jack moan with Reardon, forgetting he was supposed to be the composed one. He wanted to come. He wanted to pull Reardon there with him. He wanted to fuck his sweet prince until stars exploded behind his eyes and they woke up somewhere else.

"Please… please…," Reardon begged, and Jack's mind went blank with his own need, fingers retracting to position himself at Reardon's entrance and *push.*

Another pained gasp brought Jack to his senses.

"*Please*," Reardon said again when Jack tried to pull away.

As a lesson, as appeasement, Jack returned his head and pressed just enough to risk its breach, waiting for Reardon to tell him no.

The prince took in several sharp breaths but said nothing.

Jack risked another shift forward, a faint pop resounding as Reardon gave way and encircled him fully around his head.

Reardon bit his lip as if to keep from crying out, rocking away from Jack to pull him with him, and then back again to bring him in deeper.

The moan he released encouraged Jack, but the panted breaths sobered him. He couldn't go any harder or deeper than this, but he could do *this* and drive Reardon over the edge with him.

Not once did Jack cease his pumping of Reardon's cock, thrusting rhythmically behind him in turn but only as deep as his head. It was torture to not pound Reardon into the mattress but also bliss, because it had been so long, and no one had ever felt this rewarding to make sing.

Reardon's utterances were like pleas for mercy, but mercy to be allowed to come, not discomfort. Once Jack's urgency grew desperate too, he pulled out and slid his shaft up along Reardon's entrance instead of in, seeking friction, wetness, *warmth*, and receiving all in abundance.

"Please," Reardon continued to beg, but Jack would do no more, only increasing his pace and allowing every few passes of his cock to press its head in again.

Finally, Jack's grip brought forth a yielding cry, and Reardon sagged, deadweight beneath him. Feeling the sticky proof on his hand, Jack kept on faster, seeking oblivion and the sweet relief that only another body could provide, and then—

Jack shot across the curve of Reardon's inviting crease, staining his skin in opalescent streaks. He sagged as Reardon had sagged, collapsing atop him. At last he'd had his prince, not as fully as he wanted, but so… so good.

Pulling away to relax back on his ankles, Jack took in the sight of Reardon once more, face pressed to the sheets, eyes closed, with his ass ripe and used, now with Jack's claim all over it. Nothing had ever looked so beautiful.

"You are a sight… little prince."

Reardon smiled, half invisible against the mattress but as blissed as Jack had intended. Jack wanted to mold himself across that gorgeous form again, but first, it needed to be cleaned.

"Do not open your eyes," he warned.

"Yes, Majesty," Reardon whispered like an exhale. "I am content with your touch."

REARDON HAD never known such pleasure. No touch of his own could compare. No other indulgence either. The limpness he felt without injury—well, without dire injury, for he would certainly be sore tomorrow—was indescribable and made him incapable of movement or protest as the king lifted his spent and soiled body from the bed.

A few short moments later, he felt himself lowered into a soothing bath, smelling of lilacs, whereas the substance the king had used to ease Reardon's pleasures had been headier. The king's release that had stained him was rinsed away, and Reardon went even more boneless, afraid he might sink right down, until a firm body climbed in behind him to act as anchor.

Like that, with the king wrapped around him, Reardon could feel his scars everywhere, but it stirred no wince or need to withdraw, only a deep pity for a man who did not deserve this punishment. Maybe once he had, but not anymore.

"Majesty... if I swear to keep my head forward, may I open my eyes to see the room?"

"I suppose."

Reardon wasted no time, vision unfocused at first from keeping his eyes closed for so long. The washroom was dim but lit by candles, large and luminous, with multiple wardrobes filling the corners, the bath itself up on a pedestal, just as Reardon would have imagined for a king. His father's washroom was not nearly so grand, however.

The king was not yet fully softened behind Reardon, a solid presence reminding him of how they'd intimately but also only barely connected. Reardon understood why. Too much *had* hurt, his body unused to such experiences. He'd only ever teased himself there before, but even that brief, small conquering from the king had been incredible.

Resting gratefully back against the body behind him, Reardon fought every impulse in him to not disobey and look. This close, however, with the king's arms coming up to hold him in place, gentler than they'd held him at the desk, Reardon noticed something unexpected just out of eyeline.

A wisp of white hair.

Barely containing the smile on his face, Reardon settled more comfortably. "May I assume it gets easier with... frequency?"

"It does. Your body adapts. Is that why you came here tonight, little prince? For me to treat you like a stable boy?" One of the hands around Reardon's waist drifted between his legs where he was spent. Still, the touch made him twitch in the king's palm. "If you saw Josie and the others, I'm sure you caught them in similar states."

"M-mostly," Reardon said, mourning the king's touch the moment he returned to merely holding Reardon against him. "*Mostly* that's how I found them all, I mean, not…. That was not why I came to see you. If I had only wanted someone's touch, I could have gone to another. I didn't *want* another." He pressed his head to the king's shoulder. "I wanted my love."

The silence that answered was as torturous as if the king had brought Reardon to the brink only to leave him cold. The cynical sigh he released as he drew his hands away completely was worse.

"Is that why you asked the night for a him, some… fantasy? I am not your love. We merely shared a night of passion."

"You may think me foolish, Majesty, but it is not fantasy. Barclay had a vision."

"What?"

The pull to turn and look the king in the eyes was strong, but Reardon held still. "Before Barclay was chosen as offering, he had a vision of my love. Well, what he saw was difficult to describe, he said, but it was… *love, death, and blue eyes in a sea of white.*

"There has been much death here, Majesty, but there is still hope. Your court has all found someone to love. With Branwen and Caitlin, perhaps it is something different or moving more slowly, but they all have someone, even your sister, so content with my friend, who never thought he'd find a love of his own. Don't you understand what that means?"

"That's why you said blue eyes," the king murmured.

"Yes. It's you. You are my love, and I am yours." Reardon boldly reached to take the king's hands, that had fallen away. "We can be the final piece to breaking your curse for good."

"Close your eyes."

"All right." Reardon did so, unprepared for the sharp yank of the king's hands and push forward as the body behind him got out of the bath.

"Wait—"

"Get out."

"But—"

"You are going to dry off, get dressed, and get out of my chambers. And if you look at me, I will still throw you from the ramparts." Those strong hands gripped Reardon's shoulders and roughly lifted him to his feet, forcing him to stumble out of the bath.

"I-I cannot dress blind!" he protested.

Still rough and harried, the king brought a robe that he used to pat Reardon's skin. Then he grabbed Reardon's arm and dragged him down the steps leading from the bath, across the stones, until at last he pushed him forward and left him, just a voice over his shoulder. "Dress and stay facing forward."

Reardon opened his eyes. He was back by the desk, where his and the king's clothes lay in heaps. Much as this pained him, he grabbed his shirt and trousers. "Majesty, Barclay's vision—"

"I am *not* your love."

"But you could be!"

"You said your *Lombard* has blue eyes?" The way the king spat the name made Reardon stagger as he tried to pull up his trousers.

"Yes."

"You hoped it might be him once, didn't you?"

"N-no, I...." Reardon *had*, but— "He'd never want me—"

"If he did, you would have gladly taken him instead. And at least he could be with you during the day."

"You can as well!" Reardon insisted. "We can break the curse—"

"There is no breaking this curse!" the king's voice bellowed from only a stride behind him. "You are a silly romantic. Now get out. In the morning, you can leave for your kingdom."

Reardon snapped upright, dressed now but shaken. The king was dismissing him, but he would not let this be the end. "No."

"No?" the king challenged back.

"I am not leaving." Reardon stood firm, clenching his fists in resolve. "The secrets of this castle were only part of our deal. I said we would know one another."

"I think we know one another quite well, little prince."

The memories of that, the smell of it lingering in the air, mixed with cedar and flowers, only made Reardon more certain.

The crumpled verses on the king's desk made him certain too, though he hadn't yet read them. With the king behind him, and Reardon at the edge of the desk, he reclaimed the book he'd brought, using that more visible act to hide how he snatched the parchment too.

"I said I wanted a way to save our kingdoms from all this madness. Breaking the curse will accomplish that, and I am not leaving until I do."

"You—"

"I will prove you wrong," Reardon cut off the angry rebuttal, moving swiftly around the desk for the door. "And tomorrow, I will be ready for our next audience. Thank you for the book, Majesty. Good night." Without waiting for a response, Reardon escaped, knowing the king would not follow, and fell back against the door with a shuddered breath, clutching his prizes to his chest.

Right there in the chilly throne room, he read:

*The noble prince went on his quest....*

It was a sweet and simple tale that ended as theirs just had, only they hadn't yet managed to release the beast as the pair in the poem did. Even so, it proved Reardon right, that long before tonight, the king had wanted him, wanted more, wanted freedom and connection and the love he denied himself. He'd nearly thrown away this parchment, judging by its creases, but he'd salvaged it. He did want what Reardon offered. His heart was merely frozen.

Smiling as he held the poem and book close, Reardon slipped behind the icy throne to return to the secret tunnels. Lombard might have been his choice once, but his were not the eyes that haunted Reardon, and now, while Reardon still did not know the true form of the king, he had a picture in his mind of blue eyes on a man with an un-aging, scarred face....

And white hair.

# CHAPTER 7

JACK DIDN'T rest that night. He dressed in clean clothes, drained his bath, and hoped that the smell of the oils would overpower any lingering scent of Reardon.

They did not.

Not *enough*.

Time moved so slowly when he didn't sleep, but he still felt it in his bones when the sun was about to rise. He didn't need the sun to touch him directly, only for it to reach the castle grounds. As that moment drew near, he removed his clothes and went to stand by the door so that as little of his rooms as possible were affected by his chill.

He never wore his crown. He locked that away ages ago. Yet still, once the change took him, an icy crown would rest upon his head like a mocking extension.

It didn't hurt, but it did ache, like reaching the end of a grueling fight—only a fight waged naked in the middle of winter. One would think he'd be used to the cold by now, but that was the one thing that never got easier.

He had heard his court say that their changes merely felt like their stomachs dropped, a weightlessness overtaking them as their true bodies faded. Jack, conversely, was encased, but his body still felt like it stretched to fill his icy prison, mangled and pulled like he had mangled his kingdom.

Only, today, with his hands creaking as he clenched them into fists, there was a new ache that wouldn't go away, like a dagger lodged in his chest.

*Damn prince*, Jack thought and turned to open his door.

"Good morning, Majesty." Reardon dared darken his threshold at the very crack of dawn, prim and dressed and *smiling* as he gave his customary bow from in front of the throne.

Stomping forward with booming tremors, Jack fell upon Reardon like the monster he was, getting closer than he would have dared with one of his subjects. "Do you know how easy it would be for me to end you right here?" he bellowed, frigid breath in Reardon's face.

Like most days, Reardon didn't so much as teeter backward. "Then do it," he said with a maddeningly stable expression. "But I'm not leaving."

Jack had never known anyone so stubborn!

And he refused to listen to Josie's voice in his head saying—*he was*.

"I am not your love," Jack affirmed.

Only then did a flicker of heartache pass over Reardon's face, but that too was replaced with a determined smile. "Then be my friend. We were friendly before last night, weren't we? We were starting to know one another—truly, not only… carnally. So let us start again from there.

"Either way, Majesty, I believe this curse can be broken, but my kingdom must see reason too, or head down its own doomed path. Would you deny me that chance?"

That was unfair, like a lowly highwayman using Jack's own past against him.

Reardon kept his smile and gestured to the window—which was when Jack realized his other hand held a book. "It's a lovely morning. I thought we'd read up on the ramparts to start today's audience. Unless you're still feeling an urge to throw me from them?"

Jack could ignore him, turn from the prince in silence and disappear into the tunnels alone, but Reardon knew the tunnels now too and was not likely to be easily dismissed.

Rocking back on his icy haunches, Jack huffed with a visible snort. "I might toss you to your demise yet, so *do not* test me," he warned but motioned for Reardon to lead the way.

*Pillars of Virtue* was not a love story but, to Jack, it played out as one. The knights, Sir Waite and Sir Kent, were stationed to guard a watchtower together, and initially seemed to clash. Waite was stoic and calculating, while Kent was heartfelt and impulsive. They countered one another in every way, but because of that, they also balanced each other, and through their differences found things to admire in one another.

Their kingdom was constantly threatened by invading forces, and they were soon considered the lucky sentinels who, when on watch, always managed to ward off attacks or stop them before they became more than the kingdom could handle.

If it hadn't been for the side stories of Kent falling for a sassy barmaid and Waite's cat-and-mouse with a female rogue, the ending could have easily culminated in a passionate kiss.

Jack and Reardon didn't quite get that far into the story, with Reardon reading aloud, his voice as lovely as if he were singing another bard's tale. Instead they reached the point when the knights were first starting to display fondness for one another. Jack had been listening less closely, remembering where the story led and looking out at the distant horizon beyond his kingdom, when he realized Reardon had stopped speaking.

He turned to see Reardon watching him, the book carefully marked with a ribbon to find their place later.

"Even this fictional kingdom with its stalwart knights doesn't seem perfect," Reardon said. "There's crime, corruption, unrest inside the walls and out. Tell me, Majesty, if you could do it all again, what would you have done differently?"

"You mean, besides everything?" Jack droned.

"I'm serious." That earnest patience was very difficult to turn away from, so Jack didn't try.

"I… wouldn't have dismissed all the advisors. A few, certainly, but not the kind and competent ones. I would have stopped my philandering—well, lessened it—to focus on state matters. I would have listened to the people, not to give in to their every whim, but to deliberate and understand what I could truly provide that would be beneficial for all.

"The way things work here now, everyone gets a voice, but there must still be consensus or there would be chaos."

"Sounds like the castle is the perfect version of a kingdom."

"As is my penance."

Pity filled Reardon's face, and he gave a gentle sigh, but whatever Jack expected him to say, it wasn't quite what he did. "Why not, instead… a legacy?"

Jack already had one—the dreaded Ice King, whispered about fearfully across the lands as a monster in a frozen castle. That was his legacy. Why did Reardon insist that it could be otherwise?

The young prince shivered, and Jack noticed how high the sun had trekked.

"Forgive me, Majesty, I'm growing cold." Reardon stood from where he sat on the edge of the ramparts, gathering the book beneath his arm. "I suppose our time is up for today. I had plans to visit the alchemist tower before lunch. Shall I see you tonight?"

"I told you—"

"I'll keep my eyes closed. At least until you change your mind." He bowed, and then turned to leave before Jack could protest further.

It was one of the few times when Reardon had offered to leave rather than Jack insisting at the first sign of his potion wearing off. That would have been infuriating enough, but worse was how, more than ever, Jack wasn't ready to be without him.

He waited a reasonable amount of time before following Reardon, but when he did, he heard Zephyr's voice.

"First of all, how dare you go about as usual when something clearly happened between you and the king!"

Jack tensed, keeping hidden behind the bend in the passageway.

"It was late!" Reardon protested. "I went to bed. Then, this morning, I wanted to be early for our audience."

"Reardon!" Zephyr exclaimed, but their voices were drifting, meaning Reardon must be continuing on his path. "I heard you say you're going to see him again tonight."

*Spymaster indeed*, Jack thought.

Once he was certain the pair had moved around the next bend, he followed, keeping his steps silent and his pace even to not give away that he was there.

"Technically, I didn't *see* anything," Reardon said, and then added in a softer private tone, "but I did share his bed."

Zephyr practically squealed, while Jack continued to grimace, not that he'd expected the encounter to remain a secret. "Naughty princeling. What's he like in bed? I've always wondered."

"I-I can't speak of that!"

"Sure you can. We're friends, aren't we?"

"And as your friend, shall I remind you of what got you into trouble with your love the last time?"

Zephyr scoffed. "I have never been unfaithful to Nigel. I merely enjoy a nice view on occasion. After 175 years," he muttered, "he's more likely to get bored of *me*."

"You don't believe that." Reardon stopped; Jack heard the stutter of his feet and stopped his own forward progression.

"That I'm boring?" Zephyr returned to bright and undaunted. "Heavens no. I'll pry those details out of you yet, *friend.*"

He poofed away, he must have, for Reardon sighed like he had at Jack, and the sound of retreating feet continued.

Back to invisible like a persistent wind, Zephyr was probably fully aware of Jack's tailing now, but Jack didn't care. He followed Reardon all the same, until the prince left the tunnels to enter the alchemist tower.

"Reardon!" Barclay pounced upon him.

"What happened?" Shayla latched on to him next.

Jack could see them all through his usual removed stone. To his surprise, along with Widow Caitlin and Liam, Josie was also there, the lot of them having gathered in wait for Reardon, the meddling traitors.

"*All* of you?" Reardon voiced Jack's thoughts. Then he looked around and realized, "No Nigel?"

"He's about somewhere," Barclay said.

"And what of Branwen?" Reardon asked, looking to Caitlin. "You're his... scribe, he said?"

Caitlin had the grace to look uncomfortable, not that any of their coupling was news to Jack. He'd known from the beginning—Zephyr told him everything—and it had never occurred to him to question his court's love lives.

They deserved reprieve from the curse. They weren't at fault for causing it.

"Bran doesn't generally enjoy group gatherings unless he can have a drink," Caitlin said. "But 'scribe' is... accurate. He dabbles in verse, romance mainly, if you can believe it. He's actually very good! But he doesn't like others reading his work, or at least, not while knowing he's the one who wrote it. He has many books in our library under false names. He's not particularly fast with a quill, however, so he asks me to help."

"He asks *you*," Reardon reiterated, seeming to enjoy the close press of his other friends on either side of him, "never anyone else, to help write down his romances?"

"He is a perfect gentleman!" Caitlin countered.

"Even gentlemen have wants," Shayla said, and when Caitlin's cheeks filled with color, she added, "*and* ladies."

"Not that we need you coming around for the show again," Liam said to Reardon, electric arms visibly crossed in irritation and sparking liberally.

"Enough of all that," Josie interjected, her golden form floating a safe distance in the corner. "What about *you*, Reardon? What of my brother? Did you stay in his rooms all night?"

"N-no," Reardon admitted with a flicker of sorrow, "but I was inside them."

He proceeded to brashly tell them what he'd already told Zephyr, including his inane ideals over Barclay's vision and Jack being his *love*.

"I may have acted rashly, but I refuse to believe I'm wrong. Unless...." Reardon looked to Barclay, who had released him by now but had still been in contact with him for some time.

"I... can't say for sure," Barclay said slowly, "but it isn't impossible."

"See!"

*Fools*—all of them.

"I had to see the king straight off when I awoke," Reardon continued, "but I came here next for more reason than just to offer you all news. The truth is, I have two missions now. To break the curse, of course, first and foremost, for everyone's sake, including that of my kingdom. But as I work to melt the king, I also intend to find out what killed my mother, so that when I return home, I can catch whoever did it."

He turned imploringly to each of them, saving Caitlin for last, who didn't seem surprised.

"Will you help me?"

Reardon hadn't spoken of his mother's death since he first arrived, yet now he believed he could catch the culprit? None of those with him laughed at the notion. In fact, they each offered heartfelt agreement to help however they could, even Liam.

"It's going to come down to days, maybe weeks of experiments," Caitlin said.

"Liam's favorite pastime," Shayla teased, catching her lover's eye with a smirk. "That means more foraging together, Reardon, trying as many different combinations as we can until we get it right."

"It hadn't occurred to me to try before...," Caitlin said softer, wistful and sad, only to bolster herself and hold her head higher. "But I think we know enough to figure it out. Discovering the right alchemical combination for whatever the poison was, however, won't necessarily reveal who used it."

"I know," Reardon conceded, "but it will help me narrow down who did if the person has used the same poison since, and it would allow us to create an antidote."

"What of melting the king?" Josie queried playfully.

Reardon's smitten expression was like a bright summer sun. "When we first made our deal, he asked me what my arguments would be to change the hearts of my people once I returned home. I think I know now. If love can truly break a curse, who could say that only certain kinds of love or the people experiencing it are good and others are not? I know the truth. I just need to convince him."

*Fools*, Jack thought again. *All fools....*

But maybe he was a fool too, because it took feeling the burn of eyes on him to realize he'd been staring at Reardon so intently, he hadn't noticed when Josie turned to look at him.

She couldn't see him through the missing stone, it was far too hidden and dark, but she didn't hide that she knew he was there. Her smugness made him glance away, bringing his eyes to his obvious ice trail, frost covering the stones beneath him and on the wall.

Reardon used the tunnels. He'd see Jack's ice; he'd known he followed him, watched him, especially after Jack had admitted as much last night. Reardon must have noticed other times these past many days....

Even so, Jack stayed, unable to bring himself to retreat.

It was nearly lunchtime, so the small gathered crew only got so far as a plan for initial foraging that Shayla and Reardon would see to later. Jack followed afterward like a tether connected them, watching Reardon eat in the great hall, where he met up with Nigel, pulling him aside once the meal was done. Jack hadn't thought much of Zephyr's earlier mutterings, but Reardon clearly had.

"He thinks I'm bored of him?" Nigel said, stopping short in the hall where they'd found themselves alone—as far as they knew. "That's why he keeps trying to anger me?"

"It seems so," Reardon said with the gentle patience of a friend who'd known Nigel for years. "I wonder if he's so worried, he'd rather push you away than have you leave him first."

Nigel wasn't the type to show candid emotion, more likely to grin and joke and distract, like the charlatan he'd once been. Now he dropped all pretense completely. "The truth is... I've been fearing he feels that way toward me. How many lovers do you know who've been together almost two hundred years?"

"But doesn't that only prove your love?"

"It does for me." Nigel surprised Jack with his certainty, and then laughed. "Yet I still feared the same thing he does."

Reardon's sympathetic smile suddenly dropped, and he whispered, "What if he's listening now?"

"No, I can always tell," Nigel assured him. "Technically, if he wants to know something, he can still tap into the whispers of the wind, even if they've already faded, but I can feel when he's active. Surprising the Spymaster requires finesse, but no one is better up to that task than the man before you." He gave a little bow. "I am going to prove Zephyr is being a fool. Just like I was."

"Not exactly what I was striving for." Reardon chuckled. "But I can support that."

"Thank you, Reardon."

"Of course. You're my friend," he said without waver and pulled Nigel against him.

"Hey!" Nigel cried soon after, because Reardon had unsheathed the jeweled dagger from his belt. "You deviant!" He laughed, failing to snatch the dagger back, as Reardon held it out of reach. "Did you just use emotional connection to divert my attention?"

"You left me no choice!" Reardon said, even as he was laughing too. "I truly meant everything I said."

Nigel smacked his shoulder firmly. "I couldn't be prouder."

"That was pretty low of me." Reardon tried to give the dagger back to him.

"Oh no, you earned that fair and square. Unless I steal it again, of course." Nigel winked.

Reardon proudly sheathed the dagger on his sword belt.

"You never told me where you got that thing. Family heirloom?"

"Oh, um… no. It was a birthday present from my kingdom's master of arms."

*Lombard*, Jack grimaced. Was Reardon so fickle, or did he not realize who truly held his heart if he treasured that gift so much?

"Maybe I'll let you keep it, then," Nigel said. "Besides, I need to get to work on a grand gesture to set Zephyr to rights and prove we're idiots together. A new verse! Something especially for him. Would you help me find the words?"

"I'd be honored. And actually, I need help of my own, though more for a tune to go with something already written. Shall we go to the music room to work on our epics together?"

There he went again, being a hopeless romantic, even after talk of Lombard. Not that Jack was jealous! Jealousy was pointless when....

Wait. Already written? Jack hadn't seen Reardon working on anything lately that didn't have mu—

The poem! Jack's own verse; he couldn't recall if he'd seen it on his desk after Reardon left last night. The prince really had learned to be a thief!

As Reardon and Nigel left to head for the music room, Jack debated detouring to his chambers, but he was certain his guess was right. And it was *not* romantic or endearing!

Turning angrily to give chase through the tunnels, he had half a mind to burst into the music room and demand Reardon tear that crumpled parchment to pieces—only to find his path blocked by the golden smirk of his sister.

"Jack, what are you doing?"

"Stopping a thief."

"Of what? Your cold dead heart?"

Jack snarled and stomped the tunnel floor. "I am aware of the foolish notions that prince is trying to fill you all with—"

"Compared to what you filled him with last night, I think we're allowed to form our own opinions."

"Don't be vulgar," Jack spat, not that he could deny that part.

"Jack—"

"Out of my way."

"No. It seems you'll have to push me," she retorted, knowing full well he would never risk such a thing. "I know what you're thinking, that it's too late for hope. That hoping and being let down again might be more than you can bear. But you know Barclay's visions are always right."

"About leaks in the castle, infestations, lost items."

"And sometimes important things too!" She looked at Jack in sympathy, in *pity*, and he couldn't bear that either. "When Barclay was first ushered into the castle, with so many people touching him, he saw a multitude of visions… and one of them was of the court's forms at night."

"What?" Jack gaped.

"He didn't make it two weeks, Jack. He knew the truth before he was even presented to you that first day."

"He *lied*—"

"He didn't want to anger you! He came to my room that very night to confess, that's why I was the first to learn of his visions, and I agreed to keep his secret until the two weeks were up to avoid any rash judgments from you."

"You fooled me—"

"Because Barclay saw that it would keep the peace, and he was right. The fact that he turned out to be lovely company as well happened to benefit me."

*Fools*, Jack thought again and huffed. Love had clearly warped all his court's minds! "The prince admitted to me that Barclay is not certain of what he saw in this vision of love. It's a riddle. A guess! There is no reason to believe it has anything to do with me."

"Don't believe it, then. Maybe it isn't about you. Or maybe, even if it is, it doesn't mean our curse can be broken. But *please*—" Josie floated the smallest bit closer. "—if we're stuck with this curse forever, then at least find some happiness for yourself like the rest of us. It took me two hundred years to find my love. Don't wait all of eternity to find yours."

She left, floating elegantly away from him.

Jack was still angry, at Reardon, at *everyone*, but the bitter knots forming in his stomach made him loathe the idea of following the prince anymore today. It would only tempt him to chase fairy tales himself— like the unattainable ending to his poem.


REARDON SPENT much of the afternoon with Nigel in the music room, though neither felt their work was close to completion after only one day. Reardon wanted his tune to be perfect, and Nigel wanted his epic to be unmatchable as well. They'd continue to help one another until both pieces were just right.

Before dinner, Reardon and Shayla went out to forage for several specific items to begin testing. After learning Caitlin's story, Reardon hadn't been certain he wanted to go down this route. His father had given so much of himself trying to discover the truth of what really happened to Queen Reagan. Reardon didn't want to lose himself to it too, but as the days passed since hearing what had really happened, he hadn't been able to shake the dream that he could finally put all this to rest for everyone.

He and Shayla were late getting back for dinner, the sun setting before they had finished eating. Reardon was hurrying his dinner to more swiftly join the king, even if he thought he might discover a locked door when he finally arrived.

"What's the rush?" Barclay asked. "I thought you'd want to spend more time in the tower starting experiments."

"Discovering what killed my mother is only one of my goals. There's time for everything, but tonight, I have somewhere to be." Reardon had only just started to get up when a commotion struck.

The members of the court—sans the king, of course—burst in from the back of the room.

They were all human, and everyone in the castle knew the truth— but they didn't all know that *Reardon* knew, and several people gaped and cast Reardon nervous glances.

"Didn't you all hear?" Branwen called, leading the pack. "The Emerald Prince had a run about the castle last night."

He looked much as Reardon had seen yesterday, since he'd still been dressed at the time, in a simple sunset-colored tunic—though in Reardon's mind, he imagined he'd look quite at home in heavy armor.

The others Reardon had seen in various states of undress, so it was different seeing them in normal finery: Zephyr in similar dress to his usually transparent doublet, Liam in a long robe-like cloak befitting of a wizard, and Josie in a beautiful gown of cream and gold.

"Now," Branwen went on, as he came to stand behind Reardon at the center table, "let's see if I can teach our royal pain in the rear how to drink properly." The slap Branwen gave to the middle of Reardon's back rivaled any from Shayla, and there was a loud chorus of cheers.

"N-no, I can't—"

"You can." Branwen wedged in between Reardon and Barclay— who didn't seem to mind once Josie sat at his other side—while Zephyr and Liam joined their respective partners. "I hear you bedded the king," Branwen whispered, "yet he's still being an ass. Maybe make him sweat a little tonight."

Dissent was readily on Reardon's tongue, but his words went stale. He hadn't considered that tactic. He'd told the king he would come see him. The king was *expecting* him to try.

Maybe making him wait had its advantages.

"Seems the ruling came early!" Oliver raised his voice over the din, standing from the end of one of the long tables and raising a glass. "By decree of our own court, the Emerald Prince is fully initiated!" He thrust his glass higher in a hearty hail that everyone mirrored, a full glass of ale being pushed into Reardon's hand that he knew from experience he didn't handle any better than wine—but he was willing to try. "To the prince!"

"The prince!" the others cried, and although Reardon had begun to feel at home days ago, a new warmth filled the crowded hall.

Even those who'd sneered at Reardon, like the fierce blond and her darkly colored elven lover, toasted him and offered welcoming smiles.

As for the king....

Reardon clanged his goblet with Branwen's and took a hearty swig. The king could wait.


JACK WAS *not* waiting for Reardon.

But it had been hours since the sun set, and where in the heavens was he?

Jack had planned to lock his door, deny any future knocks, and once again threaten Reardon bodily harm if he didn't stay away. None of those things could be accomplished without the prince's presence! It was infuriating to be left sitting at his desk—where his crumpled bit of parchment was indeed missing—and tap his fingers without so much as a shuffle of approaching feet on the stones outside his door.

If it had been any other night, Jack would be in his bath, enjoying a glass of wine and perhaps some bread and cheese. He didn't require food any more than he required sleep, but he could still enjoy the taste after dark. Now he wasn't doing any of those things, too busy wondering when the prince might slip into his room again.

Two hundred years Jack had gone without touching someone or being touched. Now, after only one night of rekindling those forgotten fires, he yearned to feel it all again.

He pounded a fist on his desk in frustration.

A thud, like an echo, snapped Jack's attention back to the door. Not footsteps or a knock—a thud.

"Mmmajesty?" a voice slurred.

The knob turned—

*Fuck!* Jack leapt from his desk to intercept, realizing he hadn't locked the door after all, but it was too late, the door was swinging open with Reardon standing right there to see—

Nothing. He had a scarf that Jack recognized as Josie's wrapped around his eyes.

Reardon stumbled across the stones, nearly face-planting, and Jack reached him just in time to catch him. At the same moment, Jack swung his door shut again, in case any foolish others were daring to wait on the other side to steal a peek.

It didn't seem as though anyone had been there, but they had to have gotten Reardon close to the door before setting him loose, because he was in no state to walk, even if he hadn't been blindfolded. At least they'd removed his weapons, but he smelled like he'd taken a midnight swim in a vat of ale, and then rinsed his mouth with wine.

"Bran was tryin' to teach me to drink!" Reardon raised a hand as if to emphasize his point as a sweeping declaration, only to nearly swing himself right over, forcing Jack to lift one of the price's arms over his shoulders to steady him. "But I'm... I-I'm... I'm not very good at it," he finished with a giggle.

"Pitiless vultures," Jack growled. "They told you to come here like this?"

"Nnno," Reardon said innocently, cheeks flushed from drink and lips rosy and sweetly smiling, as he turned to Jack. "Bran and, um... Josie! And the others... tried to stop me, but I... I said I gotta! I *promised.* Did you miss me?" His prettily parted lips puckered, and he launched forward with impressive accuracy.

"*No.*" Jack only just managed to heave him backward before they connected.

"You didn't?" Reardon asked miserably.

"You're not putting your mouth on me," Jack explained.

"But I haven't kissed you yet! I-I... I bedded you before I kissed you. My first kiss...." He giggled again, and the truth of that sank Jack's stomach.

He'd deflowered a man who'd never even kissed someone. He was definitely not going to kiss him now. "There will be none of that while you'd taste more like a barrel than a man. Now, come here."

Jack hefted Reardon forward, dragging him across the antechamber. The prince was still light, but his near-dead weight did not help. Once Jack had gone a few steps and had a better handle on Reardon's limp limbs, he lifted him into his arms to carry him like last night.

Reardon rested his head on Jack's shoulder and hummed happily, too much like a rag doll to coil his arms around Jack's neck this time. His smile remained intoxicated and dreamy when Jack laid him out on the bed, a catlike stretch erupting as he settled in and clung to Jack's arms when they started to leave him.

"Will you have your way with me again?" Reardon murmured, shirt untucked and riding up his lean stomach.

"Not tonight." Jack pried the prince's fingers from his forearms.

"Tomorrow night?" Reardon reached after him.

"We'll see," Jack said. He had planned to reprimand Reardon for stealing his verses, but now was not the time. "Now, I need you to stay awake until I've gotten some water and food in you."

"Are you certain you can't get *other* things—"

"*Don't* finish that sentence," Jack ordered. His self-control was wafer thin as it was.

Reardon pouted but said no more, and Jack used the reprieve to escape. The prince's pores were practically sweating ale. A cool cloth, sweetly scented, would help.

And water.

*Much* water.

Jack forced Reardon to swallow down a glassful and half of another before he allowed him to wave it away. He even stuffed a crust of bread down Reardon's throat before picking up the cloth he'd brought and beginning to wipe at the prince's brow and down his neck. The scent of lilacs permeated, same as the bath, and Reardon took a big breath, as if to bask in it.

"A field of flowers… outside a deep wood," he said, sighing blissfully. "That's what being with you reminds me of."

Those were the most sensible words Reardon had said so far, but just poetry again, fantasy. Jack didn't know how to respond, so he chose not to. He simply wiped at the sweatier places on Reardon's skin and then laid the cool cloth to rest on his forehead.

Reardon's hands found Jack's wrists and held them, but his breathing soon evened out and the grip went slack. Slipping away would be easy then, yet Jack didn't rush to do so, enjoying the light touch of Reardon's soft fingertips. Once he was certain Reardon was asleep, he rose to put everything away and refilled the water glass should Reardon need it later—which he would.

Jack had no intention of sleeping himself, and Reardon was taking up the whole center of the bed anyway, so he pulled the covers down to fit Reardon beneath them and tucked him in.

"I still… miss her…." Reardon grasped Jack's wrists again, barely audible as he roused. "She was… so good… kind and loving. Why would someone kill her?"

*His mother*, Jack realized. If ever he'd thought there was selfish intent in this prince, he knew better now. "I don't know."

"She might have changed things… as I wish to. Because of that?"

"Maybe."

"Conspirators working against my kingdom… killed my mother. I… I must solve it and discover who they are. I must go home."

The warmth in Jack's chest returned to bitter cold. "Then you should."

Reardon smiled, and with the blindfold, Jack couldn't be sure if he was truly awake or dreaming. "When I have the answers, I will… but not until the curse is broken and you believe you are my love. Then, my king, once you are free… I will free everyone."

Heat returned with a vengeance, but not to Jack's chest—it stung his eyes, hot and wet and dangerous. Reardon was a fool—he was a fool, a *fool*—and he went limp again, head lolling to the side to show he'd once again drifted off, leaving Jack with his dreams.

Jack pulled away more swiftly than before, dizzy and feeling the need for a cool cloth of his own. He knew only one thing for certain.

He *hated* the Emerald Prince—for forcing him to hope.

# CHAPTER 8

REARDON'S BED was usually comfortable, but he didn't remember it being *this* comfortable.

Then again, beds were always comfiest when one least wanted to leave them, and Reardon did not want to leave this one at all. He struggled to recall why he was so loath to move, and the dull throb in his head reminded him.

Ale. Far too much ale. And eventually wine when they'd tried to take the ale away from him. Reardon would have been fine if he'd just listened when his friends tried to cut him off, but he'd been in such a good mood.

The only thing missing had been the king.

The *king*, who Reardon had announced he was going to see, and no amount of persuading from the others had swayed him. They'd helped him up the long staircase to the king's chamber, tied his head with a long strip of cloth, and—

Oh no....

Reardon snapped his eyes open to see—darkness.

Reaching up blindly, he felt the silken cloth still covering his eyes, even though it had to be morning, and this was definitely not his bed. Snuggled beneath the soft sheets, Reardon tentatively felt down his body but breathed relief at discovering he was still fully clothed.

"Majesty?" he called to an eerie silence.

It must be past dawn, that's why the king wasn't here, but Reardon kept his eyes closed for several long pauses after removing the blindfold before he dared peek around.

The bedcurtains had not been drawn, but he had been neatly tucked in, left in the center to slumber through the night alone. There were no windows in these rooms, so he could not tell if the sun was up, but the lacking presence of the king made him certain. He took what time he'd been granted to take in the parts of the king's chambers he hadn't been able to see the other night.

The bedroom was as lavish as the study, leading into the bathroom through a large, open archway. Everything was silver, gray, and blue, with only faint accents in gold and everything else colored so coolly. He remembered the feel of this bed now, but seeing it for the first time brought back flashes of sensation that hadn't included visuals before—the king's hands, his fingers inside Reardon, his cock in Reardon's mouth....

Reardon closed his eyes to stop the onslaught, but that only brought the memories up stronger, and his usual morning hardness pulsed between his legs for attention. That was not an option. He wouldn't dare pleasure himself in this bed without permission.

Although an audience would be interesting now that he knew the king had watched before, even if he couldn't meet the king's eyes or have him in daylight.

The king must be furious with him, though Reardon immediately doubted that thought, given how gently he'd been treated.

Then he saw the note.

Scrambling for the end of the bed, Reardon snatched up the piece of parchment, precariously balanced at the edge of the mattress. The elegant penmanship matched what Reardon had seen in the verses he'd stolen.

*Bathe and dress in what you wish. Your soiled clothes can be dropped down the chute. There are potions, food, and water on the table beside the bath. We will talk once you are finished.*

It wasn't signed, not that it needed to be, but Reardon's stomach churned at that final sentence from more than just a belly full of spirits—which reminded him how desperately he needed to pee.

Lurching up from the bed, Reardon had to wonder if he was dreaming and had merely passed out in the dining hall last night. Here he was relieving himself in the king's chambers, disrobing, and once again soaking in a hot bath already prepared for him with those same sweet-smelling oils. The dream didn't fade, however. No matter what the king said after this, he was hardly treating Reardon like a stable boy.

The wardrobes were numerous, and Reardon couldn't resist opening every single one. He'd already placed his old clothes down the... "chute," which had a basket beneath it, but was otherwise a small door set into the wall that opened to a long dark drop like into a deep well. The washing room must be directly below. Everyone else left their clothes in baskets that were picked up by whoever was on duty that day.

Looking through the multitude of wardrobes for what to borrow, Reardon wondered what the king had been wearing the night they spent together, though he knew it had been a mere shirt and trousers, not any of the gorgeous doublets with glittering accessories he found.

There were many in shades of blue which, like the décor of the rooms, didn't surprise Reardon—this had been the Sapphire Kingdom, after all—but none were embroidered with white gold or silver, which made him smile. He'd started making that secret garment in his own size since he didn't know the measurements of the king, but seeing examples now, he knew he wouldn't be far off.

It was easy to tell among the doublets, jackets, and cloaks what had been tailored for the king before versus after the curse; the signature look of the kingdom today was simple patterns in brilliant color. Any of the more luxurious articles would have been out of place, especially for Reardon to wear now, but there was a doublet in deep purple with maroon accents and matching embroidery that drew his eye.

He chose it without hesitation, a white shirt, and dark brown trousers.

Not wanting to languish too long, despite the king's hospitality, Reardon fussed with the clothes and his damp hair, which was difficult without a mirror, before downing the potions left for him—first, a mild healing potion for his headache, and then his customary draught against the cold. He finished with much water, and finally, ate every crumb of food. When it was over, all that remained was to face the king.

The sound of yelling was not encouraging when Reardon neared the door to the frozen chamber beyond, but better than it being directed at him, he supposed. The voices became clearer the moment he pulled the door open, doing so slowly to not alert the figures outside.

"I didn't pour the ale down his throat!" Branwen argued.

"You didn't do much to stop him from pouring it down his own!" the king roared back.

"It was his first night with the secret out—*second*, technically. We always get the new offering drunk after that."

"But most aren't left on my doorstep, *blindfolded*. What if my door had been locked? What if I hadn't let him in? He might have stumbled back to the staircase and broken his neck toppling down them!"

Reardon flushed at the obvious concern in the king's tone. Branwen must have noticed too, because he snorted from where he stood only a few feet from the large, hulking Ice King.

"Didn't seem there was much chance of that. And look—" Branwen turned to face Reardon, making him jump and clutch the door handle at being caught. "—seems we were right."

The king's gaze was just as paralyzing, his maw closing and his towering body tensing with tightly clenched fists.

Branwen's snort caused a burst of flames this time, as he pivoted to leave. "Not bad, princeling. Next time, maybe you'll even be able to keep up." He headed off, ignoring the king's shout after him.

It was difficult for Reardon to keep the smile from his face as he approached the king. "I am truly sorry for my behavior, Majesty," he said, offering a low bow. "Please don't blame the others. I didn't make it easy for them to tell me no."

The king dropped to all fours, but not to pound the ground or shake the throne room as he had many times before. He merely wilted, like he wished he could make himself smaller in Reardon's presence. "That does seem to be your specialty." Now that they were alone, he took in Reardon's form with a dissecting stare, eyeing the clothing he'd chosen.

"I-is this all right?" Reardon stuttered.

"It's fine. I've just… never seen anyone in those clothes."

"Except yourself." Reardon startled after he said it, remembering that the king didn't have mirrors in his rooms, and he almost never left them at night. He didn't look at himself any more than he let others look at him. "I suppose you haven't seen yourself in them either, have you? Well…." Reardon tried to keep the mood light, spinning slowly. "What do you think?"

Invited now to continue looking, the king's gaze pierced sharper, blue eyes sparkling in the depths of all that white. They were human eyes, the one part of him that remained so, and Reardon tried to imagine, thinking of Josie too, what his real face must look like.

He couldn't quite picture it, but he didn't mind that this was the only face he knew.

A low clearing of the king's throat broke the quiet. "A tad large, but they won't require much tailoring."

"Oh, you don't need to let me keep—"

"You chose those pieces out of everything I have. Call them a gift."

"A gift? After the way I acted?"

"I *should* banish you," the king said more seriously. "I should end all this right now."

Worry buzzed up Reardon's spine, and if it hadn't been for his potion, he would have shivered. "Then why don't you?"

"Because if I did, you couldn't finish your endeavor to bring your mother's killer to justice."

The breath stole from Reardon's lungs. He didn't remember everything about last night, but he did remember telling the king that. "And my endeavor to break your curse," he added.

For once, the king didn't refute him.

He stood upright and gestured at the base of his throne, where Reardon noticed their book, *Pillars of Virtue*, resting in wait. "I had Zephyr fetch it from your room. Shall we read more on the ramparts, little prince?"

It was the best outcome Reardon could have hoped for—and he also had the pleasure of getting further in that story. Sir Waite and Sir Kent were fascinating heroes, each so different and yet equally capable, proving there was no one way to accomplish anything and compromise often solved a situation best.

Reardon liked Sir Waite more than Sir Kent, if he was being honest, and he didn't fool himself over why. Waite portrayed a grouchy disposition to cover a deeply caring heart.

For the first time, Reardon stayed beside the king long past the lunch hour, since he'd eaten breakfast late, wanting to get as much time together as he could. But, like any day, once his first real shiver set in, the king dismissed him.

After grabbing a few leftovers from the kitchen to snack on until dinner, Reardon headed to his room to drop off the book, unsure how last night had ended in a win but not willing to question it. He received several stares from passersby as he trekked the halls—friendly ones but stares nonetheless—and wondered if it was because of how much he drank last night or the outfit that obviously wasn't his.

He'd been without his weapons belt when he woke up, vaguely remembering it being removed, so he half expected to find his dagger missing again, yet the belt and weapons remained, waiting for him neatly on his bed.

Reardon traded the book for his belt but decided not to change out of the king's garments. He might keep them after all.

His intended destination was the alchemist tower, but as he crossed the castle along the main landing above the large entryway doors, Oliver's wife, Amelia, came bursting inside, frantically looking for someone, anyone, it seemed, but no one was in the immediate vicinity.

Save Reardon.

"What's the matter?" he asked, hurrying down the steps.

"Thank goodness," she said, rushing forward to meet him and grasping his arms once they collided. "Shayla caught a pair of trespassers sneaking over the wall left of the gate. She's trying to hold them back, but we must warn the court."

"Zephyr!" Reardon called, causing Amelia to sag, as if in reprimand at herself for not thinking of that first.

A few beats passed, but then Zephyr appeared like always. "You know it's rude to assume—"

"Shayla's fending off trespassers outside. Tell the others," Reardon interrupted, not waiting for a response before he nodded resolutely to Amelia and took off running out the main doors, grateful once more that he had his belt.

The cold air made Reardon shiver, since his protection draught had long since waned, but he hurried onward regardless, left as directed toward the wall on the Shadow Lands side of the castle.

It was just at the far edge of the ice garden that he spotted them: Shayla with her twin daggers drawn, circling a pair of men dressed simply but each armed with a sword—and clearly wearing Emerald's colors.

"Stop!"

Shayla didn't look over her shoulder, eyes glued to the men, but the soldiers both glanced at Reardon, immediately showing recognition.

"My prince!" one of them called. "General Lombard sent us to find you, fearing the worst when you disappeared. Get behind me," he added with a sneer at Shayla. "We'll take this knave."

"You most certainly will not!" Reardon claimed his proper place at Shayla's side, staring the men down, stern and with authority he rarely used with any of his people. "Stand down. *Now.* I am not a prisoner, and you will not harm anyone in this castle."

"But…," the second soldier began, only to trail off just as a sound like the crack of thunder preceded the smell and taste of copper.

"Fiends!"

This time, Shayla did take her eyes from the soldiers. They all looked skyward, because that cry had come from above, and the sight would have been something out of a nightmare fairy tale if Reardon didn't already know what the court wizard looked like.

Liam had leapt out of the alchemist tower window, flying fast enough that it looked more like plummeting, lighting shooting out all around his already crackling form, until he landed in the courtyard with an explosion of snow and frozen dirt.

The soldiers gaped, both turning their swords toward the creature.

"Wait!" Reardon tried, holding out his hands. "No one here has to be enemies—"

"They've bewitched him," the first soldier said in horror, eyes wide at Liam, and then at Reardon. "The stories are true." He lurched forward, snatching Reardon's wrist and yanking him around behind him. "We'll save you!"

"No, I—"

"Get away from her!" Liam roared, clearly not listening either.

"Wait," Shayla said, starting to lower her daggers, but her good faith only caused the first soldier to lurch at her next, and not to grab her arm.

He swung with his sword, with Shayla barely managing to leap backward out of its path, though the swish nearly sliced the front of her shirt.

Liam swept forward—

"No!" Reardon raced to intercept.

—and fell upon the soldier with a wide swoop of his arms, as if to pull the man into an embrace.

A pop, not even a scream, was the only noise, as the man became but crackles left to dissipate within Liam's grasp.

Reardon had tried to not imagine what it might look like if one of the other court members touched someone.

He had truly tried.

"Liam!" Shayla cried, snapping Reardon back to the perils at hand, because Liam was turning toward the other soldier now, who'd frozen stock still.

"Stop!" Reardon dashed in front of him and spread his arms once more. "They know not what they do! Please! Please... don't kill him too."

The fury on Liam's elemental features was plain, but faced with Reardon rather than an enemy, he faltered, caught between his love and what he'd been trying to protect her from. The fury faded, the crackles lessening, but Reardon saw no sympathy on the wizard's face.

"I will kill whoever I must," he said, as assuredly as Jack would say, Reardon was certain.

It was the first time Reardon had looked on one of the court members, save his first impression of the king, when he thought the figure before him a monster, heartless and deadly.

"He's only one man," Reardon said. *One* because the other was dead—copper on the wind. "I will handle him. Drop your sword," he said over his shoulder, and barely a pause followed before there was a thud on the ground.

"We'll leave you to it," Shayla said, just as unsympathetic, Reardon thought, with her face a calm mask. "But we'll be watching."

She and Liam turned almost as one to head back into the castle through the front doors.

Reardon felt like he might be sick, but he had to appear strong for the sake of the survivor.

Steeling his expression, he turned to the man—though man was relative since the soldier looked younger than Reardon upon closer inspection. The other had been the superior, clearly, leaving behind a trembling figure with eyes that seemed perpetually widened.

"My prince... we thought at worst we'd find you dead at the feet of the Ice King, and instead he's.... What *was* that?"

"Not the king," Reardon said, "but the stories are not the truth of things here. You must go home. I am safe."

"Safe? Are they not monsters?"

"They're...." *They're not*, Reardon wanted to say, and yet... how could anyone kill so thoughtlessly?

How could Shayla, too, look on as if it didn't matter, even if she had called for Liam to stop?

There had been accidents, Reardon had been told. How many? How many had died here undeserving?

"It doesn't matter," Reardon said. "But you must go. You have supplies?" He didn't appear to have anything on him other than the sword he'd dropped.

"We... *I* have a camp not far, with horses."

"Then return to it, take your things, and go. Tell Lombard and my father that I am safe, and that I will return home when I deem it time."

"But why—"

"*Go*," Reardon ordered.

The soldier hesitated, pausing to lean forward and whisper, "You could come with me."

Reardon felt a terrible twist of guilt that part of him felt like he should. Part of him wondered if those cursed here deserved to be freed, or if he should simply abandon the idea after what he had seen.

But he would not only be giving up on them if he ran, and on Jack, but on his best chance to discover his mother's killer.

"I can't. I'm doing something important here. Just tell them... tell them I know what I'm doing, and do not frighten them by saying how the other soldier died. Say nothing of the creature you saw. Promise me."

"I...." The soldier's eyes went wider still. Then his voice fell once more to a whisper. "What shall I tell his family?"

Reardon winced, unable to stop the furrowing of his brow. "Tell them it was an accident, and that I send my deepest sympathies. Now go."

The soldier bowed, reclaimed his sword from the snow, immediately sheathing it, and Reardon watched him head out the gate, ensuring that it closed behind him.

He wasn't surprised to find the entryway of the castle bursting with people when he returned—along with every member of the court, save Liam.

Jack stood at the bottom of the steps that led up to his chamber, looking grave. "You let him go?"

"They didn't mean any harm," Reardon said. "They came to rescue me."

"He'll tell them what he saw," Branwen grumbled.

"He won't. I made him swear that he wouldn't."

"And you believe he'll honor that?" Jack asked.

Reardon honestly considered the question. The soldier, though young, had seemed a loyal sort, however frightened for his life. "Yes."

For the first time in ages, Reardon feared what Jack might do. Would he disagree, storm out of the castle after the surviving soldier, and freeze him into an undeserving statue before he reached his horse?

Another twist of guilt assaulted Reardon as Jack said, "All right. Then we will consider the matter closed and hope no more soldiers darken our grounds." With a simple bow of his head, Jack turned to lumber up the stairs.

Reardon felt so awful for doubting Jack that he could barely muster a smile as various members of the castle came to him afterward, including Josie, praising him for deescalating the event and keeping the castle safe.

As soon as Reardon had the chance, he pulled Barclay aside. "Where did Liam and Shayla go?"

"Back to the tower. I don't think Liam's taking this well. They never do." The sorrow on Barclay's face brought yet another twist of guilt.

Only minutes had passed since Reardon was initially headed for the tower. Now he headed there with Barclay, feeling an awful weight in his stomach.

When they arrived, Shayla was organizing the components rack and lining up items they must be meaning to experiment with later. Caitlin was mixing something that, as she finished stirring, turned green. Liam stood separate from them, purposely shooting his lightning into mixes already lined up on another table or drawing glowing runes on the glass.

Barclay took up a place beside Caitlin to begin mixing his own concoction. No one said anything about what had happened.

No one mentioned the man who had died.

"How goes things here?" Reardon asked.

"You mean how goes it working on *your* project even when you skirt your duties and show up late?" Liam sneered with a crackle of sparks leaping from his forearms.

"I am truly sorry, sir. I didn't intend for that. Please know how grateful I am for your help."

The wizard grumbled like a distant roll of thunder.

"I seem to recall at least one of Reardon's refills last night coming from *you*," Shayla said.

Another grumble responded, followed by a murmured, "He makes an entertaining drunk."

The room tittered, even with some laughter from Caitlin, and Reardon decided that this was how they dealt with tragedy. What else could they do when no one could bring back the dead?

They weren't monsters; they'd simply had to train themselves to accept what they couldn't change.

Reardon joined the workload. It was his job to catalog their attempts. He was also tasked with making the needed daily potions in their stead, such as elemental protection and healing draughts. Necessities couldn't cease just because the tower was helping him.

"What are the runes for, if I may ask?" Reardon asked as he set to work.

"Magical transmutation," Liam answered without looking up, finishing with the final vial. He returned to the start of the row of vials and tapped the first rune, which was a simple straight line. The vial frosted over, and then eventually calmed to a clear blue. "Alchemical transmutation is done differently, and therefore might have different results, so we must test both. It also tells us something about your perpetrator. Come here."

Reardon paused in his organizing of supplies to answer the request.

"The rune I activated is for ice but also means inertia or stillness. Next is its counterpart: the sun or the will and intent to change."

The second vial was marked with a more jagged line, almost like a simplistic lightning bolt, but it made sense to Reardon that it and the rigid line of ice were opposites.

"All one needs to do to achieve transmutation using magic is to first draw the rune and then activate it with an intending tap. Anyone with the most marginal of magic can do the same, even without training, as long as they will it. So… tap the rune and think of the heat from the sun as you do so."

A thrill shot through Reardon at the thought of being allowed to enact any sort of magic. He held his breath and reached out to tap the jagged line as told.

Nothing happened.

"As expected. Like we discovered on your first day—you have no magic at all," Liam said coolly. "Using runes is easier, faster, and requires fewer components to accomplish similar tasks. Meaning it would have also been easier to cover up. Therefore, if our findings lead us to believe that the poison we seek was created by alchemy with no magic whatsoever...."

"Then the one we seek might have no magic in them either," Reardon concluded.

"You see? You're less useless every day." Liam shooed him from the table. "Now get to work."

The afternoon wore on with everyone working diligently, and they eventually needed refills on supplies.

"We're going to run out of everything at this rate," Liam said. "Better dig into the winter stores. You're lucky we have plenty to spare, Emerald Prince, or I'd never allow this detour." He turned into the deeper bowels of the tower and disappeared.

It was then Reardon realized that, besides the wizard's coupling with Shayla and his role in the castle, he knew the least about Liam compared to any of the other court members.

"Liam was an elf and already a wizard with a leaning toward weather magic when the king appointed him, that much I know," Reardon said, slowly mixing a batch of healing potions, "but is that all? Everyone else has a story, yet I don't know anything more about him."

The room went so suddenly quiet, Reardon stopped his stirring to look around.

Barclay and Caitlin had turned away, so Reardon looked to Shayla, who faced him sluggishly, her usually glib demeanor more somber.

"You've wormed your way into a lot of *cold* hearts, but Liam...." She peered the direction he had gone before continuing in a low voice. "I wondered the same when I first arrived. What is the wizard's problem? Frankly, I thought he was a prick and didn't appreciate him ordering me around just because I had talents in foraging. So I decided to play a prank. *After* a month being here, so I already knew the castle's secrets.

"My plan was to sneak into his private chambers and steal his clothes, let him go without for a few nights, see if he even raised a fuss, and then return them with little pink hearts stitched into every doublet." Shayla smiled, only for the expression to quickly fade. "What I didn't expect was to find a portrait of a little girl, a half-elf with long dark hair."

Reardon thought back to when he had burst into Liam's room, and while he hadn't been paying much attention to the décor, he did think he recalled a portrait.

"He found me standing there like an idiot, and while he was as angry as you can imagine, he did eventually tell me who she was. If you want to find out, you'll have to ask him yourself."

Liam returned with a flurry and fresh crackle of lightning, a metallic taste resurging on the back of Reardon's tongue. He straightened and went back to his stirring. Luckily, he'd been nearly done anyway and hadn't ruined the batch.

"What are you all quiet for?" Liam barked.

"Doesn't the mood always drop when I say I'm leaving?" Shayla blew him a kiss.

"You are?" Only because Reardon had been here for many days did he recognize the shift in Liam's tone as disappointment. "Dinner, then?"

"If I think you've earned it," she said and winked before leaving—though Reardon wasn't sure if it was for Liam or him.

"Looking good." Liam eyed their progress as he set out the extra ingredients. It still amazed Reardon how lightning in the shape of a man could hold or touch anything without scorching it, but he knew it took intense concentration. "You two," Liam said to Barclay and Caitlin, "we'll need more containers before long. Grab a few boxes from the cellar. There's hardly anything in the stores up here anymore."

"And *you*," he ordered Reardon, "finish that healing draught and get over here to help me. I assume you can assist with non-magical transmutation."

Transmutation was one of Reardon's favorite parts of alchemy. Fire and water were opposites, air and earth, wood and metal, but lightning was the most complicated, because its opposite was like a void, pulling everything into it if left uncontrolled.

Transmutation could also turn a poison into an antidote—and vice versa.

Reardon understood why magic had been outlawed back home and alchemy heavily regulated, because both could cause much damage if dealt with foolishly. Still, he knew that fear was not the answer, and he didn't feel any as he followed Liam's instructions to add just a simple few ingredients, and then applied a little heat with a candle to the bottom of each new vial to cause a reaction.

All the vials changed in some form, some even began to swirl like a pit of endless darkness with a multitude of stars, but none caused the reaction they needed to indicate an untraceable poison.

They were closer, but they didn't yet have an answer.

"Have you ever tried transmuting yourselves?" Reardon asked as the idea struck him.

"After two hundred years? Of course. It doesn't do anything. Protection draughts for others is as good as it gets. At least until you *save us*." Liam's tone was mocking, but like with Branwen, Reardon knew that there was more to the wily wizard.

"My apologies again," he began carefully, keeping his back turned as he tidied, "for the other night, storming into your room the way I did. I hadn't realized, but I do think you and Shayla suit one another."

"So glad you approve," Liam answered snidely.

"I wondered, though... who was the little girl in the painting on your wall? There aren't any children in the castle."

If not for Liam's crackles of lightning, the room would have been dead silent, until Liam said, "Shayla's been talking, hasn't she?"

"I really did see—"

"Keep your meddling to the king."

"May I at least ask who she was?" Reardon peered over his shoulder.

"You are insufferable, you know that?"

"Many have said so."

"Who do you think she was?" Liam demanded like a floating, angry storm.

"Your daughter?"

"Who deserved better."

"And her mother?"

"She deserved better too." Liam looked away as Reardon turned fully to face him. "We married too young and fought constantly, even more after... Joslyn was born. My wife saw the old king's death as a good excuse to leave the Sapphire Kingdom. I saw it as an excuse to leave her. I took the role of wizard when Jack asked and said Joslyn could visit whenever she wanted."

"Then you still wanted to see your daughter—"

"I didn't realize they'd gone until the curse struck and I found our home long abandoned. Don't excuse being a bad husband with being a good father. I wasn't good at either."

"I just thought—"

"You thought I was the hero. That I was the one abandoned. If that were true, I wouldn't be this." He let his sparks ripple across his body. "That wasn't my first accident."

Reardon startled at the subject being brought up so suddenly. The events outside had shaken him and filled him with undue doubts, but as he looked at the grief somehow discernable even on an electric face, he didn't doubt the words that left him.

"You were protecting your love. Anyone else would have done the same."

"Oh? Or are those pretty words only meant to hide that, now, you wonder why Shayla would waste her time with me?"

"No," Reardon said without having to consider the answer. "You've grown. You've changed. You deserve the chance she's given you, because she knows you are better than you think." And than Reardon had thought for a fleeting moment too.

Nigel and Zephyr had been together since nearly the beginning of the curse, Shayla and Liam only the past forty-five years. That was still a lifetime for many, and yet doubt was a recurring theme among the court members and their partners.

Reardon didn't want to be counted among their company in that way ever again.

"You don't have to close yourself off to protect others," Reardon continued, "especially not her."

"Even if I'm beneath her?"

There was weight to that question, coming from a royal wizard about a condemned thief, despite that he had so recently ended a man's life like snuffing out a candle.

"Isn't she the one who gets to decide that?"

The silence that followed was broken by Barclay and Caitlin's return. Reardon smiled, not saying more, and went to help his friends stack the boxes before he took his leave.

When he was finally giving his farewells, Barclay gasped at the brush of their hands.

"Another vision?"

"I'm not… sure. I think you better take some extra cold-resistance draught, though, just in case." Barclay handed Reardon a small case with three ready potions, and Reardon didn't protest.

"I've been spending a little extra time in the cold, I guess. Thank you."

"We'll keep on it," Caitlin said. "Join us tomorrow?"

"Earlier this time." Reardon looked to Liam, who stared at him silently. "I promise."

He planned to head for the main halls but decided to take a shortcut through the hidden tunnels—and nearly slipped as soon as he stepped inside.

The entire passageway was coated in frost.

Reardon smiled to himself, fully aware of what that meant, but rather than spoil the game, he headed the opposite direction from where the frost settled.

REARDON KNEW. Of course he knew. Yet Jack followed like always.

He hated the allure of hope, and part of him hated Reardon for giving it to him. He'd wondered, however briefly, if seeing one of the castle's accidents firsthand would change Reardon's staunch dedication, but the prince had weathered that too, including their weather wizard. If Jack couldn't bring himself to banish the hope in his heart or Reardon, then he might as well enjoy what he could have until it was gone.

And he missed Reardon every moment he was without him. He should have shunned him when the prince rose after his drunken debauchery, but even after only one night together, Jack longed for his touch, for his company. Even if Reardon knew he was watching, Jack couldn't bear to let the prince out of his sight.

Eventually Reardon left the tunnels for the main halls. Jack couldn't always easily see him, keeping parallel with walls between them, but he could hear Reardon's steps, and as he tried to stay in line with wherever Reardon was headed, the collision that sounded when someone came speeding around a corner was unmistakable.

"Ouff!" Reardon grunted, another voice groaning in kind, followed by the thud of two bodies hitting the floor.

Jack rapidly removed the closest loose stone to check on Reardon. He appeared to be all right, but he was in a heap of long limbs, tangled with whoever had struck him.

"Apologies, friend! I didn't see... *you*," the other man said when his eyes fell upon Reardon, righting himself and grasping Reardon's hand to heft him up.

Their legs were still tangled, but they were at least sitting now, facing each other, hands clasped as both stared in recognition. The other man—an elf who'd been at the castle for decades—smiled wide, his angular nose twitching with interest.

"Emerald Prince, our new recruit. We meet again."

*Again?*

"After almost two weeks, you'd think you'd have met everyone by now, but I got the impression you were avoiding me."

"N-no." Reardon snatched his hand away, fighting to untwist their legs but making it worse on several attempts before finally pulling free. "W-why would I do that? I don't even know you!"

"Let's remedy that. I'm Raphael." The elf grabbed Reardon's hand once more before he could scramble to his feet.

*Raphael.* Jack remembered him better now; always sticking that narrow nose where it didn't belong and far too friendly. He'd been one of the few before Reardon who had tried to make nice, only to give up when Jack made it clear that he did not make friends with subjects.

Raphael clearly wanted more with Reardon, judging by the way he eyed him and let his hand linger inappropriately once Reardon acquiesced to shake.

Frost burst over the stones in front of Jack.

"Sorry I didn't say hello when we first saw each other," Reardon said with a bashful drop of his eyes. "I was hurrying after Shayla."

"I just felt bad for tripping you up. It's not often I nearly cause someone to flip over a banister."

Reardon tried to snatch his hand away again, but Raphael used the hold to hoist them to their feet, nearly knocking their heads together with how they rocked into each other's bodies from the momentum. "A-and where are you hurrying to today?"

"My duties at the stables. Lost track of time. But that can wait a few minutes."

"Stables…? You're a stable boy?" Reardon's thoughts must have strayed after Jack's frequent use of the term, though he knew full well none of Jack's conquests remained in the castle.

"I prefer to think of myself as a man. But then stable *man* doesn't roll off the tongue as well, does it?" Raphael raised Reardon's hand between them and ran a thumb over his knuckles. "Have you not seen the horses yet? They don't get ridden much in winter and can grow restless.

I could take you down to see them sometime." He raised Reardon's hand higher to place a light kiss to the back of it, making Reardon shudder. "My, you are pretty."

Another burst of cold spread over the wall from Jack's splayed palms, and then again when Raphael started to lean forward.

"I'm with the king!" Reardon wrenched away, leaving the other man's hand outstretched holding nothing.

"Not… currently." Raphael looked around in confusion.

Reardon pursed his lips.

"You mean…?"

Jack had never seen anyone move as swiftly as Raphael did to backpedal.

*Good.*

"You know… horses really shouldn't be kept waiting." Raphael continued to withdraw until he hit the wall, instantly shivering, given the other side was covered in ice from Jack angrily pressing his hands to it.

Jolting forward from the telling cold, Raphael turned and sprinted down the hall. "Another time!"

"Wait! You don't have to—!" Reardon tried calling after him, but Raphael was already gone. Holding a hand to his flushed face, Reardon laughed. "I'm with the king…," he said again.

He'd turned someone down who he clearly found attractive, someone who didn't come with any of Jack's complications, and he'd done it for Jack, for the chance at a love he didn't even know was real.

That should have made Jack angrier, but it glued him to his spot, made all the icier from the torrent of emotion that had exploded out of him. If Reardon was risking everything on some fleeting hope, and happy to do so, then maybe….

Maybe Jack owed him the same.


REARDON WASN'T sure when the king was or wasn't watching him, so he tended to imagine he always was.

Except with Raphael. Oh, he hoped he hadn't seen *that*.

Just in case, Reardon focused his time in the music room on helping Nigel, rather than working on his own piece, at least until he could ask Zephyr to inform him whenever the king was watching while he was in there—which would also ensure they knew where Zephyr was for

Nigel's sake, though Nigel insisted he could always tell when Zephyr was listening.

At nightfall, after a quick dinner, Reardon went once more to the king's chambers and tied that same scarf over his eyes before he knocked.

"I won't look, Majesty!" he called. "And I promise I haven't had anything to drink tonight."

He was ready for a fight, for silence or angry remarks, but after only a few short beats, the door opened, and a gentle hand took Reardon's to pull him inside.

The thrill of the king's touch made Reardon shiver for such different reasons than the cold of the room he'd come from. The warmth of these chambers was all the sweeter too, the look of them clear in his mind's eye now as the door closed behind him to let him know he was welcome.

"While I thank you for admitting me, Majesty, this is rather silly," Reardon said, carefully following the path the king led him on.

"You mean you coming here every night?"

"I mean you not letting me see you but still letting me in."

A comfortable hush fell until Reardon crossed what he knew to be the threshold into the bedroom. "Can't you be happy with what you're given?" the king said, the hand in Reardon's keeping hold of him, while the other was suddenly at the curve of Reardon's cheek.

"Depends on what I'm going to be given."

"Well, little prince… it seems I owe you *this*."

A puff of breath was the only warning Reardon received before the shock of descending lips. He gasped, leaning instinctively into the body before him and nearly going limp at that first brush of another's mouth. The king had touched him so intimately before, yet this made Reardon's knees far weaker.

He whined, opening his mouth wider upon the scarred softness of the king's, and sought the wetness of his lover's tongue. The king tilted his head to comply, pulling him against him tightly, his tender touch on Reardon's neck becoming a firm hold as he plunged his tongue deeper to give Reardon what he wanted.

Reardon was still shy of fourteen days in the castle, yet he'd found everything he'd ever wanted his long twenty-two years on this earth and hoped he was giving the king something worthwhile after a far longer two hundred.

"Please," Reardon panted after his breath had been stolen. "Let me know your touch again. Let me know *more*... if I can."

"Are you sure?"

"Yes."

"Then I surrender, my little prince. At least in this."

Reardon's chest felt like a jolt of Liam's lightning had hit him as he followed the king's ginger steps to the bed.

Because he had called him *his*.

PERHAPS REARDON truly believed in his devotion, but Jack knew, once the curse proved unbreakable, the prince would have to accept heading home empty-handed. And all the better, because knowing that—knowing true love wasn't real (or at least, not real for him)—wouldn't stop Jack from taking what he could.

Monsters could be gentle and giving too. Even demons garnered sympathy on occasion.

Reardon trembled and parted his moistened lips with a sigh, as if all the answers to the universe could be found in Jack's touch. He simply knew no other, but Jack would make it sweet for him and sweet, in the end, for himself too.

"You lent me your mouth, little prince," Jack said, laying Reardon down and straddling his thin hips, "now, let me give you mine."

Descending swiftly, Jack claimed another kiss. He'd forgotten how nice the simple meeting of mouths could feel, tongues caressing with demanding twirls and flicks. Reardon had little practice but more than enough passion, pawing up at Jack with equally aggressive fingers twisting into his shirt.

Jack rarely bothered with any of his doublets and hadn't again today, but Reardon wore the one he'd borrowed, with its deep purple hue. Jack loosened its ties, kissing Reardon long and slow as his hand strayed down the fabric to the start of the prince's trousers. Those ties were more important.

Once undone, Jack slid deft fingers into the opening to stroke through Reardon's fine auburn hair to the hot and hardening flesh beneath. Reardon's whine at the touch made Jack want to devour him like the beast he was.

He pulled his lips from Reardon's to do just that, shifting the lock of his thighs to slide down Reardon's body and pull his trousers to his knees. He left Reardon trapped like that, disheveled but mostly still dressed, panting deeply above him and clawing at Jack's shoulders as it must have dawned on him what Jack was about to do.

Reardon hadn't been able to see Jack when he took him into his mouth, but Jack could see Reardon as he bent to return the favor—good-sized and blushing scarlet like his cheeks and still smelling of Jack's bath oils.

He didn't taste like lavender, though; he tasted of salt and heady skin, the floral scent mixing with musk as Jack swallowed deep and pushed his nose into those russet curls.

"*Jack*," Reardon moaned without fanfare, so instantly that Jack wondered if he knew he'd done it.

Holding the prince by his hips, Jack sucked and swallowed, salivating easily and opening his throat. Too long it had been since he'd done this, but that didn't diminish his skill.

He sucked until he thought Reardon might come in moments, and then slackened, pulling slowly off to lick delicately at Reardon's head. Only when Reardon whimpered as if in pain did Jack lick boldly up his underside and return to suck him in again.

Reardon kept trying to pull his knees up, but Jack held them down. The prince squirmed, grasping at Jack's collar and begging, "Please, I... I-I need...."

"Need...?"

"*Something*."

"You wish to end things swiftly?"

"*No*, but...."

"Then be patient." Jack licked languidly around Reardon's cock, the prince's desperate whimpers growing louder, until finally he dragged Reardon's trousers down and off.

Now he let Reardon crook his knees, hooking them over his shoulders to dig his nose that much deeper into those curls, sucking almost vengefully and teasing a hand down the curve of Reardon's ass to the crease between his cheeks.

"*Yes*." Reardon's hands slid from Jack's shoulders up into his hair, curling into the long strands.

The contact was so... new for Jack, always having kept his hair short before the curse, that the sensation of someone running their fingers through it made him shudder and gasp and groan loudly when Reardon *tugged.*

"*Please*, I'm so close...." Reardon tugged again, unaware of the affect he was having, despite Jack's groan.

Tension seized Jack like he'd just heard canon fire; the intimacy, the need he felt for it, superseded everything else, and the fear of that almost caused him to flee.

Instead, the choice he made was to conquer.

"Not yet," Jack growled and roughly flipped Reardon over.

The prince shook as he got up onto his knees, willingly positioning himself and thrusting his hips back at Jack, presented lewdly and open while hanging heavy between his legs. Jack hadn't yet teased his fingers into that tight ring of muscle, and his hunger for Reardon brought his lips back to him first with a wet lap of his tongue.

Reardon's moan was encouragingly filthy.

Jack licked again, the tip of his tongue breaching the soft pucker. He spread Reardon's cheeks and licked as deeply as he could, as far as his tongue would go and that Reardon would open. The prince was as tight as before, but Jack's tongue between his cheeks relaxed him faster, and soon, Jack was plunging a finger inside with his licks.

He'd placed oils within easy reach, knowing what Reardon would ask for, but the prince's hole was already so wet from just itself and Jack's licking that nothing was needed. Jack stretched him open with a full driving finger beside his tongue and was soon ready to add another.

The resistance Jack had found before with two fingers twisting inside the prince was gone. He'd gotten this far then too, but only after careful scissoring and much more time. Managing this so quickly, Jack risked the tease of another finger around the rim.

"Y-y-yes...." Reardon's hips rocked mindlessly back and forth, fucking himself on Jack's fingers.

Jack had something better for him.

He still pressed the tip of that third finger in, only getting as far as the first knuckle and slowing his thrusts to start scissoring with all three.

Reardon cried out, but not as pained as before and fighting past the strain.

Jack hadn't removed any of his clothes yet, and Reardon was only missing his bottoms. The neediness to rut as quickly as possible, clothes or other barriers be damned, brought Jack back to his younger days, when fucking someone in the stables was for convenience more than anything—it never mattered who—because *now* was better than taking the time to bring someone up to his rooms.

He had Reardon in his rooms—the Emerald Prince who begged and mewled and deserved all the time Jack could spare him.

"Shhh...." Jack pulled his hand away to shuck down his own trousers, shifting up close behind Reardon and forming against his back with a warm slide between his cheeks—not to press in yet, just to rest there in wait.

Reaching around Reardon to bring his hand between them, Jack fumbled to connect their cocks as much as possible in this position, pumping his hand messily over each of them, adding Reardon's wetness from ready dribbles and Jack's own spit to their leaking fluids.

"I-I... want...." Reardon murmured inaudibly.

"I know what you want. Shhh...," Jack hushed again. "Relax, little prince, and I'll give it to you."

The stress on Reardon's arms to hold him up gave way, and he fell forward, resting his head against the mattress, hips still rocking to slide their skin together, hot and wet but not with enough friction.

Jack ran his hand over every bit of them colliding together until Reardon was a ragged mess, limp and quaking, so ready for any promise of release that when Jack rolled up to coat himself more slickly and returned to Reardon's stretched hole with easing pressure, Reardon swallowed him up like the hungry maw from his first song.


*YES.*

Reardon could handle it. He could take it. He—

He hissed. The base of the king was still so *much*. All that length and fullness inside him felt so good, but he knew it wasn't everything from his own cringe and the king's grunt of frustration.

"I-I'm... sorry."

"No," the king growled. "Your body is its own beast. Don't force it."

"I want—"

"I know. Relax, but if it's not meant to be yet—"

"It *will* be," Reardon insisted, pulling forward and back again to move the king inside him. That was its own magic, and Reardon loved it more than any display of power or alchemist's concoction. "Please, Majesty. I will open for you."

Another grunt resounded, desire dripping from the low utterance and making Reardon melt that much further. He was supposed to be melting the king, but melting together was just as good.

The slick slide of him was good too, the pull out and press back in of the king's cock, making Reardon smother his moans into the sheets in ecstasy. The king got so close to sheathing all the way inside him but kept hitting resistance, causing Reardon to hiss or wince, and whenever that happened, he'd relent, pull back, and fuck Reardon more shallowly.

Reardon didn't want shallow, so he focused on enjoying what he had—on the heat, the pressure, the rhythm starting to build, that little by little stretched him open more, brought the king in deeper, and gods above and below them, Reardon was determined to take him all.

And then a hard, slow thrust breached that stubborn resistance, and Reardon expected a ratchet of pain, only for the ache to give way to more pressure, and then just... fullness, such wonderful fullness, that skimmed some marvelous spot inside Reardon and made him scream.

The king pulled out, and Reardon slapped a hand back on his forearm, demanding, "*No*," gripping his wrist tight and squeezing, "more."

The next hard thrust brought the king in with a single stroke, Reardon's mouth dropping open in a silent cry. Everything burned, filling him to the brim, but it was a beautiful burn, and he wanted to chase that heat to its embers.

"*Yes....*"

Again and again the king slammed into him, Reardon's hand falling forward to clutch at the sheets for purchase. He turned his head, cheek to the mattress to let his silent cries out, and glanced back.

His eyes remained covered, so there was nothing to see, but he imagined the king's eyes on him, watching the rapture on his face growing in crescendo.

The king had to see it, had to be watching, like he always watched, because his thrusts grew more frantic, sliding in so effortlessly now, like he was made to fit between Reardon's cheeks and drive him to madness in his bedchamber.

That woodsy floral scent filled the room with sweat and musk and *them*. Reardon couldn't even push back to meet the king's slams anymore, so immobilized by how good it felt, a fluttering, tickling sensation growing in the pit of his stomach with that same incredible *heat*. He knew what it meant to pleasure himself, but it had never felt like this, and each slam built the sensation higher.

And that spot, that wonderful spot inside him, touched only ever by having the king rock with abandon, made him moan and cry and plead to finally reach the end of this incredible driving force.

Reardon's own pleasure would have been enough, but it was a haggard moan from the king, scarred hands smoothing up Reardon's back beneath his shirt and half-untied doublet, like some deep need to connect and feel him, that tumbled Reardon off the precipice.

He sank, almost falling into the spot of wetness he'd streaked across the bed, but held himself up by sheer will, back arched and thighs spread to anchor against the king's final pumps—and oh, he wanted him to stay inside forever.

"Stay…," he croaked, no breath left for anything more, but it was enough that the king didn't pull out when he hit his peak.

Another grunt came, a sharp clutch at Reardon's skin, and then a glorious warmth filled him. The king sank as Reardon had, held up just enough to not smother Reardon to the bed, both shaking and panting and sheened in sweat.

Reardon ached, more exhausted than the first time, likely not helped by his drunken slumber last night, but it had been worth every pained progress toward bliss.

"What a mess… you've made of my sheets," the king huffed, lifting Reardon's shirt to press a tender kiss to the skin between his shoulder blades.

"You'll have to clean me up again."

"Indeed." The king rumbled a throaty laugh.

After a few more captured breaths, he pulled up and dragged Reardon with him. Reardon would have needed the helping hand being led to the bath even if he hadn't been blindfolded. The ache was pleasant but definitely threw off his balance.

Once more, he found himself soaking in sweet-smelling water with the Ice King, human and comforting, at his back. A warm cloth was dragged over his body, between his legs, his cheeks, almost enough to twitch him to life again, but the touch was fleeting, and soon they were lying together with the king's arms loosely holding Reardon to him.

"Even after that… you still do not believe you are my love?" Reardon asked, resting his head on the king's shoulder.

Silence answered for a good many moments before he said, "You will find someone more worthy someday."

Reardon thought of Raphael, who was very handsome and disarming. He thought of Lombard too, but that was a child's dream. Neither of them made Reardon hesitate to say, "There is no one of more worth to me than you, Majesty."

"And what if you only think that because you already believe I'm your love without actually feeling it?"

"I'm not so easily swayed, even by Barclay's visions. I believe some things are fated, but that doesn't take away our ability to choose. If I didn't want you to be my love, you simply wouldn't be." Reardon knew that wasn't the same as saying he loved the king now, but he believed he was on that path.

"Then perhaps it is only because I am the first touch you have ever known."

"That too discounts what I liked about you long before I knew your touch. You have all the qualities I am usually drawn to."

"Being stubborn, vicious, and either monstrous or scarred?"

"I'd say… resilient, passionate, maybe a little tragic, yes, but also kind. I don't know the man you were, but I know the man you are. And I don't care about scars." Reardon turned, moving between the king's legs to face him in the large bath.

Reaching out with both hands, he found firm shoulders first, and then moved up the king's neck to the curves of his face. He could feel scars there too, but it didn't matter.

Crawling more securely into the king's lap, Reardon held his face in his palms to guide him to his lips. Kisses were written about by bards as much as lovemaking or romance. Reardon thought he could have kissed the king, mouth open or closed, well into the night and written sonnets in his head.

"Majesty—"

"Go back to your room." The king stopped him from asking the same old question to finally see him. "Sleep, little prince. You'll grow tired of me soon enough."

"I could—"

"It's best if you don't stay."

The small win was in how much more gently the king pulled Reardon from the bath, dried him, and helped him dress, before leading him to the door.

Reardon stepped outside when it was opened for him but reached back to halt its closing and said, "Good night, Majesty. But I promise you, someday soon, you will let me sleep in that bed again."

# CHAPTER 9

REARDON KNEW he was right. Even without Barclay's vision, he would have been certain that his destiny was upon him—saving his kingdom, saving *this* kingdom, and finding a love of his own at last.

No casual touches with Barclay brought forth any new insight, only the occasional frown and Barclay once again reminding Reardon to take his cold-resistance draught. Still, Reardon remained confident as the days passed. The nights were what he looked forward to most, spent in the arms of the king.

They didn't always connect as deeply when they were together, especially not if Reardon was sore, but there were so many other wondrous pleasures the king could show him. The touch of his hand or mouth on Reardon's skin, on his sex, was enough to drive Reardon to rapture time and time again.

Soon, the last few days of his two weeks had come and gone, no fanfare needed since he'd already discovered the castle's secrets, and he was nearly concluding a third week before he realized it. The king had yet to allow Reardon to spend the night in his bed again. He hoped his song might finally sway him.

Everyone knew about his nightly visits to the king. Once, the fletcher even sat beside Reardon at lunchtime and asked him straight out in a hushed voice, "Have you seen the king yet?"

Reardon forgot sometimes that only the court knew the king's true face. Even Oliver, who had been here since the beginning, hadn't been present before the curse.

"Not yet."

"And it doesn't bother you, being with someone you've never seen?"

"If you had no sight to see your wife, would you love her any less?"

Oliver reared back, but then gave a small smile. "Not even a little."

Reardon could be patient, but the problem now was that his song was finished, and he still had no idea how to woo the king with it.

"You should ask Branwen," Nigel said, close to completion with his own epic.

"I don't know if I've read any of his books, since he doesn't use his own name. Are they really that good?"

"Like a veritable god of romance giving advice."

If Reardon hadn't seen Branwen working on a book with Caitlin, he never would have believed the fiery master of arms could write verses of passionate love stories. Even so, he found him later that day like kismet, standing in the hall outside the library doors.

"Don't you want to go in?" Reardon asked.

The brightly burning behemoth turned toward him like a giant floating flame. "And risk a neglectful touch turning the whole place to cinders? Don't be a fool."

Reardon went to him, leaving the customary few feet of space, and peered inside the library. The grandness of it still took his breath away even when he remained in the hall. "Basking in its presence then for inspiration?"

Branwen grunted, and it came out like the snort of an angry bull. "It's better when you newcomers never learn that."

"Don't be bashful. Being a poet or a bard is a great calling. I don't have much skill for writing myself, only song and performance. But you *tell the tales*. That's real power. I was hoping the kind of power that you might be willing to share?"

"Meaning?"

"Do you have any advice as a great writer of love about how someone might woo their love with a song?"

Bright flaming eyes danced like flickering candles. "You want the words?"

"I have the words from another clever poet, and the tune now as well. I know I want to sing it in private, when it's just the two of us, but I'm not sure… how."

Branwen's expression shifted, showing telling signs of a smirk within his flames. "For Jack."

"Yes. The intimacy of his touch he allows, but when I speak words of love, he rebuffs me."

"And he will keep rebuffing you. What you need is to put the two together."

Reardon looked at him with a furrowed brow.

"If Jack responds to the carnal over the romantic, then give him both. Look for a book called… *Heatwave*—" Branwen nodded inside the library. "—with a dark red spine. Second row on the right, four shelves in, about eye level. Somewhere around… page 120, you'll find the example you're looking for."

"One of your books?"

"I never said that."

"If it is one of yours, Caitlin's the one who scribed it, yes? Perhaps it's time you used some of your own romantic advice." Reardon didn't wait for Branwen to refute that but turned to enter the library and followed the path he'd been set upon.

*Heatwave* was the only book with a red spine on the shelf he came to, and a couple pages just past 120 came a very romantic and *graphic* depiction of a songstress teasing her warrior love. The scene made Reardon blush like no other he had ever read, because he knew he'd have to be the one leading to make the seduction work.

And he had to do it blindfolded.

"I remember that one."

Reardon's head snapped up from the pages, and upon seeing Josie floating before him at the end of the stacks, he clutched the book to his chest as though it were a lewd painting.

"One of Branwen's steamier ones." Josie smirked, ever the breathtaking statue come to life. "Don't be bashful. I've used those books for encouragement myself, but not every evening should be spent in one's bedchambers. Mostly. Tonight, I'd like you to have dinner with me and Barclay."

Reardon's embarrassment faded to confusion. "I will always happily sit with you."

"I mean privately, in my rooms. I hardly get any time with you alone—when I don't have to keep my distance." She looked down at her shimmering form with a sad wilt of her smile. "Unless you were planning on using your… *encouragement* tonight?"

"Oh, I'm not quite ready, I… I don't think…."

"Then it's a date. Please?" Josie had a subtle hypnotism about her, sweet yet dangerous and impossible to say no to.

"A date."

JACK HAD been debating following Reardon less frequently. He couldn't use the excuse of keeping an eye on a potential traitor anymore, and it was obvious that Reardon knew Jack was watching, making it all seem pitiable and needy. Jack didn't *need* Reardon. It had just been so long since he had something worthwhile to occupy his time.

Earlier, Reardon had promised to still see Jack for their nightly audience but had informed him that he would be late, taking dinner in Josie's chambers. Like any other night, Jack should have stayed in his rooms. Sneaking out after nightfall was risky. Anyone might see him, even in the tunnels, but curiosity won out in the end, and he found himself as drawn to knowing more about Reardon as he'd been when he snuck into Reardon's room that one night to place *Pillars of Virtue* on his bed.

They only had a few chapters left before the end.

Vulnerability hollowed out Jack's stomach as he slipped into his icy throne room and scurried for the door to the tunnels like an anxious rat. At least Zephyr couldn't suddenly appear as he often did during the day, but Jack still listened with cloying paranoia before turning any corners on his trek to Josie's room.

He made it without incident, the only voices he heard being those of Josie, Barclay, and Reardon once he removed a stone to steal a peek.

They had already eaten, only Reardon left picking at a last crust of bread and drinking from a goblet of wine, while Josie gave a beginning trill on her lute. They had set up a small table to dine, Josie having pulled her chair to the middle of the room to sit while she played and Barclay turning his chair around to join her in song, as Reardon watched.

> *"Beyond the dense, dark wood*
> *Lies lands forever night;*
> *Shadows fall—and claw—and rend*
> *To see to travelers' end.*
>
> *"Oh lands possessed by demons' thrall,*
> *The Shadow Lands take all.*
>
> *"The king once sold his soul*
> *To rule forevermore;*
> *Twisted form—he stalks—and lures*
> *To further grow his horde.*
>
> *"Oh lands possessed by demons' thrall,*

*The Shadow Lands take all.*

*"Beware beyond the wood*
*For monsters made of men;*
*Darkness falls—and out—they come*
*To make you one of them."*

Josie laughed as she ended on a warning trill, Barclay's singing cutting off abruptly to laugh with her.

Most of the songs that spoke of horrors in neighboring kingdoms had been passed to Jack's people from Emerald, like dark tales of the Ice Kingdom, of the Mystic Valley, or of unknown countries and people beyond.

But songs of the Shadow Lands had been known here even before the two hundred years of the curse. No one ever ventured beyond the wood down the hill from Jack's castle. The *Dark* Kingdom was always only whispered about.

"Do you think it's true?" Reardon asked, not laughing with the others but looking suddenly sick and setting down his wine. "They never attack. Never threaten. Trade comes through sometimes, in carriages pulled by black horses with no driver. Emerald's people fear its magic, yet just like the offerings made here, the trade is taken, and we send our own supplies back.

"What if their king *does* make monsters of anyone who reaches him?"

"You believe in ghost stories?" Josie laughed again, setting her lute beside her.

"Forgive me, but I am talking to a woman made of gold during the day," Reardon said, and Barclay fought a snicker behind his hand.

"Fair enough," Josie admitted.

"But like you said," Barclay spoke up, "they've never posed themselves as a threat. Perhaps it's all stories, like what Emerald thinks of this kingdom."

"But those stories are true!" Reardon exclaimed. "They're just nicer here than we thought."

Josie bowed in thanks for the appeasement.

"I only worry because… that's where I sent the real offering for this year. General Lombard and the soldiers had fallen asleep. I'd stolen an extra key from Lombard's quarters before leaving the city. They cover the cage once it's out of view of Emerald so the offering can't appeal to their pity during the journey. It was easy to let the sacrifice out and take his place without anyone noticing.

"If I'd only known what I was going to find here, I would have simply joined him instead of sending him into the dark."

Jack could never regret his decision to trust Reardon. The young prince was a good ruler already, worrying over a past he couldn't change and a single subject he could do nothing to protect.

"You *didn't* know," Josie reminded him. "It only does you credit that you blame yourself anyway."

Reardon smiled, however somberly, and then reclaimed his drink after a moment of silence. "Barclay and I used to help put together the alchemy packages for trade with the Shadow Lands. Remember? Master Wells would sneak experiments in there just to see if there'd be any response. It's a wonder he was never given up for sacrifice. It still angers me that he turned you in. I refused to see him or stop by the shop after that."

Barclay mirrored Reardon's somberness, but without the bitter edge. "He was scared. Everyone's always scared back home. My family too."

"You forgive him? You forgive *them*?"

Josie returned her chair to the table to be nearer to Barclay and hooked her hands around his arm.

"I can't hate any of them," Barclay said. "If somehow our positions had been reversed, my friend, I don't know if I would have had the courage to do what you did—standing up to your father, seeing me to the gates, showing up here to rescue me."

"You would have," Reardon dismissed, as if all he had done wasn't a monumental collection of feats.

"Maybe, but I don't know how to use those fancy new swords of yours," Barclay said with a warm chuckle. "I'm just a scientist."

"*Just.* I doubt anyone here who uses your potions or is blessed by your visions would say you're just anything."

"Even so, I forgive Master Wells and my family. I forgive your father and General Lombard too. That doesn't mean I ever want to see any of them again." Barclay chuckled like before, turning to look fondly on Josie. "This is my home now."

She kissed him, a tender press since there was company so near, and Reardon looked on with a reverent longing that Jack had seen many times before, even when Reardon's eyes were covered by a cloth.

"When the curse is lifted," Reardon said, "your city will grow, and it will become home to many more again, blossoming into the kingdom it was always meant to be."

"And where will the Emerald *King* fit into that," Josie volleyed, "so many leagues from here?"

"I... hadn't thought about that...."

No, Reardon hadn't. Jack had been trying to tell him, but Reardon wouldn't—

"I'll just have to call both kingdoms home. Or maybe we could grow so vast together, we'll combine into one great empire." Reardon beamed as he said it, Barclay laughing at the jubilant notion and Josie looking serenely wistful.

Reardon was just a dreamer.

Always a dreamer....

"What about you two?" Reardon asked. "Would you marry soon?"

Barclay promptly choked on his wine.

"Sorry!" Reardon scooted closer when his friend's coughing prompted Josie to smack his back. "I put my foot in it, didn't I?"

"No," Josie said, "it's just.... Barclay already asked me."

*He what?*

"Do, um... people not marry here?" Reardon's cheeks flushed with color. "I thought Oliver—"

"They do." Barclay cleared his throat before continuing. "But Josie... she wants to be wed in sunlight. I understand. I can wait. Or we can live an eternity just as we are."

There were obvious reasons why Jack had never argued against his sister's choice of companion after two hundred years watching the other court members find love. Barclay might be slight and far from a nobleman or a warrior—everything about him would have angered their father, which honestly made Jack bless the couple more—but Barclay was a powerhouse where it mattered and in all the things that made Josie happy.

"It's selfish," Josie said, resting her head on Barclay's shoulder.

"Don't be silly," he assured her.

"Besides," Reardon added, "it's doable. When I break the curse, Jack can marry you in the garden, no ice statues anywhere in sight. You'll see."

"Would that suit my fair princess?" Barclay asked against Josie's soft brown hair.

"Only if Reardon puts some of that gold embroidery into my wedding gown."

Reardon erupted with a joyous laugh. "And Jack and I can wear our matching doublets in attendance!"

Jack had always known that his silly little prince meant those doublets with yellow and white-gold embroidery for them.

"You called him Jack," Josie said.

"I did. Now, if only I could muster the confidence to do so beyond… um… being impassioned."

Barclay and Josie snickered.

"When are you going to give Jack his doublet?" Josie asked.

"When I can see him in it. You two are as much an inspiration as any bardic tale or book. But I better not keep the king waiting." Reardon tipped his goblet back to finish his wine.

"You *could*, you know." Josie snickered again.

"Yes, but even after a few hours, I… miss him. Either form of him. Is that pathetic?"

*Yes.*

"No," Josie countered Jack's thoughts, smiling in her bliss. "It's familiar."

Reardon rose to take his leave, but since the happy couple had gotten quite comfortable at the table, he offered to put Josie's lute away for her. When he returned to them, he asked, "I never noticed, but your lute has a bit of patchwork to it. For decoration?"

"Oh, um… it had to be mended once. A year ago, actually. When a certain *someone* snuck into my room his first night, I hit him with it."

"What?"

"After that thief all those years ago, she was scared!" Barclay defended. "Luckily, I wasn't knocked out and hastily explained that I'd only gone to her because she seemed the most likely to listen about my visions and that they'd already shown me the castle's secrets. I was scared too, but while she kept me at a distance at first, she listened and agreed to keep my secret from the others until my two weeks had passed."

"It was the smart thing to do," Josie said, "but I also missed having someone around at night. I asked Barclay to come back every evening so I could keep an eye on him. That was my original intention, but he'd tell me stories about Emerald, about his experiments, about his favorite tales and songs, his dreams and fears, his visions, even the ones he had about me. I was smitten long before I realized." She kissed him lightly again, lingering this time far longer.

*Familiar*, she'd said. That story of a slow decline was familiar to Jack too.

"The night Barclay's two weeks were up, when he was officially initiated as a subject of the Frozen Kingdom," Josie continued, "I stole him away for the rest of the evening and never regretted it."

They stared adoringly into each other's eyes, Reardon overcome with that longing look again as he made his way to the tunnel exit. "Good night, my friends. I am very happy for you and agree wholeheartedly— no regrets."

Jack was so weighted down with guilt from Reardon's unwavering faith in him that he almost forgot he was currently standing in the tunnels Reardon was about to enter.

Nearly stumbling over his own feet, Jack hastened away, never before so relieved that there was no ice trail the way he had come from.


THAT NIGHT, Reardon thought the king sounded out of breath when he opened the door to lead Reardon into his chambers.

Eager to see him, Reardon hoped.

They kissed and touched and lay together, writhing as one with tangled limbs and inelegant, hurried enthusiasm. Reardon loved nights like that as much as any other ways they were together.

Afterward, they continued to lounge in bed, while the king read the next chapter of *Pillars of Virtue*. Usually Reardon did the reading, but oh, the king's voice was lovely and lyrical.

Reardon thought his planned singing seduction might no longer be needed, with how attentive and sweet the king was being, but when the chapter concluded, Reardon was still pushed out the door.

The next night, he had no more excuses, because Nigel was ready with his tale and had made Reardon promise that he'd perform his too— even if the only person who'd know would be the king.

Anticipation made the day inch by. Reardon's thoughts were distracted when he was with the king that morning, and far worse once they parted. Dinnertime came too slowly as well, though once it did,

Reardon felt inspired when he looked at Branwen and Caitlin sitting together hip to hip.

The sun had already set, so the pair had entered the banquet hall together. Each iteration of the experiments in the alchemist tower brought Reardon closer to discovering the potion that had killed his mother—and Caitlin's husband—and with that success, it seemed the *ice maiden* was melting just as Reardon hoped to melt the king.

Ten years Caitlin had been tethered to a ghost, called "widow" like a lifelong title, but with the mystery soon to be solved, perhaps she was finally letting go and opening her heart to Branwen.

Reardon relaxed as he watched them with a growing smile.

Just as Nigel arrived in a flurry, literally dragging Zephyr behind him.

"I'm not hungry—" Zephyr tried to protest, but Nigel tugged him along anyway.

"Yet I, my love, am hungry for the room!" He let go of Zephyr only after they were in the center of the hall and jumped straight up onto one of the empty benches to get onto the table, commanding everyone's attention. "I have the most epic of tales to tell today. Unparalleled and dramatic and spanning ages, this story is one of heartache, deceit, and love conquering all.

"Who cares to hear it?"

The usual chorus of cheers and encouragement rose at the thought of Nigel telling one of his tales, while Zephyr tried to hide his amusement by scowling and crossing his arms.

With leave to begin, Nigel started a slow stomp on the table to get the crowd pounding out a beat, and the trill of a harpsichord filled the hall. Everyone turned, Zephyr looking especially stunned, to discover Wynn sitting at the instrument in the corner—which was usually up in the music room.

Josie stood from where she and Barclay sat across from Reardon, revealing her lute tucked beneath the bench. As she joined in Wynn's song, Reardon and Barclay rose as well for their parts that came later, and Nigel began his verse to the continued beat of the crowd.

"The lovers yet to know their path begin our tale quite broken: a scoundrel found to hide his ears—" He tapped his own pointed tips. "—and a spy with wants unspoken!"

Zephyr turned his head to hide a laugh.

"The spy was once of noble blood and meant to give an heir, but hence he was sent from his home for craving *broader* fare." Nigel winked, spinning about with his usual flourish. "So too the scoundrel once was jeered at if his tricks were proved untrue. Then sent away as magic-born, a half-elf given due.

"And oh, what luck!"

Reardon and Barclay picked up the tale by singing in harmony, *"No greater love—than the first to fall!"*

Laughing outright then, Zephyr was clearly smitten, despite the embarrassed color growing in his cheeks.

"The spy was happy to be such to twist his foes about, now free but caged by skeptic's scorn that love would e'er be found. So, scoundrel came to grace his eye and maddened him for years, but madness takes so many forms and ended here in tears."

Nigel spun once more and hopped down from the table, speaking right to Zephyr as the music swelled.

"Without a captive crowd to con, the scoundrel had no call, and spy took pity with his touch to soothe him by his thrall.

"And oh... what luck." He softened, and Reardon and Barclay sang softer too.

*"No greater love—than the first to fall."*

Nigel slowed his progression toward Zephyr. "One night of passion only, the spy swore to the scoundrel, but now he'd known the taste of love and heeded not his counsel. The scoundrel sought the spy for days and weeks to come, declaring love at every turn at night *and* in the sun.

"He said it till his love believed that what they had was true—" The music stilled as Nigel took Zephyr's hands in his own. "—and to this day he loves him still—'I love you, dear, I do.'

"And oh... what... luck." He kissed Zephyr to a pause of silence— and then a roar of applause.

Zephyr pulled away with a sputter at all the attention. He was used to being mostly invisible all day and slipping around unseen, now made the center of attention. Yet he laughed and didn't draw back from Nigel's touch, that went from his hands to cradling his face.

*"No greater love,"* Nigel sang, not usually able to hold a tune, but this much he could manage, *"than the first to fall,"* and he kissed Zephyr again.

Not many loves got to survive beyond a single lifetime, but though doubts may ebb and flow, Reardon truly believed, even before the display he was witnessing, that true love was constant and unconditional.

"Now," Nigel said, louder to those watching, "if you'll excuse us, as my love said, he's not hungry yet, so I think we'll spend our time elsewhere."

Zephyr was still blushing, easy enough on his pale complexion, and several snickers and hollers arose as Nigel dragged him away, just as he'd dragged him in. They seemed blissfully young and happy and giggly, like they truly were the age they looked instead of centuries old.

Reardon turned to Barclay and Josie, but they were sharing a kiss now too. Wynn came over from the harpsichord to pat Reardon's shoulder. He knew that it was Reardon's turn to weave a tale, though his stage would be smaller.

"Have a good evening." Reardon patted Wynn's arm in turn, glancing once more at Barclay and Josie, at Shayla and Liam not much farther down the table, and at Caitlin and Branwen, less obvious but still entranced with each other, before he took his leave.

*No greater love….*

He just hoped the last to fall would be as magical.


REARDON HAD said he'd be late again but that he would indeed darken Jack's door before the night stretched on. Each day that passed, Jack knew their time grew shorter, because Reardon and the others were close to solving the recipe for that awful potion that had killed the Emerald Queen and Caitlin's husband.

Perhaps Reardon would be able to use it to find justice, but changing the hearts of his people would require a miracle—like the breaking of a curse—and as warm as Reardon made Jack feel, he didn't believe that was possible.

The knock at his door and the sight of Reardon on the other side, blindfolded as always, for the briefest of moments, still made Jack wonder….

"Majesty," Reardon said when Jack led him inside, "I would like to request something tonight."

"Oh?"

The prince was often a bundle of contradictions, equally self-assured or bashful depending on the circumstance. He was nervous tonight. Jack could feel it in the tremble of his fingers and the way he bit his lower lip. Still, he didn't let that defeat him. "I would like to lead, if you would set the stage."

"Then lead, little prince. What do you want of me?"

"Bring us to the bed, undress, position me at the foot of the bed facing it, and then lie back."

"Does the no-longer-virgin prince wish to *take* his king?" Jack smirked, already complying as he pulled Reardon into the bedchamber.

"I-I... hadn't thought *that* far." Reardon flushed brilliantly scarlet. "But I wish to prove my affections for you."

Jack didn't need anything proven, but love wasn't some magic spell—or an end to one. "Then lead," he said again, skeptical though he may be, "and I'll follow as far as I can."

It was Jack who had to lead in the beginning, bringing them to the bed and leaving Reardon at the foot of it. He slipped his trousers and shirt off and climbed onto the bed as asked, lying upon his pillow and watching his prince.

"The stage is set," he said, wondering what Reardon had planned.

Reardon smiled, nervous still, but seemed bolstered when he started to hum, and nimble fingers pulled on the ties of his doublet.

*"The noble prince went on his quest*
*To become a greater king,"*

Reardon sang—to its own unique melody—the verses he had taken from Jack's desk.

Jack tensed, though he'd known a reckoning was due.

*"Than those before who'd shamed their lands*
*And bards denied to sing."*

Drawing the doublet open, Reardon let it drop from his shoulders, slowing feathering his fingers down the center of his chest to the edge of his trousers, where he tugged his shirt free.

*"He traveled far to learn abroad*

*How other kings reigned just,"*

Reardon gripped the bottom of his shirt and drew it over his head without losing a beat.

*"But for all he found who'd earned their crowns,*
*Men made beasts ruled thus."*

Sliding a careful distance back, Reardon began untying his trousers, ensuring Jack saw every coil of those ties around his fingers.

Jack spread his legs as he looked on and reached between them, surprised, though pleasantly so, when Reardon sang a chorus not previously written.

*"Ever was, ever more,*
*Love can conquer any lore."*

Down the trousers dropped, Reardon already twitching to hardness while Jack pulsed to life in echo, barely needing the aid of his leisurely strokes. Reardon stroked himself too, once, twice, and reached forward to begin climbing up the bed.

*"He pitied one such beast*
*To turn him from his ways*
*In hopes that tenderness might win*
*And pierce the heart that strayed."*

Reardon crawled to Jack until he arrived at the spread of his legs, first rising onto his knees to feel up his own chest, and then down his hips to rake blunt nails across his thighs and stroke himself again.

*"Hearts made of ice aren't made for melting,*
*But the prince did burn so bright,"*

So bright, and next he fell forward, found Jack's thighs, and raked his nails there too.

*"That he reached the wayward beastly king*

*And found him in the night."*

Find him he had, feeling up Jack's body as he'd felt down his own. It was so rare that Reardon touched Jack more than fleetingly. Jack was the one who guided, who initiated, but now....

Reardon dragged his nails back down Jack's chest, found his hand on himself and pushed it aside to hunker low and replace that hand with lips and tongue. He could only feel his way through what he was doing, but he barely trembled now, no hesitation as he licked—

Jack gasped!

—and then continued to sing.

*"Lips and hands and hearts did touch*
*Knowing pleasures lost before,"*

He licked again, swirling his tongue up Jack's shaft and over his head, but then sat up to crawl forward, making Jack shake and clutch at him, drawing the long, lean prince atop him and spreading his legs farther to let Reardon settle between them.

*"And the prince did reach the king at last*
*As the beast became no more."*

He kissed Jack, holding his face in possessive palms and rocking his hips to slide their lengths together.

*"Ever was, ever more,"* he sang softly, *"love can conquer any lore."*

"You stole those words," Jack whispered.

"The chorus is mine," Reardon countered, looking quite comfortable atop Jack, circling his thumbs along Jack's cheekbones.

"A dreamer's refrain," Jack said, though without the bite he might have used before. "And I think I've read a similarly tantalizing seduction."

There, finally, came the blush that had faded. "You may have. Do you believe your own words, Majesty? It was beautifully written."

"Reardon...."

"I love you," Reardon said, hastily but earnestly spoken—what he'd implied so many times but hadn't yet said aloud—and reached for the blindfold to slide it from his eyes.

"*No.*" Jack snatched his wrist to stop him, seeing the instant disappointment and sorrow that marred Reardon's face. "But… you may take your king, my prince," Jack conceded, drawing Reardon's hand away from the scarf and down between their legs, lower than their connected hardness to where Jack was willingly spread and inviting him in. "You may yet change my mind."

Reardon trembled once more as his fingers grazed the puckered skin.

"The oil is at your right," Jack said. "Make all the mess of me and my bed as you wish."

However Reardon had hoped his performance would end, Jack knew it hadn't been this, but he took what he was offered, found the oil, and coated his fingers.

There was many a stable boy, nobleman, or passing nobody who'd had Jack bent or folded and begging for it. Demanding it, more like, since Jack had rarely if ever been sweet or needy when with others in that manner. With Reardon, however, he gave what he'd so often been given by his plaintive prince—the quick breaths and pleasured moans that meant, *Yes, this is what I want and what I need*—and let Reardon lead.

Reardon had poured more oil than needed, but that merely made the slide easier and the stretch respond faster, as his tentative but strong fingers found Jack's entrance, circled his rim, and pressed inside. Reardon knew from experience now the right pace, the right depth, and every few moments, when he asked, "Is it all right? Is it enough?" he only pushed Jack closer to catching the pleasure he chased at having Reardon inside him.

Not ready for Reardon to see him, he'd thought this would be impossible, but Reardon didn't need to see to feel Jack and bring him to the edge. He had two fingers scissoring inside Jack when he dipped down to lick up Jack's length again.

"Is it—"

"*Yes.* I won't break."

Reardon's confidence resurged with a wicked chuckle. "I wish I could see you… spread open and sprawled for my viewing. The feel of you…." He kissed Jack's tip as he continued to stretch him with harder and faster thrusts, and then sucked him in as far down his throat as he could.

Jack's cry caught on his tongue.

"Mmm… the broadness of your shoulders…." Reardon licked Jack's cock again. "The lean firmness of your muscles… it paints an appealing picture, Majesty, and one day you will let me see it."

Sliding his fingers free, Reardon returned with the push of his head, slick from the extra oil on his fingers but with a wonderful added stretch that Jack hadn't felt in ages, the stretch of his own fingers or any salacious tool he used as replacement never able to compare.

"The way feels smooth...." Reardon panted, one hand guiding his cock, knuckles grazing Jack's cheeks, and the other gripping the back of Jack's thigh as he slowly pushed in. "But...."

"*Reardon.*"

"I-I... I can't tell if you cringe, Majesty. I don't want—"

"*Take me,*" Jack echoed what Reardon had first said to him, because Jack was no virgin, and he lifted just enough to grip the wrist of the hand on Reardon's cock to squeeze and let him know he meant it. "You won't hurt me."

The bulb of Reardon's head pushed deeper inside Jack in answer, and the rest of his shaft widened where it sunk in farther, until Jack felt undeniably full.

Then Reardon pulled back to thrust inside again.

Jack moaned—and for one wild unchained moment, he wanted to tear the scarf from Reardon's eyes and let him see him.

He couldn't... he couldn't. Soon, he truly couldn't, as Reardon's thrusts sped up, the hand on his cock no longer needed and falling to Jack's thigh like the other, tilting back his hips to sheathe in deep and make Jack incapable of anything but mewling pleas for more.

Jack wished he could see Reardon's eyes in all their beautiful emerald green, but the flush to his cheeks and sweet part to his lips as he took Jack as expertly as he'd ever been taken was still breathtaking.

Reaching between his own legs again, Jack started pumping himself to the rhythm of Reardon's rocking. Reardon must have felt/ heard/sensed it, because his brow scrunched, and he asked, "Majesty, I can—" but the hesitation to reach for Jack meant his thrusting slowed.

"No," Jack huffed. "Keep on. It's everything I want. Don't stop."

Reardon listened, keeping his attention singularly focused, as Jack did the same—only Jack had the pleasure of a view. Witnessing his prince take him with such powerful force, the tingling burn growing hotter inside him and building his release quickly, made Jack cry out when he finally came, spilling over his fingers.

Hearing him finish spurred Reardon to go harder, faster, intensely claiming and thriving in it and eventually ending with him spilling hotly inside Jack too, a surprised, embarrassed look overtaking his features that Jack read all too well. Reardon hadn't warned him or asked, but Jack didn't care. That warmth was not something he would ever want to go without.

"Well done... my little prince," Jack soothed. "You are a man of many talents."

Reardon snorted, relieved as Jack wanted, and then pulling away to pitch to the side and lay exhaustedly beside him. "I would offer to wipe away our mess, Majesty," he said, "but I'm afraid I can't see."

*Brat*, Jack thought with a snort of his own, both of them tumbling into laughter. Jack wanted to let Reardon see him but also didn't, and in the end, he was too afraid to say yes. "Let me catch my breath... and I can still clean us."

Reardon nodded but couldn't dismiss his frown.

The guilt Jack felt most days was so much stronger when he made Reardon look like that. Whatever love truly was, its pull was as strong as magic and hurt just as much too.

Jack cleaned them in silence but didn't pull Reardon into a bath. He collected him in his arms and held him on the bed. He couldn't give Reardon what he wanted, but he didn't want to let him go either.

"May I ask something, Majesty?" Reardon said.

"Yes?"

"You enjoy reading romance, but you didn't know more than carnal pleasures in your youth?"

"Do I have any lost loves, you mean? No. I didn't allow myself that. It was only later, after the curse, that I began to realize what I had gone without and would never have."

"Jack," Reardon said, catching a gasp in Jack's throat at it being uttered so plainly for once, "I do love you."

Closing his eyes, Jack squeezed Reardon tighter against him. "Sometimes, my prince... I believe you."

REARDON WOKE slowly, confused at first by the large bed beneath him and the darkness when he opened his eyes. It was like waking while still within a pleasant dream.

Warm arms were wrapped around him as he lay on his side, a firm and even warmer chest against his back. Reardon smiled as he realized he'd gotten his wish and slept in the king's bed again, but this was so much better than sleeping alone, with the presence of the king not yet having turned to ice with morning.

*Morning.*

The surge of joy Reardon had begun to feel receded, replacing the warmth of the king with increasing cold.

"Majesty!" Reardon cried, realizing what was about to happen and struggling to get away and rouse the king before—

"Hm?"

—the sun finished rising outside the castle walls, with Reardon left scrambling to escape, blind and desperate and feeling the worst pain of his life crack like whips across his back, so cold it *burned*.

Reardon screamed.

# CHAPTER 10

*No!* JACK thought as he snapped awake—*awake*, because he'd allowed himself to sleep beside Reardon in an unthinking act of carelessness, and now it was morning!

He cringed, an extra spike of pain shooting through his body at his futile attempt to stave off the change, being twisted and hunched and covered in stinging cold as the ice took him. He was still on the bed, for the first time in all the decades since the curse was cast, causing him to freeze a part of his one human sanctuary, destroying the sheets, and then the bedpost that he reached for to get up and away as fast as he could.

It was too late, though, he knew, because he'd been wrapped around Reardon when the curse took hold, and he'd heard the prince scream.

Transformed and frosting everything around him in his distress, Jack stood, unable to move farther at first save the tremors wracking his limbs, knowing what had to be on the other side of the bed where Reardon had fallen.

The young prince might be in pieces after his own futile scrambling, if he'd turned to ice before he landed. Even if he was whole, Jack had most certainly killed him, creating a new statue, all for one selfish act of wanting something he didn't deserve.

Clenching his icy claws, Jack forced himself to stomp around the bed. He had to see. He had to accept what he'd allowed to happen and look at Reardon—

Who was whole and not made of ice!

Jack surged forward but stopped before he got too close. Reardon was still flesh and blood, but his naked back was an angry swath of frozen skin like the worst frostbite. He was unconscious, likely from the pain, but still breathing.

"Zephyr!"

REARDON REMEMBERED pain—so much pain. He could still feel it as an awful ache across his back beneath a warm numbness as he tried to rouse and focus.

His blindfold was gone, but he was still naked, covered only by a sheet, lying facedown on a bed far smaller than the king's. There were voices around him, but not the king himself.

*Zephyr*, who'd found him.

*Oliver*, whose strong arms had carried him to wherever they were now.

*Caitlin*, barking orders, with the occasional caress of her delicate fingers rubbing something soothing over Reardon's half-sore, half-numb skin.

And others, Nigel maybe and others with elven blood, offering a healing touch.

Through the din and constant shift between feeling content, nothingness, and pain, Reardon remembered what had happened. All he could think was that the king had to be so worried, while also blaming himself, which was why his voice wasn't among the rest.

"That should stabilize him," Caitlin's voice came more clearly, Reardon finally picking up on real words, as he turned toward the sound and blinked with blurred vision. "Reardon," she said, her face swimming into view, "you're going to be fine, but the damage to your skin… it might never completely heal. How do you feel?"

"F-foggy." Reardon struggled to move his mouth.

"That's normal with everything we gave you to help the pain. Once it wears off, you shouldn't need more, the wounds are no longer open or necrotic, but…."

"Scars don't bother me." Reardon curved his mouth into a smile—or as much of one as he could manage with a heavy head. "The king? Is he…?"

"He's in his throne room," Oliver said from nearby, but Reardon couldn't lift his head to look.

Beyond Caitlin, Reardon thought he could tell where they were now, in a back corner of the alchemist tower, on a healer's bed that was almost never used, since no one in the castle ever fell ill.

"He won't go into his chambers," Oliver continued, "even with the bed destroyed and so much of it iced over already. It was strange being there. Besides Zephyr, first on the scene, Caitlin and I are the only ones to ever enter those rooms since before the curse.

"Well, besides *you*, Emerald Prince. If Zephyr hadn't fetched us so swiftly—"

"But I *was* swift," Zephyr's windswept voice interrupted whatever Oliver might have said. "And now I can tell the king that his fretting is for naught. His little prince is fine."

"Wait," Reardon croaked, turning his head the other way, though it took much effort, his mind as sluggish as if he'd drunk a bottle of wine. He wasn't certain if Zephyr's ghostly form floated before him or not, but he said, "Tell the king it's okay. Not just me. *We're* okay. Nothing has to change. I know how he must be blaming himself, but *I* don't. I have no regrets, not a one, about being in this castle or with him. Promise you'll tell him?"

Zephyr was quiet, and Reardon feared he'd already vanished until he whispered, "All right," and then he did vanish, removing some of the haziness from Reardon's eyeline.

"There are others who are worried," Oliver said, a strong hand patting Reardon's ankle. "I'll let them know. Heal well, Emerald Prince."

"Thank you."

The combination of treatments Caitlin provided were more than enough to soothe Reardon, and while some of the numbness might be as permanent as the scars he hadn't yet seen, the pain eventually ebbed. Soon he could sit up and look around, confirming where he was, though Caitlin insisted he rest and avoid lying on his back until evening.

It was annoying, staying on his front or side, but Reardon wouldn't have minded if the hours hadn't ticked by without Zephyr bringing any return message from the king. Eventually Reardon was able to stay sitting up for longer periods, and did so in the company of good friends.

Liam had come in by then too, since it was his tower. He feigned lack of concern, but Reardon knew him well enough now to notice the relief in his voice when he said, "If you can sit up and chat, I hardly believe you can't be useful and work."

"Liam," Shayla warned, sitting at Reardon's bedside with Barclay and Nigel.

Reardon smiled, but his heart wasn't in it. Although he was grateful for his friends, he ached to see only one face today.

Nigel had tried a few new tales to cheer Reardon up. Shayla had tried jokes. Barclay had excitedly told Reardon of the day's most recent experiments. None of it lifted Reardon's melancholy.

Wynn visited too, among others, even Raphael, who'd peeked his head in with a wiggle of his nose. The visits from the court members, however, made Reardon sadder, because they and his other closest friends all made up couples that he envied.

Liam and Shayla ribbed each other ceaselessly but always managed to share a warm smile that spoke of their deeper connection.

Zephyr and Nigel were lighter in their teasing and often fell into somewhat vulgar—yet adorable—promises for when night fell.

Josie and Barclay were sweet and affectionate, even during daylight hours when they couldn't touch.

And Branwen and Caitlin were just as sweet, however subdued, now that Reardon had seen them together more often. Branwen would grumble like usual, but then call her "Caity" so offhandedly, and she'd smile in a way Reardon hadn't seen any signs of his first week at the castle.

It just made Reardon more aware that one person hadn't come to visit him like the rest.

"Nigel, can you call Zephyr for me?" Reardon asked.

"Call me yourself." Zephyr appeared. Even now, Reardon forgot sometimes how easy it was to catch the Spymaster's attention.

"Are you sure the king didn't have a message for me?" Reardon asked in a small voice, feeling exposed with such a vulnerable question spoken with an audience, but then, most of his visitors had stopped by before someone finally brought him trousers.

Zephyr's features pinched, unmistakable no matter how transparent his face was. "He didn't say anything, not a word, even after I passed on what you'd said. I'm sorry."

It had been a fool's hope, knowing the king as he did now, but one mistake was not going to ruin what they had found together. "Caitlin!" Reardon called. Even tucked back from the main part of the tower, he could still see the edge of the worktables and Caitlin and Liam's bustling forms.

She leaned around the corner with an inquisitive brow.

"I feel fine. Sore and tired, but I've rested enough. Please, may I have your blessing to leave?"

"I suppose." Her brow pinched like Zephyr's. "But if you feel unwell or notice any returning pain—"

"I will come right back here. Zephyr, tell me where he is." Reardon tossed the sheets aside. He was meagerly dressed in trousers and a simple untucked shirt, but he didn't care how unkempt or casual he looked.

Shayla and Nigel both scooted back their chairs to give him room, and Barclay jumped up to help Reardon stand. Barclay's eyes widened when their skin touched.

"What is it?" Reardon asked. "Was it something important?"

His friend's face seemed alarmed and almost pale despite his dark complexion. "I, um… no, it's nothing. I just realized this must be why I kept thinking you needed more cold draught. I hate when I don't understand my visions enough to help."

"Don't blame yourself. But are you sure that's all?" Reardon had known Barclay a long time, and there was more than regret on his face.

That was fear.

"It's nothing," Barclay said again, covering his trepidation with an anxious smile. "Go see the king."

Reardon knew his friend would tell him the truth in time, but for now, he had somewhere to be.

Zephyr told him the way, and Reardon accepted the supportive nods from his friends before leaving the alchemist tower on determined feet.

JACK HAD sat on his throne for hours, staring at nothing, even when Zephyr floated in to tell him that all was well and delivered Reardon's expectedly naive message.

When Zephyr pressed for an answer, Jack had simply sent him away. He'd already known Reardon would live after seeing him on his bedchamber floor, but the cost, how close things had come to turning out so much worse, was unforgiveable. Couldn't Reardon see that?

Jack wasn't in his throne room any longer. He'd finally gotten up, only to discover the scarf that had once covered Reardon's eyes lying on the floor in front of the still-open door to his private rooms. He couldn't touch it, couldn't go into those rooms and see the damage he'd done just by being in there. He had to get away.

Maybe he should have gone to the ramparts or the garden, but his monstrous feet had brought him into the secret tunnels and to the library. More hours passed, and he hadn't turned a single page. He barely remembered what book was on his pedestal before he and Reardon had started reading together.

"Shall I have Zephyr fetch *Pillars of Virtue*?" Reardon's voice nearly caused Jack to topple over backward.

"What are you doing here?" Jack demanded, hunkered in his trench, as Reardon came in, looking weak and all manner of disheveled without a doublet or even shoes. "You should be resting. Are you mad?"

"So you keep trying to claim, Majesty, but I know what I am doing and what I want." Reardon's eyes held all their usual emerald brightness. He sat, tired and frail as he looked, right at the edge of the trench and far too close to Jack. "I'm fine," he said, as though Jack were a child needing comfort. "I really mean it about the book. I can rest sitting right here, have Zephyr fetch it, and we can—"

"Get out." Jack rose, so furious at the young prince's negligence that he could barely see clearly.

"Majesty—"

"We are no longer having audiences. Not in the mornings, not now, and not when the sun sets."

"You'd run?" Reardon yelled after him, when Jack tried to turn and flee. "You'd run like a coward and turn me away, after we—"

"After I nearly killed you?!" Jack howled back, whirling so fast and fierce, a burst of ice filled the trench about his feet, proving the threat he was to everything around him. "Yes, I'd run. I'll get as far from you as I can, until it finally sinks in that you will only find despair here, and I will not let you make me be the cause of it. I've caused enough.

"Go home." Jack swallowed the catch in his throat that Reardon's eyes filling with moisture conjured so easily. "Once you've solved your precious potion, go home. Tell your people that I will accept no more offerings. Build a new kingdom that never thinks on us again."

"No." Reardon sucked in several breaths to stay his tears. "Love can beat anything. If only you'd—"

"There is no love for you here!" Jack cried, clutching the cracks of his icy chest to indicate the hollow shell beneath. "There is nothing but a cold, unfeeling thing that wants to be left to its prison.

"There will be no more audiences. There will be no more words between us. Do not waste your time on me any longer. Finish what you started to find justice for your mother, and then. *Go. Home.*

"There is no love for you here," he said again, "only regret, only misery, and scars you didn't earn."

"I don't care about scars," Reardon choked on the sobs he could no longer keep at bay, standing on shaky legs and moving closer to Jack along the edge of the trough with tears streaming down that stopped when he got too near and froze on his cheeks. "Not mine or yours. It was an *accident*."

Jack slid backward, putting as much space between them as he could with a stride. "Next time it might be your life. If you follow me," he warned, even if the threat fell far flatter than it once would have, "it will be." He tried to make it to the tunnel entrance in only a few steps, but Reardon called brokenly after him.

"Jack, please... I love you."

Jack couldn't turn. If he did, his frozen tear tracks would be visible. "Sometimes love isn't enough."

For once, Reardon didn't follow. Even so, Jack couldn't bear being in the tunnels, in his throne room once he reached it, or near his ruined chambers. He went up to the ramparts and looked out toward the Mystic Valley, wondering if the Fairy Queen, hidden by some invisible veil that made the lands look empty, was staring back, witnessing his suffering and laughing.

"DID YOU hear us?"

Reardon blinked from gazing down at his bowl of soup. He should be starving. He hadn't eaten much of anything yesterday while recovering in the alchemist tower. He'd barely slept last night. Now it was lunchtime, his back feeling no more pain and the most scarred parts feeling nothing but numbness, yet he'd still hardly touched any food.

Jack refused to see him. He wouldn't last night or for their regular audience that morning. He was set on his words to end this and had become a retreating ice trail everywhere Reardon sought him. The only words he'd spoken were to tell Reardon once again to go home.

"Sorry, can you repeat what you were saying?" Reardon smiled somberly at his friends. He, Barclay, and Shayla had all come from the alchemist tower, where Reardon had tried to bury himself in work, but he'd been too distracted to be of much use.

The others had been fruitful, however—more than he'd realized.

"We said," Barclay explained softly, "that with only a few more ingredients and hard work for another day or two, we should finally have the right combination to identify the potion used on Caitlin's husband and your mother. We're almost there, Reardon." He smiled, but it was so obviously pitying for everything else Reardon was going through.

"That's wonderful." Reardon tried to smile back anyway. "Do we have everything we need for the final tests?"

"Some extra hemlock would be useful," Shayla said. "We've narrowed it as one of the last ingredients. I was going to forage for some after lunch."

"Would you mind if I went to get it?"

"We'll go together."

"I'd prefer to go alone."

Shayla and Barclay exchanged pensive looks.

"I'll be fine," Reardon insisted.

"Reardon," Shayla tried, "you know we don't usually allow—"

"Please, I need to think, to clear my head, and... I could use the air." Everywhere in the castle was a suffocating reminder of the king's avoidance, especially when Reardon found ice. "I'll have my weapons with me. I'll be careful, I promise."

They exchanged more troubled looks, like so many inhabitants of the castle had been acting around Reardon, as if it was his first week all over again.

He was ready to plead his case further when Shayla said, "Okay, but if you're not back in time for dinner, I'm siccing Liam after you."

Fragments of a real smile twitched at Reardon's lips, but fragments couldn't form a complete picture. "Thank you." He stood and grabbed his soup to dump it.

"Wait." Barclay reached across the table. "Maybe I should—"

"No." Reardon flinched out of reach. "Sorry, but if it's all the same, right now I don't want to know what comes next."

He expected Barclay to follow him, expected every second of his trek to collect his weapons belt and cloak that Barclay would catch up and try to stop him, or suddenly appear and grab his arm to read his future.

*Love, death, and blue eyes in a sea of white.*

It was all true, it was all *here*, but if death was how this ended, no matter how much Barclay had said things didn't have to turn out the way that sounded, then Reardon didn't want to see it coming.

He hurried out of the castle. He was rarely ever alone inside its walls, and he hadn't been alone outside since before Shayla took him on his first forage. It was the end of January now and reaching the bitterest temperatures. Besides taking his cloak, Reardon had downed an extra resistance draught to protect against the elements.

It had snowed recently, and his boots sank deep into the mounds covering the path he and Shayla took to reach the edge of the wood. He didn't have to look up to know the way, only down at his feet to keep steady. The bag slung over his shoulder would soon be filled with hemlock and whatever else he found that was deemed worthy to add to the tower stores.

Anywhere but the Frozen Kingdom, hemlock wouldn't flourish until early spring, but here, within the grounds of the castle, various greenery and flowers could be found all year round, even peeking out of snowdrifts. Reardon knew exactly where the grounds ended, because there was a hard line where that strange mix of life and death stopped. He could see it in the first line of trees, still mossy or budding, only for the second line to be completely barren.

Sometimes Reardon forgot that, technically, his weeks here hadn't aged him. Nothing here aged, and yet the seasons came and went in their own way like a mockery.

Reaching several sprigs of hemlock, almost hidden with their white flowers so similar to the snow, Reardon began to pick them as he'd been taught and carefully bundled them away. The monotonous action cleared his mind as he'd hoped, but the melancholy he felt only seemed to set in deeper.

How could he prove the king wrong if Jack wouldn't even speak to him?

Or maybe Reardon was the one who was wrong….

Only when his hands ached from the cold did he realize it had been hours, his bag full and his potion losing its potency. He glanced back at the castle up the hill, pristine and beautiful when once he'd thought it ominous. He had a duty to his own kingdom, to his mother's memory, but there was so much more he could do here.

He knew, selfishly, that the real reason he didn't want to go home was because he'd finally found his love, and in a place where no one shamed him for it.

Could he really just leave?

The crack of a stick whipped Reardon's attention back to the trees, where a pair of glowing eyes locked with his. Without moving any other part of him, Reardon slowly reached for his swords.

The glowing eyes drew nearer, and soon a familiar form stepped into the light from out of the wood—a thin but slightly less emaciated wolf than how Reardon had last seen him.

Another stick cracked, even though the wolf had stopped moving, and a second wolf slipped out from behind the first. This wolf was smaller but still fully grown, a *mate*, if Reardon were to guess, judging by the way it nudged the larger wolf's side and then began to growl at Reardon.

But the first wolf nudged back and didn't growl in kind, as if to say, *No, there is nothing to fear.* The wolf that had nearly killed Reardon all those weeks ago had been healed, nourished, and left in peace to try at survival again, and with that gift, he'd found another.

"Mercy begets mercy…," Reardon said softly, thinking this a very magical place indeed. "I am happy for you, lone wolf, that you're not alone anymore."

The wolves' heads snapped back into the wood, picking up on something Reardon couldn't hear, and then they took off running the opposite direction down the line of trees.

Reardon hefted the bag over his shoulder, turned where the wolves had looked, and finished drawing his swords all in one smooth sequence. He feared a bear, if the wolves were running, but in the darkness of the trees, the figure coming toward Reardon appeared to be a man.

Memory of the original sacrifice struck Reardon all at once, who he'd let wander into those woods alone. Could it be him, running from a horde of monsters he'd found once he reached the Shadow Lands?

"Here!" Reardon called, waving one of his swords in greeting. "Are you well? Do you need help?"

The figure kept hurtling toward him, the wood so dark, Reardon couldn't make out anything save his outline, but it was definitely a man. Reardon started to put his swords away but hesitated.

"Hello?" he questioned, because the man hadn't called back, and it was only when he burst from the line of trees that Reardon saw him fully—*not* the sacrifice he'd saved but a dirty and wild-looking highwayman with a dagger drawn as he pitched himself at Reardon.

Reardon swung his swords up in an X that caught the dagger before it struck him.

"Stop! What do you want? I—!"

The man howled, hair bedraggled and beard so bushy, Reardon could barely see his eyes. The man pulled his dagger free and swung at

Reardon's side, but Reardon brought his swords sharply to the right to deflect the blow, parrying the man once more.

"Listen! If you need coin—"

The man rushed him while Reardon's swords were pointed down, using his body to knock Reardon off balance. The potion might have kept Reardon's feet from slipping normally, but it had long since waned, and the slickness of the snow sent him tumbling backward. The man fell upon him, and Reardon barely managed to get his swords up into another X to stay a downward plunge of the dagger.

"Please!"

And then a sharp pain stabbed into Reardon's side—from a *second* dagger he hadn't seen. Reardon pushed with the force of his connected swords to throw the man off him, but the second dagger stayed in his side, abandoned and dug in deep to the hilt. Reardon easily could have bested the man, but he hadn't wanted to hurt him.

*Mercy merely means you might end up the dead man instead*, he heard in Lombard's voice.

A howl from the man broke the afternoon quiet, as he swung the first dagger over his head to fall upon Reardon yet again—

—only to be caught, mid-leap, by his throat in an *icy* grasp.

The effect was instant, a wave washing over the man as if he were a matte surface on the ground and someone had spilled a bottle of oil that burst over him, catching rainbow colors in the light. But it wasn't oil, and the man was far more than a soiled floor, dead now, turned to ice.

His neck cracked as the Ice King tightened his grip and threw the frozen highwayman into the snow, where he broke into dozens of shattered pieces. Reardon's stomach lurched, but then he hissed, because the real pain was buried deep in his side, and there was no time to mourn the madman who'd attacked him.

"You fool," the king said, his hulking form towering over Reardon.

"Y-you… came for me," Reardon sputtered, vision dimming and the chill of the snow feeling strangely warm.

He must have passed out, though he remembered rousing when someone lifted him, then again from the bob of his body being carried up stairs, and once more with Caitlin's face hovering. The sun was far from set, so the king must have fetched someone to rescue Reardon.

Time drifted like a lazy river, until at last, Reardon sprang awake fully to find himself in his own bed.

"Jack," he exhaled, wishing so desperately to see him.

Had he dreamed it all? But no, he wore only loose trousers with his chest bare, and there were bandages about his waist where the dagger had pierced him. It was after dark now, and only a lone candle flickered on his nightstand.

"You fool," the king answered, echoing his words from before, but his voice was different now—*human.*

Human and in Reardon's room.

A rush of air came at Reardon, upsetting the candle and casting overlapping shadows and light over the face of a man, right there above him, with firm hands planted on either side of Reardon's shoulders upon the bed.

"Why do you keep putting yourself in danger to save someone who doesn't want to be saved?"

Reardon stared. The wolf? The bandit? But no, he knew the truth. Because he could finally *see* him—the man who didn't want to be saved.

"Jack…," Reardon whispered with trembling hands reaching up to cup that elusive face.

The scars felt the same beneath Reardon's palms as when he was blindfolded, and the eyes, oh, those eyes could belong to no one else. Now the rest of the picture was painted before Reardon in candlelight.

Jack tried to pull away, eyes darting to the sheets as if he wished he could hide, having allowed this without meaning to, it seemed, but Reardon held firm.

His features were perfectly symmetrical—straight nose, high cheekbones, firm jaw—with wavy locks of snow-white falling into his eyes, even with white eyebrows, like a lasting part of the curse clinging to him even at night, same with the scars that covered so much of him.

Reardon had been prepared from what he felt, but now he could see them—over Jack's lips, his eyebrows, everywhere. No battle-hardened warrior knight could compete with all that damage.

But to Reardon, he was beautiful. The scar tissue, the despair in his eyes that he didn't deserve to feel, none of that mattered. Reardon took in everything before him and loved it all. He would wipe that despair away and prove to Jack that he was right.

"I loved you before I knew anything more than the wonder of your eyes. Now I can say without falter, *Jack…* that I love you, *all* of you, and I will never stop trying to save you." Reardon stroked his thumbs over Jack's cheeks and pulled him down, forcing Jack's eyes to meet his. "Thank you. For saving me, and for giving me this." He kissed him, closing his eyes only for a moment, and then drew away to look at Jack again.

Maybe Reardon was blinded by love. Maybe loving someone made them beautiful regardless. Either way, though Reardon knew he could never understand the grief Jack felt or why he'd hid for so long, that wasn't his duty. His duty was simply to love Jack and to show him that love however he could.

"Please, my king, believe me this time when I say—I love you."


JACK HADN'T thought, hadn't paused even for a moment to consider what he was allowing, until it was too late. Reardon had seen him now, but he'd done nothing more than smile and kiss Jack in the aftermath.

No one else had seen Jack. Others had come for Reardon at the tree line, carried him and cared for him until his wound was closed. Only after it was deemed safe to leave Reardon in his bed did Jack tell everyone to stay away so that, once the sun set, he could enter Reardon's room as himself.

He'd wanted to berate him, to end this once and for all, to scream at Reardon all the reasons why this would never turn out the way he wanted. But now Reardon was looking into his eyes while holding his face—his *human* face, scarred with all the wrongs he'd committed during life, and Reardon still said the same words.

"I love you."

How he could see Jack and still say that?

"Don't push me away. Don't tell me to go home. Let me show you that this curse can be broken if only you'd let me melt the ice caging your heart." Reardon's hold on Jack's face became gentler, loose enough that Jack could have pulled away if he'd truly tried, but then Reardon slid one hand to the back of Jack's neck and drew him down again.

His lips were always soft and warm. Jack had feared, with so many scars covering him, that knowing someone's touch again would be the real curse, because he wouldn't be able to feel it through the numbness. But he could feel Reardon, every nerve igniting at the barest brush of skin.

Jack clambered up onto the bed to get closer, falling deeper into the kiss. The covers had fallen to Reardon's waist, and Jack climbed atop him in the mere trousers and shirt he'd snatched from his chambers before diving back into the tunnels to get here. Reardon was in trousers only, but Jack's hands sliding from the mattress to his chest and lean stomach reminded him of the bandages where he'd been stabbed.

"You're hurt," Jack panted between delves of their tongues.

"Then you... will be gentle," Reardon panted back and dug his fingers into Jack's hair to bring him down again.

Jack had to be gentle. He could be gentle. Reardon was strong and could usually handle however Jack might flip him or roughly pin him to the bed, but no matter how effective the healing potion Caitlin had given him, Jack had to be gentle now, unless he was willing to walk away, and he... he couldn't.

He should. He should retreat and end this, but the thought of that hurt more than any jagged pierces of ice entering into his skin when morning came.

Keeping his hands on the bed or tentative down Reardon's hips, mindful of the wound in his side, Jack straddled the prince's waist and ground into him, kissing him deeply once more. Each twirl of Reardon's tongue was rapture, though he always pulled away between presses of their mouths to look at Jack and smile again before he claimed his lips with another press.

The longing in Reardon's emerald eyes spurred Jack to sink against him. Reardon shoved his trousers down, and then shoved Jack's down too, clawing at Jack's shirt like he'd never been so desperate to be rid of clothing. Jack tore and kicked it all away, until they were bare and grinding and kicking down the covers too.

But Reardon stopped, grabbed hold of Jack, and rolled them. He spread Jack out, taking in the full form of him, head to toe, like taking nourishment in the view.

Jack hadn't had anyone's eyes on him this intimately since before the curse. The rest of his body was as scarred as his face, worse, and even the hair between his legs had been turned white from the ice so deep-seated within him when once he'd been as brunette as Josie.

Reardon saw it all and continued to smile, no guile, just contentment, as he drew a hand from Jack's face down his neck and chest and hips to his thighs, and then farther between his legs. Jack gasped as the prince's fingers curled around his length. It was hardly the first time Reardon had touched him, but it was the first time with his eyes on him.

Slowly, Reardon started to stroke, shifting closer to lift one leg over Jack's hips and straddle his thigh—only to hiss and fall back with a twinge.

Jack moved after him, concerned at first, but then amused by Reardon's pout. Carefully, Jack pulled Reardon to him, but it was then that he felt the far too similar scars covering Reardon's back.

Jack ran a hand up and down the expanse. Across Reardon's shoulder blades, down the center, and as low as his waist, the scars Jack had caused could be felt like the surface of an oil painting. Jack didn't have to see them to know how they must look, so like his own bare skin.

"Reardon...."

"I don't care," Reardon said, smoothing a palm over Jack's chest and resting it over his heart. "All that matters is this."

Jack's heart was beating wildly, and as he slid his hand from Reardon's back to mimic the gesture, he felt Reardon's pounding just as fierce.

He rolled Reardon onto his back, Reardon's hand returning to between Jack's legs and joined by Jack's own, connecting their heated cocks. With Reardon sprawled and comfortable, Jack straddled the prince's thigh instead, rocking their slick lengths together while his hand curled around Reardon and Reardon's remained on him.

It was a synchronized clash of fervent pumping through budding wetness, with only so much movement allowed without risk of hurting Reardon, but it was enough. Anytime Reardon's eyes closed, they opened again, locking on Jack's or straying down his body. He truly seemed to love and want everything he saw, even though Jack was ruined and had ruined him too.

"*Reardon*," Jack gasped again, foregoing the use of his hand to rut with more urgency, half at Reardon's side and half atop him, thrusting with a maddened need to release while those emerald eyes were on him.

"Jack... oh, Jack," Reardon mewled back, weak and struggling for breath but still pumping upward to meet him. His hand fell away too, leaving them as two mindlessly grinding bodies, slick with sweat and the moisture from their cocks, until Reardon's gasps grew harsher, and then Jack's did too, and they finished, almost overlapping.

"I love you," Jack said, too caught up in the moment to hold the words back.

The smile Reardon graced him with was more breathtaking than any Jack had yet seen. Reardon took Jack's face in his hands once more, kissed him again, and held him close, never once believing that this bliss between them wouldn't last.

Jack knew better, but oh, how he wished it could.


REARDON AWOKE with a creeping feeling of déjà vu, but there was no body wrapped around him and no increasing pain from deadly cold.

Of course, Jack hadn't stayed in bed with him after what happened last time, but when Reardon rolled over, he found Jack, human still, sitting in a chair and looking at Reardon with a soft expression.

They'd done it, Jack would see. The curse was lifted now that Jack had confessed his love for Reardon and....

And....

And then the sun rose outside the castle walls, prompting Jack to stand with a wince and move for the door so he wouldn't leave too long an ice trail when the curse finished taking him and remade him into the beast.

Take him it did, the first time Reardon had seen the change happen, when he had thought... he had hoped that he could be enough to end it.

It looked so painful, the strain on Jack's face and tension in his steps that stuttered and stopped when he reached the door. His beautiful, scarred, naked body seemed to grow the ice out of itself, stretching and deforming him and causing Reardon to shiver from the expulsion of cold and pull the covers tighter around him.

The Ice King wasn't ugly to him, never had been, but now the sight of him made Reardon's heart sink. Jack looking back at him with so much sorrow and shame in his expression only made it worse.

"But I... I love you," Reardon said miserably.

"And I you," Jack repeated without taking back the words he'd said last night, "but as I told you, my little prince, sometimes love isn't enough."

He left, and Reardon stared at his now iced-over doorknob, wondering what he'd done wrong to fail his love so terribly.

# CHAPTER 11

"LIAR!" REARDON kicked the gate leading out to the Mystic Valley.

He had bathed and dressed and carefully removed the bandages protecting wounds that potions had already healed to smooth scar tissue, but every monotonous act only fueled his rage.

"Witch!" he cried, because this was the Fairy Queen's fault! She cast the curse without following her own rules! "Why are you doing this to him?" He kicked the gate again, and then grabbed its bars and shook them in his fury, nearly upsetting the frozen-over latch.

"*My*, you have a temper."

Reardon reared back with a gasp, instinct bringing his hands to his hilts, as he looked up—upon a radiant figure perched on the castle wall.

Reardon had heard stories of the power and beauty of the queen of elves—beauty that could swindle and corrupt, for the tales painted all elves and anyone with magic as sinister and vile. He hadn't believed it, but his anger at her now made him wonder if those stories were true.

She certainly was beautiful. Dark skin and eyes, her hair in lovely long waves pinned even more intricately than Shayla's and twisted into a thick braid over one shoulder. Within her hair were flowers and delicate vines, as well as a crown of golden antlers that could easily have been mistaken for demon horns. Her gown was made of such rich shades of violet, indigo, and blue that the silk flowing from her skirts and sleeves did indeed make her look more like a fairy than an elf.

She had no wings, however, just her pointed ears, adorned in cuffs of glittering gold that matched her crown. She looked as much like a goddess of the wood as a high queen. The only exception was her dainty feet, bare beneath her skirts as she dangled them from her spot on the wall. She was smiling, but Reardon held his guard. He had never believed his angry ranting would actually reach her.

"You mean to mock me?" He clenched his jaw to keep from stuttering, hands still on the hilts of his swords, even if a swipe of steel might mean nothing against her magic.

"I mean to talk to you, Emerald Prince. It hasn't been often enough that you've come this close to my gate."

"As if you'd need such formality, *Majesty*."

She clicked her tongue at him, leaning back on the wall, as if she weren't an ethereal vision, but a simple peasant girl enjoying a nice day outdoors. "Such venom. No need to call me that, or 'Fairy Queen.' Those are just titles. May I call you Reardon? Because please, call me Mavis."

The tension in Reardon's stance faltered. It was said that true names could be powerful among those who wielded magic. Had she given him hers?

But then, Reardon had no magic himself, only science, and only his swords and dagger on him now.

"You wish to talk to me? Why?"

"It seemed you wished to talk to *me*."

Reardon fidgeted in the snow. "I thought you had long since moved from these lands, but the king implied you were still out there. It all looks empty." He glanced through the bars of the gate.

A thud drew his attention back to her, where she stood in the snow, having leapt from the wall, her bare feet hidden by her gown. Being so close to a figure he had thought mythical only a few weeks prior reminded him of when he first met the Ice King.

With her glowing smile, she opened her arms, gesturing him to her. He hesitated but figured he had nothing to lose.

Her hands were warm as one curled around his back to lead him forward, the other taking one of his hands to wrap around a single bar of the gate. As soon as his fingers closed, it was like being thrown through the castle wall, hurtling blindingly fast down the hill and into the valley below.

Reardon knew his feet hadn't left the castle grounds, but he saw it all as if he had, like a soaring eagle. Reaching the edge of the valley that indeed looked abandoned like the Frozen Kingdom's adjoining city and villages, ripples appeared in front of Reardon. The ripples parted like the sheer drapes of the king's bedchamber, revealing so much beyond the veil that he could hardly take it all in.

Cities and towns stretched there too, but bustling ones, both outside the forest edges and within. The woods there were lush and magical, far removed from the Shadow Lands on the other side of the king's hill, with all sorts of dazzling sights in every direction.

There were humans, elves, half-elves. Reardon thought he even saw fairies—real fairies—dancing in the wind. He realized, however, that among all the people he saw, no one ever drew close to the veil. He assumed it was so that they wouldn't be seen by those outside it, but realization grew within him that they were in fact trapped. Happy with their lot but unable to leave.

His vision zoomed forward again to a glittering castle, then inside, where he saw the Fairy Queen's throne. She sat upon it, eyes closed, as if to show Reardon that the real her was there, and the one with him was a phantom.

Beside her throne was a smaller one with a human man in equal finery to hers but with a smaller antlered crown. He was handsome, gazing adoringly up at her, blond and blue-eyed, but clean-shaven and far more sweet-faced than Oliver or Liam. If that was her husband, Prince Consort to her kingdom, then Reardon understood why a younger Jack had tried to court him.

"You too, hm?"

All at once, Reardon returned to himself, staring at his hand on the bars.

"I think he's quite handsome too," she said, "but he is taken."

Reardon pulled back, shrinking away from her and turning to look upon her form once more. "You're not real?"

"I'm real. Think of it as a long-distance conversation with a nicer view."

"Why can't you leave the valley?"

"I can't tell you that, I'm afraid." She cringed. "Magic has its rules. But I can tell you to not give up. This kingdom, yours, and mine all have something to gain. King John told you the words of the curse?"

Reardon's heart was still racing from the rush of all he had seen, and he was skeptical that he could trust the source of all this misery. "Yes. I don't remember exactly, but… I know he said you told the others that when his heart melts and he is a true king, the spell will be broken." He felt his anger resurface at the memory and spat back at her, "Is loving me not enough to prove his heart has melted?"

"Toward you?" she said, soft and compassionate. "Toward his people, his family, and friends? Of course. But a true king sees value in himself too."

"He... he loves me, and he is a good king, but he doesn't believe he's worthy of either. I should have known. The ice that remains is because he has yet to forgive himself."

"Yes."

"Then I will continue to prove to him that he is wrong." Reardon squared his shoulders before the Fairy Queen—*Mavis*. "But that does not absolve you. This curse is cruel and unfair."

She tilted her head, a sad smile upon her lips. "You keep looking for a hero in this story. We simply all made choices, and I do not regret mine."

"Then hero or no hero, *you* are the villain," Reardon snarled. "Jack is a good king, but you trapped him in a life he never wanted."

"He had to accept responsibility. After his father died, as the new king of these lands, he could have changed anything he wanted. He could have taken a prince, if that was his desire, changed the laws to pass his kingdom to his sister, renounced the throne for another leader to take his place. Instead, he chose to be carousing, irresponsible, and apathetic, and he has paid for it."

"And his sister and friends and far too many others paid for it too!"

Still, she did not rise to Reardon's challenge, her voice calm. "Are they so miserable, or have they each found their own happiness?"

"That isn't enough. What of those who died unjustly? The accidents? What of all the years lost? What about *my* kingdom? All this only perpetuated a fear of magic and the idea that people are disposable."

"Those choices are the responsibility of those who made them, but not everything is as it seems, Emerald Prince. This was never meant to have gone on for so long." Again, she looked sad, even though she said she wasn't regretful. "My magic is not infallible. I cannot explain everything, but I came to tell you that the curse can be lifted. You must do what the Sapphire King could not and trust—"

"Reardon!"

Reardon's attention snapped away from her toward Oliver, racing from the castle, followed by a dozen of the strongest fighters Reardon knew, all armed, with Barclay trailing behind in a hurry.

They must have seen—

He startled when he turned back to Mavis, because she was gone, and he somehow knew that if he told the others about his audience with the Fairy Queen, none would say they had seen any sign she had been there.

Trust? Trust what?

Trust *who*?

"What's happened?" Reardon asked of the others when they joined him at the west gate.

"Emerald banners," Oliver said with a hard edge, bow in hand. "There is a platoon approaching the castle."

"It's Lombard," Barclay panted. "He's leading them. The soldier must have told Lombard the truth, or he didn't believe him."

Reardon had known it was only a matter of time, but he hadn't believed Lombard would bring fifty men to counter the initial two.

"If they try to get in, we'll have to open fire," Oliver said. "They won't understand. They expect monsters here, and honestly, we need them to believe that. If they find only a hundred simple people trying to live their lives, and five poor cursed souls, they'll wipe us all out as easily as they sent us here as sacrifices."

They would. They would assume everyone here was bewitched, the elves and half-elves worthy of death simply for what they were. Reardon had only been thinking of Barclay when he came here, but he had stayed for selfish reasons, and now, disaster was at the gates.

"I'll talk to them."

"You can't." Oliver grabbed Reardon's arm before he could move past them. "I promised the king I would never let anything else happen to you."

The earnest admission made Reardon smile. He had been lucky; the only reason he hadn't frozen on the spot the other morning was because the king hadn't been fully transformed when he pulled away. If it hadn't been for Oliver and Caitlin, and Zephyr who fetched them, Reardon still might have died from the shock or been far worse off than merely scarred. Then Oliver had saved Reardon again when he carried him from the edge of the wood after being stabbed.

"You won't fail that promise," Reardon swore to him, gripping his forearm in kind. "Lombard would never hurt me."

"Reardon, wait." Barclay grabbed after him, not gasping at the contact but taking in a deep breath as a new vision appeared to wash through him.

No, not new, Reardon realized. The resignation on Barclay's face said it was one he had seen before.

"I don't know what it means, or how to prevent it, but what I saw yesterday, and what I just saw again… was everyone in this castle dead." Barclay let the weight of that sink in, twisting Reardon's insides with nausea. "It was carnage, everything completely razed, but you… you had a shadow over you, like the future is not yet set. I saw your father, Lombard, and Master Wells. Wells was making a potion…."

"The counter potion?" Reardon pressed. The High Alchemist was gifted. Perhaps, with his help, Reardon could finally succeed in solving his mother's death.

Barclay didn't answer, seeming unsure, but Reardon felt more resolute than ever.

"That's why I have to go." He pulled Barclay in tight against him, embracing his friend like he had the last time he saw him in Emerald before the guards took Barclay away. "If I don't, they'll storm in and prove that vision true, but I can stop it."

"Open the gates!" Lombard's voice rang from the castle entrance. "We know you have our prince! You were given your allotted sacrifice! Now, release the prince at once!"

"You see?" Reardon squeezed Barclay once more before pulling away. "It'll be all right. Lombard thinks I've been kidnapped. He'll see reason if I go out there. I was always going to have to go home to explain, to change my father's mind. Please, don't stop me." Reardon gazed imploringly at Barclay, and then at Oliver.

Oliver nodded.

"Wait," Barclay said again, but when Reardon readied a protest, all his friend did was push a piece of parchment into his hands. "Take this. It's my notes on the last version of the potion. It's not finished. We know we're still missing something, but if you don't come back…."

"I will come back," Reardon promised but still took the parchment, tucking it into his cloak.

He looked up at the castle. Much as he longed to see a familiar hulking form, he knew it would be foolish for the king to be up on the ramparts. There was the brief blur of movement anyway, but that was others staying hidden while readying bows on Oliver's orders, no doubt. The king was nowhere to be seen.

Reardon hoped Jack understood.

With his swords, dagger, and cloak, Reardon didn't need to return to his room, and there wasn't time if he'd wanted to. He believed, however, as he finally made for the gates, that someday soon, he would return.


STAYING OUT of sight when strangers were within eyeline of the castle was one of the Frozen Kingdom's most important tenets. Let all who would look upon their prison from afar think it a mystery too terrifying to breach.

Jack followed that rule now, but that didn't mean he wasn't watching from his throne room, remaining carefully in the shadows, as Reardon marched to the castle entrance.

Jack hadn't slept at all the other night, just cleaned what he could of his chambers and turned his bed into kindling, so that now he had nothing in that spot anymore where a bed had once been. He didn't need sleep, after all, and he hoped he never dreamed again.

"Zephyr," Jack said low beneath his breath, "carry their words to me."

Without turning to see Zephyr appear or obey, Jack felt the rush of a bitter breeze, and with it came the distant voices of those at the gates.

Reardon was a smart prince, ensuring the entrance closed behind him quickly so that none of the soldiers outside could catch too much of a glimpse of the castle grounds—though the ice sculptures were difficult to miss.

Jack saw many of the men shift uneasily on their horses.

"General Lombard!" Reardon called to the armored man at the front, who wore a full helmet that obscured his face.

*Lombard.*

"There's no need to go any farther. I am not a prisoner, and I will return with you. We shall retreat now, for I have much to discuss with my father."

The soldiers shifted once more, only Lombard holding firm as he looked down on Reardon from his horse.

"This place is known for dark magic," Lombard said, "and you have been gone for weeks. Prove you are our prince."

*Not a fool*, Jack thought, and Reardon wisely nodded, understanding Lombard's cynicism.

At first raising his hands to show he held no weapons, Reardon slowly reached down to retrieve his dagger and held it aloft. "When you gave me this on my eighteenth birthday, you told me to keep it close, always. I may have misplaced it a time or two, Bardy, but I did not fail you."

There was a long pause, yet Lombard must have deemed the dagger and Reardon's words enough, for he dismounted, removed his helmet to set it on his saddle, and approached Reardon.

He was handsome, about Reardon's same height, like Jack, and built similarly too. He was older, a few years older than Jack had been before the curse, but proud and dashing.

As Lombard neared Reardon, Jack was ready to leap from the window and launch an icy attack if this was a trick, but all the man did was loose his hands from the hilts of his weapons and embrace Reardon boldly.

"I have missed you, my prince."

Reardon hugged him back just as tightly. "I missed you too. Let's go home."

A stinging chill pierced Jack's chest like the first rays of dawn.

Lombard led Reardon to his horse, replaced his helmet, and helped Reardon into the saddle behind him. Reardon was leaving without a fuss—without saying goodbye.

"Majesty!"

Jack turned slowly to the entrance of his throne room. It was Oliver, and Jack expected to see Zephyr, but Josie and the rest of the court had arrived too.

"Barclay had a vision," Oliver said. "The prince believes he must return to the Emerald Kingdom to prevent a war. I have my men on the ramparts, awaiting orders. What should we do?"

*War?* Maybe that was true, but Reardon would have had to go eventually anyway. "There is no need to fire on them or pursue. The prince is going of his own accord. Now leave me." Jack turned back to the window to watch the retreating horses.

Not once did Reardon turn back, but held on to Lombard's waist.

Jack could no longer hear them, and the eerie silence dug the ice in his chest deeper.

"It's a ruse," Zephyr said. "To bide time and speak with his father."

"We didn't finish the potion," Liam announced. "He has to come back."

"Of course he's coming back," Branwen growled.

Jack didn't say anything.

"Jack?" Josie spoke more softly than the others.

Still Jack said nothing, staring after the emerald banners until they were but specks in the distance. He heard the others start to leave and finally turned his head again.

"Oliver," Jack called, halting the fletcher's leave. "Accompany me to the library to replace the book on the pedestal." He nodded to *Pillars of Virtue* lying closed but with its page marked with ribbon on the steps leading up to his throne. "I would like to read today."

"Of course, Majesty," Oliver said. "Zephyr...."

"I'll let the archers know to stand down." Zephyr nodded and vanished with a frown.

Josie, Liam, and Branwen were all without words as Oliver came forward to do as Jack had asked. Slowly, Jack trudged into the tunnels with Oliver following. There was no point in waiting for Reardon to finish the book, and besides, Jack knew how the story went. It was not a happily ever after between star-crossed lovers but came to a practical end.

Like everything in the real world.


REARDON HAD nearly forgotten the drudgery of the days' travel to and from the Frozen Kingdom. Almost three days normally, and still a long two if moving swiftly, the journey was grueling. Reardon had no potion with him to help against the cold, only his cloak and extra blankets packed by the soldiers.

The heat of Lombard's body helped more than any blanket draped over his shoulders, but even that heat wasn't much comfort, because the chill in Reardon's heart grew colder the farther they got from the castle.

They rode all day, with minimal stops, and not once did Lombard ask anything about Reardon's time away. Reardon couldn't tell him the truth anyway. He'd promised to keep the secrets of the castle and its curse until he saved them from it.

Reardon had to foster change, prove all was well, and return to Jack to break the curse once and for all.

At nightfall, as they set up camp, Reardon felt exhausted but couldn't imagine curling up on a bedroll yet to sleep. He sat by a separate fire, asking the others to give him space, so he could study Barclay's notes.

Something was missing from what they'd experimented on so far, but he couldn't figure out what. More testing would have led them to the answer eventually, but Reardon didn't have that luxury on the road. Hopefully, Master Wells could help him.

"May I join you, my prince?" Lombard came over, prompting Reardon to tuck the parchment away. "I know you requested solitude, but—"

"It's all right," Reardon said, smiling as the general sat beside him on the blanket he'd placed before the fire. "I don't mean to act like a brat and refuse the company of my own soldiers, I just needed time to think. I know I need to sleep."

"You do, but there is something we need to discuss." Lombard's tone drew Reardon's eyes to his face, the firelight flickering over his handsome features. "I wanted to be sure we had put at least a day's travel between us and that... place, before I told you the truth."

"Has something happened?"

"We weren't sure what to think when you went missing. I sent soldiers to pick up your trail."

"And I sent one back to explain that I was safe. Why did you not listen?"

Lombard turned to Reardon with greater worry on his face. "My prince, neither soldier ever returned. That is why I followed."

"But I...." Reardon trailed off, realizing how foolish it was to send a lone man on such a long journey, especially one so young, armed or otherwise. "Something must have happened to him. You're sure he never made it?"

"Master Wells didn't report anything. They were meant to see him first upon their return, in case they had been enchanted."

Then that was a second life Reardon felt on his conscience more than he would ever blame another. "There are highwaymen about, wolves. I should have gone with him."

"I am glad at least that *you* are safe, but the fate of my soldiers is not all I need to tell you." Lombard closed his eyes as if greatly pained. "My deepest sympathies, my prince, but your father has fallen ill."

"What?"

"It seems to be very like what killed your mother, only working slower. We know that's why the Ice King took you along with the other sacrifice."

"No, I...." Now Reardon clenched his eyes in pain, because he had set all this in motion. "That is not what happened. I traded places with the sacrifice. I followed you that day and chose to go to the Ice King's castle. He and his people have nothing to do with whatever is happening to my father."

"You can't know that," Lombard said staunchly. "The Ice King's power is vast. Has he bewitched your mind—"

"*No*," Reardon said again, turning to face his mentor fully. "Bardy, I swear. That castle, that fallen kingdom, is not what you think. I wish I could tell you more...."

"Then tell me. If it is not dark magic cursing your father, then what?"

"I don't know exactly, but it isn't magic. It's alchemy, and I've been working on figuring out the exact ingredients. If I can finish a copy of the potion, maybe I can reverse it to save my father and find whoever did this. And who first did it to my mother."

So often was Lombard the voice of reason trying to pull Reardon back from his musings and the rants he used to throw at his father, but the furrow to his brow was contemplative now, not dismissive. "You're certain? You're close to having proof? Some sort of... potion caused it all, even without leaving traces?"

"There is no doubt in my mind. I should have stayed in the Frozen Kingdom." Reardon lamented the distance between him and the castle now. "I was so close to finishing what I'd started. But I may be able to finish the potion at home, with Master Wells's help. I must. My father...." He returned to Lombard in trepidation. "How bad is it?"

"He was bedridden when we left, but Wells and the physicians believed he had several more days, if not weeks, before the situation would be dire."

Reardon sighed in relief. There was time. "Trust me, then, please? When this is over, I will tell you everything."

Lombard scanned Reardon like he had upon his horse before accepting him as the prince he knew. "You look cared for, well-dressed and well-armed, and you don't seem as though you've been bewitched. Yes, my prince, I will trust you, but you must know that no matter the truth, you are treading dangerous territory."

"I know, but if I'm right—about a number of things—it will be worth it."

Trusting in Reardon as he always had, Lombard nodded. "I'm glad you are well," he said again and rested one of his cool bare hands atop Reardon's between them, far more intimate than Reardon could ever remember him allowing before.

The contact made heat rush to Reardon's cheeks, his heart beating rapidly despite himself, unable to deny the pull Lombard had always had on him. "I-I'm glad you're well too," he stammered.

Their eyes met, and in the firelight, with so much darkness around them, Lombard's face and golden hair looked almost... white.

He pulled his hand from Reardon's and stood, like he hadn't meant to be so uncouth. "Sleep, my prince," Lombard said, leaving Reardon with guilt stirring unbidden in his stomach. "If we ride hard tomorrow, we'll reach Emerald before nightfall."

A KNOCK drew Jack's attention from where he leaned against his desk, staring at where his bed had once been. Even a few days ago, with the sun set, he would have yelled at whoever dared disturb him.

Now... nothing seemed to matter.

He opened the door without hesitation. "Yes?"

"Jack!" Josie exclaimed, standing on the other side of the door with an expression of shock, carrying two brightly colored doublets over her arm. "I didn't think you'd actually... oh, Jack." She dove forward, throwing her free arm around his neck to pull him close.

He had forgotten how beautiful she was, with her long locks of brunette waves, and the feel of her was such a different comfort than Reardon's embrace.

He'd missed it.

Tears filled Josie's eyes that she wiped away, but then she returned her hand to the back of Jack's neck and hugged him again, before moving her palm to his scarred cheek. "You never needed to hide this from us, from me."

"You all have enough reminders of what I did to us." Jack's voice came out hoarse from disuse the past couple days. He hadn't realized how much more talking he'd been doing with Reardon around.

His sister's eyes, blue like his own, held only sympathy and love. "Will you never believe the fault was not yours alone?"

"Not likely," he tried to say with levity, twitching a grin at her.

She laughed but swatted his chest. "Not funny. However, if I'm allowed to have a true audience with my big brother at last, then even better than dropping this off at your door, I insist you try it on for me."

"Try it on?" Jack frowned as she breezed past him into the chambers. He shut the door and watched as she laid the doublets on his desk.

Jack recognized them now—or the fabric and thread they'd once been when Reardon asked his opinion on their embroidery. One was emerald green with yellow gold, the other sapphire blue with white.

"The green one's Reardon's, obviously," Josie said. "He didn't get to finish it himself, so I did it for him. I thought it would be a nice gift for when he returns."

"Josie…."

"The blue is yours." She turned back with a haughty smile that allowed no reproach. "He made sure to finish that one first, but didn't want to give it to you until his was also done. I'm sure he won't mind me giving it to you early if you wear it when he comes through those gates again. Now, let me see how it looks on you."

The certainty in her words left Jack too brokenhearted to refuse. "Allow me to change into something that will match better at least." He rarely took much stock in what he wore, only bothering with clothes because he felt wrong without them while human at night—when he wasn't in bed with Reardon.

After selecting a white shirt, black trousers, and his nicest pair of black leather boots, Jack returned, allowing Josie to help him tie up the doublet. For a prince, Reardon was a good tailor, seen in the intricate embroidery and even stitch work.

The doublet fit Jack well, and after finishing the ties, Josie stood back to take him in without any sign that his scars or white hair distorted the kingly picture.

"I wish you could see yourself," she said. "We could always go out to find a mirror."

"I'm not up for that." Jack smiled at her attempt.

"Next time, then. Though trust me, it looks wonderful on you. When Reardon sees you in it, he won't be able to contain himself from putting his on too."

"Josie…." The ice over Jack's heart was still in place, because he could feel it cracking.

"They're beautiful, aren't they?" Josie said, picking up the green doublet and holding it to her chest. "The yellow- and white-gold threads. It never would have dawned on me to try such a thing with my touch, but

Reardon has a marvelous way of seeing beauty in the things we take for granted as terrible."

The tears she'd banished before pricked her eyes again, and Jack didn't stop himself from going to her. It had been too long since he held his sister.

She sniffled against his chest with the second doublet crushed between them. "He will be back, you'll see," she said, even as her tears fell.

"Barclay said, did he?"

"He said… there are different paths, and he doesn't know which will come true, but each one leads to Reardon being back here, however else it all ends."

*However else….*

"I hope, dear sister," Jack said as he hugged her, "that if Barclay is right, it is a happy reunion."

But that would never be the ending Jack expected.


REARDON COULDN'T help it; as soon as Lombard's horse reached the castle grounds, he leapt from the saddle and took off running for his father's chambers. Everyone parted before him, some whispering loudly about the return of the prince, but nothing mattered other than reaching Henry.

Reardon burst into the room, unhindered by guards, to find several physicians, including Master Wells, at Henry's bedside. He dismissed them all for now and raced to his father's side, falling at the edge of the bed and taking his father's hand.

"Reardon…?" Henry croaked, a shadow of his former self, pale and gaunt, in only a dressing gown beneath the damp sheets from what must have been a constant shift between chills and awful sweats.

"I'm here. I am sorry I've been gone for so long, but I had to go."

"Go…? Where? Did the Ice King truly take you?"

"No. I was there, in the Frozen Kingdom. I went to find Barclay, but I was treated well, shown kindness, and asked to stay to better understand that place and end all this nonsense of offerings and fear over magic. I've learned so much, Father. Please, let me explain. I may yet be able to save you."

He longed to tell his father everything about the castle and its curse, but he stuck to simpler truths about its people and the wonder of magic that was nothing to fear—and eventually, he explained the hardest part, that he had fallen in love with the Ice King and had always longed for male company over a future queen.

"Surely, he bewitched you."

"Everyone keeps saying that, but I swear I am in my right mind, and I know the truth of my heart. It has always been a man I longed to have at my side, Father. Please understand."

"You're young, confused, and wary of the responsibilities ahead of you."

"I am not—"

"It's the evil allure of magic," Henry insisted, lifting his free hand to cup Reardon's face. "You may not believe that now, but when its power fades, you will think clearly again."

Tears pricked the edges of Reardon's eyes, and he drew back to let his father's hand fall. "Mother never condemned those who loved the same gender. She followed the old ways but hated them and might have changed them if she'd lived."

"Because she was too kind and didn't want to believe that love could be corruption."

"Because it *isn't*."

"Reardon—"

"I never thought I could tell you. I feared I'd marry and live a hollow shell of a life as king. But if I can show everyone here that magic is not all dark and sinister, perhaps I can change more than I ever imagined and prove to you that love is *never* corruption, no matter what you think.

"First, I am going to work on the potion to save you."

"Reardon...." Henry clung to his hand before he could rise.

"I love you, Father, even if you are misguided." Reardon bent to kiss his father's forehead, but then pried his hand from Henry's grasp and turned to leave without giving an ear to another word his father might have said.

His destination now was the alchemist tower.


JOSIE LEFT, but Jack still wore the blue doublet. He held Reardon's emerald one in his lap, seated at his desk, wondering at all the different ways Reardon might return.

To say goodbye.

To start a war.

To be a new sacrifice if his father and kingdom shunned him.

Perhaps that could be a good ending, and the two of them could shutter away here forever. Jack didn't need the curse broken, if he could have Reardon with him.

But the knights in *Pillars of Virtue* didn't find their way to each other, and those knights, in that fairy tale, were righteous men. Jack had never been that and didn't deserve a happy end.

He didn't think so much as let his feet carry him from his chambers, like he'd let them carry him to Josie to hold her. Slipping into the tunnels, Jack kept his steps quiet and his ears alert for anyone he might encounter but came across no one and snuck into Reardon's room.

Once there, he placed Reardon's doublet on the bed, then walked to the bathing area, where a mirror hung over the washbasin. He hadn't looked in it when he was last here. As much as he'd forgotten Josie's beauty, he hardly remembered his own face, but something pulled him forward to see.

The sight was not what he expected.

His hair was fairly neat, long as it had grown, white and stark against his tan skin. The scars were many, but his eyes burned bright, and wearing the doublet Reardon had made for him, Jack felt a little like a king. All he needed was his crown.

He had locked it away once, though he barely remembered where. The only crown he was used to was the one made of ice—the one he'd earned.

"I don't know why you would ever wish to come back to me," Jack said to his reflection, trying to imagine Reardon's face instead of his own, "but if you do, if you'd still have me, I will never let you go again."

There was no Reardon to answer him, and with the quiet came sorrow deeper than any before.

Jack hung the doublet in the wardrobe so he could lie upon the bed and breathe in Reardon's fading scent, until the hour grew late.

REARDON'S VISION was swimming, but he had to find the answer.

"My prince, please," Master Wells implored him. Reardon had begged him to help him discover the missing ingredient or alchemical property that would finally make the right potion, but Wells kept refusing, demanding answers about the Frozen Kingdom.

"I don't have time to explain," Reardon snapped, taking Barclay's notes that he had memorized by now and pushing the parchment at Wells. "I need your expertise, not your doubts or curiosity."

"This is Barclay's handwriting…."

"It is." Reardon didn't spare a look at Wells but heard the man's quiet sigh and soft crinkle of paper. He had tried several more experiments, but he feared he was going in circles. "Barclay also *saw* you making a potion. I don't understand why you keep refusing…." Perhaps it was his franticness or determination to push past his exhaustion, but the most awful realization struck Reardon, and he turned slowly to look back at Wells. "In a vision, he saw you making a potion… but that doesn't mean it was the cure."

"What?" Wells looked up from the parchment, as if he hadn't fully heard Reardon.

The truth was all so clear then. Barclay had visions, something very dangerous to someone who had something to hide. If Reardon thought about it, even before Wells condemned Barclay as a witch, he couldn't remember ever seeing Wells touch Barclay or allow himself to be touched.

He was an alchemist, set against magic.

At the time of Reardon's mother's and Stevie's deaths, ingredients were missing from *his* shop as well as Caitlin's.

He had access to the castle and everyone's trust.

The soldier Reardon sent home was supposed to report to *him*.

"Guards, take Master Wells to his shop and lock him inside."

"*What?*" Wells spouted, lowering the parchment and looking around anxiously as the two guards at the door came forward upon Reardon's request. "My prince, I am doing everything I can to help your father. If this is about Barclay—"

"*Now,*" Reardon said without further explanation. Technically, he had no proof, not yet, but the answer seemed so obvious.

As the soldiers seized Wells to take him away, Reardon snatched the parchment back from him and tucked it into his tunic. Once he knew for sure, he would deal with Wells as the man deserved.

"My prince." Lombard came in not much later, though when Reardon looked over, he thought the candles had burned down much lower, and he couldn't be sure how long it had been since Wells was taken away.

"I don't have time to stop—"

"It's nearly *dawn*," Lombard said firmly. "I've been told you sent all the physicians away and had Master Wells confined to his shop. I know you mean well, but if you don't rest and take care of yourself, you'll be of no use to anyone, least of all your father. Now eat something." He set a plate of bread, meat, and cheese on the table where Reardon was working, as insistent as he'd been when Reardon was a boy, lost in studies or a good book. "Then please, you must rest."

Reardon turned, slumping back against the table, and in that moment with his eyes finally away from the vials and flames and components he'd been testing, they felt as heavy as though literal weights clung to them, and his stomach rumbled from the smells on the plate. "I... I know you're right, but I feel like I'm so close, and there's no telling how much time my father has left."

"He has more than hours," Lombard assured him. "Eat. Rest. Your work will still be here when you wake." He pushed the plate closer to Reardon, expression stern until Reardon acquiesced to snag a piece of meat. Then Lombard leaned back against the table too, casting a curious glance at the mess Reardon had made. "And what is your work, exactly? Master Wells and the physicians *have* been searching for a cure."

"Master Wells may be the one who caused this."

"You believe that?"

"I... it has to be him. Even if it's not, he and the physicians don't know what I do."

"Which is?"

"Finding a cure requires finding the cause."

"You're making *poison*?" Lombard stared.

"If it can help save my father, yes. Once I create the right poison, simple transmutation can make it an antidote." Reardon was ready to argue, quick to anger, given his hunger and fatigue, but Lombard merely smiled.

"It's a wonder anyone ever managed to tell you what to do. You are tenacious, my prince, but you will rest, even if I have to haul you to your bedchambers myself."

Before his time at the Frozen Kingdom, hearing Lombard say that, however jokingly, would have made Reardon feel....

*Still* made him feel a warm stirring in his gut.

"Wh-what about you?" Reardon blurted to change the subject. "You haven't slept either."

"I'll sleep when you do, which means if you do not wish to be cruel to your old teacher, you should show me mercy." Lombard smiled, something so rare when he was usually so serious, and that made him look even more dazzlingly handsome.

Reardon glanced away. He needed to remember his purpose: to save his father, and then to do everything he could to get back to Jack and save him too.

"First, I expect you to clean this plate." Lombard tapped the table.

Reardon couldn't help smiling back at him and began eating with more fervor. He really was hungry, but each bite also made him feel more exhausted. Lombard was right. "I'll sleep, but only for a few hours. Maybe a break will help the answer come to me. Thank you, Bardy. You really don't need to babysit me like this, though. Surely there are more important things you could be attending to?"

"Than my prince? Never." His smile remained, directed solely at Reardon.

It made him feel awful that he'd lied to Lombard for so long—and still was. "There's… something I always wished I could tell you," Reardon said, setting down the last bit of bread. "But I fear, after you hear it, you'll wish me exiled."

"Reardon?" Lombard's smile vanished. "What could possibly make me think that?"

"I suppose I have to start somewhere, don't I, if I wish to change things? You see, I love magic. I have none of my own, but I find it beautiful, wonderful, not something anyone should fear."

"I know," Lombard said as if it were a trifling confession. "Everyone knows. You were never very good at hiding it. But you are young. You don't yet understand how dangerous magic—"

"Anything is dangerous in the wrong hands. My swords—" Reardon gestured to his weapons belt on a chair atop his cloak. "—alchemy—" He waved at the worktable, and then drew his dagger. "—this too. But loving magic isn't my real secret."

He set the dagger on the table, fingers gently caressing the jeweled hilt and keeping his eyes there to avoid looking at Lombard.

"When I was little… *more* than when I was little, I never longed for a queen. I longed for the company of others like me. Boys. *Men.* For a long time, I…." He clenched his eyes shut. "I longed for you."

The silence that descended made it impossible to open his eyes, but it wasn't a harsh word or touch that roused him.

Lombard's fingers, cool on Reardon's chin, tilted his face toward him. Reardon gasped and had to open his eyes then, surprised and unsure what to do at finding *want* in Lombard's expression.

"Reardon, I knew that too," Lombard said and pulled Reardon into a kiss.

# CHAPTER 12

LOMBARD WAS kissing him.

Lombard was kissing him!

It was like all Reardon's adolescent fantasies come true....

But *no*—this couldn't be real! Lombard was the one who found the city's deviants, who locked them away or made sure they were banished.

"Stop!" Tearing his lips away, Reardon pushed at Lombard's chest. "I-I... I'm imagining this or... or I've fallen asleep!"

"No, my prince," Lombard whispered, so close despite Reardon's wriggling, still holding his chin and smiling. "You are very much awake and seeing nothing but the truth." He tried to kiss Reardon again.

"It's against the law!" Reardon sputtered, shaking Lombard's fingers from his face. "I've watched you cart people away who were caught with another as we just were."

"I know," Lombard said with pain in his expression, relenting finally and pulling back. "I am a hypocrite. I would never, ever have acted if you hadn't confessed first. You're like your mother and wish to do away with the old customs, don't you?"

"Yes," Reardon said softly.

"Then know this, my future king." Lombard lifted his hand slowly, allowing Reardon to deny him if he so wanted, but when those cool fingers touched Reardon's chin again, he stayed frozen within their grasp. "I will not condemn you if you do not condemn me."

It was everything Reardon had ever wanted. "Never," he said, and had his breath stolen when Lombard renewed their kiss with an eager lunge.

Passion was easy to feel springing to life inside Reardon with the tightening of Lombard's grip, his other arm looping around Reardon's waist to hold him close and his tongue boldly seeking Reardon's own. The worktable they leaned against shook from Reardon sagging more weight against it, and he heard the vials he'd been working with clink in their holders.

He'd only ever known one other man's mouth and tender touch, and this felt... different.

Lombard's hand at his back tugging his shirt from his trousers, his whole body encompassing Reardon's as he kissed him deeper, felt different too.

It felt *wrong*, with a twist of shame in Reardon's gut.

The vision could mean Lombard. It could mean anyone. Lombard's face had looked so white last night, and his eyes were beautifully blue, but that was when Reardon realized the truth, as his stomach bottomed out at the mere thought of his love being anyone else.

Because, deep down, the vision didn't matter. All Reardon cared about was how he felt, and *he loved Jack.*

"I can't." Reardon tore away once more, more harshly and certain in his dissent.

"You can—"

"No. I can't." Even held tight in Lombard's embrace, a place Reardon had once longed to be, he pulled his head out of reach. "Not because I think it's wrong. I don't. I never did. And please, please forgive me, but... I'm in love with someone else."

Lombard stared, not seeming to understand. "Barclay?"

"No! Barclay and I are merely friends."

"Then someone else at the Frozen Kingdom? One of those monsters?"

"They're not monsters!" Reardon defended. "They're... not what you think. I swear, Bardy, I found my love there. I'm sorry."

Lombard drew back, the hand that had held Reardon's face so sweetly falling to the table, though his other remained loose around Reardon's waist. "I never expected this. No matter, though."

Reardon meant to apologize again, but his words caught in his throat as Lombard continued.

"I only thought to do something nice for you before the end."

The pain was so abrupt and cloying, Reardon's mouth fell open in a silent scream.

"Shhh...."

Lombard's hand on the table had claimed the dagger and stabbed it into Reardon's heart.

"I know it hurts." He used his grip to twist the dagger hard, springing tears to Reardon's eyes. "But it won't kill you. Yet. This dagger is special. It will keep you very much alive, until I'm ready to use you."

Reardon stared, and within Lombard's clear blue eyes, a darkness seemed to swirl, cold and terrifying.

"Let the spell take hold," Lombard whispered, hefting Reardon from the table, kicking his sword belt from the nearby chair, and setting him down upon his crumpled cloak. "If you do try to remove it, rest assured, you will bleed out and die in even more agony than you're feeling now. If you want your suffering lessened, then don't fight."

Moving back to the worktable, Lombard left Reardon as a splayed heap, frozen from the pain, arms dangling at his sides, as the dagger he'd loved with such naivete stuck out of his chest. Lombard, meanwhile, acted completely unfazed, not only from having been in a heated embrace with Reardon moments before, but from stabbing him with his own gift.

He didn't even look at Reardon.

"You'll be able to move in time, but every step will be excruciating, so I don't recommend it. That's why I told you to keep that dagger close. I never knew when the time would be right after you came of age. That time is now." Lombard lifted one of the vials to inspect and glanced at Reardon finally with a wicked smile. "You're quite close. You might even have already gotten the answer if you'd trusted Wells instead of falling for my misdirection. I killed that soldier, by the way. Such a pity.

"You knew to test transmutation. Impressive. Would you like a hint?"

The slow advance of Lombard back to Reardon churned his stomach, as he remembered that he'd kissed him and loved him, even if it wasn't the same love he felt for Jack.

"The correct answer is transmutation into fire, which you would have realized eventually, but what makes any trace of this deadly poison vanish after the person dies is... well, I guess you'll never know."

The tears in Reardon's eyes were from far more than pain, as Lombard dared to stroke his cheek before returning the vial to the table.

"Wh-why...?" Reardon croaked. This man had heard every plea Reardon ever made to his father, begging for magic to not be blamed for his mother's death, and internally, he must have been laughing all the while.

"Your mother wanted to change things." Lombard leaned against the worktable, as casually as if they were still talking civilly. "But I wasn't ready then. I needed the condemnation of people with magic and the yearly sacrifices in order to quietly siphon their power without anyone caring what happened to them."

"For... magic?"

"I was born without any, like you. That wouldn't do, not if I wanted to live forever. When I was younger, centuries ago, I went to the Fairy Queen and pleaded to be given eternal life. She said I was welcome to stay in her lands, and that, there, I would never age. But then I would have had to *stay in her lands*, giving up my freedom. I wanted immortality I could take with me, and she could grant me that, but she refused.

"I knew there were other ways to get what I desired. Alchemy is so useful for doing what magic can't." He turned his sly smile to the worktable. "I started siphoning power from others to add to my life. But killing and having people constantly going missing gets tricky. The first bit of alchemy I learned after I drained the magic from a young elf was how to change my face."

A ripple came over Lombard's features, and he was one of the guards, then a wizened merchant Reardon remembered from the square, then the tavern innkeeper, then Reardon's own father, before he returned to the handsome blond that Reardon couldn't even say was Lombard's original face.

If he even *was* Lombard.

"Did you... kill the real Bardy?" Reardon asked.

Lombard grinned terribly.

"Y-you... replaced him? When?"

"Does it matter?"

Reardon supposed it didn't, since the switch had to have happened before his mother's death. The man he had first thought he loved had never been that man at all.

"The right face can make anything effortless," Lombard continued. "Start a war here, point fingers there, and everyone turns on each other. It was simple to twist people against magic and those who wielded it. And once those unfortunate souls were in prison, they'd die so easily, I'm afraid, and no one suspected it was because I was sucking the magic from their bodies.

"I couldn't have your mother interrupting that, or your father in his grief over your disappearance when I was so close to finally being done with all this. You thought you fooled me when you replaced the sacrifice? I knew. You've made this all so much easier, because you've helped set the stage. Those sacrifices are my true purpose. They've been getting fat on the power of their cursed land, enough now that it is time to cull it—through you."

"What?" The limpness in Reardon's body started to fade, allowing him to lift his hands into his lap instead of dangling. Even moving that much made him ache with a pulse of the dark power working within him.

Lombard tilted his head, like every cringe of Reardon's was amusing. "The Fairy Queen never paid much mind to the distant Emerald lands, compared to the Sapphire Kingdom so much closer to her own. She had no idea what I was doing, but I was always watching her. When she cast her curse, I made my move. She'd set things in motion for me perfectly, and I'd gathered enough power over the years that, once she returned home, I erected a shield to lock her away. I wasn't strong enough to fight her, no, I couldn't risk that, but I could keep her from interfering and force her to watch.

"Then all I had to do was keep the status quo, fed from the sacrifices ever since the first, when I chased a drunken nobleman's son to the Ice King's door."

*Oliver.*

"I merely needed to wait for all that power and immortality to reach its pinnacle and for the right vessel to filter it into me. Only someone completely without magic will do. Do you know how rare that is? The people trick themselves into believing magic is gone, but it is never gone. You and I are the rare ones, Reardon.

"But I also needed it to be you, the Emerald Prince, so that when the people see you destroyed by magic after being corrupted by the Ice King, they'll embrace me as their new ruler without question."

"You—"

"Shhh," Lombard shushed Reardon again, pushing from the table to saunter toward him. "You're staying here, I'm afraid. The dagger will do its job no matter the distance. When it's over, there will be no dagger or wound remaining, and everyone will assume you died from magic like your parents. All I need now is to pass the Ice King's gates and complete a simple incantation tied to the alchemy that made that dagger, and it will begin.

"I'll bring the whole army this time, so that when I—pure of heart, as they'll believe—breach the castle, and all its inhabitants fall dead at my feet, I'll be lauded a hero."

"P-please... have mercy," Reardon tried.

Lombard bent over him, never before having seemed so looming. "My prince, do you not remember what I taught you? Mercy merely means you might end up the dead man instead—and I never intend to be the dead man."

One of Reardon's tears stubbornly streaked down his cheek. "I... would show you mercy."

"I know. That's why I won. I will honor you, though, I swear. After this, the laws can finally be changed." Lombard crowded in closer, so that Reardon knew long before his lips descended what cruelty he meant to inflict.

He kissed Reardon, and Reardon fought through the pain to turn his head away.

"Don't... touch me."

"So unkind?" Lombard breathed upon his cheek. "I'm going to let you say goodbye to your father. You should be grateful." He hooked one arm around Reardon's shoulders and the other beneath his knees to lift him. The jostling filled Reardon with so much pain, he gasped, especially when Lombard draped his cloak across the dagger to hide it. "You know, I only made them hate magic. Their hatred for *you*, simply because you long for another man's touch, that they learned on their own.

"I never could have predicted you'd fall in love with one of those cursed creatures. Or is it merely one of the sacrifices?"

Reardon didn't answer.

"No matter. They'll all be dead soon."

Every step Lombard took to leave the tower filled Reardon with more shooting pains throughout his chest and limbs and *everywhere*. It was becoming too much to bear, and he was so tired. He could feel his head swimming with the urge to sleep, his vision dimming.

"Now, as far as anyone knows, I am carrying you to bed, and I will tell them that you'd like to stay in your father's room and not be disturbed by anyone, no matter how many days pass. Don't fight, Reardon. I've already won."

Reardon could barely move, let alone call to any guards. Darkness was taking him swiftly, and he almost longed for it, if only to be free for a few brief moments from the pain—in his body and his heart.

Reardon used to think that all men could be reasoned with. No longer. He had doomed everyone in the Frozen Kingdom, thinking he could somehow be their salvation, and his own kingdom was doomed now too, for he was going to be caged with his father, the both of them left to die by the hand of a friend.

JACK HAD returned to his chambers before sunrise, but now he left for his throne room like any other morning, surprised to find that he was not alone.

"Barclay," he rumbled at the diminutive man who stood ringing his hands in front of the throne. "What do you seek of me at such an early hour?"

"I'm sorry, Majesty." Barclay bowed. He looked haggard, like he hadn't slept. "Terrible dreams kept me awake, concerning my last vision."

"Oliver said the Emerald Prince left with his soldiers to prevent it, your vision of a war."

"Of worse than war—our destruction. Reardon thought he could fix things by leaving, but he'd be home by now, safe in the Emerald Kingdom to see his father, and my vision hasn't changed."

Jack didn't truly believe Reardon would return at the head of his own armies, leading a war himself, but he had to wonder—who else might they have to fear from that kingdom?

"Tell me what you've seen." Jack took his throne with a creak of the ice that made up his long limbs. "Tell me exactly."

REARDON ROUSED, wishing it all had been a dream, but when he tried to move, the searing pain through his chest proved how real the torture was. He'd fallen asleep, overtired and aching, but that didn't change the truth.

Lombard was a traitor. He'd killed Reardon's mother, Caitlin's husband, and was trying to kill Henry, and Reardon was helpless to stand against him. His old mentor was readying Emerald's armies that very moment to leave for Jack's kingdom.

As Reardon painstakingly moved his head to take in his surroundings, he saw that Lombard had laid him on the lounging sofa in his father's room. He could see him upon the bed, frowning within what looked to be a fitful sleep. At least Lombard hadn't lied about that much; he had brought Reardon to say goodbye.

But Reardon couldn't accept this literally lying down. He couldn't say goodbye from so far away. No matter how much it pained him, he had to make it as far as the bed.

"Ah!" Trying to sit up resulted in him immediately falling back onto the cushions. Lombard hadn't lied about that either, that moving would be excruciating, as if, from the point of entry of the dagger's blade, Reardon's own blood had turned against him and seared him from the inside out.

It wouldn't kill him, though, and if pain was all he had to fear, he had to face it.

"Ahhhhh!" Reardon broke off his howl through clenched teeth. He'd call for the guards, but voices didn't carry well through these walls, and he didn't know if he could trust anyone.

Lurching up into a sitting position took much out of him, but he eventually got up, and moved with tears in his eyes the entire way, until he collapsed at his father's side upon the bed.

"F-Father…?"

Henry did indeed appear to be in a fever dream, looking far worse than Reardon had seen earlier. The right transmutation for their final version of the potion was fire. Reardon would have come to that conclusion himself, but what made it undetectable? Conflicting transmutation would simply cause the potion to evaporate right away, which wouldn't give it enough time to have any effect.

*Sea of white.*

Sea of white….

Wraith's teeth!

*Ice.*

"Of course," Reardon said, taking his father's clammy hand in his, much as that movement and any utterance of words made him wince.

Other opposing elements would have a similar effect, but only ice could work latently, melting over time. Once everything mixed in the victim's bloodstream, it would eventually cancel out and vanish like vapor. In Henry's case, Lombard must have been poisoning him slowly, with very little of the potion each time, to hide his tracks.

There was a cup beside Henry's bed, and Reardon knocked it to the floor with a pained cry. Lombard might have poured more down Henry's throat before he left. Reardon's father may only have hours. Minutes. And now Reardon knew how to save him but had no way to make the cure.

Lombard must have enchanted the Fairy Queen to not speak of what kept her and her people behind a veil, but she'd tried to say all she could. She'd told Reardon to trust… something. Obviously not Lombard.

To trust something that Jack hadn't….

*Himself.*

Reardon had to trust in himself as future king. Lombard didn't think he could handle so much pain to be a threat, and oh, it did hurt, but Reardon had to act. He had to. He had to save his father and hurry on to save Jack.

Rising with a whimper, Reardon looked to where Master Wells and the physicians had been trying out possible cures. A handful of healing potion variants and herbs lay on a table. It wasn't enough to make the potion Reardon needed or the subsequent cure, but it might be enough for something else.

Looking to his father once more, Reardon forced quiet words to pass his lips, "I love you… and I will defeat our enemy and prove my love for Jack is worthy."

JACK HAD gathered his court in the throne room, as well as his best advisors—Barclay, Caitlin, Nigel, Shayla, and Oliver. There was little time, and the humans in their midst shivered to be so near Jack without having taken resistance draughts.

"None of us believe the Emerald Prince would betray us, but we know a traitor lives in his kingdom," Jack declared. "Many of you have worked on the potion to prove it. If his presence returning home has not changed Barclay's vision of a dire future, then that means Reardon is the one who has been betrayed. We must expect an army and a battle ahead that we might not win."

"What should we do?" Josie asked, golden before Jack, and while she was always lovely, he kept picturing her true form, now that he'd finally had the honor of seeing it again.

He longed for her to be like that always. His friends too.

"Everything we can," Jack said. "Prepare the people. Fortify the castle. Have lookouts at all times and keep our fortune-teller on hand to keep telling fortunes." Jack looked to Barclay with reverent respect, who tensed nervously but nodded. "If the future begins to change, we must know immediately."

"If they're turning right around with reinforcements," Oliver said, "we can expect Emerald troops within two days."

Not everyone in the room was a fighter, but each person's expression hardened as Jack gave the final order: "Then be ready."


REARDON BURST out of his father's room, and the pain was so blinding, he feared he would collapse, but he refused to lose faith.

"My prince!" a guard cried, taking hold of him. "What have you done?"

"General Lombard warned you were unstable," another said.

"But to *stab* yourself—"

"No time!" Reardon screamed as he threw them from him, simultaneously hurling a concoction to the floor that burst with a cloud of thick smoke.

The guards scattered, and Reardon pushed onward. It caused more pain than he had ever known, but he knew this castle better than any guard. He could get to the alchemist tower blindfolded; through smoke was easy.

The physicians had been sent away, not a soul left in the tower when Reardon reached it—but his work was gone too! Lombard must have returned and destroyed it all.

"No," Reardon lamented, resting against the worktable with a suffering sag. There were barely any ingredients around to be of any use. He needed alchemist supplies. He needed....

Master Wells's shop. It wasn't far from the castle, but the journey would still be arduous. Royal tunnels led from the palace, like the secret tunnels in Jack's castle, and could bring Reardon close, but he had to hurry and be discreet. Lombard could have the whole kingdom against him.

Every step was agony, and covering himself with his cloak to hide the dagger put stinging weight on it, yet Reardon persisted, vision swimming all the while, until he met the cold air of the brisk winter morning. It was *morning*, but it was late. Lombard might have already left.

Hurling himself onward, Reardon snuck around everyone he could, hoping that those who spotted him didn't recognize who he was in such a rumpled state.

He found the shop blessedly unguarded but locked as he'd requested. Thankfully, Zephyr and Nigel had taught him a few tricks for remedying that, and he'd come prepared. Once inside, he raced to find everything he needed. He knew his way around this place almost as well as the castle, and soon had the poison simmering, adding in Wraith's Teeth that immediately began to melt.

Before the ice was gone, Reardon had to transmute the entire potion once more in order to create a proper antidote. With such singular focus, the pain that lingered was not nearly as important as his goal. He couldn't be certain how much time passed before it was all complete, but with a triumphant puff of smoke rising from the vial, he knew he'd succeeded.

"Yes!"

"What are you doing?"

Reardon spun, cringing at not having taken the movement slowly. It was Wells, standing at the bottom of the stairs leading up to his private quarters with wide, accusing eyes. "Please... I had to—"

"You are bewitched, aren't you?" Wells backed away. "The Ice King controls your actions and would have you poison us all...."

"*No*, I—"

Reardon fell forward at moving without thinking, the cloak already loosed from so much shuffling, finally unwinding from his shoulders and falling open.

Wells gaped—and turned to run.

"No!" Reardon snatched the antidote and sprinted after him, gritting his teeth as the pain renewed tenfold. "Please! It's for my father!" He ran, but the pain spiked so terribly, he stumbled over the unwound cloak and crashed to his knees, barely keeping the antidote from crashing to the floor with him.

Pained breaths kept Reardon from passing out, but he saw the darkness encroaching.

"Lombard… did this to me… *please*… please believe me…." As Reardon pitched forward, a sudden firm pair of hands grabbed hold of him.

"That can cure the king?"

"Yes…." Reardon looked up, still swaying within Wells's hold. "Forgive me for believing you caused this. Lombard made you look guilty, but I should have trusted you. Whatever else you believe… please make sure my father gets this." Reardon thrust the vial toward Wells with a shaky hand. "If something happens to it… use Barclay's notes, transmuted into fire, then add Wraith's Teeth. Before the ice melts, transmute it again."

"Barclay's notes…?" Wells repeated, accepting the vial with deeper remorse.

Reardon handed that to him as well.

"He's safe then, at that castle?"

"He is."

"There hasn't been a day I haven't thought of him. I knew, so much longer than I admitted, about his visions. I didn't want to turn him in, but a customer was beside me when Barclay saw something and blurted what he'd seen without thinking. I feared if I didn't act first I'd be called a conspirator. I am so sorry…." He was a good man, always had been, if somewhat stern. Now he looked filled with the shadow of regret.

Reardon understood. "He forgives you, but you owe him, happy though he may be, and he *is* happy. If you don't trust me… trust him."

Wells gave a solemn nod and helped Reardon to his feet. "I will," he said, and seemed as though he might try to pull the dagger from Reardon's chest.

"You can't." Reardon pulled away from him and moved to the door. "But I swear my mind is my own. Thank you," he said, before hurrying outside.

A solid body stood in Reardon's path, and he crashed into it and nearly ended up on his knees again.

"Highness!" the guard cried, seizing his shoulders.

Reardon had to keep him away from Wells, or risk the cure never reaching his father. "I… I must see Lombard!"

"He's left to slay the Ice King in time to free you and your father," the guard said, eyes widening at the sight of the dagger's hilt. "It's true…. Please, Highness, you must—"

"No!" Reardon fought to shake him away, but his vision spun again, everything around him a bright blur in the morning light—or perhaps that was the many colors of the crowd beginning to gather. "He lied to you!"

"You're delirious—"

"I'm not!" Reardon fought that much harder, but realized quickly how futile it was, because he looked every bit the madman, and struggling only made him weaker and the pain that much worse. "I... I must reach the square. Let me tell the people what is happening. Then, if you're still against me... you can take me to wherever Lombard told you."

Through Reardon's hazy vision, the guard looked sympathetic, as loyal as any could be after whatever lies Lombard spread. "I suppose it can't hurt to let you speak, but... the state of you—"

"I'll manage," Reardon said, allowing the guard to loop an arm around his waist and carry him toward the center of the city.

It was only him and that single guard. The small crowd that had gathered at their exchange gasped and whispered, but whatever they thought the dagger in their prince's chest meant, they followed with eager interest to learn more.

Allowing only a furtive glance back, Reardon saw Wells slip out of the shop and head for the castle entrance. That was one burden lifted, even if Reardon failed the rest.

Other guards they came across went silent at the sight of Reardon. There weren't many. Lombard likely had most of them with him as part of the legions headed to conquer the Frozen Kingdom.

Word spread of the wild, wounded prince before they reached their destination, and by the time the guard brought Reardon to the center of the square and up the merchant platform, the streets were crowded and the din of voices hushed.

"Your prince is not dying!" Reardon called, weak but forcing each word to be as loud as he could. "Whatever you've heard... this dagger *is* enchanted, and it will kill me, but not from the wound. And it is not the Ice King who wielded it.

"General Lombard betrays us. The villain is him, not me, and not our neighbors. He wielded this magic and means to take more from the Frozen... from the *Sapphire* Kingdom to the north. Yes, that is where I've been these many weeks, but I am not bewitched."

"Then where are our men?" someone called—a woman, old enough to be someone's grandmother. "Two men went missing looking for you!"

"I know. I saw one of them die," Reardon admitted, "and I am so sorry for it. So is the man who killed him. The soldier threatened a member of the castle at sword point, and her love merely meant to protect her. Would you have not done the same?"

The woman might have been that soldier's mother, or the mother of the younger soldier, but though grief claimed her features, she didn't speak again.

"The other was killed by Lombard to prevent him from telling my father that I was safe. He is your enemy, not the Sapphire Kingdom or its people. I have seen our loved ones that were cast so cruelly there, and for what? Magic? Destitution? Love for another that does not fit the molds of the many?

"If you need to steal to survive, then you have not failed your kingdom. Your kingdom failed you. And who someone loves or what power resides within them, however frightening it may seem, is not worth condemning. I... I have no magic, but...." Reardon closed his eyes to take a breath and steel his nerves to finish this, though it was not the same as admitting his deepest secret to a kinder kingdom weeks before. "Should I be your king someday, I would stand before you with a prince or other king at my side, not a queen."

"Deviant!" a voice said in alarm, and when Reardon opened his eyes to look, he could not say who had cried it, for many more rose up to call similarly punishing things.

"Corruption!"

"Cursed!"

"The Ice King controls him!"

"*No*," Reardon snarled, lurching forward from the guard who held him and nearly toppling right off the platform. "No... I am no more worthy of vile words or banishment than any other! And I know I'm not alone. Not only in my passions, but magic exists among us, as prevalent as in any age before."

He said it without thinking but knew it to be true as soon as the words left him.

"Lombard uses magic in the despicable way you fear, but he did speak one truth before he plunged this dagger into my chest. He said I was the rare one, having no magic at all, which means far more of you than those put in chains or sent from our kingdom as exiles and sacrifices have magic within you, right here amongst us."

That stirred the crowd to cast their accusations on each other.

"Do you wish to hide? To pretend forever? To wait for Lombard to return victorious, claim the throne, and continue to pick you off? If you have elvish blood or some hidden ability you think dooms you, know that I will never allow someone to be sent to the dungeons for such things again.

"Speak! Show yourselves! Please.... And we can be a larger army than those who call us corrupt. If you don't... then I have no one to help me stop Lombard, and when he destroys our neighbors, he will destroy us too."

Reardon sank down on weak legs, but the guard was there to catch him. Expecting a few more volleyed insults, Reardon was surprised to hear only silence, eerie within the square when it was usually so bustling.

Perhaps silence was worse....

"I have magic," the guard blurted.

Reardon tilted his head up at him, and the guard shucked the helmet from his head, revealing a handsome *elf* as the glamour lifted from his ears, rippling like the veil of the Mystic Valley, to show how they were pointed.

"My whole family are elves, taught to hide it until a time when the ruling power would learn sense. I'm also in love with a fellow guard."

Reardon laughed. He didn't mean to, but he'd never expected—

"Me too!" someone called. "Well... not the guard part, but I'm a half-elf! Most of my family is at least a quarter!"

"I see spirits!"

"I can transmute without alchemy!"

"I want to court the grocer's daughter!"

The chorus grew into such a frenzy, louder than the jeers against him, that Reardon hardly caught it all, but his smile continued to grow. The racket wasn't without dissension and wary glances from magicless humans, especially when more and more pointed ears were revealed, but the silent majority wasn't being so silent anymore.

"Please!" Reardon tried to hush them.

"Quiet!" the guard yelled, and the chorus fell to a murmur.

"Master Wells delivers a cure to my father, but the only way to save me and our kingdom is to stop General Lombard. I must give chase. And so I ask you all, as your prince…."

He'd feared for most his life admitting half the truths he'd spouted today, but without anything hidden from his people any longer, he saw most of them looking back at him with pride.

"Who will join me?"

NOT AGING made it easy to ignore the passage of days, never truly feeling them, but for Jack, waiting on his prince, the days since Reardon's departure moved at a crawl.

Barclay's vision never once changed, save to say that the shadow over Reardon seemed darker as the expected time for the prince's return grew close. Whether that meant good or ill, Barclay didn't know.

Even so, with the castle fortified and Jack's people as ready as they could be for whatever might be coming, everyone had a remarkable way of staying in good spirits.

It was in realizing that the approaching night might be Jack's last, his final moment to be the man Reardon believed him to be, that he asked Josie to meet him in the passageway behind the great hall after sunset.

"Are you certain?" she asked, taking his arm. "You haven't shown any of the others yet. I didn't tell them you'd shown me. Not even Zephyr."

"You don't think he knows?" Jack grinned, dressed in a simple blue doublet, saving the one crafted by Reardon until his prince was at his side again. "If he doesn't, he's about to find out, and everyone else with him."

Together, they entered the hall through the doorway that usually only admitted the court on the first night of a new sacrifice. With stalwart steps, Jack walked with his sister to his center seat at the head table.

The rest of the court was out amongst the people, feasting and drinking as one. As a hush fell over everyone gathered, Jack sought out Branwen, Liam, and Zephyr first.

It was no surprise to find them with their loves—all three at the same table with Caitlin, Shayla, and Nigel respectively. Barclay was with them too, though contrary to the surprised gapes they all wore, he was smirking.

"I may have told Barclay, though," Josie whispered.

Jack shook his head at her, but he was smirking too, because for the first time since they'd been cursed, he stood before his kingdom as himself and didn't feel the need to hide his face. "What are you staring at?" Jack called, making sure to maintain a pleasant tone. "Aren't we here to enjoy dinner and drink, or are you going to gawk all night?"

Without being asked, Oliver and Amelia rose to fill fresh plates to deliver to them, and Jack allowed the gesture, since they looked so pleased to offer it.

Barclay came forward too, bringing goblets and a jug of wine.

When Josie curled a finger at him to join them at the table, the young fortune-teller retrieved his plate and wine to sit at Josie's side.

"I think this calls for a toast!" Nigel stood, raising his glass, to which everyone followed. "Not only for our king's handsome face, of course, but for whatever tomorrow brings. Hear! Hear!" he cried, and again, everyone echoed him.

"Hear! Hear!"

"Also!" Nigel said before the growing mutters could rise to a normal dinner din. He set his goblet aside and moved to approach the head table, bringing his hands behind his back where Jack couldn't see and then bringing them out again with a flourish. "I believe this belongs to you, Majesty. No idea how I acquired it."

Jack's *crown*—glittering silver with inlaid sapphires.

He hadn't seen it in decades. He'd grown more used to his crown of ice.

Josie rose to take the crown and gently placed it upon Jack's head. It weighed more than he remembered but felt strangely… right.

"What say you, Majesty?" Nigel bowed. "Shall I spin a tale?"

Only one came to mind, since it was the beginning of this adventure and seemed fitting to be part of the end, whatever tomorrow brought. "Let's hear once more of the fletcher," Jack said, and a cheer rose up like always, with Oliver bowing his head from where he'd reclaimed his seat.

Fitting indeed.

Even more so the next day when it was Oliver, the first sacrifice, who sounded the alarm.

# CHAPTER 13

IF REARDON thought the long journey home from the Frozen Kingdom was more grueling than he'd remembered, then doing the same journey once more with a mystical dagger plunged into his chest was the worst torture he had ever known. At least this time he had the comfort of a wagon, though every bump in the road made him wince.

The only thing that would be worse was if he failed to catch up to Lombard in time.

Reardon and those who'd chosen to join him couldn't push onward without resting, however. They camped briefly the first night and were doing so again before the final leg to the castle the following morning. If Reardon had calculated correctly, they were set to arrive right on Lombard's heels. He wished that gave him comfort or eased his pain as he lay down, trying to rest.

This time, he had asked for space, because he hated to see the discomfort on his people's faces when they looked upon the dagger or saw him cringe. He tried to keep it covered, but anything touching it, even just his cloak, made the pain worse.

He lay beside a fire with the dagger aimed upward at the open sky. Eating and drinking was a chore as well, but he'd choked down what he could. Now he longed for his exhaustion to let him sleep, if only for a little while, so he could forget how much his heart hurt—from so many things.

"Your Highness, I fear I know the answer, but I must ask... is there nothing that can be done to ease your suffering?"

Tilting his head, Reardon took in the visage of the elven guard who'd helped him, the first to speak up and bolster his fellows to do the same. Lombard had taken most of the guards with him, and Reardon had had to leave some in Emerald, but his company was still made up of a great multitude, just mostly artisans, shopkeeps, and farmers.

Watching them all beyond the elf who stood before Reardon reminded him of his first night at Jack's castle. He'd been awed then to see so many elves and half-elves, to see men cuddled close to men and women holding hands with other women. Now he was seeing that same miracle in his own people.

He tried to smile at the guard, who was handsome without his helmet, his elven ears still prominent without whatever glamour had hidden them. He was tall and dark and stoic, with a poise to his stance that spoke of the honorable man he was. He'd even fetched Reardon's sword belt from the palace before they gathered at the city gates and left, though Reardon doubted he could put his swords to much use in his sorry state.

"I wish I knew," Reardon said. It still hurt to speak, but it didn't hurt much less to stay silent. He glanced down his body at the dagger, bejeweled and beautiful, a once treasured possession. "Lombard said… I'd die if I tried to remove it. Perhaps… that is what I should do. If I die before he completes his plan, he can't succeed."

"Highness." The guard stepped closer, as if ready to stop him.

Reardon didn't bother lifting a hand to try. "If it comes to that, I might have to… but not yet. I need to reach those gates, to be sure everyone is well." He clenched his eyes shut, and a tear streaked down his cheek.

The guard still hovered when Reardon opened them.

The guard. The elf.

"I don't know your name," Reardon realized. "I usually remember everyone in the castle. Are you new?"

"I was a city guard until recently. Robert, the man I love, is a city guard as well. I feared we were more likely to be caught if we worked too closely together, so I petitioned to serve as a castle guard instead. I've only been assigned there a week. My name is David, Highness, house of Zheck."

"What a week," Reardon remarked. "Your love knows of your feelings and lineage?"

"He does."

"Is he here?"

A spark of remorse marred David's strong façade. "I bid him farewell before we left. I begged him to stay behind and keep peace in the city. A few guards had to remain, and I…."

"You worried for him."

"He's more suited to be an artisan than a guardsman. He's human, no magic, but he feared that anything other than picking up a spear would have made it too easy to tell... what he was."

*What.* Even now, among friends and knowing that Reardon himself had admitted attraction to men, David said it in a hushed voice. "No longer," Reardon said with an aggrieved raise of his head. "I swear."

"Maybe I've left Rob to a worse fate, if those who still fear us rise up in our absence."

"Our numbers are greater," Reardon assured him. "And once my father is well, he'll see reason after learning what saved him."

"I hope so, my prince." At last David allowed some of his tension to recede. "Your love is at the frozen castle?"

Reardon had explained as much as he could to those who followed him, about the once formidable Sapphire Kingdom, and while not giving the details of the curse as he had promised Jack, he explained that some of the people there might look like monsters, but they were not, not any more than an elf or a person with magic. He also hadn't made it public that his love was the Ice King. He feared that might give credence to Lombard's lies that Jack controlled him.

So Reardon kept his answer brief.

"He is. And I am going to save him. I am going to save all of them."

"*We* are, Your Highness." David bowed his head once more and offered a steadfast smile.

Reardon nodded gratefully back at him, and David took his leave to let his prince rest.

JACK STOOD on the ramparts, not trying to hide his looming form, with all his court lining the walls with him. Oliver was farther down along another ledge to lead his archers, many others standing guard at any potential entrances onto the grounds, prepared to launch a strategic attack and volley magics they usually saved for quiet, domestic use.

Of Jack's subjects, only Barclay stood with him and his court as they surveyed the approaching army.

Jack looked to Barclay then, who shook his head. Lombard led the Emerald soldiers, but Reardon wasn't with them. Still, Barclay's vision said that he would arrive eventually with a shadow hanging over him and his impending fate. All Jack could hope to do was hold off the soldiers until that path became clear.

"Zephyr," Jack said, returning his eyes to the arriving troops, "when the fighting begins, if they be so foolish as to declare war, remind everyone to avoid killing unless they have no alternative. We will use fear more than force and hope they see reason. Now, carry my words to their leader."

"Yes, Majesty," Zephyr said.

There was a gentle rush of wind, and Jack knew when he spoke that his voice would boom forth as if from the gates themselves or a god calling down from the skies.

"You have your prince!" Jack declared. "Why do you return?"

The line of horses came to a stop with a simple raise of Lombard's fist. There was a decent expanse between them and the gate yet, closed tight. Like Lombard, everyone at the front wore helmets, though many farther back did not, simple city guards brought along to fill their ranks.

Jack did not wish them any harm.

Lombard was another matter.

"You cursed our prince!" Lombard replied, loud enough that Jack would have heard him, however distantly, even without Zephyr magnifying his words. "You cursed our king! We come to avenge them and free them from your power!"

"I have no ability to curse," Jack spat. "I merely bear my own."

"Lies!" Lombard drew a mighty long sword that glittered in the sun. "We will no longer serve your whims! All magic must be eradicated! Only with the fall of your kingdom can ours be saved!"

A cheer rose up from the soldiers, echoing loudly over the castle exterior with Zephyr's power amplifying their voices. Lombard didn't elaborate. He didn't need to; he'd clearly bolstered his men by filling their heads with falsehoods, and no one would listen to the words of the damned.

Jack wished he knew what had become of Reardon, but until that revealed itself, he would defend his people and his home with everything at his disposal.

"So be it," Jack said and rose to his full height atop the ramparts. He saw the Emerald soldiers, with and without helmets, falter back at the sight of him. "If you wish to eradicate magic, then feel its wrath."

"Ready!" Oliver ordered, and as Jack gave a nod, he continued, "Aim!" and a row of bows pointed skyward along the wall below the court.

Next to Jack, Branwen waved a fiery hand toward the archers and set each arrowhead ablaze.

"Fire!" Oliver finished, and the arrows arced like falling stars toward the front line of Lombard's forces.

The horses reared up, frightened by the glow and whooshing sound, but the arrows struck the ground in a nearly perfect line, not hitting any people or creatures, simply creating a barrier of flames.

One by one, the court rose into the air, soaring downward to the front gate, Zephyr to pass on orders and the others to fight. Branwen kept the barrier lit, and Liam fired lightning bolts at the horses' feet to drive the soldiers back.

Atop the gate wall, previously hidden people rose up on their knees, bearing dull, rounded shields that angled above their heads, as Josie flew by with an elegant touch, alighting the center of each one. The shields caught the sun so unexpectedly with their sudden golden sheens, that Emerald soldiers and horses alike were blinded, staggering back another meter.

As they stumbled and hesitated but didn't yet retreat, Jack's own riders appeared atop the few horses they had, led by the young elf Raphael. Behind the cavalry poured their meager but brave infantry, made up of fighters and wielders of magic. Some even ran right through Branwen's fire, having taken protection draughts against it.

A few Emerald soldiers tried to flee the unexpected barrage, those that held steady looking horrified at the elves and humans alike casting spells to transmute swords into planks of wood or put horses into a dead sleep in the snow.

These men knew nothing of real magic, cast as easily as a bard telling a tale.

"Stay strong!" Lombard cried. "Their wickedness cannot stand against our cause!"

Liam shot a strike of lightning at his horse's feet—but it bounced harmlessly away and fizzled into nothing, like hitting an invisible shield.

To the soldiers nearby who witnessed it—a miracle.

"To me!" Lombard ordered, riding through Jack's ranks like parting reeds, with his soldiers swarming in behind him.

As quickly as spells were cast or elemental magic rained down upon Lombard, it all dispelled and fell away like he was blessed. Branwen's fire even snuffed out when Lombard rode through it, and soon the expanse to the gate was mere meters.

"Now!" Liam ordered from where he floated above the courtyard—above the trebuchet Wynn had constructed.

Liam had told him what compounds to add as ammunition, and Wynn had complied, a full arsenal at their disposal. Nigel was there as well, preparing future rounds, as the first flung forward at Liam's cry, launching what appeared to be a boulder but broke apart like dust, raining colorful speckles upon the approaching army.

They were too near the gate now, despite those trying to hold them back, and Jack watched Liam call down rain with a roll of dark clouds and thunder filling the sky. The second the water hit the dust that had coated the Emerald soldiers, the reacting combination turned the dust to sticky sludge.

Soldiers off their horses fell to the ground as if wading through muck, and the horses themselves had it worse, knees buckling and causing them to throw their riders.

As before, only Lombard seemed immune.

"He's using magic?" Barclay darted to the edge of the wall beside Jack. "Or is it alchemy?"

"It doesn't matter," Jack growled, stepping onto the ledge to finally leave his perch.

"Wait!" Barclay cried. "What of my vision?"

"If your vision changes, we will all learn the truth long before you can warn anyone." Jack turned his monstrous maw toward Barclay. "The soldiers know not what they do, but *him* I am not afraid to touch."

With a crunch into the stones of the rampart wall, Jack leapt off to begin his descent, creating an icy ramp in his wake. He slid down the length of the castle at speeds that eventually launched him like the trebuchet had launched its weapon.

Jack landed with a similar crunch upon the front gate wall far from the line of golden shields, but close enough to where Lombard charged that Jack dropped right down in front of the gates and bellowed.

"Give room!" Then he stared Lombard and the other charging horses down as they all stopped short. "Any who dare touch me will earn an icy grave. So please, *accuser*, let it only be you."

He could see Lombard's eyes through the man's helmet, blue and vibrant like his own.

"Jack!" Josie called from above him.

She had refused to use her touch as a weapon and was fearful of what Jack might do—or what might be done to him—but he could not be cowed. Around Jack, and farther out in the field beyond their gates, he saw so many good people fighting the army at their doorstep.

Like Shayla, a wickedly fast fighter with her twin daggers, cutting painful scratches into dozens of soldiers, one after the other, before they could counter, making them hiss and retreat—but not causing fatal harm.

And Caitlin, with her own elemental power, throwing icicles from her palms that hit soldiers' ankles or shoulders, or she would cover the ground in ice that caused their horses to slip.

Everyone was doing what they could to keep from killing these men, but no one would mourn Lombard, who or whatever he truly was.

Jumping down from his horse, Lombard dropped his helmet into the snow, a cruel echo of when he'd last been there and embraced Reardon in front of those same gates. "You wish to challenge me directly, Ice King?" he said, squaring his stance with his long sword pointed outward.

"Gladly," Jack growled and barreled forward with a mighty leap.

The sword struck his icy palm, holding him at bay, but no normal weapon could harm Jack, and he gripped it firm as he swiped with his other hand at Lombard's head.

The ricochet stung more than Jack could have expected, his arm bouncing to the side, deflected like Liam's lightning. While Jack stared in furious shock, Lombard heaved him away as though fighting with the strength of ten men.

Jack leapt at him again with a roar, but while the sword could strike Jack, whenever Jack tried to reach any part of Lombard, he was repelled. He swung and swung and swung at Lombard anyway, battering at him with palms and fists, each successive blow making him grit his teeth at how much it *hurt*.

Try as he might, Jack couldn't touch him.

"You see! These demons cannot touch the righteous!" Lombard called—and then grinned, adding quietly for Jack's ears only, "Did you think this would be easy?"

Attacking Jack with similarly vicious, battering strikes, Lombard hacked and hacked at him to drive Jack back. It didn't hurt the way striking that magical barrier did. It barely chipped away even the tiniest flecks of Jack's ice, but seeing their leader holding his own against the starring villain in their darkest tales, Lombard's men rallied and began fighting back harder too.

Jack couldn't allow it. He and Lombard weren't even able to hurt each other, but he was being backed up to the gate. If the courtyard was breached, there was no telling what Lombard was capable of.

With a mighty stomp at the ground, a burst of ice poured forth from Jack, enough that Lombard's footing faltered, and Jack was once again able to catch his sword on the following blow. Jack grabbed it in both hands and held firm, allowing his naturally frosty presence to creep upon its blade.

Lombard's grin widened as they stared each other down, blue on blue, with barely a hand's width between their faces. "You only make the tales they'll sing to honor me more epic. Just like Reardon."

Jack's stomach plummeted.

"It's you, isn't it, the love he spoke of? Such soft skin and lips, that prince," Lombard continued in a whisper, no strain on his face or in his arms as he continued to hold Jack at bay. "So easily shaped to my will. I would have been kinder to him if he'd only bent willingly, but he chose to stay loyal to you."

"What have you done to him?" Jack demanded, with everything but Lombard giving way to his power, as even the snow turned to mounds of ice.

"He is far, far away, and when I claim your castle, he will be dead."

Lombard hurled Jack to the side with such force, Jack toppled, collapsing to the ground and leaving the way clear to the gate. Once Lombard reached it, he used his sword like a battering ram and split the doors apart as though a cannonball had struck them.

Jack's subjects along the wall scattered, holding their golden shields up to protect them from splintered wood and twisted metal fastenings. Farther above, Jack saw Branwen and Liam both hurling their fire and lightning again at Lombard to no avail. Even Zephyr appeared, trying to blow Lombard over with the force of his wind. Jack feared even Josie would dive down and foolishly try to turn him to gold, but she merely stared in horror.

Lurching back to his feet, Jack felt an awful sense of dread watching the slow pace of Lombard moving across the broken threshold into the courtyard, but before he could race after him and pound upon that shield until his arms broke apart in chunks if need be, Jack heard his name cried out like a scream of agony by a voice he had deeply missed.

"Jack!"

REARDON'S CLOAK was wrapped around him as he rode full pelt, ahead of David and the others, toward the ensuing battle. Once they had neared the castle, he couldn't lie in his wagon anymore.

Every gallop made more tears spring to his eyes, and calling to Jack with such force had come out more like a howl of pain—because it was one. He couldn't let his own anguish stop him, however, not when he could see wounded soldiers and friends littering the expanse around him that he knew could so easily become casualties.

"Stop!" Reardon cried, riding past familiar faces on both sides, and in their surprise to see their prince, the soldiers who'd followed Lombard gave way and let him through. "Stop this! Lombard betrays us! These people are not our enemies!"

Many of them dropped their swords and stared, but enough kept fighting that Reardon knew he had to reach the gates to end this for good.

Jack was there, and Lombard was already moving into the courtyard.

As Reardon pushed on, he could see Shayla amid the soldiers, whirling like a graceful dervish with her daggers, Caitlin tripping up horses and men alike as though she too were a born fighter, and the tall, angular elf, Raphael, atop one of the horses, fighting bravely to drive the invaders back.

Subject after subject of the Frozen Kingdom was defending their home, including the female couple Reardon remembered best from his first night in the castle, one blond and one dark, working in elegant tandem as lovers should.

Reardon wanted that too, to at least reach Jack, even if he could barely raise his swords to fight beside him. He was so close but still felt leagues away.

It was at the sound of a wild, hysterical howl that Reardon looked up, seeing the court members first, floating above the chaos to rain down their elements or offer support, but then, soaring through the air from beyond the castle walls, came the source of that war cry.

*Nigel*, flung as if from a catapult—no, a trebuchet—hurtled into the throng with his own sword and dagger drawn. Reardon thought him absolutely mad, coming down far too fast, only to hit a cushion of air and float gently the rest of the way down like the wind had caught him.

The wind had.

Reardon watched as Nigel joined the others, brought into the battle by his love, who floated with the rest of the court to keep from touching anyone directly.

"Don't you see? They wish you no harm if you'd only stop!" Reardon tried once more as he rode that much harder forward, reaching Jack at last and sliding so swiftly from his horse that the jostle pitched him to the side, and he nearly fell into the snow.

"Reardon!" Jack rushed to him, almost forgetting himself and grasping Reardon's shoulders before he stopped.

He couldn't touch him. If he did, Reardon would turn to ice like the awful garden of evildoers in the courtyard. The same courtyard where Lombard stood, right where he needed to be upon the cursed grounds, looking back at Reardon with a nasty grin.

"Ahh!" Reardon dropped to his knees, his cloak falling open to reveal the dagger, glowing and burning inside him with a white-hot pain even worse than before, as Lombard's lips began to move, speaking his promised incantation.

"Reardon!" Jack cried again, dropping to his knees in kind to be closer to Reardon, so that, with the snow beneath and Jack right there in front of Reardon, all he saw was white.

And Jack's beautiful blue eyes.

Far beyond the gates, up on the ramparts, Reardon caught a glimmer of Barclay, looking distraught and trying to call to him over the battle. Reardon couldn't hear the words, but he didn't need to. He understood now what the vision meant. He knew what he had to do to save them all, even if *all* might not mean him.

His friends were all around him, some above, all fighting so hard while trying not to cause harm to their attackers. The fighting seemed to quiet, though, and Reardon couldn't be sure if the Emerald soldiers were stopping or if the pain of Lombard's spell was making him deaf and blind to everything but what was right in front of him.

"I… love you," Reardon choked out. "*You*. L-Lombard tried…."

"It doesn't matter," Jack said. "I love you too. What has he done to you?"

"Promise me." Reardon cringed. The pain was growing so excruciating that he knew his time was short, but he had to ensure that he saved Jack and the others like he'd promised.

"Reardon, we need to—"

"*Promise*."

"Of course. Anything."

"Forgive yourself. B-believe… you're a good… king… and move on."

Tears tried to form in Jack's eyes, but when they crested his cheeks, they froze. "I showed everyone my face."

The pain forced Reardon forward onto his hands, yet still he smiled, because hearing that gave him a brief, stuttering beat of peace. "I'm glad… but say… y-you promise."

Reardon could hear Lombard now, though he didn't think anyone else could. The voice seemed to come from the dagger, echoing into his head, words he didn't understand but that were unmistakably malicious.

More tears spilled onto Jack's cheeks and froze. "I promise."

"Thank you," Reardon gasped, and using the last of his wavering strength, he heaved upward against the pain, reached for Jack's face with both hands, and kissed his icy lips.


JACK COULDN'T express the horror of having Reardon kiss him, knowing what would happen.

It was unfairly slow, Reardon able to pull back and smile before the ice washed over him, freezing every part of him, sword belt and cloak and all—but not the dagger.

Thudding to the cold ground, the dagger was the only part of Reardon spared, because it was enchanted and had no place killing him anymore or fulfilling whatever sorcery Lombard had planned.

Reardon was already dead.

A howl exploded from Jack, so earthshattering that he almost expected Reardon to crack. The wail echoed long after he'd stopped releasing it, but afterward, everything else was silence. The soldiers, Jack's subjects, they'd all stopped fighting, staring in wonder and horror at the frozen prince and the monster who would mourn him.

The dagger had been glowing while pierced in Reardon's chest, but now it lay dull and dormant on the ground. Jack picked it up, and in his grief, he found rage, spinning around to see a similarly seething Lombard, who had rushed back to stand beneath the ruins of the castle gates. Whatever he'd been doing, Reardon's sacrifice had stopped it.

Jack launched himself forward with a vicious cry, not trying to use his touch, just the dagger, and when the blade struck Lombard's barrier, it didn't bounce but caused a glowing crack to form like a bolt of lightning hanging midair.

The snarl vanished from Lombard's face.

Jack struck with the dagger again, relentlessly stabbing into the shield as fiercely as he had tried to pummel Lombard before, and with each blow, the cracks in the magical armor began to multiply.

"Stop!" Lombard tried to scramble backward, but Jack kept at him, hitting again—again—*again.*

The shield shattered like translucent glass, and in one fierce movement, Jack grabbed Lombard's shoulder, digging his icy claws into flesh, and stabbed the dagger downward into Lombard's chest, piercing right through his metal armor like the blade was a white-hot poker.

Lombard was too stunned to cry out, Jack's touch finally doing to him what it did to everything else. He froze right there with terror in his expression, a counterpoint to how Reardon had let it happen with a smile.

Finally, this time, the dagger too turned to ice. With the force of Jack ripping it free and tearing his claws out of Lombard's frozen shoulder, Jack broke the ice that made up that awful man until he crumbled into pieces.

It should have been satisfying, dropping the frozen dagger onto the chunks of his enemy, but all Jack felt was numbness. He stared downward, not wanting to turn and see the statue of Reardon outside the gates.

"Majesty," Oliver called, soft but also strangely loud with the battlefield silent.

Jack looked up, and Oliver, who had been on the ramparts with the archers, stood before him now, bow in hand. The court had all floated down too, in an arch surrounding Oliver, waiting on Jack's next order.

"What say you?" Oliver asked, an arrow nocked and ready should Jack tell him to raise his bow and fire into the soldiers outside.

Now Jack had to turn and see how bad the damage had been to everyone else.

"If even one of our people has been maimed or killed…," Branwen warned, his grumbling voice making many Emerald soldiers cower now that the energy of battle had dissolved.

But there were no prone bodies, only people limping or holding small wounds with the light pressure of a palm. The only casualty among the innocent was Reardon—smiling still like he was made of crystal instead of ice.

Stepping back out the gates so everyone could see and hear him, Jack rose as tall as he could. "Did you follow that man out of loyalty or fear? Because I never asked for the sacrifices you sent me. I took in your rejects and made them welcome in my home. You might see monsters, in them and in us, but you were also following one, and your prince chose to sacrifice himself to stop Lombard's plan. I don't even know what that madman wanted…."

"Immortality!" an unknown voice called.

All heads on the battlefield turned toward it, as a man came forward on horseback, leading all those who had joined the fray behind Reardon. When he stopped in the middle of the converged soldiers, he took his helmet off to reveal elven ears.

Those who had been with Lombard shared further looks of confusion.

"I am David, house of Zheck, a castle guard for Emerald. Prince Reardon told us everything he could. Lombard sought immortality, and as someone born without magic, he believed acquiring it from others was his only way to continue cheating death. I am happy to explain the rest to you, Majesty, but I say to you others, the Ice King speaks the truth."

Others who had come with Reardon shed their helmets to proclaim their lineages to their fellows. Reardon had gathered his own army. He must have been so relieved, so proud, to have found allies in his own city.

Jack was still angry, still deeply grieving, but he knew that the one who deserved blame was already dead. "Throw down your weapons," Jack called to the Emerald soldiers, "promise peace and no one else needs to die."

He wasn't sure if that would be enough, or if a few would be so terrified and bigoted against them that they would continue to fight or try to run.

None did, and after the first few dropped their weapons into the snow, others followed. Jack would invite them all in through the gates, but first he had to face the one part of this that he wasn't sure he could stand.

Looking upon Reardon, glittering in the sun, Jack had to say goodbye. His eyes felt hot, but his tears were unable to become anything more than icicles on his cheeks.

Slowly, he walked back toward Reardon and spoke aloud, not trying to hide how his voice caught. "I am so sorry, my love. You asked me to forgive myself and move on, to see in me what you always did, and I will hold true to that promise. I *am* a good king, and I will be a good king hereafter, for you, for them, and for me."

As gentle as he could, Jack reached his clawed hand to Reardon's cheek, wishing he could feel its warmth one last time against his skin, but all he had to touch him with was ice.

Jack gasped at sudden cold—*cold* because he was touching ice, but his hand was starting to melt, and beneath was his human hand.

Snatching his hand back, Jack gaped, seeing the ice melt away rapidly. The relief was instant, the jagged edges and harsh cold of the ice that normally encased him vanishing from his body far more dramatically than he had ever seen it when night fell. In mere moments, he stood in the snow, naked but human.

"Jack!" Josie called, and when he looked back, he saw that she too was human—and so was everyone in the court.

They stood there—dressed, since their forms had always turned their clothing to their elements—gazing down at themselves in jubilant disbelief. They had changed forms just like Jack, and so too did the ice sculptures that filled the courtyard, melting away into nothing to join the dampness of the snow.

Those vile villains, along with Lombard's pieces, returned to nothing because they deserved nothing, like the thief Jack had shattered the day he met Reardon—and the first thief who taught him about betrayal.

There had been others, though, too many, who had suffered the effects of an elemental touch without deserving to go up in flames, or fizzle, or turn to gold. Jack faced the courtyard leading to the castle and saw the doors as they burst open to let out not the archers or anyone remaining from the ramparts, but familiar faces that had once been thought dead, their remains shut in the cellar.

Even the Emerald soldier who Liam had touched appeared right where he'd been slain, at the edge of the courtyard wall.

Then a gasp, like an echo of Jack's before, sounded from behind him, too close to be any of his subjects or the Emerald soldiers. Jack almost dared not turn, but he had to know.

Reardon was melting, not into nothing like those who had earned their fate, but having the ice melt from him, leaving him damp but whole again, standing before Jack with a relieved sigh and that same sweet smile.

Before Jack could move, Reardon tackled him, without any trace that the dagger ever existed save a tear in Reardon's shirt. He threw himself at Jack so fully, they almost toppled over, but Jack steadied his feet upon the cold ground and held Reardon tight.

"You did it!" Reardon sobbed into his shoulder. "I wasn't sure if it would work, if it would be enough, but you did it! You finally believed in you."

Jack squeezed Reardon tight and kissed the side of his neck. "I did, but only because you believed in me first."

As soon as Reardon lifted his head with that glorious, tear-stained smile, Jack kissed him. He kissed him as fiercely as he ever had and wished upon every power that existed that this not be an illusion.

Reardon's warmth, his soft lips, his lithe body against Jack's, felt better than any time before, standing in the light of the sun.

"Y-you're naked!" Reardon exclaimed when they parted, hurrying to remove his cloak and wrap it around Jack.

Jack clasped it closed but couldn't bring himself to care that dozens of people from two different kingdoms had just seen a naked Ice King with all his scars.

A triumphant holler came from the courtyard, and Jack and Reardon looked back to see Barclay finally having descended to join the others, Josie close at his side, as they were surrounded by the happy faces of the people returned to them—including the elf who had once tried to save Josie and paid for it.

At last, their curse was truly and finally—

Light erupted in the center of the battlefield so blindingly that, even though Jack and Reardon had been turned away, they still had to shield their eyes. Once it began to fade, they looked to where it had originated, and where the light dimmed stood a figure.

*Her.*

"Now," the Fairy Queen said, in all her beauty and finery, "*that* is the ending I've been waiting for."

# CHAPTER 14

REARDON FELT the way Jack tensed at the arrival of the Fairy Queen—
*Mavis*—in the center of the battlefield, or rather, what *had* been a
battlefield, but that Jack had diffused into a peaceful standoff.

None of the Emerald soldiers looked likely to take up arms again,
though a good many looked nervous or at least in wonder at the great
queen of elves proven as real as the Ice King in their midst.

What exactly had transpired, Reardon couldn't say. He'd known
only what he had to do and had kissed Jack boldly in goodbye upon his
icy lips, but what he'd expected to be as excruciating as the dagger once
pierced into his chest had proven to be a peaceful chill that overtook him
like falling into a deep sleep.

Then, in what had seemed like moments, he woke again, the cold
turned to soothing warmth like that of a summer sun. The dagger was
gone, and the pain with it, which meant, especially with Mavis's arrival,
that Lombard must be gone too. Reardon would mourn him eventually,
but for now, all he could feel was joy to have the curse lifted and the
battle ended without further bloodshed.

Even if Jack was stark nude in the middle of it all beneath Reardon's
borrowed cloak.

"You *dare* show yourself the moment we earn freedom!" Jack
roared. He wasn't in as delighted a mood and pulled Reardon behind
him as if to shield him from her power.

"Jack—"

"I won't let you touch him or any of my people again!"

Mavis clucked her tongue, walking toward them with her indigo
gown fluttering elegantly as she moved and everyone in her path giving
a wide berth. "Such a temper—for a barefoot man in the snow."

Reardon couldn't help but notice that she was barefoot again too.

"You did this," Jack seethed.

"I did some of this, and for the part I played in a too long and
lasting torture, I beg forgiveness." She bowed, and whatever smugness
had donned her face fell away.

Jack didn't seem to know how to respond.

"My love," Reardon tried again, moving to stand beside Jack and taking hold of his hand, "her curse may have been cruel, but she has not been idle watching, laughing at your struggles. She couldn't do more than watch because of Lombard. She didn't close off her lands, hidden in the Mystic Valley to mock you. She was a prisoner just as you were.

"And... well...." Reardon glanced down, marveling at their connected skin in the sunlight, though that paled in comparison to being able to look up and see Jack's face in the day. "Are you really angry to be here now with subjects and friends who are more like family? Are you angry over the lessons you've learned and all you have gained?" *Like me*, he thought, though he already knew that answer.

Jack's human face, however scarred, his white hair falling in windblown strands across his forehead, was so beautiful to Reardon with sweet resignation and fondness upon it.

"I won't take back what I did or why." Mavis drew their attention back to her. "But I swear I would have been kinder had I the chance." She took another step closer and extended an arm to Jack. "Can you forgive me, Sapphire King?"

Even with so large an audience, all the air seemed to escape Jack in one great sigh for how everything had led to this one exchange between monarchs.

"If it hadn't been for our curse, my fellows and I wouldn't have all we do." Jack looked to Reardon first, tightened his hold on Reardon's hand, and then returned to the queen. "What say we forgive each other?" he said and reached his free hand to clasp her forearm.

Reardon expected a cheer, but all went silent, because Jack began to glow.

The light lasted only a moment, but when it faded, Mavis pulled her hand away, and Jack stood there, free of all his scars. He noticed immediately, because his outstretched arm was bare outside the cloak.

"You didn't need to do that," Jack said, turning his hand in the sunlight. "I—"

"*You* don't have to play martyr," Mavis said. "We all carry enough scars. Accept the gift. And try not to flirt with my husband this time."

Reardon laughed, and as he turned to look where the queen inclined her head, he could see them. A caravan approached from the Mystic Valley, and at its head was her handsome human Prince Consort.

"I'll try my best," Jack joked, and then cleared his throat as if to shake away whatever sentiment was cloying there too tightly. "Come! All are welcome here. Let us get inside to be warm and clean and freshly fed. I am sure we all have much to tell each other."

Reardon was glad to see that the Emerald soldiers didn't hesitate, perhaps too weary or too stunned by all they had seen to imagine slinking away. It was an easy task to move for the Frozen—no, the *Sapphire* castle.

As they went in through the gates, and Reardon saw how spacious Jack's garden looked with no ice sculptures to adorn it, he remembered where Lombard had been standing and wondered if that was where he had fallen, though there was no trace of him save the melted ice.

"What of Lombard?" Reardon asked, turning to Mavis, walking in step beside him and Jack. "He seemed a twisted and cruel man, but all he wanted was what you have."

"Do you blame me for his corruption?" she asked.

"No, I... I just wonder if all this could have been avoided if he'd gotten what he wanted when he asked."

"Or perhaps it would have been much worse. All I did was tell him no and look where it brought him." She gestured to the same cold ground beneath their feet. "If people can take immortality with them, it changes them. Surely, the people here changed, but they could have left their immortality behind and traveled beyond these lands. Choice is key, Reardon. People choose whether they want to be better or worse versions of themselves every day."

"With the curse gone," Jack said, as though a sudden weight sunk within him, "this place will no longer keep everyone alive."

"But children can flourish again," Mavis said. "Or I could compromise the power here to allow children without anyone losing their immortality, like my own lands. Or, if you'd prefer this place stay untouched by such magic, yet some of your subjects aren't ready to give immortality up, they are welcome in the Mystic Valley, same as before."

Reardon saw how the unknown future ahead weighed on Jack, so he pulled in closer to his lover's side, feeling the firm lines of him through the cloak and how he shivered in the snow.

"I will have to think on it and pose it to my people," Jack said. "I have lived a long life, but I don't know if I'm ready for it to be shortened."

He leaned against Reardon in reply. "Many of my subjects from the start of my reign are in your valley, aren't they?"

"Some. Some moved on to live simpler lives before our lands were locked. Those who stayed might even want to return here."

Barclay and the rest of the court were ahead of them but had slowed their gait upon nearing the castle doors. Reardon knew they had done so to listen in, because Zephyr would no longer have his ability to spy anywhere he pleased.

Since they had overheard, however, Liam rushed toward them at those words. "Do you know if…." He trailed off, his face pinched with uncertainty, yet still, he tried. "I… had a daughter."

"Children age in the Mystic Valley until they are grown," the queen said. "Her mother is gone, not one to live forever, but the girl chose to stay. Quite lovely now, isn't she?"

Reardon watched Liam turn to look at the arriving caravan pouring into the courtyard, one young woman clearly catching his attention, though she must look so different from when he'd last seen her.

She was beautiful. A half-elf with dark hair and large almond eyes.

When Reardon looked back at Liam, Shayla had joined him, and she held his hand as he stared in awe until his eyes met those of his daughter. She must have recognized him, her expression placid at first, tense, but when she—*Joslyn*, Reardon remembered—smiled in hopeful encouragement, Liam and Shayla went to see her.

"Reardon?"

Reardon turned back, realizing he'd been left at the bottom of the steps, and hurried inside the castle after Jack, who was picking at the edges of the cloak. "Oh! Of course. You need to dress. I'll run to my room as well and meet you in the hall?"

Jack nodded and drew Reardon in close to kiss him. Mavis was gazing at Reardon fondly when Jack headed away.

Everything was as it should be, Reardon's friends all around him, embracing and talking happily, still waiting to pounce and embrace him once he ventured from the Fairy Queen's side. They tried to pounce on Jack, but while he accepted a few half hugs on his way to his chambers, he begged to be allowed to get clothes on first.

Reardon smiled, but one question still plagued him before he could leave the queen. "Lands can be cursed with immortality. Could you give that to a person, but you simply refused Lombard?"

"I could," she said, taking him by the elbow and leading him away from the entrance that would soon be filled with others, "but nothing comes without a price."

"But *you* are immortal no matter where you tread?"

"Yes." She smiled cryptically.

"Other elves only live forever if they are on your lands. What makes you different? Just your type of magic?"

"I'll tell you a secret, Reardon." She leaned in especially close to whisper, "I'm not an elf."

Reardon jerked back. "You *are* a fairy!"

"No." She laughed. "There are other things in this world—and outside of it. Does it matter what I am if this is who I want you to see?"

She clearly had no intention of divulging what she truly was, but Reardon couldn't help a wave of curiosity. Maybe someday he would learn the truth, but regardless, with the promise of all he had ahead of him, he bowed and answered plainly, "It doesn't matter what anyone is, only who they choose to be."

JACK TOOK longer than he should have getting ready, dirty from being outside naked in the snow and wanting the warmth of a hot bath before he changed. It was surreal, knowing the sun shone outside.

For once, he wished his private chambers had windows.

Part of him kept waiting to wake from a long dream, and it would be that morning all over again, only Reardon wouldn't heroically come to his rescue and change everything with a kiss.

But Jack never startled awake. Reardon had changed everything and ended the curse with the simple press of sweet lips and a love he had chosen to embrace against all odds.

Jack dressed in the blue-and-silver doublet Reardon had made for him, donning his crown and heading through the secret tunnels at last, where he could hear much merriment the closer he drew to the hall. He was last to arrive at the head table. Additional chairs had been added to accommodate every court member and their consort, including a seat beside Jack's for his prince.

"You found it," Jack said, taking in what Reardon wore. He had almost forgotten he left the green-and-gold doublet in Reardon's wardrobe.

Reardon flew into his arms as wholeheartedly as he had when they were first reunited.

Then everyone else did too.

"Oh Jack!" Josie embraced him next, as radiant as ever in a golden gown.

Barclay was dressed rather princely himself, in clothing that bore more of Josie's previously spun gold thread, but he was more reserved toward his king and merely clasped Jack's forearm.

Liam and Zephyr held no such reservations and clobbered Jack from either side. Zephyr looked like a true courtier again, prim and stately, and Liam wore robes of opulent purple.

Shayla was there then to bow and kiss Jack's cheek, in matching purple to Liam's, though she remained in trousers instead of a skirt. Nigel didn't bother with a bow or curtsy, wearing even more varied colors for his mismatched clothing than usual, but he kissed Jack's cheek all the same, to which Jack laughed.

He expected Branwen to do no more than pat his shoulder, but his master of arms drew him in for a crushing hug, pulling Caitlin along with him to crush Jack further. They were dressed grandly too, taking this as the celebration it was, with Caitlin's brunette hair done up in pinned curls.

Reardon returned to Jack's side after he had been thoroughly accosted by everyone else. Jack took his seat and tugged Reardon onto his lap.

"Jack!" Reardon said with a blush, but Jack kissed him—his cheek, the side of his mouth, his lips directly, and willed Reardon's embarrassment away.

"My prince may do as he pleases, but his king would like him to stay right here."

A smile from Reardon still lit up the hall like no candlelight ever could.

The others took their seats. There was an *extra*-extra chair beside Liam. For his daughter.

The lovely half-elf looked overwhelmed to have been invited to join them, but then, Liam looked overwhelmed as well and happy for it.

Jack realized that who he had expected to be at the table was not.

"What of the Fairy—" he began, but as soon as he looked out at the hall, he saw her.

Moving through their great gathered masses, she floated like her namesake, creating extra tables and chairs with mere waves of her hands, until the room was near bursting with people from all three kingdoms, yet there was room enough for everyone.

Her consort sat amongst the people, not at all put out that there wasn't room at the head table. There was feasting and drinking as grandly as if it were evening, though it was barely midday.

Reardon wriggled to get out of Jack's hold when food was served, but Jack clung to him stubbornly.

"Jack!" Reardon protested again with a giggle. "This is very sweet, but I can't eat here, and I'm starved. I'll have you know that dying is very hunger-inducing."

That shouldn't have been funny, but Jack laughed and let Reardon go. "Fair enough." It still warmed him and his melted heart whenever Reardon cast him a loving gaze.

As they were settled now, Barclay reached over to pat Reardon's shoulder—and immediately let out a gasp. Anxiety cloyed at Jack's chest where his thawed heart was far too tender to take bad news.

"Anything I should know about?" Reardon asked, the twitch of his smile betraying that he was wary too.

"Yes," Barclay said, smiling without guile. "You are going to be a great king. Your father awaits you back home for coronation."

Reardon's face lit up even more brightly, learning truly that his father was well despite Lombard's scheming. Then his expression dropped. "I'll have to leave... won't I?"

"True," Josie interjected, "but kingdoms join forces through marriage all the time. A few days travel isn't too far between homes."

"I think that means we have ourselves an engagement celebration!" the Fairy Queen declared.

She had finished making room for everyone in the hall and approached Jack and his court as though gliding on air.

"Perhaps for more than one wedding." She cast her conniving gaze down the full length of the head table, until she caught the eye of a madly grinning Nigel. "Bard! Let me teach you something new for the occasion." After striding closer to where he sat, she leaned over the table and tapped him on the nose, causing his eyes to light up as if he had been given a great gift.

Nigel jumped to his feet and leapt right up onto the table. "Shall we hear of immortal love between two unlikely souls?"

The room hushed abruptly, and then someone cheered, and an echo of encouragement followed from the Sapphire subjects, who knew Nigel's talents well. Zephyr, beside him, looked equally exasperated and admiring.

Nigel began a steady beat upon the tabletop, and others stomped or pounded their tables in kind to lead him into his verse.

> *"Our tale begins, alas, with strength, which many seek*
> *to gain,*
> *but sometimes power births its spawn before it's split in*
> *twain.*

> *"A creature born of magic wild may seem corrupt et al,*
> *but aren't we all wild magic born when set upon our*
> *call?*

> *"Our hero, almost villain told, fell madly into love.*
> *Not once did this wild creature think of happiness*
> *thereof.*

> *"Tragedy did follow thus,*
> *love's road is tough for all,*
> *but a hero knows no right or left,*
> *only forward toward their fall.*

> *"Into love,*
> *into tragedy,*
> *but all we ever need.*

> *"The hero called defeat and vowed to make a great*
> *amends,*
> *assuming love would never rise to mend their heart*
> *again.*

> *"Yet oh, the fates have other plans for those who beat*
> *the odds,*

*and love will find its way again when power finds a*
  *cause.*

*"This power might have culled the lands but chose to be*
  *a balm,*
*and in their worthy sacrifice, they found a brighter song.*

*"In their love,*
*in their destiny,*
*who finally came to be.*

*"So, heed this tale*
*for where you fall*
*may not be all they sing."*

Nigel ended with the usual flourish and deep bow, sending the room into uproarious applause. Once he jumped back down from the table, he blinked as if he had been in a sort of trance but smiled and took his seat to a sweet kiss on the cheek from his love.

"Was that your story?" Reardon asked the Fairy Queen, who remained standing in front of their table. Reardon had seemed enamored but also clearly affected by the depressing nature of the tale that eventually led to a happy end for a creature not quite human—or elf or otherwise.

"Perhaps," she said, "but the best fairy tales are not told merely once." She bowed, and then turned to descend back to the people, taking a seat beside her prince.

She was certainly enigmatic, but what mattered to Jack was his own happy end seated beside him.

They feasted and enjoyed themselves, seeing so much warmth and comradery between everyone. The harpsichord was still against the wall, and before long, music filled the hall as well. When the food was gone and only wine and ale poured, the tables were pushed aside to make room for dancing. Eventually, even the members of the court went down to dance with the others.

Jack hesitated, not because he would ever deny himself the opportunity to hold Reardon close, but because he wanted to look upon his people, mingled with others he never thought he would see here.

When Reardon pulled him from the head table, Jack went with him but sat them down at the edge of the elevated stage to survey the merrymaking.

Branwen, who had once been thought too brutish to be a kingdom's master of arms, was delicately twirling Caitlin, a woman who had been preceded by the title of "widow" for so long, Jack never would have thought he'd see her smile with the rosy glow of new beginnings in her cheeks.

Shayla was dancing with Liam's daughter, though they snatched Liam by the wrists to force him to join them. He had a chance to make up for what he had once neglected, and Shayla, a starving thief, would never go hungry from lack of food or love again.

Zephyr was as drunk as Jack had ever seen him. Although once he'd been exiled by his parents simply for wanting the company of another man, now he was starting to untie Nigel's shirt right there on the dance floor. And Nigel didn't need to use his tricks or bardic tales against others, he needed only to make them smile.

Jack's own sister, Josie, who had followed him in his selfish ways, now cared far more for her people and the man on her arm than she ever had for fancy dresses and jewels. Barclay would make a fine addition to their family, the seer who'd lost his own only to find another in his banishment. The pair was taking a break from dancing to talk with some of the Emerald soldiers.

Oliver had Amelia in his lap, both warmed by ale and telling some story or another to elves from the Mystic Valley. The fletcher hadn't been the same spoiled rich boy who first darkened Jack's doorstep in decades, but Jack could see the added ease in his expression at the thought of being able to visit his home city again someday.

It was as raucous as any party Jack and his court had thrown when they were squandering the kingdom's wealth for their own pleasures, only this was how it should have been, *for* the people and earned.

Jack even spared a kind eye for Raphael, dancing with Wynn, who he'd snatched up as soon as Wynn took a break and let someone else play the harpsichord for a while.

The Fairy Queen and her prince were dancing too, as if they were the only ones out there—though when the prince caught Jack's eye, Jack couldn't help winking, and the handsome blond laughed and lost his footing.

To think, once Jack would have chased after a man like him, after any man who caught his eye without care or consequence, yet now he couldn't bear the thought of being with anyone but the man beside him.

When Jack finally turned from the crowd, Reardon was gazing back at him. His sweet Emerald Prince reached a hand toward him to wipe away a tear that Jack hadn't even realized had formed. It was a happy tear, because this was what his kingdom should have been from the beginning, but it had taken a long time for him to understand what being a good king meant.

"You are so beautiful," Reardon said, "but I thought as much when the scars remained."

"I know. It was a thoughtful gift." Jack nodded at the Fairy Queen. "Since she caused more scars than she intended. But my hair is still white."

"Perhaps that is a gift for me." Reardon coiled a finger through a fallen strand. "It was the first thing I ever saw of you, just a glimpse over my shoulder when we were in the bath. Now I could look upon you forever."

"That... is an option."

"Well, the queen did call this an engagement party."

"She did. And you, Reardon, would you be my king and I yours to unite our kingdoms? Do you think they could handle that?"

Reardon shifted to look out at the others. "If you'd asked me that before I spent those few days at home, I'd have said no, I don't think my people are ready. But when I spoke the truth to them and begged their aid against Lombard, they answered my call. Not all of them, granted. There will be dissenters, but we have to start somewhere."

With a gentle touch at Reardon's cheek, Jack drew his attention back to him. "Then I'll ask again: Would you be my king and I yours?"

"Yes." Reardon's smile brightened.

"And would you want forever, truly, as the Fairy Queen could offer it?"

"I... I think so, knowing that should we ever grow weary of this world, we could simply wander to new lands and begin a different adventure. What say you, then?"

"Yes," Jack answered, "I would like nothing better." He kissed Reardon, and the music and loud chatter dimmed like a distant background swell.

They kissed so long and deeper by the moment, that when they finally parted, Reardon was panting.

"Would you... care to dance, my king?"

"Yes, but elsewhere."

Jack didn't give Reardon time to ask what he meant. He took Reardon's hand and stood, and instead of dropping down to the main floor to join the others, he pulled him into the tunnels.

REARDON MARVELED at the throne room when they reached it. Jack had melted, the court members all flesh and blood too, but he hadn't thought the places once touched by the Ice King would melt as well.

The room was cool, for it was still vast and made of stone, but it was a soothing cool instead of chilling. The throne wasn't a throne anymore without a coating of ice to make it imposing, simple in design like Jack's chair in the hall, instead of the grand throne in Jack's chambers.

Jack took a breath and surveyed the room as if he hadn't truly taken it all in when he came up here to change. "I suppose it's time to move my true throne out here again. Although, if you're going to be king with me, we'll need one for you as well."

Reardon moved into Jack's body and took his hands. "I think we can both fit. Shall we test it out?"

"I thought you wanted to dance," Jack teased.

"True." Reardon encircled Jack's waist with his arms, feeling Jack encircle him in kind, and led them into a slow sway. "In the place we first met."

Jack pressed his cheek to Reardon's. "Indeed. But we haven't any music."

"Well then...." Reardon cleared his throat.

*"And the thief cried on,*
*Swallowed up by greed,*
*But the hungry maw*
*Had enough.*

*"So, beware the vice that will feed the story's end,*
*for the next year comes again too soon...."*

Jack pulled Reardon out in front of him and sang the end, *"And the Ice King sings the final tune."*

Reardon laughed. "I suppose we'll need to change the words, since only that last line is true."

"I'm sure you and Nigel are up to the task. Now come—" Jack backed them toward his private chambers. "—let's see if we can fit on that throne."

Reardon didn't think Jack was being serious—Reardon hadn't been serious when he suggested it—but once they entered the chambers, Jack led them straight to his desk and to the ornate throne behind it.

Which afforded Reardon a clear view into the bedroom.

"You don't have a bed!" he exclaimed.

"I've been sleeping on yours. We'll have to end there all the same tonight, but first…." Jack sat Reardon down, which confused him, until Jack squeezed in between the desk and Reardon's legs and dropped to his knees in front of him. "We can worry about fitting in that chair in a moment."

Seeing Jack in the dark of Reardon's bedroom their last night together couldn't compare with seeing him now, in a room fully lit, as his beautiful hands untied Reardon's trousers and pulled him out right there on Jack's throne. There was reverence in the act but also want, deep and fully focused on Reardon with Jack's eyes on him.

*Blue eyes in a sea of white.*

The white was more a frame around his handsomely tanned face now. The truth of Barclay's vision had been what Reardon chose for himself to save his love.

A love whose soft lips parted now, drawing Reardon in between them, a king on his knees for Reardon, licking and sucking on Reardon's length and spurring him to hardness.

Reardon's instinct was to flutter his eyes closed at the warmth, but he didn't want to look away now that he could truly, fully see Jack.

He watched his handsome king swallow him down until Jack's nose touched the base of Reardon's curls. Reardon reached with his own reverence to run his fingers through Jack's hair. A crown of white gold and sapphires sat upon Jack's head, glittering from the many lamps in the room.

"Perhaps it should sit upon your head, my little prince," Jack husked with warm breath on Reardon's tip, and then licked slowly up his length to make him shiver.

Reardon felt like *he* could melt. Neither of them had enjoyed more than a few sips of wine, the flush inside him building from something far better.

He plucked the crown from Jack's head and set it upon his own, heavier than the gold diadem he sometimes wore at home. This freed him to dig his fingers that much deeper into Jack's hair, soft as silk and white as the winter snow, encouraging Jack in his careful work bobbing up and down Reardon's cock.

It had been too long, Reardon wound as tight as an artisan's clock about to burst its gears. He'd been nothing but a bundle of anxiety, and now, finally, here was salvation.

But he didn't want to be saved too soon.

"Jack," Reardon panted, feeling Jack's warm hands at his hips, holding him steady.

Jack seemed to understand and pulled away, but continued to lightly lick at Reardon between words, while also undoing the ties of Reardon's doublet and sliding his hands up beneath his undershirt as if desperate to touch him. "I am going to worship you as you deserve. You kept your word." Jack kissed Reardon's belly, Reardon's doublet falling open and his shirt drawn up by slow, precise hands. "You saved me, came back to me, even sewed and sang for me." Jack rumbled a laugh before licking up between Reardon's pecs, and then leaned in to kiss his lips.

He soon dropped back to his knees, returning to Reardon's trousers to pull them down his legs. Reardon lifted his hips to allow it, watching his boots get removed, then the trousers, but not expecting Jack's sudden return to swallow Reardon down—once, twice. Then Jack slowed to gentle sucking, as he brought his fingers to Reardon's lips and prodded for entrance.

Reardon opened his mouth to pull in Jack's fingers, rolling them across his tongue. He coated them wetly, enjoying the feel of them in his mouth, while simultaneously being sucked on with slower and slower bobs.

"*Jack*," Reardon whined with a plaintive drop of his head against the throne when the fingers fell from his lips.

"As you wish," Jack said and tilted Reardon's hips so that his feet left the floor, finding purchase on the edge of the throne and presenting Reardon boldly before Jack, where he brought those wet fingers down.

Reardon trembled at the first tease of a fingertip circling him, slick only from his own mouth but enough to ease its way inside. The hums and moans that left him as Jack sought to stretch him open were impossible to stifle.

"I've missed those sounds filling this room." Jack pressed a kiss to Reardon's thighs, licked around the heavy drop of his balls above his entrance, and when Reardon tightened at a deeper thrust of a finger, Jack added a lick and sweet suck at Reardon's tip.

Reardon tightened again, and then relaxed and opened further at the prospect of what came next.

"Does my little prince want more?" Jack flicked the tip of his tongue at Reardon's head, twisting a second finger inside and spreading them apart in tandem.

"Please…." Reardon quaked.

At last, Jack pulled away and stood, leaving Reardon shaking with his feet propped. The ties of Jack's trousers were deftly undone, the garment dropping and being kicked away, and his boots kicked away as well, but while he also untied his doublet, he merely let it fall open, his thick and heavy cock bobbing just beneath the line of his shirt and dripping at the tip.

Jack stroked it, smoothing the wetness up his length, and jutted his hips toward Reardon in offering. Reardon righted himself on the throne, feet dropping down so he could suck his king's cock as eagerly as he had sucked his fingers.

While the taste was the same, the view made it so much better than when Reardon only had darkness as a guide. He could swallow Jack down and look up his smooth, firm chest at those beautiful eyes looking down at him. Jack's lips had the most mesmerizing curve with a tiny, smug smile, shimmering with wetness.

Reardon sucked and sucked and opened his throat to bury his nose as deeply as Jack had with him, loving the fullness it gave him and the promise of being further filled in due time.

"And how… would my king… like to have me?" Reardon spoke between teasing licks.

"Together on our throne, of course." Jack halted him and left the close quarters of being behind the desk. "I'll be but a moment. Stand, remove your doublet and shirt, but keep the crown."

A tremor pulsed through Reardon at the order. His footing wavered when he stood, but by the time Jack returned, Reardon had complied. Jack's shirt and doublet were gone now too, and he held one of the bottles of bath oils.

Reardon made room for Jack to sit this time and accepted the oil when Jack handed it to him. Like this, Reardon could see all of Jack, naked and full before him, and had the pleasure of coating his love while touching him anywhere he wanted.

Reardon didn't waste a moment, pouring the oil on Jack's tip to dribble down his cock and coating it with a swift hand, while exploring with the other. The feel of Jack's skin was different without the scars. Reardon had mapped the feel of him in his mind, and now the terrain was new, but no less beautiful, no less desirable, and all his.

He wanted Jack to know how stunning he found him and took his time tracing every muscle, curve, and divot, stroking Jack all the while, until he could handle it no longer and had to have Jack inside him.

There were no arms to the throne, so climbing atop Jack to join him was a simple act. Reardon spread his legs to straddle his king and used one hand on Jack's cock to guide him in where he had already been slicked and open.

The scent of a forest clearing with a field of flowers, the feel of Jack tight and devoured within Reardon, the connection of their thighs and Reardon's hand pressing to Jack's chest over his heart to a steady, warm beat, were but a prelude to experiencing this with their eyes locked.

"You see... my king," Reardon huffed, sheathing himself completely and basking in the fullness of being with his love, "we fit."


YOU DON'T *deserve this*, tried to chorus in Jack's mind, but damn those thoughts, because Jack *did*, and he would do everything in his power to continue proving it.

He thrust up into the heat of Reardon, not feeling any of the shame or self-hatred he always thought he would to have someone's eyes on him, and he knew that, even if his scars remained, he would feel the same. He wanted Reardon's focus, his adoration, his lithely moving body rocking atop him on their throne.

Reardon kept touching him, a hand over his heart, on his cheek, in his hair. He was no amateur any longer, but moved slowly, muscles tightening in tempo, his thighs wide and clamped around Jack's hips. He used the hold he had on Jack's hair to tilt Jack's head and kiss his neck with an open mouth, licking and biting lightly enough to fill Jack with tremors.

Holding Reardon around his waist as they rocked in synchronization, Jack enjoyed the minutes ticking by with neither of them hurrying toward an end. That slow rhythm couldn't last, however, and when Reardon drew close, his pace increased, and he leaned back enough to grasp one of Jack's hands at his waist and bring it between his legs.

Jack gripped Reardon hard, pumping through the wetness already leaking down his shaft, and with each increased breath and added whine released to the air, Reardon hastened and clenched and finally cried out a beautiful litany of praises.

When, after several moments, Jack had yet to follow him, Reardon lifted Jack's soiled hand to his lips and licked his own release from Jack's fingers.

Jack came almost instantly, feeling and seeing the filthy slide of that silver tongue. Barbed at times too, Reardon's tongue had charmed him as much as it had scolded him. Jack kissed the taste of Reardon right off that tongue and wrapped Reardon in his arms.

No stable boy had ever made Jack's heart flutter with the same intensity. This young prince would be Jack's king, the one who'd saved him, who'd believed he could save himself, and who never lost hope no matter how many times Jack pushed him away.

"I love you," Jack said, whispering against damp lips.

"I love you," Reardon echoed, still panting. "And loving you, my dear Jack, is more than enough."

The words were almost chiding, as if to say, *I told you I'd be right*, but Jack didn't mind. It *was* enough, and he was glad to have been proven wrong.

He might not have a bed, but he did have his bath, and once they had grown tired of their sticky embrace with lazy kisses having passed between them, he coaxed Reardon to get up so they could clean themselves and soak.

"Are we going to while away the rest of the day here?" Reardon asked.

"For a bit." Jack no longer needed to keep Reardon faced away from him, but he still held him against his chest, arms wrapped around him from behind. "Then we can rejoin the others in their merriment."

"And if they ask where we got off to?"

"We'll tell the truth," Jack said, grinning when Reardon turned to him with a wry expression. "We were consummating our engagement."


REARDON KNEW the road ahead would not be without its challenges. Finally returning home afforded him many a dark, wary, or disgusted look from his people, some even daring to spit at the feet of his horse.

But those were the minority, for most cheered to see their prince alive with no disaster following in his wake.

He did, however, have a king riding beside him, whose white hair despite a young face made whispers spread quickly. Once they reached the palace, it was clear that everyone knew their prince had returned with the Ice King.

*Let them stare and whisper and wonder*, Reardon thought. All he cared about was seeing his father.

He leapt from his horse and rushed to meet him, embracing his father tightly on the palace steps. Master Wells was there amid the court physicians, for Henry did appear weak, however revitalized.

"It will take some days yet for the poison to fully leave me, but I am well, my beautiful boy, all because you are a sweet, stubborn prince who refused to admit defeat."

Reardon laughed, because he couldn't deny that he had made it this far largely due to stubbornness. "Father, this is King John of the Sapphire Kingdom," Reardon introduced when Jack dismounted and came to join them. Henry bowed, as did Jack, but Reardon did not mean for this meeting to be formal. "He is also Jack, my betrothed."

Henry looked startled, though not dissenting as Reardon feared. "That is… truly what you want, my son?"

"It is. I will accept my responsibilities as king, but I also have a responsibility to our neighbors, to our people shunned and wrongly called witch or banished, and to my love and all the friends I made. Don't think too terribly of me for being selfish that I want a love as potent as what you had with Mother."

"Never," Henry said with a weak but caring smile. His hand quivered slightly as he reached for Reardon's face. "I missed her so much, I didn't think of what my mourning cost. I fought for nothing but the voices of the loudest, forgetting that those without a voice need their king too. Now that you are home, I can rest easy.

"I am guessing you both have much to tell me. Come. Let us leave prying eyes and ears to themselves."

Not once did Henry rebuke Reardon when he explained all that had transpired and what he wanted for the future. It was only the three of them in Henry's private rooms, with Jack having been welcomed in like any neighboring king should be.

"This is your kingdom, Reardon," Henry said, "and I know your mother would be proud of what you wish to do with it. I only wish I had been brave enough to do more myself, but know how proud I am as well that you will be a far better king than I ever was, no matter who is by your side or how you fight for what you believe in."

It was all Reardon had hoped to hear, and he grasped Jack's hand as they sat before his father united. "That warms me greatly, but I was hoping you would continue to be King Regent when I spend time in the Sapphire Kingdom, as Jack's sister will be Queen-Regent when we are here."

"If you so wish it," Henry answered with a smile.

"Should the time come when you no longer want that title, we will let the people decide who will be regent and who might one day succeed us. It is all going to be very different, and some might speak against us, fight or rally, even simply leave. I am no longer going to fear that. This is my kingdom—ours—" Reardon squeezed Jack's hand. "—and we're going to make it a better one."

The surrealness of having Jack with him in Emerald, human and vibrant, was almost like a dream, seeing him speaking with Henry and getting along easily, or showing him around the city to many stares that eventually became excitement.

Elves and half-elves were no longer hiding themselves, and many, after a time, came up to Jack to ask the truth of his story and his castle. Those that heard it looked relieved to know that no one undeserving had died since the first sacrifice was sent to Jack's door. Reardon was even able to watch the lost soldier who Liam had zapped from existence reunite with his mother, though Reardon wished the younger soldier that Lombard killed could have had the same homecoming.

It was a start, despite the less hospitable glares and whispers that followed them, and nothing would change that Reardon and Jack's kingdoms were going to be joined with the marriage of king and king.

Once, Reardon thought he'd loathe his future royal wedding. Now it filled him with joy, penning invitations to send throughout Emerald, in Sapphire, the Mystic Valley, and other lands beyond, for all were welcome if they chose to celebrate the joining of the two Gemstone Kingdoms.

Reardon and Jack didn't stay in Emerald long, however, for Reardon wanted their wedding in the castle where they met.

"Shall we go, my little prince?" Jack asked the morning they planned to depart. Henry and many others would traverse to Sapphire for the wedding, but for now, it was a small party setting out.

David, the castle guard, had insisted on being Reardon's personal escort, though this time his Robert would be joining them.

Wells was joining the caravan as well, partly to meet Liam and trade alchemy secrets, but also to see Barclay and apologize to him in person.

Perhaps Barclay's family would venture to Sapphire someday, when it was *his* wedding to attend. Reardon hoped they would, though he knew Barclay was plenty fulfilled with the family he had found.

"I suppose I should start calling you my little *king*," Jack amended.

"Do you know what I realize standing close to you?" Reardon pursed his lips. "*I'm* taller. Not by much, but that name only worked when you towered over me. I am hardly a 'little' anything compared to you now."

Jack leaned in close to whisper at Reardon's ear, "Little king it is."

Reardon would have laughed if Jack didn't steal the sound with a kiss—right there in the streets of Emerald. It was freeing to no longer be afraid of that.

They were about to mount their horses when something caught Reardon's eye. The carriages from the Shadow Lands were in the square. They had already been unloaded, and the merchants were finishing reloading trade goods for the trip back.

"One moment," Reardon said to Jack and hurried over to one of the carriages before it could depart. He wasn't afraid of the black horses or lack of visible drivers. He had learned well that nothing was as it seemed.

So he placed one of the wedding invitations with the goods being sent off and penned a quick note in addition, asking if the young man he had sent there had arrived safely and been welcomed. Perhaps, someday, they could finally learn the truth of their other neighbors as well.

"I'm ready now." Reardon rejoined Jack and their convoy with a smile. "For whatever happens next."


*SEVERAL WEEKS EARLIER*


LEVI HID his face with the hood of his cloak before entering the market. He didn't think himself ugly, but compared to everyone else here, surely he was almost…

Ordinary.

He crept down the stone steps into the market square. Behind him was the entrance archway, covered in a black glittering awning with two glowing crystals in silver sconces on either side. These crystals were warm orangey-red, though light sources throughout the Dark Kingdom could be many colors. Crystals in lampposts along the market path were green, blue, even violet like the Source Crystal in the town square at the center of the market.

Farther behind where Levi came from, someone ascending the steps could turn left toward the residential area or right toward the trees. The long road through the townsfolk's houses eventually led to the Shadow King's castle. The other direction passed by Braxton's tower at the edge of the wood, where Levi lived.

Braxton Leviathan was Levi's master. His creator. It was difficult sometimes being only a few weeks old, but Braxton insisted that Levi's shyness would one day fade. That's why Braxton had tasked Levi with doing the shopping, and because using steps was difficult for the enigmatic inventor.

As Levi descended the long stone staircase, the voices of the bustling people below were welcoming, as if it was a midday bazaar. But there was no day in the Shadow Lands. Eternal night shone above, with ever-present stars and a never-waning full moon.

Levi didn't know what day looked like. Many people who lived in the Dark Kingdom had never seen it, and those who existed before the curse that had changed these lands barely remembered what the warmth of the sun felt like. Levi only knew "sun" and "day" existed because he had been told.

"Newest silks from Emerald!" a man at one of the first stalls shouted as soon as Levi reached the bottom. The merchant had the appearance of a fish with bulging eyes, though his fins were still shaped into something like webbed fingers, and he had legs, as well as gills on his neck to prove he could leap right into the Black Lake and not resurface until he wished it. "Who knows if the next carriage will contain more! Get it while you can!"

Levi pulled his hood lower and scurried away. He was meant to engage the sellers, for how else could he conquer his shyness, but did they have to be so loud?

"Careful!" a woman with a forked tongue hissed at Levi when he nearly ran into her. Unlike the fish-man, she had no legs but moved like an upright snake, a naga with slit eyes and hair plaited as though made of scales like the rest of her.

"S-sorry!" Levi hurried onward, trying to keep his face hidden while taking more care with where he was going. He liked the people, the swarm of them here, all so different, never two exactly alike, but it was also overwhelming when any of them paid attention to him.

He'd start with Daedlys's shop like usual to calm himself. Daedlys spoke in a naturally pleasant whisper—as long as he wasn't screaming, but he didn't scream often since it could be painful to others, being a banshee. Plus, Daedlys was friendly and had doted on Levi ever since he first ventured out of the tower.

"If it isn't our sweet Stitches," Daedlys said like an echo on the wind when Levi entered the shop. As a general store with many various wares, it was one of the few businesses inside a building rather than a stall.

Levi threw his hood back when he saw that no one else was inside, revealing his red hair, wavy and messy, that curled around his slightly pointed ears.

Daedlys could see through things anyway with his pit-like black eyes. The banshee had long white hair, his face gaunt and body thin, fading where feet should have been to a wisp almost like the tail of the naga woman outside, though Daedlys floated, translucent, wearing an equally translucent black robe. Daedlys could wear anything, but whatever he put on his body became as see-through as he was.

"Hello, Sir Daedlys. I have a list today," Levi said, carefully pulling it from his cloak. Usually he kept his hands hidden, too, while trekking through the market, afraid that someone might find his blue skin or the stitches holding his parts together off-putting, but Daedlys had called him "Stitches" with a smile ever since they met. It made Levi less self-conscious of his appearance while in this shop.

"Lyssy, my love?" Daedlys's husband, Klarent, called before entering from the back.

Klarent almost seemed to float too, though that was because his tentacles carried him across the floor. His arms were also made of tentacles, three each that worked in tandem like large fingers. Tentacles made up what might have been hair as well and covered his face like a beard. Levi distinctly heard a voice, however, not one in his mind, so he knew a mouth had to exist beneath the tendrils somewhere.

"Levi!" Klarent exclaimed when he saw him, loud perhaps but cordial, and not so loud that Levi shrank back or regretted removing his hood.

Levi remembered how surprised he'd been to discover the two were married, given the vast difference between their species, but then, everyone in the Dark Kingdom was a different species.

"Perhaps you can offer your opinion as one untainted by too much life experience." Klarent approached Levi, holding out a beautifully bound tome edged in gold with a depiction of the Source Crystal on the front.

"Tainted, he calls me," Daedlys scoffed.

Klarent waved at him in dismissal, focusing on Levi. "What do you think?" He coiled a tentacle toward the cover, and the painted picture of the crystal glowed with violet light like the real thing. "Too ostentatious?"

Not everyone in the Dark Kingdom could cast magic. Levi could only minimally, being a construct. Even fewer understood alchemy the way Braxton did, but enough were attuned to magic to keep the crystals glowing so that it was never dark in the land of night.

Levi might have guessed that the Source Crystal itself gave illumination to the other crystals, but the great amethyst was the source of the kingdom's curse, not its magic or light.

That was another reason why Levi kept his face hidden, because his eyes glowed violet like the crystal.

"It's lovely, Sir Klarent," Levi said. "What does this one chronicle?"

"Why, the story of the Source Crystal and the curse that afflicts our lands, of course, and how King Ashmedai rallied the people when we might have descended into chaos. I think this shall be a gift for him come Festival Day."

"Suck-up," Daedlys muttered fondly.

Klarent turned on him with a huff that upset his mouth tendrils. "I am the official chronicler of our history!"

"Which you appointed yourself a few hundred years ago. And we have endless accounts of the night of the curse, my love—most by you."

"Am I not allowed to make improvements over the years? After all, some things get better with age."

It was only playful banter, Levi knew, for he had experienced the pair many times now and was not surprised when Klarent coiled his arm tentacles toward his husband, slithering them up and around his ghostly form so that Daedlys seemed to emanate bits of mist wherever he was touched.

"Darling! Not when we have a customer."

Klarent laughed. "What are your thoughts then, Lyssy? Too much?"

Daedlys shivered with a ripple of his form that almost made him disappear. "I think the glow is a nice touch."

"Thank you."

They were like one being for a moment, not kissing or embracing exactly, but something unique to them and equally as intimate, before Klarent released Daedlys.

That sort of closeness seemed such a precious thing to Levi, and he wondered if he'd ever get to experience it.

"Gather whatever you need, sweet Stitches." Daedlys returned his attention to Levi. "I know Braxton is good for any trades. What's he have for me today?"

Levi removed the item from his pack and set it before Daedlys and Klarent on a nearby table. It was a black crystal that Braxton had crafted with alchemy.

"Brace yourselves a moment," Levi warned. He touched the crystal, and all the other crystals inside the shop went dark, plunging them into shadow. Levi touched the crystal again and the light returned.

"Fascinating!" Klarent declared.

"Master Braxton said he can make more for you to trade at the shop if you like it," Levi said.

"A master switch to dim every crystal in a room?" Daedlys carefully studied the black crystal, which was no larger than a goblet.

"Within the walls of any building, more than just a room."

Daedlys stared until the black of his eyes mirrored the black brilliance of the crystal. "Every home will want one," he said breathlessly. "You bet I'll take more. Pick out something for yourself while you're at it. This is the best invention yet!" He snatched the crystal up, though touching it this time did not sink them into darkness.

"You must will the lights to darken, so there's no risk of setting it off accidentally," Levi explained, refilling his pack with the supplies on Braxton's list and then hoisting it over his shoulder again as he began to look around the room with more scrutiny.

There were always wondrous things in this shop, but food and supplies were plentiful elsewhere. What caught Levi's eye were fabrics and jewelry and all the ways he might make himself look more like a denizen of the Shadow Lands instead of a newborn creation.

"I should chronicle this," Klarent said, watching Daedlys inspect the crystal, and then setting his tome aside to gather paper and a quill and sit at the desk where he did the shop's bookkeeping. "Braxton invents so much, I can hardly keep track."

Only half paying them as much mind, Levi tentatively touched a violet tunic on display. "Is this silk from Emerald?"

"Indeed it is. Don't listen to Gordoc at the steps," Daedlys said. "There's plenty of silk yet and more likely to come with the next carriage. You go right ahead and claim that, darling. It would look lovely on you."

The tunic was far more ostentatious than anything Levi had worn before, with long sleeves edged in silver thread. It was slightly longer on the left and right sides, where it would drape near his knees, almost like a skirt, bound together at the collar with deep purple cord, and bearing a hood with similar silver embroidery as the sleeves.

"Claim a belt as well," Daedlys added.

"Oh!" Levi snapped back from touching the tunic. "I can't actually take this. Master Braxton—"

"Can let you indulge if I'm offering. He treats you too much like a servant. Honestly, just because he made you in his lab."

But Levi was a servant. It was his place. He owed his life to his maker.

He wasn't planning on taking the tunic or a belt, but at the last second, he shoved both into his bag, just as the shop door opened to admit someone new.

On instinct, Levi drew up his hood. Everyone knew about him, he just... didn't like the way most people stared.

"Ash!" Klarent proclaimed. "We were just talking about you."

Levi's eyes snapped to the man who had entered.

Ashmedai.

The Shadow King.

Every time Levi saw him, it was as if his stitched-together limbs were about to unravel, and he felt both unable to move and as if he might collapse to the ground in pieces at any moment.

The king was just so beautiful. Levi didn't even know if he understood beauty, but to him, Ash was it.

His skin was white as bone, his hair long, straight, and ebony black, with black in place of the whites of his eyes and white irises. He had long nails, almost like claws, all his teeth were razor sharp, and he had pointier ears than Levi's subtle tips, like Levi had read about elves.

Like Daedlys, Ashmedai wore all black, but with deep purple stitching and accents in purple and gold. He looked so royal, with a brocade tunic and long cloak. He wore no crown, but when he moved, the shadows moved with him, as if drawn to his regal presence.

Levi could relate.

"Daedlys, my friend, I'm afraid my sword belt is in need of mending, possibly replacement, before next week's hunt. What do you recommend? And what's this about talking about me?" He turned with an amused smile toward Klarent.

Ashmedai's voice was deep and penetrating, so much so that Levi could feel it rumble through his chest. Ashmedai was king, yet he acted toward his people as though they were all equals, allowing anyone who wished it to call him "Ash" and consider him friend. From what Levi had been told, Ashmedai had always been that way, for hundreds of years, since the start of the curse, when the once Amethyst Kingdom's prince brought calamity upon the people and Ashmedai became king in his stead to save them.

Levi watched Klarent try to inconspicuously hide the book he meant to gift Ashmedai, rising in the same motion to draw attention elsewhere.

"Why, we were saying how much you'd enjoy learning of Brax's newest invention. Show him, my love."

Daedlys did so, touching the black crystal he'd already set on display with intent this time and briefly shrouding them in darkness. When the lights returned, he said, "Can you imagine how convenient it will be to turn out all one's lights at once before going to bed? Tell you what, my king, I'll give you a deal on the first one, so long as I can keep it on display until Brax sends me more."

Ashmedai approached the crystal, eyeing it with the same subtle smile and a curious tilt of his head. He didn't float like the others but carried such a commanding presence in his steps, Levi's breath was lost again and again while looking at him.

The white on black eyes Levi was staring at suddenly turned toward him, likely having felt the weight of his gaze, and all at once, Levi could move again—because he had to.

"Th-thank you, Sir Daedlys," Levi stuttered, half muffled by the fabric of his hood. His feet reacted before he'd consciously considered running, because the panic of being perceived by the king made him desperate to get out from under those eyes.

"Hang on, Stitches, have you met—"

"Another time!" Levi all but shrieked and ducked his head to scurry from the shop, and then just as quickly fled from the market.

But that is another story.

AMANDA MEUWISSEN is a bisexual author with a primary focus on M/M romance. She has a Bachelor of Arts in a personally designed Creative Writing major from St. Olaf College and is an avid consumer of fiction through film, prose, and video games. As the author of LGBT Fantasy #1 Best Seller, *Coming Up for Air*, paranormal romance trilogy, The Incubus Saga, and several other titles through various publishers, Amanda regularly attends local comic conventions for fun and to meet with fans, where she will often be seen in costume as one of her favorite fictional characters. She lives in Minneapolis, Minnesota, with her husband, John, and their cat, Helga, and can be found at www.amandameuwissen.com.